Opal Song

ADELE LANDE

Published by Michael Baigent Pty Ltd

Copyright © 2021

ISBN: 978-0-6452895-0-3 (paperback)
ISBN: 978-0-6452895-1-0 (e-book)

First edition, 2021

For book orders and enquiries, contact:
MBPLpublishing@icloud.com

A catalogue record for this book is available from the National Library of Australia

Part One

Manguri

South Australia

Foreword of the first edition of
The Magic of Opals by WO Brown 1972

Only WO Brown can truly claim the title of the "Wizard of Opals". He was the first opal miner to understand the deep connection between the Australian landscape and man, and this has influenced his writings on opals for the past 50 years.

When WO Brown was a young man, he made his first trip to the Australian Outback, where he prospected for opal near the new township of Manguri, in South Australia's far north. Although his prospecting yielded little over the years, knowledge of the local Aboriginal tribe's history and traditions was his treasure to keep. Perhaps Manguri is where he began to appreciate the spirituality of the opal gemstone. After all, memories of ancient seas are locked within the stone's fiery milieu. Each type of opal has particular qualities, reflecting the changing moods of those oceans.

WO Brown has long held that anyone can access the magic of opals, even the most skeptical. He often experienced ridicule for his claims that opals call troubled souls to their ancient sea beds. Although this precious gemstone can be more valuable than diamonds, I agree that many miners do not just dig for riches, but rather to heal a perturbed psyche. I should know, for the last 22 years I have prospected for opal in Manguri.

In the pages of this thoughtful, entertaining and inspiring book, the history and hitherto secrets of opals are shared by my good friend, WO Brown. Believe in magic or not, opals bring joy to anyone, wearer or not, alike.

Dimitriou Scoumbros, Manguri mayor and miner, 1972

CHAPTER ONE

Cari

1/9/2015

Opals can be beneficial for anyone; they bring luck. Any of these colorful gems promote healing, whether it be from the pain of suppressed memories or from the torment of frustrated love and desire. It has been said that the wearer is released from inhibitions, allowing passion to enter their lives.
(*The Magic of Opals by* WO Brown 1972, p. 4)

If I could have read the faces of my colleagues and friends after they learned I'd bolted to Manguri all those years ago, what would I have seen? Curiosity, worry? Fear? Or perhaps, a quiet happiness and relief? *Finally!* they'd think. She's woken from her coma of blissful ignorance and is at last escaping that philanderer's slick clutches. After all, the people I'd known then were wise about things I didn't have a clue about. Not until that day, when the brutal truth about who Richard really was smacked me hard across my backside and then sent me scurrying north to a different fate.

Ironic isn't it? A doctor *and* a trainee surgeon. You would think I'd have known better. I was always considered the bright girl when it came to facts and figures. Scholarships and prizes paved my way, sealed by a good work ethic. I like to think I had always been a good diagnostician, a good medico. I had never been great at the touchy-feely hold hands bravado. Anesthetized patients I understood, not the walking, talking variety. Sick people trusted me to do the right thing; I always delivered. But when it came to matters of love, the heart and romance and all that gooey stuff, I was and sadly still am—even now, 18 years after Richard—a total klutz.

You know what? Most people think surgeons are the superheroes of the medical world. We've all seen the pictures on TV—scalpel-wielding surgeons in army field hospitals, battling insurmountable odds, almost dropping with exhaustion, while bombs rumble outside and lights flicker. What's not to admire about a doctor who can save a life or limb with the simple knot of a ligature? It's little wonder many a young doctor harbors a fantasy to join those elite ranks.

But that's not why I started training as a surgeon. For me, it was because the body is knowable—it follows rules. And I did like that idea—that I could remove diseased flesh and destroy terrorist malignancies with deft cutting, attention to detail and fancy needlework. But that doesn't mean my skill to prune malevolent growths extends into my personal life. I wasn't so great at severing the manacles chaining me to my pathological relationship with Richard. Like an aggressive cancer, he came back. Some surgeon, hey?

I had no idea that day, when I sprung him in that nondescript storeroom, that Richard's actions would catalyze a chain reaction resulting in my flight to the deserts of the Australian Outback. Or that some years later, I'd visit two hospitals in southern India and repair my damaged friendship with Samson, my Manguri colleague and mentor.

I often reflect with the passage of years, how my life could have taken a different path, were it not for one simple mistake on my Manguri contract—only discovered on my arrival. If that hadn't happened, Richard and I would have had very different fates. We would have quietly slipped away from each other. But the mistaken substitution of one town name for another by the agent who organized my placement, on an otherwise exemplary document, changed everything. And Richard, Samson and I therefore ended up in that remote mining town: it was an intersection that would change all our lives forever.

My recollections have become blurred through the dulled lens of time. Faces and names no longer take form in sharp focus. But I still remember that journey to Manguri as if it was yesterday. I was 25 years old, a Brit with no experience in bush medicine. The fact that I took that drive shows how desperate I was. It also shows how little I'd thought about what could happen; how inexperienced I was in most aspects of life. But I will never regret my years in Manguri and, even today, it is a rare day when my memories are not tugged back there by a random sound, a smell, or even a smile, taking me back to the people I knew then.

Chapter Two

8/9/1996

The Fire Opal is a playful opal; it is said to incorporate the energy of fire. It stimulates libido and action; lovers needing an energy boost are counseled to wear this fiery gem. But the benefits of the fire opal don't stop there. It can attract customers to a business and can stimulate initiative.
(*The Magic of Opals* by WO Brown 1972, p.150)

It was mid-afternoon, on that first day all those years ago, when I turned off the main bitumen highway onto the potholed narrow road leading into the small town of Manguri. Puzzling brown and white jagged earth mounds bordered the road. There was no green foliage to be seen, only red sand and gray gravelly earth. And, other than the odd rusting car wreckage every few miles, there was no sign of human existence. When my friend Linda said Manguri was "out the back of beyond", I didn't question her. Yet this reality was more desolate than I could have imagined.

I had purchased my red second-hand Ford Escort in Adelaide only a few days before. A car mechanic had checked that it would make the distance: a journey of about nine hours from Adelaide, the capital city of South Australia, which I would need to complete over two days.

Gusts of strong wind buffeted my small car as I drove north. I was glad to escape onto a secondary road, away from the road trains that thundered past me with a scary regularity. Some were three trailers long, causing my little car to become momentarily airborne, as if trapped in one of the red whirly whirlies that I could see agitating on the horizon.

I'd set off the day before in the early afternoon. To my surprise, I found the journey itself to be mesmerizing. The landscape was full of dramatic contrast. An hour after I left Adelaide behind, I was passing rippling fields of green wheat, rich with a promised harvest of grain. Ghostly white wheat silos appeared to float above the plains in the distance, overshadowing small farming communities. Later, the mountains of the Flinders Ranges, glowing red and purple as the sun set, formed a spectacular backdrop to the town of Port Augusta. I turned off there to spend the night. I stayed in a boxy but clean motel unit, before setting out the next day to make the six-hour drive to Manguri.

As I drove I often noticed my pulse was beating fast and my mouth was dry. An effect of adrenalin surging through my bloodstream, no doubt. Was it brave or foolhardy to go bush with my limited experience? Best not to think about it, I decided. This didn't change anything and was pointless rumination.

Soon I was passing expansive salt lakes, shimmering in the glaring sunlight. These gave way to vistas of gray scrublands with black-stemmed scraggy trees. As I headed further north, the terrain became more barren and hilly and the soil now turned shades of red mixed with ochre. A pack of haughty emus strutted across the road at one point, causing me to brake suddenly. Some of them stopped and glared at my car; I was a trespasser on their territory.

After driving for five hours, I stopped to rest and to gaze from a lookout over the undulating floor of a long-dried antediluvian sea. I struggled to identify the feelings that were aroused by the magnificence before me. This landscape was so different to the rolling green hills of the Wales of my childhood. There, there were markers of civilization wherever you looked. Then I got it: what I felt was inconsequential—I was dwarfed into insignificance. This ancient landscape almost frightened me with its beauty, its destructive power. Seemingly empty, yet full of hidden life.

I needed to keep moving. A breakdown in these parts could be catastrophic. The swooshing growl of the road trains gave cold comfort. The dust clouds mushrooming in their wake seeped into my car through the air vents and furred the interior; I could even feel dust forming a fine grit between my teeth. The tinny music of a local radio station blared from my car radio. I sang to stay awake and to stave off niggling worries. On this second day signs of human habitation became very rare. I passed only a few small settlements, with the odd roadhouse and caravan park.

After several hours, I turned off the main road and headed into the township of Manguri. As I drove this final leg, I recognized the emotion that swelled within me. It was raw pride—I had done it. Even though logically there was nothing to suggest I wouldn't or couldn't, I still allowed myself to experience that warm sensation. I'd left Richard and our life together behind. And, more to the point, I had made it.

Chapter Three

*I have often reflected how the sunsets of the Australian opal
fields are mirrored in the colors of the gemstone. Every opal has
all the colors of a rainbow, if you look closely.*
(*The Magic of Opals*, by WO Brown, 1972, p. 1)

I spent the first night of my Manguri adventure at an underground hotel, just off the main street. Cafés, shops selling souvenirs and clothes, a supermarket and a few restaurants lined each side of the thoroughfare. The town seemed so foreign—I couldn't relate it to anything I'd seen before. Dusty, was my first impression. Four-wheel-drive vehicles parked in the road were blanketed by the fine red powder which coated everything. Fronts of houses and hotels seemed to rise up out of walls of red earth with their bodies submerged underground. The streets were strangely empty. I later found that, shockingly, most of the townspeople and tourists were spending the daylight hours partying in underground hotels.

It was late afternoon by the time I arrived, and I headed to the hotel I'd booked through the local tourist bureau. The hotel foyer looked more like a jewelry store than a hotel's reception. Glass cabinets housed opals of all shapes, sizes and value, including one fiery red opal. It reminded me of a crimson light flashing outside a house of ill repute. I felt my cheeks grow warm. On a whim, and unusually for me, I purchased it, a small ring with a gold band.

Exhausted, I ate dinner in a hill-top restaurant overlooking the town and offering a panoramic view. The sun setting behind the hotel transmogrified the valley below from red and brown to a super-saturated orange-red, the same color as the stone in my ring. The sky turned cerulean and purple, before stars gradually began to sparkle over the eastern horizon.

Walking back towards my hotel along the main street, I heard the screams of a distant fight that sounded like it was between two women. I quickened my pace to enter by the hotel's side door, then descended a flight of stairs. Soon I was back in the soothing protection of my underground room. I suspected that living underground, as I had read people did in Manguri, would suit me. The inside temperature was always the same: 23 to 25 degrees Celsius (or 73 to 77 degrees Fahrenheit), hail, rain or shine.

The next morning, I arrived at the hospital earlier than needed. I took a taxi (also thick with dust) driven by a man with a Yugoslavian accent. Perched on top of a steep red hill, the hospital building was visible from all over town. The exterior looked run-down. The white paint on the balustrades and posts was peeling and faded; the cement footpaths badly cracked. Clearly, someone wasn't doing their job. Maybe, I thought, I should bring this to the attention of the hospital's director.

The letter from the recruitment agency asked me to meet with the Director of Nursing at the main reception desk. I carried a copy of the contract in my handbag.

"Good morning," I said to the young woman seated behind the front reception desk. I gave her a toothy smile, this always assisted with enquiries. "I have an appointment to meet with the Director of Nursing at nine o'clock. My name is Dr Cari Rainsford."

The receptionist blinked a few times. "I'm sorry, she's not here. She just left to go down to the Aboriginal Health Clinic. Is there someone else who can help you?"

"No," I said, using my Pleasant Voice. "I have an appointment with the Director of Nursing."

"Oh." She looked me up and down. "Hang on a tick. I'll just find somebody else who can speak with you."

She disappeared for a few minutes, then returned with a largish woman wearing a nurse's uniform of white shirt and blue slacks.

"I'm Jo Robertson," she said, offering me a hand, which I reluctantly shook. The latest research suggested that bacteria and viruses were readily transmitted by hand shaking and should be banned in hospitals. But, in this remote place, she may not have read the journals yet. "I'm the clinical nurse on today. How can I help you?"

"I'm Dr Cari Rainsford. I'm the new doctor assigned to work here. I have an appointment with the Director of Nursing at nine o'clock."

I pulled the contract with the covering letter out of my bag and tapped it loudly with my finger.

Jo hesitated, before asking, "Are you sure it was Manguri, you were supposed to be? We've just had a new doctor sent to us. He started two weeks ago."

I felt a surge of irritation. Of course it was Manguri! The hospital's address was printed in black and white, along with the starting date of my appointment. There was nothing to argue. I thought about Dr Smythe, my psychiatrist in Bristol many years ago. Her words still echoed in my head. *Now Cari, I want you to smile. Best not to start off on a wrong note.* I therefore smiled and again I showed my teeth fully, before saying, "Yes, I'm quite sure. I organized this placement through the recruitment agency only two weeks ago. Look—it's all here."

I passed over the small bundle of papers and Jo scanned it, her eyes widening. She looked up and passed the document back to me. She turned and called out to the receptionist I'd spoken with. "Ange! You'd better ring clinic. Tell Dee to get back here right away." Under her breath, she said to no-one in particular, "She won't believe it. Two doctors in Manguri at the same time. That's going to be a first."

Jo seated me in the staffroom to wait for "Dee the DON". A pin-up board fixed above the sink was decorated with photos of people at parties, looking extremely silly and grinning. I stared at the images: most of the partygoers appeared to be in fancy dress, holding bottles of beer and toasting the camera. No wonder the building was crumbling if this was the culture of the workplace. I made a mental note to also discuss this sad state of affairs with the hospital's director. Perhaps it was just as well I *had* been assigned to Manguri.

Soon a small woman came rushing in, followed by a short brown-skinned man of slight build.

"Hello, I'm Dee Edwards, the Director of Nursing," she said, after taking a few calming breaths. I stood and introduced myself.

"And this is Dr Samson Cherian," Dee continued, "who is… who has also been sent to us by the recruitment agency."

Dr Cherian extended a fine-boned hand which I shook somewhat gingerly. Surely as a doctor he knew the risk of passing contagion on by shaking hands? He smelled of coconuts and strongly of something else, which I later recognized as Brut 33 aftershave.

"How do you do?" he said.

Dee sat down next to a table and spoke before I had a chance to instruct my new colleague about the importance of hand washing. "We have a problem, however," she said. She tapped her fingers on the table and appeared to be thinking. "We were only supposed to be sent one doctor, not two." She glanced at Samson. "Truth be told, I was only expecting Samson to fill our vacancy."

Smile Cari! Dr Smythe instructed from the deepest reaches of my brain.

I summoned up a grin. "I'm sorry? I don't understand. I have a contract to work here for three months."

In fact, I didn't feel sorry at all. I was just putting Dr Smythe's lessons in how to conduct appropriate social intercourse, from all those years ago, into practice. *I had a contract.* And that was it as far as I was concerned. Find another placement for the other doctor.

Dr Cherian sat down. He twirled a gold ring on the mid-finger of his right hand. "I also have a contract, Dr Rainsford," he said quietly. "And I have come all the way from India especially to work here, for two years."

"And I came from Wales," I retorted, "which is further away."

Keep calm, Cari … Dr Smythe whispered, "*and smile!*"

The Indian doctor and I eyed each other warily. I was still standing. My hand hovered over the contract in my handbag at my side, as if about to grab a loaded gun from its holster. His head gave a slight wobble as if he had an unstable neck fracture. He looked nervous. Even I could see that from his tensed, rigid stance. His thick black hair was slicked down and parted on the side above chunky black-rimmed glasses that could easily have doubled as miniature picture frames. He wore a short-sleeved shirt with a gray leather tie. How ridiculous, I thought, eyeing that useless ribbon of fabric dangling from his neck. That could carry multiple strains of bacteria or viruses and infect half the hospital! Several ballpoint pens bulged from his shirt's top pocket, which was tucked into high-waisted mud-brown polyester trousers. He looked like he'd wandered off the set of a 1970s police drama TV show.

"Now, doctors," Dee said, softly. "I'm sure this can be worked out. There must be some kind of mistake. I'll ring the agency straightaway."

She departed, leaving Dr Samson Cherian and I to stare in silence at the pin-up board with its stupid laughing faces. I decided this was not a good time to remind him that sloppy hand-washing techniques and the wearing of ties could be the genesis of a pandemic. That advice could wait for later.

A few minutes later Dee returned. She was rubbing her (hopefully sanitized) hands together.

"Well, there's been a monumental cock-up," she said. "The agency put the wrong town's name on the contract. Cari, you were actually supposed to go to Maitland. But, as it turns out, they also recruited another doctor for that post by mistake. He's already working there. So, Cari, it looks as if we may get to keep you—that's if the health department will allow it. And, presuming you wish to stay of course."

I nodded. This was indeed a plausible explanation, exonerating her from fault. Dee disappeared again, to make more phone calls. Dr Cherian announced he had work to do and indicated in a friendly manner that I was welcome to join him. At a loss to know what else to do, I found myself following him. He collected Jo and the three of us started a ward round.

Watching Dr Cherian's interactions with the patients, I noticed his tense manner soon change to one of unruffled purpose. He went about his work with a minimum of fuss. In contrast, when I thought about it, my extraverted ex, Richard, also a doctor, had acted like a one-man oompah band. Covert trumpets blared and cymbals crashed on his ward rounds, nurses and patients equally entranced by the rollicking fun and festivity of his manner.

It dawned on me after a while that my new colleague felt pleased—and maybe even relieved—to have my company. Although Dr Cherian's clinical skills were excellent, I was more up to date on certain treatments. I spent some time explaining to him the recent recommendations regarding smoking-related lung damage, for which he murmured his thanks several times. Given this obvious show of appreciation, I then regaled him with the new evidence regarding rare occupational lung diseases, just announced in *The Lancet*. However, Jo cleared her throat just as I reached the climax of this explanation and informed me that ward duties did not allow time for doctors to pass time in idle chitchat. I was shocked at her flippant remark. The ward was clearly not busy. I pointed this out to her, using my Pleasant Voice. Samson quickly agreed with me that this was indeed important information and that when we were finished, he would be delighted to learn more. Maybe, I hoped, this response was a sign that we would make a good team.

After arranging for the discharge of several patients and assisting Samson with writing drug charts, it was nearly lunchtime. He insisted I should call him by his first name, impressing that he was not one to stand on formality. I noticed that the nurses, however, all called him Dr Cherian.

Dee returned an hour later. Her face was quite red, I took this to be flushed with success. She'd endured a series of telephone brawls with several health department officials in Adelaide. After verbal combat with the heavies in their ivory towers, the bureaucrats, worn down by their own ineffectual and circuitous arguments, had eventually conceded defeat. I was going to stay.

"They're all overpaid, those public servants. Especially that pea-brained idiot who is head of HR, in the health department." Dee laughed and did a little jig on the spot. "Ha! But I won in the end. So Cari, we get to keep you. Isn't that terrific?"

Just after lunch, a short, rather stout woman, who introduced herself as Barb, came to take me to a dugout that was to be my new home. This was only a short drive from the hospital down a steep dirt road. I drove my car. Barb liked to talk and also seemed very inquisitive. She asked me repeated questions about where I came from and my reasons for moving to Manguri. She obviously enjoyed delving into the personal histories of her coworkers. I immediately liked her; I also liked seeking out information from people I had just met. However, I remained silent about Richard, even though she asked me several times if I had a boyfriend.

"This was where the agency sent me," I replied. "My previous relationship has ended." My face reddened and I swallowed. *What a stupid thing to say!* "But of course, you know that already, if I said it was 'previous'. That means it is in the past."

Barb gave me a strange look as if she felt confused and opened her mouth as if to say something. Fortunately, at that moment we arrived at the dugout.

"Doctor Cari, you do need to be careful in Manguri, and use your common sense," she said, after we'd opened the front door. "Be careful if you go and visit the minefields. Don't go alone, and always tell someone if you plan to go sightseeing. Just in case you break down."

I looked at her, incredulous. "Why would I want to sightsee down an opal mine?"

Barb laughed. "Well, plenty of tourists do, you know. Although something tells me you're not typical."

We brought my bags in from the car and Barb led the way through each room, opening cupboards and pointing out the amenities.

"See, you have a TV, washing machine, everything. Nice, don't you think?"

"Yes, it is."

She filled the kettle and found two cups and teabags. "Did you wanna cuppa?"

"No. Thank you."

"Dr Cherian is such a nice man, don't you think?"

"Well, I hardly know him—"

"He's popular with all the staff and patients. It can't be easy for him though, everything being so different and all. And I wonder why he didn't bring his wife from India. Maybe she's sick or something."

"Why don't you ask him?" I suggested.

Barb carried on as if she hadn't heard my question. "And fancy that! We now have two doctors. *Two doctors!* The Department of Health must be scared of Dee, I reckon." She paused to draw breath. "That woman would be more fierce than a Jack Russell down a rabbit hole if you let her loose with one of those health officials. Don't reckon they'll close the hospital down now. And that's good news for the town." She filled the cups with the boiled water and found some milk. She pushed one towards me.

"I said before that I didn't want a cup of tea. But thank you for making it."

"Oh, yes you did, sorry …" Barb reached over and tipped the brown liquid down the sink. "Is there anything else you think you'll need?"

I shook my head.

"Are you sure?"

"Yes, quite sure, thank you."

"It's no trouble. I can pop in later and we can have that cuppa then."

"Yes … I mean no— I'm fine …" I felt my cheeks flame.

Smile and just say "Another time", Dr Smythe said.

"I'd love to, another time. I'm just a bit tired now."

Well done, my dear …

"All you have to do is call. And then you can tell me all about yourself and I can fill you in about Manguri. Well then," Barb stopped and looked at me, as if waiting for something. After an awkward silence, she said, "We'd best get back."

"You didn't drink your tea," I reminded her.

She patted my hand and smiled. "I'll make another then, dear."

We walked, without speaking, back up the red hill to the hospital's back entrance, next to the ambulance parking station.

On our return Samson informed me that Dee had invited Samson and me for dinner at her dugout, to welcome me to the town. She drove us there in her utility vehicle, the three of us squashed into the front cabin.

Dee lived in a modern dugout on the western side of Manguri and some miles out. Chrysanthemums and sunflowers growing under shade cloth made a fine display outside her front door. On entering her home, I was impressed by the cleanliness and orderliness of the interior.

Her husband Stan attended to the cooking, with Dee issuing regular instructions.

"I'm not very interesting, I'm afraid," Samson said later when I asked him why he'd migrated to South Australia. "My wife is the one who is keen to live here. But we need to raise the funds first, before she can come."

"When did you arrive?" I asked.

"Two weeks ago. But what about you? Why are *you* here?"

"I failed my primary surgical exam and I need to study for it." I found myself telling the bare truth. Somehow, I had already almost forgotten this unfortunate fact. I didn't tell Samson the real reason, which was because of Richard. It was unusual for me to not reveal truths in their entirety and I found this new behavior perplexing and somewhat disturbing. I made another mental note to debate this later in private.

"I am most sorry to hear that," Samson murmured.

"So, I decided to try again. I also thought this would be a good place to gain experience. I could learn a lot while working."

"Oh, bravo! I would be most delighted to teach you all I know."

"Don't forget, we don't have an ICU … or even an anesthetist," Dee reminded him. "Anything more serious than an ingrown toe nail we have to send away."

Samson lowered his gaze and took a sip of wine. But then he said softly, "It is of no matter, Dee. We will help Cari pass her examinations with first-class honors."

Thank him for those kind words, Cari, Dr Smythe reminded. (Did she ever take a break?) *He is a kind and decent man.*

"You are a kind and decent man, Samson," I said. "I thank you for your reassurance and assistance."

Stan suddenly made a strange snorting noise and had an urgent need to wipe his mouth with his serviette. Dee stared hard at him and he quickly gathered up some dirty plates and left the table. Dee then launched into the story of how she and Stan had settled in Manguri

15 years before and how she had eventually taken over running the hospital.

"It's all about playing to people's strengths," Dee said. "The people in Manguri work hard and look after each other. If I look after my nursing staff and the people of the town, in turn, they look after the hospital. Manguri is a good town—"

"—with good people," Stan pitched in as he rejoined us.

"The doctors who have come to work here since Dr Arthur retired a few years ago didn't give the town a proper go," she added. She gathered up the remaining dishes and headed off to the kitchen. Samson and I were left in silence. The sour smell of anxiety that we would also hotfoot it out of town when the going got tough, hung in the air. Obvious, even to me.

"Cari," Dee began when she returned, "tell me about your trip here. I heard you drove your car. It's such a long way though, isn't it?"

I nodded. "It was manageable over the two days. But I have never tackled such a distance before."

"And what about you, Samson? That must have been some journey, coming all the way from India?"

"Oh Dee," he replied. "Such a wonderful flight here from Adelaide! I enjoyed the trip immensely."

Dee smiled and sighed. "Oh, we are kindred spirits, Samson. I also love it when you fly up here. Especially when your plane banks and comes in to land. My heart begins to sing, and I don't even know why."

Samson suddenly coughed uncontrollably until his face went quite red. I passed him a glass of water. Alarmed, I then stood behind his chair in readiness to deliver the Heimlich maneuver, but the offending piece of food thankfully shifted just in time.

"Please … I am fine," he gasped, waving me to sit down. He sipped at his drink again and added, "Such a wonderful plane ride here, Dee. I will never forget it …"

CHAPTER FOUR

Samson

23/8/1996

Many visitors are taken "noodling" when they visit the opal fields of Outback Australia. The areas visited by tourists to sift through surface earth are considered safe but are usually emptied of precious opal. However, more likely than not, the sharp-eyed will find a piece of potch. This opaline material is considered worthless, but I beg to disagree. Memories of ancient oceans can exert a quiet magic. Bearers of this milky stone may notice heightened awareness.

(*The Magic of Opals*, by WO Brown 1972, p.14)

That Monday spring morning, I, namely Dr Samson Cherian, of Tamil Nadu in India, was seated in a small plane, about to land at Manguri. The aircraft banked at a sharp angle and my limbs gave a violent twitch. I had not habituated myself to being cooped up in such a small space. Only when we were safely parked on the tarmac could I unclasp my aching fingers, knotted in my lap since leaving Adelaide Airport two hours before.

Through the window it looked like dollops of an acrylic rust-red paint and another darker, almost black pigment, had been squirted haphazardly onto an illimitable canvas, then smeared across it, only broken by the straight lines of empty roads. The terrain reminded me of the crinkled velvet of a stomach's rugae. Crusted open sores of white lakes blotted the parched red earth, looking like gastric ulcers I'd excised in my operating theater in Vellore. Not a pleasing picture to hang on a wall, I thought.

"All right Doc?" the young man next to me asked.

I gave a polite but cursory nod, before turning away. After our earlier conversation, I didn't want to be questioned for a second time by the muscular young man seated to my right. Unlike me, he was a seasoned traveller. When we climbed aboard the 12-seater in Adelaide, he'd stowed his duffel bag into the compartment above us and lobbed into his seat with an easy grace.

My face, in contrast, would have looked a portrait of anxiety. I'd only been on a plane three times in my life. As far as I was concerned, that was three times too many. But most of all I feared what was in store for me on my arrival in Manguri.

I'd introduced myself to my greasy-looking neighbor not long after take-off.

"Good morning. My name is Doctor Samson Paul Cherian. I am from Tamil Nadu in India. I am most delighted to make your acquaintance."

"G'day Doc. How you goin'?"

He introduced himself as Jack, also known as "Diesel Jack", to the local town folk, son of "Chicken Pete". I'd get to know his dad soon enough, once we arrived in Manguri. I had trouble understanding Jack's slow nasal drawl. He spoke with a broad Australian accent: "You" sounded like "ya" and "all right", was pronounced "aw'right".

I discovered Jack was a 23-year-old diesel mechanic. Originally from "up north", he was returning to help his "ol' man" out with a spot of opal mining over the spring and summer months. This would explain the black smudges ground into the skin of his forearms and his calloused, scaly hands. Deep pits and indurated scars gouged his face, characteristic of not-long-healed acne. Blonde scruffy hair melded with a straggly beard below.

We'd shaken hands at the start of the flight, my well-manicured surgeon's fingers soft and pliable in his firm rough grasp, before an adolescent-looking pilot leapt into his seat. He said a cheerful "G'day" to the passengers whom he clearly knew well. Then the sound of the motor chugged over and the propellers on each wing growled into life.

"Thank bloody god," Jack said, after I explained my reason for going to Manguri. He wore red-stained shorts and scuffed brown leather boots; his legs stretched into the narrow aisle of the small plane. A faint smell of astringent oil mixed with body odor emanated from his denim shirt. "Manguri never has a doc who stays more than a few weeks. We haven't had anybody regular for 'bout two years. We bloody need a bloody good doctor."

"Why is that?"

"You know …"

My silence implied that I didn't. Only my head gave an involuntary wobble.

Jack appeared to squirm; he was probably wondering if he had said too much. I knew I was deplorably uninformed about Manguri and its residents. I only had a postcard with a photograph to fuel my imagination: a picture of a glowing sunset with a piece of mining equipment creating a startling silhouette against brilliant oranges and blues. The recruitment agency had sent it to me. *After* I'd signed my two-year contract.

He shifted in his seat. "Well, most of the doctors are like you, Doc. When they land, they freak out a bit, and run hell-for-leather back to where they came from."

"Why would they do that?"

"Oh, come on, Doc!" It was Jack's turn to look shocked. "Didn't they send you any information?"

"No... I mean, yes … Of course, they did." *But they simply sent me what I wanted to hear.*

Jack frowned and said no more.

Fear began to surge through my veins. I was an experienced surgeon, but one used to well-equipped theaters, with highly trained anesthetists and nursing staff on standby. Here, I would be the only doctor in town. Also, there had been no regular doctor for two whole years. No-one had mentioned the high attrition rate of doctors in Manguri when I negotiated my contract. I chastised myself; I should have asked more questions. I'd just accepted blindly, without probing too deeply, that I'd be deployed to an area of medical need. I didn't expect any choice in the matter of my final destination. And, at the time, that seemed perfectly reasonable.

"Manguri is a good place, with good people," Jack said. His gaze dropped. "The trouble is …"

"Yes?"

"You people, as I said before."

I swallowed. "Indian doctors?"

Jack shook his shaggy head. "No, no. It's nothing to do with being Indian. It doesn't matter where you come from. It's just that … you're all from overseas. Pakistan, India, South Africa, Russia … You name it, we've had 'em." He sighed. "You take one look at the place and then you do a runner."

Was I too going to be one of "those" people? I thought. I searched for words.

"Yes, yes... But why?"

"Dunno. Maybe it's the heat, or the flies. P'raps it's the isolation …" A melancholic tone crept into the timbre of his speech. "Some of the mining accidents can be pretty nasty, you know. Legs and hands sometimes get blown off. The car accidents can be pretty messy." He gave a mournful shake of his head and smiled wistfully. "There was a whole family of Aboriginal people killed just last week. A hundred klicks out of Alice, six of 'em. Rollover. All dead at the scene …"

As Jack spoke, a slideshow of uninvited and ghastly scenes began to flit across my mind's eye, slotting into view, one after the other. First frame: a twist of bloodied bodies lying within the charred remains of cars strewn across a highway. Next: an exploding mine catapulting amputated limbs into the air in all directions. On it went: next a dog with slavering jaws snatching up a splintered fly-blown femur, half-buried in the red soil …

"Not to mention the tourists," Jack intoned. "They drive off into the desert without any water or petrol. Then they break down and they try and walk it. They're usually found cooked to a cinder, often just meters from an Aboriginal water hole..."

I looked at my neighbor, aghast. More horrific images crowded my brain: pictures of the corpses of sun-scorched tourists sprawled along outback roads. A legless miner hobbled alone into the distance, a crutch under one arm, his blood-stained stump of a leg resembling a gigantic bandaged toe, a black cloud of flies swirling about him …

Jack chuckled. "You know, they also fall backwards down the mineshafts. Quite often, I'm afraid." He whispered as if he was divulging a little-known secret. "At least once a year. They're usually taking a photo or something, and don't look where they're going... Swedish tourist, young girl, just last month. *Dead.* We always warn them, but still they don't remember." He flashed a bright smile and said more loudly, "Sad, isn't it?"

My head swayed unsteadily. I was sure my face had become beige rather than coffee-colored, as my blood seemed to drain away.

"But don't you worry, Doc," Jack said. A grin spread across his face. "Manguri is a good place, with good people. We'll look after you!"

I wondered if it was too late to beg the pilot to let me out; after all, we were still stationary on the tarmac in Adelaide. But the plane's engine was revving for take-off, the doors bolted and cross-checked, or whatever it was they did to stop errant foreign doctors trying to make a last-minute break for it. The alarm must have shown on my face because the diesel mechanic became mercifully silent.

After a few minutes he spoke up as if to clarify matters. With his booming voice the whole plane would have heard him. "I'm only joshing you, Doc! Only kidding! That stuff only happens sometimes." He slapped my thigh good-naturedly with his oil-stained hand.

A loud guffaw, from an equally dusty-looking gentleman in the seat behind, did little to reassure me. Lost in my fears about what lay in front of me, for the rest of the flight I speculated how long it would be before I earned the record for the fastest departure ever from Manguri by an IMG—an international medical graduate.

The plane began to make its descent onto the landing strip, and I studied the scene below. Manguri consisted of mostly gray and terra-cotta-colored sheds, with conical mounds of yellow and white rock and shale studding the surrounding landscape. Gray bitumen and white dirt roads criss-crossed the red terrain. Large galvanized iron rainwater and fuel storage tanks stood or leaned against each other in the middle of nowhere, as if dumped. The flatness was broken by the pyramids of rock scattered as far as the eye could see, some as high as a building. Machinery towered alongside, like posturing praying mantises. Unbidden, a question sprang into my thoughts: How could anyone in their right mind live in such a place?

Looking at this strange vista, I recalled a favorite lunchtime game I'd played in the dirt of my schoolyard in Madras. My friends and I scrabbled for antlion nests among the yard's few shrubs. A fine pyramid of dust next to a hole signaled an antlion to be resident. We captured black ants and dropped them, one by one, into the predator's lair. Enthralled, we watched as a life-and-death struggle went on below. Churned-up dust got flicked about, adding to the powdery pile alongside the hole, as the pincered lion claimed his prey. Eventually, the sacrificed ant would be completely sucked into the quicksand, its black limbs trailing behind. *Gone.*

Now the memory of those boyhood pranks disturbed me. With my schoolmates I'd killed innocent creatures. Admittedly only insects, but nevertheless, living beings. Each one was fed, brutally and without compunction, into the nobbled jaws of an antlion.

It was early afternoon when we finally disembarked. The airport building was little more than a tin shed, with galvanized iron roofing and chicken wire fencing surrounding a small carpark. After I'd collected my bags in the airport's combined arrival and departure area, a late-middle-aged woman with a friendly smile approached. A frilly pink apron did little to disguise her protuberant abdomen. Short stringy gray hair framed her round face.

"Dr Cherian? Hello!" The woman pumped my hand; she had the same accent as Jack. "I'm Barbara Rogers. Everyone calls me Barb. The Director of Nursing—we call her the DON—asked me to meet you. Did you have a good trip?"

"Yes, fine, thank you. It was most satisfactory." I glanced furtively at Diesel Jack who was now striding out of the waiting room, his duffel bag slung over one shoulder. "That young man and I had quite a long chat."

Barb's eyes followed the direction of my look and her mouth twisted into an apologetic grimace. "Oh, Jack," she said. "Don't believe everything he tells you. Him and his old man are full of hot air. Some days I worry his old man is going to blow up, he's so full of it. When he's full … If you know what I mean."

"I'm sorry, I don't quite understand."

Barb picked up my two large bags before I could protest and led the way out of the airport.

"He's an alky, Doctor." My face must have revealed my complete confusion. She shook her head slowly and explained. "You know, alcoholic. His dad Chicken Pete often disappears for weeks at a time on a bender, then comes back into town to dry out at the hospital for a few days. Young Jack comes home from the city to help out for a bit, just to make sure Chicken's eating and has enough money to live on. But Jack does like to tell porkies, I mean … he likes to tell a bit of a tale. *Embellish the truth*. Is that the right word?"

I willed my head to stop wobbling.

"Don't worry, Doctor. Manguri's a good place, *with good people*. We'll look after you."

At these now familiar words the dewy calm of reassurance I'd briefly enjoyed, following the revelation that Jack was a pathological liar and I shouldn't believe a word he'd said, evaporated in an instant.

At the carpark Barb opened the passenger door of what looked like an ambulance, and I climbed in. The cabin reeked of cigarette smoke. Small sticky flies followed me into the vehicle and zoomed in to feast on my eyes. I tried batting them away.

"You drive an ambulance to collect people at the airport?" I asked.

Barb started the engine. "Yup. Don't use this one too often, so it needed to have its battery charged. Thought I'd kill two birds with one stone by coming to get you."

"Yes, that is most sensible." So, the ambulance doubled as a taxi service. "Tell me, I'm curious. Why is Chicken Pete called Chicken Pete?"

Barb was by now guiding the ambulance through the gates of the airport carpark.

"Dunno. Most of the miners here have nicknames. Especially the ones who've been here a long time."

"Why is that?"

"The miners in Manguri came from everywhere in the seventies. It was a bloody United Nations: Yugoslavian, Slovakian, Croatian, Italian, German, Greek, Scottish, Australian... You name it. And they're just the ones I can think of. They all got nicknames, because nobody could say or remember their names. Chicken Pete is Croatian. They're called that because of something they did, or just how they look. Chicken Pete used to run away from a fight in the early days. Or it might have been because he once won the chook raffle at the Italian club."

"Excuse me. What is a chook?"

"A chicken." She laughed, a moist-sounding burble.

"Oh, of course." I mulled over what she had just said. A raffle must be a form of local gambling.

"Manguri had a lot of mining accidents in the early days, but the opal's dried up in recent years. The miners don't take the same risks they used to, so we have fewer accidents nowadays."

"What happens now?"

"A lot of the old ones keep going until they fall over, more or less" (images of crippled amputee geriatric miners falling backwards down mineshafts flashed across my imagination—Jack's words had obviously left a powerful impression upon me) "but usually they just stop working and open a hotel or café or opal shop or something. Some of them run tours. Tourism has become big business here over the last few years. The young ones usually head off to the city to work."

We sat in companionable silence as the miles slid by, allowing me to reflect on our short conversation. The landscape here was so desolate, so oppressive. Why would a tourist travel over 900 kilometers to visit this uninviting place? I could only imagine the heat of summer. And now I'd discovered the swarms of dreadful flies, still flitting about the ambulance's cabin, dodging my pathetic attempts to swat them. I glanced over at Barb. Her eyes were fixed on the road ahead, but I detected the trace of a smile.

Soon we were driving along the dusty main street of Manguri. A petrol station stood at one end and restaurants and cafés lined both sides of the road. She turned down a side road and a vista opened up of low reddish-gray hills slashed with jagged crevices. Close inspection revealed a line of verandahs projecting at regular intervals out of the hillside. These skirted conventional-looking houses, with carports adjoining. Along the summits of the hills, thin vertical pipes stuck out from the ground looking like missiles ready for launching but strangely topped with what looked like "Chinaman" hats.

"Those are dugouts," Barb said, pointing to the house exteriors. "Those pipes are for ventilation."

"I'm sorry?"

"You know, people's homes."

"People actually live underground?"

Barb looked amazed at my ignorance, as if to say, "Gee doctor, you don't know much about Manguri!" However, she just said, "They certainly do! There are some lovely places there. Some of them with five bedrooms. Cool in summer, warm in winter. No need for air conditioning. It's the best way to live up here."

I wondered how I would deal with the terror I experienced whenever I was in dark confined places. This was probably a hangover from an episode of solitary confinement I'd experienced at the children's home where I spent my youth.

"There are even some beautiful churches here underground. Stained glass windows, everything."

Well, I thought, at least I could pray to the Lord for help while dealing with my subterranean anxiety.

Minutes later we climbed a hill and pulled up at the front of an impressive-looking modern red-brick building. A sign announced we had reached the Manguri and Districts Hospital. Barb killed the engine. "Here you go, Doctor," she said. "I'll just take you in and introduce you to Dee the DON. She'll look after you. Oh, and by the way, you're getting the flat at the bottom of the hill." I smiled with relief: no dugout then. "So, I'll take your bags down and drop 'em off at the front door. OK? Either me or Dee will take you down there after she's shown you around the hospital."

In the main entrance I was introduced to Dee the DON, who, like Barb, sprang forward with an open smile to greet me and shake my hand. In contrast to Barb's slow and casual manner, Dee moved about more like a mini tornado.

"Dr Cherian, welcome! My name is Dee Edwards. I am the Director of Nursing. We're *very* pleased that you've come here to work in Manguri."

Dee looked to be in her mid-forties. She was small in stature, but she filled every room with a sense of authority wherever she swept. Her dark hair was cropped short, and looked almost like a bathing cap. A lanyard around her neck held her name tag and attached pen efficiently.

"I thought I'd give you a tour of the hospital and introduce you to some of the staff here. Then I can show you around the town. But let's have a coffee first."

She didn't wait for my reply before leading the way into the staffroom, the keys pinned to her dark blue waistband jingling as she walked.

A large pin-up board on the wall dominated the room. It was covered with photos of parties and the portraits of previous hospital staff. The partygoers were silly and laughing, slack arms flopping over one another. Some were dressed in ludicrous costumes; a few wags were evidently Christmas elves. Dee placed a coffee before me and then sat down at the table opposite me. She began to shoot questions.

"You trained at Vellore Christian Medical College in Tamil Nadu? By all accounts I understand this is an excellent teaching hospital," she said, to which I nodded in agreement before I had a chance to reply.

"You trained in general surgery but have done some pediatrics as well. All good experience." Then she suddenly leaned forward, looked me in the eye, and asked quietly, "But Samson, why choose to come here, of all places on earth?"

Her direct manner and informality in using my first name so soon, took me aback.

"I approached a medical recruitment agency in Chennai and they negotiated my contract here. I passed the examination for medical entry to Australia as required."

"I see. You wanted to work in Australia and this was the easiest way?"

"Yes. The recruitment agency advised I had no choice as to where I would be sent."

Dee sat back in her chair then and laughed mirthlessly. "Did they now? That's not entirely true. But I'm delighted you have joined us. A hospital can't really function without a doctor on staff."

"I hear there has been no regular doctor in the town for two years. Is that true?"

"'Fraid so."

Dee, the one-woman interview panel, appraised me for a few seconds, her close-set brown eyes unblinking.

"On first impression Manguri looks like a rough place," she said. "Some of our previous doctors were too inexperienced—I don't know which government idiot thought they were—so they shot through virtually straightaway. Others were highly qualified, but didn't understand our on-call system, or were just plain lazy."

We sat for a few minutes, sipping in silence, each lost in our own thoughts.

"Samson," Dee looked at me very directly now, setting her cup down on the saucer with a gentle clatter. "Manguri is a good place—"

"—with good people," I repeated the mantra under my breath.

"Sorry?"

"Oh, I was just agreeing with you; Manguri does seem to have good people."

A relieved smile lit up Dee's face. "I'm very glad you think that. I do hope you will be a stayer."

Next, Dee took me on the grand tour of the hospital, to introduce me to the nursing staff on duty, and to show me the general layout of the building. There were only ten single rooms for patients, rather than shared wards. All of the rooms and corridors seemed to be empty.

"Where are your patients?" I asked, astonished. In India, hospital rooms and corridors were always crowded, not just with patients but with their relatives as well.

"Well, we only have one inpatient at the moment, Dirty Harry. But he's outside having a smoke."

"You have a patient called *Dirty Harry*?"

Dee laughed. "You'll find out soon enough why. And don't worry, Samson, you're going to be kept busy. The hospital will fill up soon enough."

The staff I met, kitchen hands, cleaners and nurses, all looked busy, restocking cupboards and cleaning. They greeted me with giant smiles and came forward one by one to shake my hand. None of this joviality counteracted my growing sense that I had made a very big, intractable mistake.

Then Dee took me on another 20-minute tour, this time of the town, in her utility that was caked in the pervasive chalk-like dust. We drove up and down sun-blasted streets, past shops and the supermarket on the main strip, a public pool ("It's closed for winter," she informed me) and a school. Dee told me who lived in the dugouts and who had done well out of opals. A few Aboriginal people rested in the shade of tin sheds along the way. Gray spindly eucalyptus trees lined the main street, the only visible vegetation. Squawking white corellas squabbled and darted playfully in and out of the trees. An occasional car prowled past, mainly four-wheel-drives bristling with radio antennaes, all of them covered in dust or dried mud. Strange black pipes emerged from their bonnets, which I later learned were snorkels, to allow the vehicles to cross flooded waterways. Peeling souvenir stickers from remote places were stuck onto back windows and bumper bars: *Karoonda SA. She purred like a cat as she rode my tractor face at B and S ball! Darwin. If this van is a rockin' don't come a knockin'!* The odd snatch of rock music pounded from the open windows of vehicles crawling past, leaving a musical vapor trail.

"The main drag's busy for a Tuesday," Dee said.

"Really?"

"Must be a party somewhere. That means we'll be busy tonight."

My throat tightened.

Once we left the main street, we saw little sign of any human habitation. So different to the streets of Chennai where I'd grown up, and more recently, Vellore. I disliked this feeling of emptiness, this lack of comfort in numbers. When we stopped at a lookout, the highest point from which one could survey the town, a suffocating cloak of nervousness tightened steadily around my shoulders. Bar a squealing motorbike and the faint noise of an engine in the distance, all I could hear was the sound of pervading emptiness. There was nothing to see except a jumbled collection of sheds and vehicles. My head began to throb. The glare of the afternoon sun brought a hazy quality to the town undimmed by my dark sunglasses.

I half-expected a noisy protest of disgruntled placard-waving miners, protesting their lack of decent opal finds, to swarm from hidden dugouts and start throwing rocks or setting off sputtering fire crackers. The only time I'd seen streets abandoned like this was when a riot at the local temple erupted in Chennai. Then, gun-toting policemen roamed the streets and banged on doors at random to round up masked bandits.

Dee broke the silence and asked me if I'd seen any opal before. I'd viewed the green and blue gems hanging from the necks of well-heeled Indian women, but I'd never seen the stone in its raw state.

"Why don't I take you out for a spot of noodling?"

My blank expression affirmed I had absolutely no idea what she was talking about. She chuckled and we drove to an abandoned mine site ten minutes from the hospital, off the main road into the town. The scene resembled a science fiction movie, set on Mars. A cold breeze whipped up a brown dust cloud against the bleak afternoon sky. Random mullock mounds stood like sentinel guards to the entrances of the mine's yawning black caverns. Obstinate tussocks of grass clung to the earth here and there.

Dee pulled over next to a large roadside sign. "DANGER! MINING AREA! KEEP OUT! BLASTING!" the notice said, in large black letters next to a small illustration of a bomb fizzing. "OPEN SHAFTS!" it helpfully informed, alongside an illustration of a stick figure falling headfirst down a vertical hole. Directly behind, making a fitting backdrop, lay a crumpled burned-out car wreck, its rusted parts scattered across the red dirt. Was this wreck a remnant of one of those multivehicle pileups Jack had mentioned? As I pondered, a squadron of sticky small flies zeroed in for another attack.

Dee passed me a zip-lock plastic bag. "All you do is sift through whatever the blower has tossed out from the mine. It's the dirt that's vacuumed out from the bottom, after the walls have been blown up or dug out." She walked over to a dirt pile and picked up some small grubby stones and peered at them sitting in her palm. She called out to me over her shoulder, "Sometimes you can be lucky and find something quite valuable. But … Just watch your step."

I stumbled across to where Dee was foraging and stooped down reluctantly. A tenacious fly was determined to excavate the conjunctiva of my left eye, ignoring my frantic waving to dislodge it. My hands immediately got filthy as I scooped up a few stones for inspection. One small quartz-like rock drew me to examine it more closely; it glinted in the sun with streaks and flashes of emerald and azure.

My heart lurched. "Look, look! I found one!"

Dee tossed her handful aside and came over to give her verdict.

"Sorry, Samson. That's just a piece of potch. It's worthless, I'm afraid. Although it's a good start."

Instead of throwing it away, I thrust the milky-white stone deep into my trouser pocket. Sometimes—I recalled the saying—true beauty is locked up deep within a seemingly worthless exterior.

Chapter Five

*If you are fatigued or suffering malaise, green opal is the gem
to wear. Known for its energy boosting qualities, green opal
can strengthen the immune system. Bearers may even report
enhanced spiritualism and appreciation for life.*
(*The Magic of Opals* by WO Brown, 1972, p. 67)

Dee dropped me back at the hospital. After bringing me chicken sandwiches and a slice of butter cake from the kitchen, she announced I should rest before attending the dinner to officially welcome me, which was to be held at the Greek restaurant. All of the hospital staff were invited. As if summoned by magic Barb reappeared, oblivious to my mild panic at this sudden news, and escorted me to Dee's utility in the hospital carpark. We drove down the hill and almost immediately turned into a carport. Before me was the entrance to a dugout—*a dugout!*—with walls of red earth, an aluminium window and front door complete with mesh fly-screen. A white timber pergola framed the front door. A few faded terracotta pots containing straggly succulents and decorated with ancient spiderwebs, stood sentry next to the pergola.

We got out of the car. Barb produced a key.

"Here ya go. This is the doctor's flat. There's an identical one next door, if we're ever lucky enough to get another medico. That's a bit of wishful thinking I'm afraid."

After yanking at the cobwebbed metal frame of the front door, which squealed loudly in protest, she led the way into a pitch-black room. I felt my pulse quicken.

"Just find a few lights… there we are," Barb said. The room flooded with yellow light. "See? Nice ya reckon?"

I surveyed the room before me and, tentatively, I had to agree. The yellow and rose-tinted earthen walls were coarsely patterned, reminding me of the swirly weave of a crocheted doily; the floor was covered in a kind of green, waxy linoleum. Several clumsy paintings of eucalyptus trees and Australian river scenes hung on the walls. A bright orange sofa faced a TV. A white-tiled bathroom opposite the kitchen was pleasingly clean.

Barb broke my silence. "The walls were tunneled out by a digger. If you want another room, we can just get Steely Dan—he's married to Sally, one of the kitchen hands—to dig you another. He won't mind. He did Dee's extra bedroom."

"Thank you, but that won't be necessary."

"It's no bother, really. Just sing out anytime."

I quietly willed Barb to leave so I could nurse my pounding head and slow my shallow breathing in private.

"Well Doctor, now that you've been introduced to your new home, I'd best take you back to the hospital."

"I'm sorry? I thought Dee wanted me to rest this afternoon ahead of the dinner."

Barb's face became deadly serious, her mouth tightly compressed. "You are expected to do a ward round and we also have a full clinic booked for you," she said. But then, seeing my pained face, she burst out laughing. "Only kidding Doctor! I'm just pulling your leg. You have a nice rest and then I'll make you a nice cup of tea and then—"

"No, no, I'm fine, really," I said. Murmuring my thanks, and with some relief, I shooed her out the door. It would take me some time to get used to the Australian sense of humor.

Although I'd had a day's stopover in Adelaide after my flight from Singapore, my whole body ached. Ignoring my two suitcases full of mostly books, various medical paraphernalia and a few clothes, I fell into an exhausted sleep on the double bed, lying atop its slippery purple nylon bedcover. I made sure I left the bedside lamp on.

The shrill ringing of a phone on the bedside table roused me from a deep slumber. I fumbled for my glasses and sat up, disorientated. It was a reminder: Dee was picking me up in 30 minutes. I'd been asleep for nearly two hours. After a quick shower, with all the interior lights glaring, I tried to decide what attire would be appropriate for a meet-and-greet with my new work colleagues. Dressed only in my underpants I took a moment to regard my reflection in the full-length mirror on the back of the wardrobe door. In a sudden burst of energy, I curled my fists and air jabbed my mirror image, hopping about in imitation of boxers in the Hollywood movies. I hummed the theme of a film I had once seen: *Rocky*.

At 35 years old and in my prime, I indulged a little self-admiration. My muscles were rippling and defined. I could be an anatomist's dream model. My wavy, jet-black hair was thick and lustrous, despite a most annoying cowlick on the right side of my forehead that resisted copious and daily applications of *Parachute Advansed* coconut hair-oil. I was also blessed with a perfectly straight set of white teeth in my chiseled—some would say manly—jaw. Now completely dressed, I thought my white nylon shirt contrasted beautifully with my deep brown eyes and prominent black eyebrows. Tan trousers toned nicely with my black leather jacket, belt and shoes. (Barb had warned me about the bitter cold of the desert night air.) To complete the look, I discarded my usual gray tie and pulled a more dressy, shiny red one out of my suitcase.

Minutes later Dee knocked on the door. She took in my outfit and an eyebrow lifted as her gaze rested on my tie.

"Am I dressed appropriately?" I queried.

She appeared to be smothering a smile. "I think you can lose the tie, Samson. Around here no-one wears one."

I quickly removed the offending item, grateful to receive my first lesson in the local dress code.

We walked out the front door (somehow, I had forgotten that my new home was 50 meters under a hill) and then I stopped dead in my tracks. The view from under the pergola looking west was breathtaking. The sun, now an orange orb, cast a lingering pink glow over the red earth and a riot of color spread up into the sky. Flames of reds, oranges, purples, like the vivid dyes of silk saris, exploded, alongside foaming clouds of gray and pink that rippled in a radial pattern across the sky.

"Oh, my goodness," I said, otherwise dumbstruck.

"Lovely isn't it? I'll never get tired of Manguri sunsets."

We stood for a few minutes admiring the view then I reluctantly climbed into Dee's vehicle. She drove us into the town, and within five minutes we arrived at Joe's Greek Taverna at the top of the town's main street. As we entered the restaurant, we had to push our way through multicolored plastic ribbons hanging in the doorway.

Seeing me, Barb called out, "G'day Doc!" She was seated at a large brown laminex table and was patting the seat of an empty chair next to her. The restaurant was crowded with at least 30 diners, all dressed in T-shirts, jeans, flip-flops and sandals. I soon met more nurses, who had not been on duty at the hospital earlier that day, and an assortment of husbands, partners and children. Platters of Greek food appeared. Dips and breads, wafting garlic smells, lamb kebabs and grilled seafood. Waiting staff strode in and out through the constantly slamming kitchen door. Dee sat on my far side, her husband Stan alongside. An older bearded man with a generous paunch urged me to try the local beer. Not wishing to appear rude, I accepted what looked like an enormous glass. I tasted the tart cold liquid that was the color of dark honey, with an ice cream-like froth on top, and found it surprisingly good. Before I knew it, I had quaffed half the glass. More people came over to shake my hand and clap me on the back, and to tell me how pleased they were that Manguri had a new "quack". Names, faces: Jo, Kath, Marg, Kym, Di, Rae, and more. (How would I remember them all?) All smiling, laughing.

My misgivings soon evaporated and I started to enjoy myself. The friendliness of the people and their unreserved welcome was infectious. My headache eased, even though the chatter around me had grown louder. Soon I was laughing at most of the jokes; even the ones I didn't understand. Waitresses brought more trays of beer, then small glasses of an exotic liqueur that tasted like aniseed. The faces of the people seated near me were starting to blur. I could not suppress belly-shaking hiccups. I giggled when Dee told me I would need to be on duty at eight o'clock sharp the next morning. And that I was down to run a full clinic in the afternoon. "Time for bed, Dr Cherian," she said.

Steely Dan helped me to stand. "Up you get, Doctor."

Swaying, I responded, "Thanks for giving me such a warm welcome … Manguri is a very good place … *With very good people.*" I lifted my glass in salute.

A chorus of resounding agreement filled the restaurant:

"Hear, hear Doc!"

"I'll drink to that, Doc!"

"On ya Doc!"

Dee then half-carried, half-pushed me out the restaurant's door, to bundle me into her utility. I found her small face quite enchanting—how had I not noticed this before? A sudden desire to kiss her pursed lips came across me—an urge I only just managed to restrain. I leaned against the car door in a state of happy delirium, unable to wipe a soppy grin off my face.

"I'm the first doctor to work here in two years!" I repeated several times as she drove me homewards.

Soon she was pulling into my pergola with screeching tires. Muttering to herself, she hauled me out of the car and pushed me, staggering like a drunken sailor, through the front door. I toppled forward onto my still made-up bed.

"See you in the morning, Doctor," was all she said, as she slammed the front door behind her.

I heard the car start and pull away. Around me the room was starting to spin. And then, I heard a voice, inside my head, its volume waxing and waning in and out of my consciousness. I realized it was the voice of my wife, Mercy. "Samson! You were supposed to call me when you arrived in Manguri, remember?" She harrumphed and then sighed. "You never keep your promises."

The last thing I remember was vomiting aniseed-flavored yellow liquid all over the gaudy purple bedspread, still fully dressed, with hair oil staining the pillow dark and my thick-rimmed glasses teetering on the end of my nose.

Chapter Six

Opals bring a sense of peace and wonderment to any wearer.
For those of a depressive disposition, the light of ancient oceans
radiates and enlivens the souls of even the most melancholic.
(*The Magic of Opals* by WO Brown, 1972, p. 1)

In the nightmare I endured that first morning in Manguri, I was back in the streets of the Old Tambaram of my childhood. My uncle, Mama Guna, was chasing me, and not in a playful way, but like a stray cat chases a mouse. I ran panicked, through alleys and past stinking rubbish tips, yet my dash was blocked—by a cow. The beast stood chewing its cud and stared blankly at me with my wife's dark and gentle eyes, its tail switching to displace a black cloud of outback flies. I screamed, terrified. I wouldn't be going anywhere with this ungulate creature acting as a bollard. Mama Guna flew at me seconds later and pinned me down. But, strangely, by then he'd transformed into Diesel Jack in a stained dhoti, his breath a sickly concoction of coconut and aniseed. Rough hands wrapped around my neck, to squeeze tighter and tighter. I couldn't get any air; my breath came in hot, desperate bursts. He tightened his grip. But then, his expression softened to one of kind concern. He said, in Barb's rasping voice, *"Doctor! Doctor! You aw'right?"*

I woke with a start, to the sound of an insistent rap on the front door; breath rushed to fill my lungs. My bedside alarm clock informed me it was seven o'clock. The events of the previous evening flooded back as I located my glasses in the sheets. I gave up the struggle to sit and instead collapsed on the bed, groaning as a searing pain lanced my temples. Sweat soaked my armpits, my nylon shirt clung to my torso. My head felt as if it was being repeatedly split in two by an icepick. My mouth must surely have been swabbed dry with cottonwool while I slept.

"Doctor! You in there?" Barb called again. "Good morning! Time to get up. You don't want to be late for your first morning."

The room stank of vomitus, oddly sweet and acid. I stared in horror at the wet stain with drying yellow food particles smeared over the pillow and bedcover. I stumbled to the door. I was confronted by dazzling morning light and a bright-eyed Barb, holding a plastic bag full of breakfast provisions.

"Good night last night, wasn't it? You enjoyed yourself, didn't you?"

She barged past me and dumped the food items with a clatter onto the mustard-brown kitchen bench. "Dear, oh dear," she clucked as she eyed the yellow vomit stain on my white shirt. "You poor old chook. Go and have a shower, Doc. Clean yourself up. It's lucky I thought I'd come down and make you breakfast … After all, it's your first day."

"Thank you but—"

"No buts, Doctor. You have 40 minutes before ward round starts."

I moaned. Light and noise pummeled my brain. Barb passed me three small white tablets.

"Dee thought you might need these. Something for the head and to stop you being sick."

"What are they?"

"Dunno. But Doctor, always do what Dee says. She's a good woman that one. She'll look after you. If she says these are the best tablets for a hangover, then you better believe it. That, and bacon and eggs."

I swallowed the pills dry, without argument.

So dismissed, Barb turned her back to me and busied herself. She lit the gas stove and found a frypan and cups, all the while opening and slamming drawers crammed with jingling cutlery; each crashing noise another blow of the ice pick into my skull.

A short while later, dressed in clean clothes and freshly showered, with the pain in my head subsiding to a tolerable ache, I faced Barb across a plate of greasy food. She had tactfully left the front door open so a cool breeze ventilated the room. She sipped from a cup of tea as I tentatively started to eat.

"All right Doctor?"

I nodded as I swallowed the runny yellow egg and toast. I had to agree I felt a lot better; my stomach no longer felt like a churning cement mixer.

"Barb, what is your actual job at the hospital?"

"I'm just the all-round general dogsbody."

"Pardon me?"

"Sorry, Doc. I keep forgetting you don't speak Australian. 'General dogsbody' is like someone who does boring jobs, like cleaning out cupboards. I help the girls, the nurses that is, do other things too, like feed the oldies."

"Then you are on the payroll?"

"Nah, of course not. I do it because I love the girls up there," Barb inclined her head in the direction of the hospital, "and I like keeping busy. Me husband Merv died up there. Had cancer. 'Bout three years ago. When Dr Arthur was still in town. Dee and the nurses looked after him right up to the end. They did a bloody good job too. He couldn't have wanted a better way to go. So, instead of going home after he died, I just kind of stayed on."

"You live there?"

"Nah—mind you, the food's good. I have a dugout about five minutes away. Merv dug it out for us when we first moved here in the seventies."

I imagined Barb as a fresh-faced young woman, one of the few in town. "That must have been a most interesting time," I said.

"You're dead right there. No police overnight, with just one copper for much of the time during the day. Too much grog flowed when a miner had a good find; there were lots of fights and accidents then. But Manguri is a tamer place nowadays. Lots of people have moved away. Poor Dee keeps arguing with the health department. Because of the falling numbers and the difficulty in keeping doctors, they keep threatening to close the hospital."

I stared at her. "They are thinking of closing the hospital? When?"

"Dunno. Hopefully it won't happen now. That's why Dee's so pleased you're here. She told me that you signed a two-year contract."

"Yes, that is correct."

Looking at Barb, all thoughts of "hot-footing" it out of town as soon as possible seemed reckless and even cruel. Instead, I felt weighted by a new responsibility. I could single-handedly stop the hospital being closed—it was up to me. I smiled my approval as I ate my breakfast, although the toast tasted like cardboard. Barb smiled back cheerfully.

My savior had parked her own small Torana in the carport area adjoining my pergola. After I'd finished eating, we got in the car to make the 500-meter ascent back to the hospital. My stomach felt queasy again, but this time I couldn't blame the after-effects of a debauched night out. A rabble of butterflies was congregating in the lower reaches of my gut. Maybe I wasn't up to the job? Maybe they had changed their minds—hospital closure or no—after my performance the previous evening. Maybe the patients hated Indian doctors!

I glanced at Barb expertly steering the car up the steep dirt road over potholes and jaw-shattering corrugations. I steadied myself against the dashboard. The people of Manguri *were* good people. They didn't deserve a doctor who became a mawkish drunkard on his first night in town.

I cleared my throat. "I'm very sorry about my behavior last night. I hope I didn't cause offence."

Barb looked over at me, humor dancing in what I could see of her green eyes, which were half-closed due to a lifetime of squinting into the outback sun. With her leathery folds of facial skin and sagging double chin, she resembled one of those wrinkly dogs I'd seen in a *National Geographic* magazine.

"No worries, Doctor. Don't give it a second thought. We're just glad to have you here in Manguri."

I sighed and held my head; it was throbbing again.

Barb dropped me off at the front entrance. I was beginning to wonder if Dee and Barb were members of a relay team and the baton being passed back and forth was me. Dee came out from the main reception desk, all efficient smiles still, a clipboard in hand.

"Good morning, Samson." She raised a wry eyebrow. "How are you feeling?"

"I am quite well, thank you." My tone was sombre as I said, "Thank you again for making me feel so welcome last night. Needless to say I most truly apologize if I behaved inappropriately." An alarming memory of my incipient ardour toward Dee flashed into my consciousness.

"Samson, you were a perfect gentleman. It was lovely to see you enjoying yourself. And, as I predicted, today we are quite busy. Shall we begin?"

Dee led the way. The hospital was now fully occupied, although it still looked empty compared with what I was used to. Our first patient was a young tourist, a boy, aged about eight. His mother, who had been dozing on a trundle bed placed next to her son, awoke with a start when she saw me.

After introducing myself, I examined the boy's abdomen. Dee was most correct in her diagnosis of food poisoning. He had recovered though and could now be discharged. I looked at the boy's rosy cheeks—he probably felt peachier than me. His mother asked me the usual questions, such as when he would be fit to travel. And Dee answered her competently and confidently.

"All seems to be in order here, Sister," I said. "Good work. Carry on."

She straightened; arms folded. "Yes, Dr Cherian. All *is* in order."

I glanced sideways at her. Was she parodying me? She smiled warmly at the boy's mother. "I think you can take young Lewis back to your caravan." She produced the required paperwork. Feeling slightly foolish, I signed my name against orders that had been written by the nursing staff and jotted down my clinical findings.

We continued the round. I began to wonder why I was even present. The nursing staff had diagnosed and treated a number of ailments, including a weeping leg ulcer, painful infections and a case of mild asthma, to name just a few. They had followed standard protocols and their judgement was excellent. I met the patient known as Dirty Harry, a Greek ex-miner with the leg ulcer. He clearly enjoyed the nurses' attention and, disgracefully, was not averse to making the odd loud lecherous comment in their presence.

We walked towards the next room, to be assaulted by a fetid smell, and another odor I could not place. Dee later explained this was the smell of wine and *rakija*: a type of Serbo-Croatian brandy.

"This is Chicken Pete," Dee said as we stood in the doorway.

"Father of Diesel Jack?"

"Yes! How did you know that?"

"I met Jack on the plane coming here."

"Did you? That's a coincidence. Jack brought Chicken Pete in this morning. He's been too uncooperative to shower as yet. We already commenced him on the Diazepam regime for alcohol withdrawal. His scores have been off the chart. He last drank about ten hours ago. Poor Jack had been trying to get him to eat and to clean him up, but Pete became abusive. He even took a swing at Jack."

"What do you mean, a swing?"

"Pete tried to punch Jack on the nose, but then fell over instead. I've known Chicken Pete a long time. I've never seen him this bad before."

I peeped into the room and willed myself not to retch. A man I judged to be in his mid-sixties lay supine on the bed, appearing how I imagined a skinned kangaroo would look. Sinewy ankle and wrist tendons were clearly visible beneath his filthy yellow skin; his untied blue hospital gown only half-covered his emaciated body. With his swollen belly, he could well have been gestating some kind of desert-spawned alien. My mouth went suddenly dry. I'd had scant experience with the treatment of alcohol dependence in India. I was a surgeon, after all.

"G'day Dee! Long time, no see!" Chicken Pete called out from behind his curtain of dirty silver hair. His symptoms had eased as the medication took effect. He was unexpectedly chirpy, though his words were slurred. "Gotta new doc 'ave ya?" He reached up and pushed a clump of hair away from eyes that fluoresced yellow with jaundice. Then he scowled. "Christ. Another bloody darkie," he said. "How long you gonna stay here for then, before you bugger off back to where you and all the others bloody come from?"

I bristled. I'd never been spoken to like this before—by anyone.

Dee reared up. She looked not unlike an aggrieved Indian cobra, her eyes beady and glittering, her fangs bared.

"You mind your manners, Pete. Or so help me, you'll be out of this hospital and back in your dig as fast as you—"

I stepped forward; my palms held upwards in a placatory gesture. "It's OK, Sister. I can handle this."

Dee retreated, still frowning.

"Mr—" I began, instantly at a loss for words. What was his real name? Did I call him Mr Pete? Or Mr Chicken?

"Call me Pete, Doc. Everyone else does." He chuckled and smiled a toothless grin; his mood had oscillated now towards ebullience. But he still radiated pent-up restlessness. If not for his severe health issues,

I'm sure he would have already scarpered out the hospital's sliding front doors.

"Mr Pete, I can assure you I have no intention of leaving Manguri in the near future…" (However, I thought, I would have given a different answer yesterday.) "You are suffering from alcohol withdrawal and showing signs of liver failure. Please be so kind as to cooperate with the nurses. Have a shower and a light meal. I will examine you when you are feeling more comfortable." I spoke with a calm authority, my accent soft and melodic, compared with Chicken Pete's rasping mix of Australian and some Eastern European language. "We will then need to treat you and make sure there is not another cause for your liver not working properly. Are you agreeable to this plan?"

"Do whatcha bloody well have to. Won't do any bloody good though. I'm dying, Doc." Chicken Pete's head flopped back, all opposition leached away, like a morose caged animal that lies flat and refuses to stand up. The pendulum of his mercurial emotional state had swung back into a bleak depression.

"Certainly not!" I said. "It is premature to say this."

Dee flashed me a warning look.

"Let's wait and see how you get on, shall we?" I said, in my most cheerful tone. "In the meantime, please have a shower."

Dee left me then to attend to her administrative duties. I was now assigned another nurse, the capable Jo. I realized that without the help of the staff I would be floundering. I liked Jo. She was a big cheerful woman with black hair bundled up in a large topknot on her head, an opal necklace glinting in the hollow of her neck like a drop of blue-green sea water. She took me to see a young man with a dislocated finger in the emergency room, the A&E. All I needed to do was put his crooked digit back into position.

This was more like it—I could do this in my sleep. No sign of a fracture on the X-ray, I tugged on the finger after administering a ring-block anesthetic. With a reassuring click the finger joint slipped back into place. I felt jubilant. I'd just treated my first emergency case in Manguri, and competently too. Other patients began to roll in: nasty gashes from falling off motorbikes, a punch-up at the pub with a broken nose, a dog bite that I hesitated to suture, worrying about the risk of infection. All the while Jo was there to steer me.

Midmorning, an elderly man sidled slowly up to the triage desk as I was writing notes in a patient file. Leaning over the desk he whispered, "I've gotta problem with my waterworks, Doc. Reckon you could take a gander at me old fella?"

I looked around. Where was his old fella? He was the oldest man present in the department. Perhaps he was experiencing the disorienting effects of dementia?

"This is a hospital, sir. Perhaps Sister Jo here can direct you to the town's waterworks?"

Jo, who was standing nearby, spluttered laughter. "He means he's having problems passing urine, Dr Cherian," she said between gulps of air. "His 'old fella' is his penis."

She took his arm. "Come on then Bill," she said. "Let's take a gander at your waterworks." Still chuckling, she led the frail old chap away to a cubicle. Shuffling past, he softly chortled to himself. Red-faced, I returned to my work.

Later, sitting in the staffroom, I considered how my earlier negative assessment of the hospital could have been so wrong. "Sister Jo … Now I have spent the morning here, I don't know how you lasted so long without a regular doctor. I am full of the most sincere admiration."

"Yeah, it's been pretty hard and frustrating at times," she said. "Dee's been under enormous pressure. We've had the odd doctor turn up for a few weeks here and there. But no-one permanent. We'd usually send patients off to Port Augusta, anything we couldn't handle, or Adelaide, if they were really sick. But we knew if we just had a doctor, we could admit those same patients here. You know, for things like pneumonia and blood pressure, instead of always sending them away. That's why we're glad you're here." She didn't smile as she made this final statement.

We finished our tea in silence, Jo leisurely turning the pages of a *Woman's Day* magazine. She didn't look up again.

After a lunch of chicken sandwiches from the kitchen, and more stewed tea, I was taken to another part of the hospital, where I was going to run an outpatient clinic. This filled me with even more dread. I'd never worked as a general practitioner before—a doctor who was expected to be the gateway for any complaint.

News of a doctor being in town had traveled fast. I already had ten patients, all rough and tough souls with reddened and weathered faces, booked to see me. Thankfully Jo was there to assist. She gave me a quick lesson on how to use the computer, which was parked like a space pod on the office desk. Back pain, tonsillitis, strange headaches, blood-pressure troubles, persistent belching—anything and everything drifted in that day. I did the best I could, the stoic patients themselves patient and tolerant of the many gaps in my knowledge.

Feeling drained of all reserves of energy and in dire need of a strong cup of tea, I took a break and then, in the late afternoon, I returned to the hospital to review Chicken Pete. Hopefully he was feeling more optimistic, or at the very least, a little more convivial. The old Croatian miner was sitting up on pillows when I entered his room. Its window offered a panoramic view of the corrugated iron-roofed town. Shiny cars snaked along the highway in the distance. A coil of smoke curled up into the sky from a rubbish burn-off in the valley below. The sky was sapphire-blue and cloudless—a perfect outback day. Shaved and showered by a bossy nurse (hopefully blessed with a poor sense of smell), Chicken Pete had managed to eat some soup. Uncharacteristically taciturn, he merely grunted consent to my request to examine him.

Starting with his hands, I observed the classic flapping tremor due to the release of toxins from a liver in its terminal state. His eyes were stained yellow; even his tear-film seemed to have taken on the pigment. Amber-colored skin was now visible following his cleansing shower. A few broken, rotten teeth indicated he'd not seen a dentist for 20 years. This could account for the necrotic halitosis emanating from his mouth. However, heart and lungs sounded normal and strong through my stethoscope, his blood pressure having normalized with medication.

I progressed to the abdomen and was not surprised to see the star-burst of superficial veins radiating out from the umbilicus, known as *caput medusae*. This was further evidence of Chicken Pete's severe liver failure. Small hemangiomas, tiny blood vessels like upside-down spiders, stippled his skin. Nor was it unexpected when I felt his massive knobby liver, which was three times bigger than normal. I didn't examine his testicles. These would have shrunk to the size of walnuts or large peanuts, a side-effect of a liver unable to metabolise a build-up of female hormones, not a problem in a healthy male. His hairless chest and armpits provided further confirmatory evidence for my diagnosis.

"Mr Pete, you have an abnormally large liver. This could be caused by the alcohol you drink, or there may be other causes. How is your bowel habit, sir?"

"My what?" Chicken Pete roused himself enough to try to understand my words.

"You know..." How did one put this in to the "Australian" way of speaking? "How are your stools?"

"My *what*?" Chicken Pete said, looking even more confused.

My voice became high pitched. "Your bowel motions, Mr Pete ... Your *feces*?"

He stared at me blankly.

"*Your poo, sir!*" I roared.

Dee entered then, and I cast her a look of humble gratitude.

"He means: What has your shit been like?" she said calmly.

"What do you bloody wanna know that for?" But before I could respond, he added, "Well, if you must know Doc, I've been shitting blood every day more or less for the last few months."

Dee's mouth tightened in concern. "Why didn't you come and tell us? Jack could have taken you down south to see somebody."

"Ah, just put it down to 'roids, Dee. You know, miner's curse, and all that."

"He means hemorrhoids," Dee whispered in response to my equally perplexed looking expression.

"Rectal bleeding can be caused by hemorrhoids, Mr Pete. But I'm worried that you may have some kind of tumor bleeding inside your back passage."

"My what?"

"Your arsehole," Dee translated.

"I will have to do a rectal examination."

"He means he has to put a finger inside you to see what is bleeding."

"Nobody is sticking his finger up my arsehole!" Chicken Pete bellowed.

After some cajoling by Dee, with the promise of a "ciggie" outside when he was up to it, Chicken Pete eventually rolled over on his side, and the deed was done. My hunch was correct. Chicken Pete had a large craggy tumor, solid and bleeding profusely just inside his hemorrhoidal backside. It was also likely that he had tumors in his liver from the spread of a cancer, and if so, his days were numbered.

After I'd disposed of my gloves and Dee had ensured Chicken Pete was as comfortable as could be expected, I ushered her into an empty room.

"I'm afraid the news is very, very bad," I said. "Mr Pete has a nasty rectal tumour. He is also in severe liver failure, most likely due to his alcohol dependence and from his cancer spreading."

"I'm not surprised, Samson. Chicken Pete stopped looking after himself when his wife ran off with his best mate. Sandy, her name was. They had a daughter too, Rosie. She was ten when her mum left Chicken. Sandy took Rosie, but left Jack behind. He was only eight years old. Chicken Pete took up drinking full-time and Jack was more or less raised by the rest of the Manguri townsfolk."

My head gave an involuntary wobble of sympathy. "That is very bad."

"Chicken Pete was a lot older than Sandy. I didn't think she'd hang around for long, to be honest. But to run off with that no-good-for-nothing piece of— I mean … that not very nice person."

"When did this happen?"

"About 15 years ago. Chicken Pete's never been the same since. He became a hermit. He spends most of his time nowadays out on his dig, coming into town every month or so. He's dried out here a few times, but then goes back to drinking as soon as he leaves. Jack tries to give him a hand, but I think he's beyond help now."

I remembered Barb telling me that Chicken Pete was an "alky" and that Jack returned regularly to Manguri to help him.

"So when shall I tell Jack his father's cancer diagnosis?" I asked.

"It would be better if Chicken Pete told him, I think."

"You wish me to tell Mr Pete first?" I was momentarily lost for words. "Are you not worried his family will be concerned? He will give up all hope?"

"Well, given that Chicken Pete hasn't seen his wife or daughter for 15 years and he only has Jack left, I don't think that's such a big problem, do you?"

I had to concur, but this was very different to my experience of informing of bad news in India. There, most of my patient's relatives were steadfastly intent on the medical profession not divulging any upsetting news to the patient—often not an easy gambit to pull off. Dee and I discussed quietly what strategy I should recommend.

We re-entered Chicken Pete's room. He cast me a suspicious look. "Well, Doc, how long I got? Give it to me straight."

Dee nudged me, I shifted uncomfortably.

"I'm afraid it does look as if you have cancer, Mr Pete. I don't know how long you have. I will fix you an appointment in Port Augusta for a series of X-rays, and to see a specialist. The specialist will talk to you about treatment options."

"Don't be bloody ridiculous," Chicken Pete said, before belching. "This is my home. I'm staying put. No bloody treatment. I'll go back to my dig and sort things out when I've dried out. But this town is where I'll die, Doc—"

Dee interjected, "We will respect your wishes, Pete. But we'll have to tell Jack what you have decided. I'll ask him to meet with us tomorrow morning. OK? Do you want us to tell him your diagnosis, or do you want to?"

I waited nearby, a useless bystander. This discourse reflected the lack of medical hierarchy of this place. Nurses stood their ground here and dared to express different opinions from their seniors and doctors. They did not hesitate to speak up, loudly and assertively. Patients being told of their terminal diagnosis, before family? So strange, so foreign.

At seven o'clock, Barb came to the front reception and announced that it was time "Doctor knocked off", and that she was taking me home; she held a tray for my supper in her sunspot-riddled hands. Dee emerged from her office, which adjoined the main entrance and touched me lightly on the arm. "I just wanted to tell you—you did an excellent job today, Samson."

For the first time since I'd met this bundle of fizzing energy, I sensed a mood of resignation or regret.

"Today was busy," she added, as if this statement was an adequate excuse for every doubt I'd experienced since my arrival. She ran a hand over her face, smoothing for a moment her forehead's fine lines. She smiled a philosophical smile, as if to say, there would be no ill-feeling felt toward me if I just packed my bags and buggered off like all the others.

I couldn't help but be affected by Dee's dedication to her hospital and her staff. By then I knew that although I would find my work in this remote mining outpost challenging, the town badly needed a doctor. I owed it to Dee and her staff to stay. Somehow, I would endure. I would "stick it out" and not "bugger off", or "do a runner". The hospital, built to serve the good people of Manguri, would stay open. This resolution filled me with a fine ambition, even a loftiness. There was a greater purpose. *Yes!* The hospital will be saved, thanks to the noble actions of Dr Samson Cherian!

But a new gloom settled over me on the way back to my new home. I still needed to telephone my wife, whose image in my head had begun to remind me of a languid fat cow dressed in a bright green sari. In this vision I could see her heavily hooded gentle eyes, gazing out through wire-rimmed glasses, her bovine mouth moving in a mechanical fashion. She would then frown at the shrill of the phone, knowing the caller was likely to be me. She would pick up the phone and, in contrast to a cow's gentle bellow, violently spit out her contempt for me. "You might save a hospital Samson, but you are not capable of giving me a baby. You are a useless, infertile fool, husband—nothing but *a useless, infertile fool.*"

CHAPTER SEVEN

Madras City, Tamil Nadu

1967

Thirty wriggling children, temporarily hushed by Miss Bhagyalakshmi Subramaniam—but that didn't stop sneaky digs in the ribs from a neighbor's elbow, or unwitnessed little pushes or pinches—were sitting on the floor of the *Karunai Illam* (House of Mercy) Children's Home, metal plates before them. Girls on one side of the room, boys on the other.

An elderly kitchen lady appeared, Chandra Amma, her hair white but her movements agile, in spite of her advanced age. A vanilla sponge cake materialized from the back kitchen, a slice of which was placed before each child. A generous anonymous benefactor had provided the sweet treat, in honor of the donor's own birthday. It didn't matter that the children didn't have a clue who they were singing birthday salutations to—cake was cake. And besides, chances were, as Miss Subramaniam reasoned, there was a high probability that one of the children unknowingly shared the same date of birth as their benevolent patron.

Miss Subramaniam was an older woman of average height, moderately dark skin and small, shrewd eyes, with a firm but kindly disposition. Chalky patches of decay on her front teeth resembled a dental prosthesis. Everyone, adults and children alike, knew her as "Miss". And having run the children's home in Old Tambaram for close on 20 years, she also called herself this. Presiding over the children in her fuchsia-pink cotton sari with antique gold neck chains tucked under her blouse and thick gray hair tightly plaited and extending like a ship's rope down to the small of her back, she ensured there was no cakey thievery. The children then dutifully sang "Happy Birthday", in honor of this auspicious occasion. When all were finished, it was time for play. There were few books and no toys or games.

To be residents of this institution, the children needed to be aged between six and twelve years. After their twelfth birthday, they were usually reclaimed by members of surviving family if not already adopted out elsewhere. Many simply returned to the squalor of the streets. Miss was known for turning a blind eye when the fateful birthday came and went. As she often argued, how reliable is a birthdate document anyway?

Vijay was six years old. He had been brought in, abandoned, six months earlier, his parents having died two years earlier. The boy quickly realized that life in the orphanage was a good deal better than begging on the streets. He had been living near *Ramani Theru*, with Mama ("Uncle") Guna. Guna was a cruel man. There had been no love felt by the small boy for his uncle, or vice-versa. Vijay's mouth was just another to feed.

A quiet boy, Vijay soon became the resident unofficial peacekeeper at the orphanage. Known for stepping forward to help resolve disputes with calm reason, his interventions were usually successful. The child was well-liked by most, but not by all.

One late afternoon an oafish older boy, Sanjay, saw an opportunity. He sneaked behind Vijay as the boy hastened to the rarely used Indian toilet hidden in a noisome cubicle out back. This insult to Indian plumbing, with its porcelain bowl cracked and stained with globs of ancient feces, sat like a throne above a constantly and mysteriously wet floor.

Vijay squatted in position when the room plunged into blackness. It sounded like a crate was being pushed outside against the cubicle's heavy door. "What are you doing?" he shrieked.

Sanjay called through a crack in the door. "This might shut you up for a while, shortie. Think you are top dog, don't you?"

Vijay shouted, "Please! I have homework to do! Let us talk about this!"

Sanjay had gone. Only a stinky silence met his cries. Cooped up in that putrid place, it would be a long time before his release. School homework was done between six and eight o'clock in the evening, and only then. Lights out at nine. Miss wouldn't allow him to open his books if he missed that time slot—regardless of the reason.

Vijay started to panic.

An hour later Chandra Amma released him from his solitary confinement. When Miss saw the tear-stained face of her favorite charge, she cried out. The cowlick of Vijay's black mane stood bolt upright and the boy had vomited his distress down the front of his shirt. Out of the corner of her eye Miss spotted his antagonist creeping upstairs. "Sanjay!" she growled. "Come here. Right this minute."

Sanjay's punishment later that night—after he'd done his homework to Miss's stern satisfaction—was to clean that same toilet, brushing away the remnants of the younger boy's undigested *tuvar dal*, his victim's dinner from the previous evening. And just on this one occasion, Miss invited Vijay to study in her private office, where he completed his school work undisturbed.

Every week on a Monday afternoon, Dr Paul Cherian, a doctor of medicine, closed his small surgery in nearby *Reddiarpalayam Theru*. "I'm off to see how Miss and the youngsters are faring," he announced to his wife, just as he did every week at two o'clock on the dot, before setting off on his 20-minute journey to the orphanage.

Clutching his black doctor's bag at his side, Dr Cherian always followed the same route, past JJ Motors and then the Malliga Kidney

Stone Centre after crossing the busy bitumen road outside his clinic. He ducked out of the path of bicycle rickshaws and dodged sputtering motorbikes and buses, before stepping onto an uneven pavement congested with small shops selling groceries and incense. Further along, he passed food stalls and carts laden with coconuts and bananas. As he hurried by, women wearing brilliant saris sweeping doorsteps looked up and smiled in recognition, and men seated at tables on the footpath playing cards and drinking chai called out greetings. At times Dr Cherian needed to step over overflowing sewerage oozing in black slime from drains or weave around poles strung with telephone wires like tangles of spaghetti. Flea-bitten scruffy dogs fossicked in the piles of rubbish that littered the sidewalk. The odd cow roamed into traffic, causing much beeping and tootling of horns.

Dr Cherian was a short rotund man, with wheatish-colored skin and a luxuriant black moustache, which complemented his thickly coiffed black hair, now streaked with gray. Each day he would spend a patient ten minutes teasing his tresses upwards and backwards into a bouffant style, his one and only concession to a little vanity. With two adult daughters now married to doctors and settled abroad, Dr Cherian was content. He loved his diminutive wife Rosalind; theirs had been an arranged marriage, but one that worked well. Rosalind was not as educated as Dr Cherian; nevertheless, he thought she was almost as intelligent. They often discussed books and argued different points of view. Rosalind kept a spick and span home for him in a small but comfortable residence behind the clinic. She attended to bookkeeping and answered the telephone. She kept her face unadorned, which her husband liked. He was suspicious of women who felt a need to tamper with the gifts God had given. And she would never wear trousers, like those floozy and uncivilized Western women. "So uncomfortable, so unflattering!" she would say, if this ever came up in casual conversation.

Dr Paul Cherian made all the important decisions in their marriage. Rosalind, for her part, did not bother her husband with trivial matters, such as household staff disputes or leaking taps and the like. Or, for that matter, unpaid patient accounts. She was, in her opinion, a much better arbiter of these trivial matters.

So, for the good doctor, life was satisfying. Business prospered. He was held in high regard by his loyal band of patients, due to his superior listening skills and dispassionate nature.

The doctor had offered his services without fee at the children's home for the last 15 years. The Cherians had never adopted themselves, although Dr Cherian had assisted with finding the children good homes from time to time. In his eyes, all of the residents at the home were equal. So, when Rosalind had occasionally expressed a desire to adopt a child, he had resisted. To give one ward a home would reject another, equally deserving. However, his resolve was sorely tested and his heart-strings were regularly tugged whenever he was timidly presented with *chai* by one of the younger children, who would look up at him with those thickly-lashed eyes, like limpid black pools.

Despite Dr Cherian's desire to remain egalitarian, he was known at the home for his generosity. Every year on Christmas Day he dressed in a Santa Claus outfit and presented each child with a chocolate and a small bag of colored pencils. Miss secretly thought Dr Cherian looked a little silly, with his cottonwool beard and suit that was too small for him and his thick black hair peeking out from under his red floppy hat.

Thanks to Dr Cherian, the orphanage was well stocked with medicines. The youngsters generally enjoyed reasonable health, once they had been wormed and nourished with three meals a day. However, one child, Vijay—Dr Cherian didn't know if he had a second name—was not thriving as expected. Every week Dr Cherian auscultated the six-year-old's chest with his stethoscope. Each time he heard moist noises, suggestive of established bronchitis. He also had chronic ear infections and thick mucus, like green jelly, dripped persistently from his nostrils. Antibiotics didn't help. Dr Cherian was beginning to think that maybe it was time he asked a good friend, Dr Vikas Koshy, a pediatrician, to see the scrawny child, whose ribs were starting to protrude like the flat slats of a xylophone.

One humid afternoon, Dr Cherian loosened the shirt of young Vijay, and placed his stethoscope. A few children lay listlessly on the floor, watching proceedings. The doctor sighed with exasperation. Musical snaps, crackles and pops rang out loud and clear from the boy's barrel chest. Dr Cherian instructed Vijay to exhale. A soft, prolonged expiratory noise gusted from his chest, sounding like the low notes of an aged bassoon.

An exasperated looking Miss had slipped into the room. She waited until Dr Cherian finished, before ranting to the small child in rapidly spoken Tamil. The other orphans lazing nearby sat up, pleased for some light entertainment.

"Not again! Bad, bad boy!"

Miss threw some pieces of paper at Vijay, which fluttered to the floor at his feet.

Vijay's eyelids drooped and his bottom lip gave a faint quiver.

"What do you have to say for yourself? Do only your own work, Vijay. Is it because Sanjay is bullying you? Is he giving you food if you do his work?"

"No, Miss," Vijay mumbled.

"What is the problem?" Dr Cherian interrupted.

"Vijay keeps doing the older boys' homework!" She threw her hands up. "His teacher now recognises his handwriting. You *must not* do their work, Vijay. You will be punished!"

Vijay continued to study the floor. A large teardrop trickled down each cheek.

Dr Cherian squatted down next to him. "Vijay, why are you doing work for other boys?"

Vijay remained silent.

"Are they beating you?"

Vijay shook his head.

"Are they giving you extra food?"

The boy gave another definite shake of his head.

"Then why? You heard Miss. You know you will get in trouble."

Vijay wobbled his head in acknowledgement. "I … I just like doing their work, sir," he stammered.

"What do you mean?"

"I find it interesting, sir."

"You find your own schoolwork too easy?" A shocked Dr Cherian asked.

Vijay's head wobbled again.

"Have you told your teacher? Does she give you extra tasks?"

"I have tried, sir. She tells me that she does not have the time, and it is wrong to treat me as special."

Dr Cherian turned and addressed the home's mistress. "Is this true, Miss? Have you spoken with this boy's teacher?"

Miss pursed her lips. "No, Doctor," she replied. Hands on hips, her eyes met Dr Cherian's, until he felt a touch uncomfortable. Her steely gaze said it all. *You may be a medical man, Doctor, but this is my domain.* She would never say that out loud though. Dr Cherian's opinions were not to be questioned, especially by a member of the fairer sex.

Feeling despondent, Dr Cherian returned home later that day. Before he left he took the time to examine young Vijay's work and indeed, the standard was more befitting a 12-year-old student's, not a six-year-old's. He urged a mulish Miss to approach his teacher and get her to challenge Vijay with extra homework and the like. She stared glassily back at him; there was no point in persisting.

Later, a sense of pessimism washed over the learned doctor as he tried to eat his evening meal. It was clear the boy's future was mapped out and virtually set in stone. Not only was he likely to return to the streets, but a fine young brain was going to be wasted through sheer lack of opportunity. He also felt puzzled; he'd thought Vijay to be one of Miss's favorites.

A week later, Dr Cherian returned to the orphanage as usual. He arrived earlier than was scheduled. He'd been thinking a lot about the young boy. Unusually, he'd spoken of him to Rosalind. His heart started beating a little faster than usual. (*I must not allow myself to become overexcited,* he reminded himself. *A racing heart is not good for one's constitution.*)

He examined one by one the children who had been earmarked by Miss as needing medical attention, including Vijay. The boy's chest was again resisting any attempts to achieve a medical miracle. The vibrato of his wet, raspy breaths sounded louder than ever. Dr Cherian had brought with him some old school textbooks that had belonged to one of his daughters. Vijay's face lit up when the doctor presented him with the two books: one in English, a geography book; the other in Tamil, a Standard Eight mathematics book.

"Sir, I can't speak English."

"I know. It is of no matter. You can still look at the pictures."

Other children running amok squabbling and yelling—one young imp had managed to untie his shoe laces, and was proceeding to pull his shoe off—wearied him. He felt the beginning of a squeezing, dull headache. He accepted a cup of *chai* from a somewhat churlish Miss; she glowered as she set the hot drink on the table beside him with what he thought was more force than was necessary. Feeling suddenly in extreme need of a nap, he stood to leave, his tea untouched. Already, one pimply older boy known as Sanjay had seized the English book and it was zooming around the room, held aloft like an oddly shaped plane. Dr Cherian noted that Miss made no attempt to intervene.

"You must not give any one child special treatment," she said firmly later, as he closed his doctor's bag. She flicked her head at Vijay, who was sitting quietly nearby.

Dr Cherian stopped, astounded by her audacity.

"It is not fair to the others," she added.

"He is a clever boy," Dr Cherian argued, when he'd found his tongue. "And capable, given the right guidance, of doing very well. Maybe he could become a district administrator or something similar?"

"Humph," was Miss's only response.

"I will see you next week then. *Bhagyalakshmi.*"

Miss opened the squeaky iron gate leading to the narrow street outside. She lowered her head and placed her hands in the prayer position, but with an air of dismissal.

And so, the following week, Dr Cherian returned to find there was no sign that the textbooks he'd gifted had ever existed; it was as if they had vanished into thin air. (Dr Cherian suspected that probably they had been incinerated in the alley outside.)

Nor had Vijay's medical condition improved.

Week after week, Dr Cherian produced more books, and week after week they disappeared as quickly as they arrived. There was no point in denying the obvious. For Vijay to reach his potential, he needed to be removed to a loving home.

The doctor began to make discreet enquiries among his colleagues and friends. On two occasions Vijay was visited by potential adoptive parents. But, after taking one look at the emaciated child sitting mutely before them, each couple muttered hasty apologies and departed without a second glance. This happened despite Dr Cherian's attempts to coax Vijay out of his silence and to act bright and amusing, like a circus monkey.

A few weeks later they took Vijay to see Dr Vikas Koshy, a pediatrician. He agreed with Dr Cherian's medical treatment but also suggested increasing the doses of Vijay's medications. He informed Rosalind and Dr Cherian that Vijay was not only woefully underweight, but his height was also stunted.

"Well, we need to adopt Vijay," Rosalind declared later, as the trio climbed into a rickshaw to return to the orphanage. Only that afternoon she had insisted she accompany Dr Cherian and Vijay to the appointment at the clinic. This was after a sheepish Dr Cherian had confessed to her, following much probing, the reason for his recent distemper: he believed he had failed in his care of the young boy.

"Hush, dearest. We can't do that. It is most unkind to the orphans left behind," he said.

"Don't you think this is unkind to Vijay?"—Here she indicated Vijay sitting between them— "And you can perhaps explain to him why every week you give books, and yet he isn't even allowed to study them?"

The rickshaw creaked along the road. Rosalind crossed her arms over her chest and leaned her slender body away. Vijay meanwhile, seated between them, stared ahead, his face a blank study. Rosalind turned back to add, "Oh yes. Miss told me all about it when I took some food to the orphanage yesterday. She is very upset! She thinks you are being unfair to the other children by continuing to favor Vijay!"

Dr Cherian inhaled deeply. He was glad he wasn't sitting next to her so could avoid her dark, accusing eyes; he'd stupidly assumed his wife had no knowledge of his clandestine book-supplying activities. With a sinking feeling he knew she was right—she was morally correct to suggest adoption. If he remained at the home Vijay's physical health was unlikely to ever improve.

Yet, how could a man in his late fifties, with a wife only a few years younger, manage, educate and entertain a young child? He'd grown to enjoy his peaceful evenings reading the latest medical journals, his wife always seated in her favorite chair nearby, perusing magazines or devouring light novels, or brushing her silver hair. The only household noise the chinking of crockery as the maid washed up after their meal. However, looking at the scrawny quiet child, he suspected his peace would not be too disturbed. Vijay only spoke if he was spoken to, and he displayed little interest in the noisy games of his peers.

Dr Cherian had to admit it would be satisfying to raise a boy as his son, even if physically the lad would never be a Mister Universe. But the idea had another appeal. If Vijay was as bright as he appeared to be, there was a chance he just may, with the right instruction, follow in his footsteps and become a doctor. God willing, Vijay may even take over his practice eventually. And if Vijay were to study medicine, and later become a surgeon (Dr Cherian had once secretly fantasized about this eventuality for himself), then this would also be a most satisfactory outcome.

At length they pulled up at the orphanage. Dr Cherian paid the driver and opened the gate. The cacophony of squalling, tired and hungry children reached them even before he led his wife and Vijay down the steps into the crowded playroom. The boy solemnly thanked his benefactors before slipping into the throng of children. Miss was nowhere to be seen. The dinner bell clanged. After much jostling and shoving, the waifs formed a line at the kitchen door. Smells of fragrant sambals, potato-fry and rice drifted though the room.

"Wait, Vijay!" the doctor called out. Unknowingly, he had clapped his hands.

Vijay approached and silently stood before both of them, an expression of bewilderment on his gaunt face.

Dr Cherian had to shout above the clamor. "Vijay, how would you like to come and live with Mrs Cherian and myself as …our …" he cleared his throat and his final words came out as a barely audible squeak over the noise "… adopted son?"

Vijay's head wobbled slowly, his eyes widening in surprise. A pulse throbbed at the base of his thin neck. Rosalind clutched at her husband's arm. "Did I hear you right? Did you say Vijay would be our son?"

Dr Cherian nodded, now rendered mute.

Rosalind addressed Vijay. "We will call you Samson," she said, brushing her husband aside. Her eyes glistened with tears, yet she smiled. "You will grow up to be strong. And you will break down the pillars of temples, not with your muscles, but with your mind." She placed gentle hands on the boy's shoulders, before pinching his thin cheek playfully. Vijay—now Samson—had no idea what she meant by biblical pillars and temples, not having received any religious instruction in his short life.

Dr Cherian, still unable to say anything suitable, turned his back in case Miss should arrive and observe a crack in his demeanor. Rosalind continued to smile at Samson, and he smiled shyly back. Miss eventually appeared from the kitchen and arrangements were finalized.

Afterwards, Rosalind stepped forward to touch Miss's hand. A fleeting look passed between the two women.

"Thank you, Miss. You have been so very helpful," Rosalind said graciously.

No she hasn't, thought Dr Cherian. But he had the good sense not to express this opinion out loud.

Miraculously, as the family stepped through the gate, the rickshaw was still waiting outside and, without further ado, they climbed in and traveled together to the Cherian family home. The doctor would have to forgo his usual evening stroll.

Later that evening, after Miss had locked the gate, she observed the peaceful faces of the boys sleeping on their mats in the playroom, one bed empty. Now she had the bother of what to do with all those textbooks cluttering her office cupboard. She shrugged and smiled with satisfaction; she could still see Vijay whenever she visited her good friend, Rosalind, at the Cherian's home. The books could be dealt with later.

CHAPTER EIGHT

Cari

7/10/1996

*Opals have long been known to induce a heightened spirituality.
Miners who have returned from prospecting have reported
finding self-compassion and acceptance. Others have reported
a stilling of mood, just as the ancient seas once sedimented to
form its brilliant fossil. Beware though—the allure of opals can
sometimes create a giddiness or elevation of the spirit. Fools in
love should be extra careful.*
(*The Magic of Opals* by WO Brown, 1972, p. 18)

I slipped into my new Manguri life without any fuss. The small dugout was perfect. I loved the comforting silence and darkness that enveloped me when I turned off my bedside lamp each night. My dugout was almost identical to Samson's; his was only 20 meters away. Each morning we met out the front of my flat and we trekked together up the steep bumpy incline to the hospital. Huffing and puffing, we realised how unfit we were. We resolved to walk daily during our lunch break, allowing for weather and patient-care demands. Slowly, we began to learn about each other.

I learned that Samson was eager to listen, especially to all the medical information I thought he needed to know. I also found I could open up to him about my personal life, a topic that was not always easy for me. It was during one of these walks, about two weeks after our first, that I divulged to Samson some of the difficulties I had communicating with other people. There was something I liked about his non-judgmental manner and the quiet way he just listened. He didn't feel a need to offer solutions or to buck me up with empty reassurances.

I explained to Samson, as I had to my friend Linda some months earlier, how I struggled not only in reading other people's body language, but with expressing my own feelings as well. Often I found I couldn't curb my own bubbling and brewing moods. Too often I would explode, a pressure cooker popping it's regulator valve, when internal tension reached a certain pressure point.

A standout example of the disconnect between my facial muscles and my intentions occurred during my student pediatrics attachment. A young boy I'd been asked to examine took one look at me and started bawling. The doctor looked like a witch, he wailed. And yet I was simply trying to put on a cheerful face. I didn't get a good mark for that rotation. A comment on my feedback sheet recommended I needed "to temper my facial expressions so as not to frighten young patients."

"I have Asperger's syndrome," I said one morning. "Have you heard of this?"

Samson shook his head. "What is this condition?"

When I was 15, I explained to him as we trudged along, and still a student at Wistow Grammar School for Girls in Bristol, I was taken for the first time by the headmistress and my parents to see Dr Edith Smythe, a psychiatrist. The school had arranged that I consult her for an opinion about my unusual style of relating to others.

Dr Smythe had the housewifely manner of Mrs Beeton, and the smell of baking scones wafting from her back kitchen only served to reinforce that impression. She saw me most weeks in the front parlor of her home, only a short walk from the school. To my teenage self Dr Smythe looked quite old, but in fact she was probably only in her mid-fifties. She sported a blue-rinse hairstyle that looked like a helmet that had been molded and then dried on a blown-up balloon, *papier-mâché* style. Her white-powdered face contrasted with deep pink lipstick and an impressive strand of pearls worn over a white nylon blouse completed the somewhat old-fashioned look.

This dowdy matron became my hero from the very first meeting, when she informed my parents that they were completely ignorant as to what was best for me. My father had said that my appointments would only be allowed to proceed if the school picked up the cost of my therapy, given that I was "the school's problem". As far as he was concerned, my sessions were going to be a complete and utter waste of time and money.

Notwithstanding that rocky start, I actually found the one-hour sessions stimulating. I saw Dr Smythe weekly for almost a year. We discussed issues such as, "When is it OK to lie?" (My answer: "never".) And, "What do you do if you are given a present you don't like?" (My answer: "Be upfront and honest, tell him or her why you don't like it, immediately.") Dr Smythe taught me amazing things about people's expectations for small talk and other social conventions.

But she never really explained what was wrong with me.

One day, I overheard a hushed conversation between her and Mrs Barber, the headmistress. Dr Smythe explained I had "mild Asperger's syndrome". She detailed all the symptoms I was aware of but struggled to make sense of, such as my need for a rigid routine. My whole day was planned, from the minute I awoke to when I closed my eyes at night. This led to problems getting along with people, if my schedule was upset in any way. She explained how I needed things to be just so, giving the example of how I liked my desk to be organized. Another example was how I tended to become fixated on a topic of interest, always something to do with science, and why I was unable to understand others' cool reactions to my enthusiasms. I would explain facts over and over, in meticulous detail; these could be as clear as daylight to listeners, if only they showed the slightest interest. Instead my classmates preferred to gossip about stupid rubbish girls' things, like pop stars and clothes.

Dr Smythe explained that I was only slightly afflicted. She said I was exceptionally bright and, in the right environment, I could flourish. However, I was also vulnerable to being exploited by the unscrupulous—because I believed everything I was told. If someone was "a rat dying of terminal deceit at my feet", as she put it, I wouldn't recognize it. She also pointed out I had a keen sense of humor. I was capable of happiness and love. Life would not always be easy for me, but I could be highly successful "given the right conditions". I accepted the truth of what Dr Smythe said. To get along socially, I needed to put into practice certain skills I was being taught—such as smiling at people when meeting them for the first time, modulating my voice, and remembering to compliment others.

I put the doctor's advice into effect immediately. I developed a compliment schedule with all my classmates where each day of the week I would praise a different friend, at least once. School holidays always upset this timetable, however. At the start of each new term I would have to do a catch-up on the first day, glorifying each of my school buddies with up to seven compliments at a time. I couldn't interpret the quizzical expressions of my schoolmates in response to this, until one girl took me aside and told me I was "weirding her out". Unfortunately, I didn't have—and still don't—a glossary of terms to decipher frowns or glib smiles. Nuances of behavior were mostly lost on me. Dr Smythe advised me there was a fine balance between genuine admiration and empty statements, and not to overdo it. She also told me it would get easier for me with time. (It didn't.) I also practiced watching and imitating the emotional responses of others. Television was a rich source of examples. Learning at the age of 15 about my affliction had, in some ways, been a relief to me but despite that valuable tuition, I still felt poles apart from my classmates.

"That is hard," Samson said, when I'd finished. "To feel different. I think I know a little of how you feel."

"Really?" I said. I would never have picked that Samson knew about struggling to be accepted. "You know, I sometimes feel like I'm an alien—from the Planet of Ice Queens."

Samson stopped abruptly, and spun to face me, his mouth hung open. "You feel like you're an alien ice-cream?"

"No, Samson … An alien *ice queen*." Fancy him thinking that I was an iced confection from outer space!

His features flooded with contrition. "Oh … Silly me."

We continued our promenade in silence along the ridge behind the hospital, the red plains below us stretching away from Manguri into the crazed distance.

The weeks passed. The days were warmer and stretched out longer. Red dust blew daily, coating clothes and skin. The quiver of heat glazed the air that hung above the north–south bitumen road that bisected the town. Each night there was a sunset more vivid and spectacular than the last.

Samson and I imitated the rituals of an old married couple. Every evening we scraped rusted metal lattice chairs over the yellow dirt, to sit at a wobbly table under his pergola. We spoke little. The only noises were the hiss of each small bottle of ice-cold beer we opened, then gentle slurping, alternating with the slapping sound of Samson swatting flies; we'd discovered a mutual fondness for the bitter brew. Together we watched the incandescent inferno of color that haloed the flaming sun, before its dive behind the western hills. Usually, we shared the evening meal. This could be leftovers from the main kitchen, or occasionally a curry Samson scraped together with the basic selection of spices available from the local supermarket. My own cooking left much to be desired, so he cooked, and I washed up afterwards.

One evening, Barb turned up at Samson's dugout bearing a large ceramic pot containing a foil-covered chicken curry, complete with sultanas, chopped bananas and desiccated coconut. Barb proudly announced she'd followed a recipe from *The Australian Women's Weekly Cookbook* circa 1975, give or take a few ingredients. She worried that Samson must be wracked with a dreadful case of homesickness, "Everything being so different and all", so she did her best to emulate the cookbook's recipe. *Keen's Mustard Powder* was a close substitute for turmeric. I watched my new friend chew the sickly concoction with slow deliberate mouthfuls. He ate a whole plateful, congratulating Barb fulsomely the next day, "Such truly excellent flavors. I thought I was eating my mother's cooking." She blushed with pleasure.

We established a mutually beneficial working relationship. We shared most of the clinical duties, such as taking turns with the overnight on-call. We conducted ward rounds daily. Each evening, after dinner, my nights were left free to study. The nursing staff rarely disturbed us after hours, only when an emergency situation called for a doctor's attendance.

At the end of the three months, Dee organized for an extension of my contract. I'd be staying longer. I loved the fierce beauty of the landscape and I enjoyed the work. I related to the honesty and dry humor of the locals, although sometimes I struggled to know when I was being teased. When this happened, unfailingly, some contrite outback character would slap me on the back, saying, "Don't ya worry, Doc. Only joshin' you."

More patients began to trickle in from far flung places further north, often driving six hours or more. Dee told me that she also had, for the first time in two years, answered enquiries from other doctors wanting to work in Manguri—medicos wishing to experience the outback and to work at the true, rugged coalface of medicine.

One of the patients I cared for during my early weeks at Manguri was a loud-mouthed, rough-opal character only known to the staff as Chicken Pete, his Croatian surname forgotten years ago. Samson knew him already. Chicken Pete had discharged himself after he'd been weaned off the booze, only to turn up again two weeks later. Now, he was a mere skeleton of his former self, apart from his pot belly. Unable to keep anything down, he smelled of bitter vomit. His body was filled with toxins. He was dying—and on his own terms.

"What's a bloody young sheila like you, doing working in this bloody dump?" Chicken Pete said one day, his voice barely louder than a whisper.

I'd just finished inserting a drain into the side of his squelching belly, to remove liters of orange fluid. The gown and sheet shrouding his distended torso were stained with the spills of his bodily fluids.

I didn't know what to say. Be truthful, or white lie/humor him?

Humor him, Dr Smyth said.

"I came here to look after *you*, Pete." I'd put on Richard's teasing voice that everyone had seemed to love.

"Bullshit! What a load of crap!" he spat.

I drew back.

"Sorry, love. Didn't mean to scare ya." His voice softened. He slumped his jaundice-yellow head back onto his pillows, his breathing made easier with the expansion of his diaphragm. He inhaled and exhaled deeply, in and out, clawing agitation puffed away, like he was smoking a joint.

"No-one comes to Manguri unless they're running away from something. No-one." He opened one jaundiced eye and regarded me with a lizard's stare. "What's ya real story then, eh?"

Before I could answer, Dr Smythe piped up. *My dear girl. Remember what I told you—the truth is not always appropriate. Tell him some other reason.*

I struggled to think of a plausible excuse, but luckily Chicken Pete continued on to confess in a dreamy tone, "You know, I killed a man once …"

"You what?"

"Yup. Bloody well deserved it too."

"Should you be telling me this? Did you tell the police?"

"What does it matter now, Doc? 'Course I didn't bloody report it."

My curiosity aroused, I sat down next to his bed.

"Bloody Bob Emerson." Chicken Pete whistled through his teeth, then made a spitting gesture, but lacked the strength to collect a saliva bolus in the cracked toilet bowl of his mouth.

"Was Bloody Bob his name?"

"Nah, sorry Doc. Just Bob. He tried to run off with me missus, you know. Bloody got what was coming, he did." He stopped to catch his breath. I didn't dare move. "Bob came out to my dig, late one night. Middle of winter. Wind as cold as if it had just blown off snowfields. No-one around, just me and him. Bob must have thought I'd finished for the day. Decided to have a go at my pickings, he did. But the stupid bastard didn't know I was waiting for him. I'd followed him from Manguri. I waited and waited, quiet as a bloody little church mouse, in me car, down the track, when I saw him come up, with a bag full of stuff slung over his shoulder. Like he'd been shopping like a girl. So, I goes up to him and says, 'What the hell, Bob? You having it off with me missus, ain't that enough? You gotta get me gear too?' And he said, 'Yer wrong Pete. Me and Sal are just bloody friends. I'm just a bloody shoulder for her to cry on, you useless piece of shit.' And then I pushed him, Doc. I didn't think twice. I pushed that crooning son of a bitch—yup, he used to sing with a band at the pub, where Sally worked—down that bloody mineshaft. And I walked away. If *I* couldn't have Sally, there was no bloody way Bob was going to have her either." Chicken Pete took another big breath, his bottom lip was shaking. "Sally pissed off straight away, the next day. She didn't go to the coppers. She probably thought Bob had done a runner on her too. But she took my daughter, Doc." Gulping, he spluttered, "She took me little girl, my little Rosie, Doc. My little angel. She left Jack behind—he was a good kid, but he needed his mother, he did. Barb looked after him for a long time, her and Merv. Other good people too. I just sorta gave up. I don't know why Jack is still here. I was a shit father to him, Doc."

He was now blubbering great racking sobs. I stood by, a useless spectator.

Pass the tissues, Cari! Show him you are listening, Dr Smythe whispered.

He pushed my hand away.

"Don't bother, Doc. You're a good kid and you wanna help. But I deserve every bloody thing that is wrong with me. Just sit with me while I go to sleep, Doc. I'm a bit buggered now. You remind me of Sally, you do. She was a good girl too, but I didn't treat her right …"

Chicken Pete dozed off; his memories vanished into the ether in the blink of an eye, his breathing now freer.

After a while, I stood up shakily and made my way to the nurses' office.

A deathbed confession … I thought that kind of thing only happened in movies.

"Need any help, Cari?" one of the nurses asked.

"No, I'm good, thanks. I just did Pete's ascitic tap."

The nurse, Marg, looked at me hard. She was a long-term resident of Manguri. Her bullshit meter was obviously squealing, the dial jumping up into the red zone. She was not buying any of it. "What did that old bullshit artist tell ya?"

"I'm not sure I should say." I wondered if Chicken Pete had regarded me as his confessor and the information he'd shared should stay within his room's four walls.

Marg stood before me, hands on hips.

"Let me guess. He murdered a man, Bloody Bob. Or was it Bloody Bill? Yesterday it would have been he'd murdered Bill. Drowned the man, off the Gold Coast. The day before, Bob. He also told me one time that he was a millionaire in Croatia when he was 20, and that the mafia were after him—even now. Pete's always been good for a tall story. But with the alcohol, it's really screwed up his brains. It's all bullshit. His wife Sally did run off with that man, Bloody Bob—Bob Emerson, that is—but they split not long afterwards."

I sat down to document my findings in Chicken Pete's case record. It took a while, but finally the lightbulb located in the frontal cortex of my brain sparked into life. Of course! Chicken Pete had a form of alcoholic dementia. His memory cells were pickled over the years by the effects of ethanol. No wonder Richard had such an easy ride with me, telling me those outrageous lies I'd believed. I was a silly, gullible little fool. Even a first-year medical student would have seen through the moth-eaten hole-riddled net of Chicken Pete's confabulated story. *But no.* Gullible Cari believed everything anyone ever told her.

I groaned. Marg looked up. "All right Cari?"

"Yes, Marg, thanks." I remembered to smile, in response to her look of concern. "I'm just fine," I said. I sat straighter and looked her in the eye. "I'm perfectly fine, really …"

Well done, Cari, Dr Smythe whispered again. *Excellent. I think my job is nearly done.*

CHAPTER NINE

Llanishen, Wales UK

1977

"Mrs Evans! Mrs Evans!"

Mrs Dora Evans pushed her horn-rimmed spectacles onto the thin bridge of her nose and looked up from a page of marking. Young Joe Maloney was standing mute in the doorway to the teacher's classroom, tears coursing down and blurring his features, his fists opening and closing.

"Heavens, child. What on earth is the matter?"

The teacher pushed the children's work away. She had been looking forward to peace and quiet over the lunch break. She heaved her portly frame from her desk and lumbered over to where he stood.

"It's Cari Rainsford," he said after a minute, between gulping breaths. "She's got my frog!"

Mrs Evans followed Joe through the schoolyard, past children milling about or playing hopscotch, curious faces turning to observe the commotion. She struggled to keep up with Joe, who ran in bursts, stopping briefly to allow Mrs Evans to catch up, to a back corner of the yard, next to a sandpit. Pint-sized Cari Rainsford, all of six years old, her long straggly hair obscuring her face, was standing stony-faced over a piece of cardboard propped against the trunk of an oak tree, holding a pair of scissors. A shriveled brown frog lay spread-eagled before her, pins piercing its limbs. In an oversized brown dress with arm raised, implement shining in hand, she looked up to the sky. She reminded her teacher of a pagan worshipper about to plunge a blade into her sacrificial victim. Dappled shadows from the tree above fell over the yellow sand; a rustle of patchwork orange and green leaves whispered encouragement for this propitiatory act. A group of delighted boys stood nearby, egging her on. Several girls also watched, weeping and clutching their hands to their hyperventilating chests. Cari was oblivious to their presence, as if in a trance.

"Cari Rainsford. Put that pair of scissors down right now."

The child's arm dropped. She slowly turned a sour face toward her furious teacher. Joe Maloney had buried his sodden features into the folds of his teacher's skirt.

"Classroom, now!" Mrs Evans said, grabbing her by the shoulder. She disengaged Joe and gently pushed him in the direction of the sandpit. "There, there, Joe. Take your frog and … I'll speak with you shortly. Girls, look after Joe." She pushed Joe, who was still noisily sniveling, toward the group.

The girls, now finding a new purpose, promptly bustled around the boy. Mrs Evans suppressed a small smile, thinking that this clutch of local farmers' daughters would one day make fine wives and mothers.

"Weirdo," one of the boys taunted Cari. She just stared ahead, her arms dangling by her side, her weight shifting from foot to foot. Some older boys who had drifted over started to fall about laughing, pretend scissors in hand. They savagely stabbed the air while shrieking *Eeek! Eeek! Eeek!,* a perfect rendition of the shower scene from the movie *Psycho.*

"Boys!" Mrs Evans said. The lads fell silent.

The teacher tried to frogmarch Cari to the classroom. Cari however, tended to walk in a directionless, staccato manner and appeared to be distracted by the sight of moss growing between bricks and masonry.

"Hurry up, child!"

Finally, she shepherded the girl into the class room and sat her on the other side of her desk.

"What did you mean by this?" Cari in response stared down at the desk. "That was Joe's frog."

"The frog was dead, Mrs Evans," she replied in a faraway voice. "Joe forgot to put water in its jar."

In the hush that descended, Cari started to fiddle with a lock of hair. Squinting at her index finger, she twisted a selection of strands of hair around its tip. When her nail turned a dusky blue, she released the tourniquet, then selected another lock for the same treatment. The rest of her thin mousy hair, roughly basin-cut, hung over her pale freckled face.

"You still mustn't … interfere with other people's property, Cari."

Cari looked at her teacher with undisguised disdain. "I wanted to look inside its stomach to see what was there," she said. Her lip momentarily curled into a slight sneer. "Not to *play* with it." Her face promptly resumed its usual blank expression.

Mrs Evans experienced a pang of pity. At that moment she realized how little she knew about the small plain child seated before her. Shunned by the other children—she would never be a specimen of beauty either—and she was such an odd little thing. The teacher didn't worry if children were unable to read or spell at this tender age, but she prided herself on her ability to spot a shining star. Was this an act of childish barbarism? Or had Cari been motivated by scientific curiosity? Was she underestimating the little mite?

"You must make more effort to play with the other children. You shouldn't spend every day in the library, either. It's not healthy for a growing girl. And you should have asked Joe before you took his frog."

Cari, who was resigned that she would be picking up papers for the rest of her lunch break, glanced up and breathed a tiny sigh of relief as her teacher's lips thinned into the shape of a star. Just like a cat's anus, she thought. She'd been let off lightly.

"But Mrs Evans … I don't like their games," she said with a soft lisp. "I like to read in peace. The others won't leave me alone."

Mrs Evans knew that in reality the other children in her form were fearful of Cari and avoided her. Thornier than a gorse bush, everything always had to be done her way—Cari's way. An autocrat when it came to rules, she became upset and even antagonistic if others ignored a minor infringement. And she turned huffy when the other girls wanted to play their silly dress-up games. Some of the older children teased her. Mrs Evans had apprehended one bullish thug after he threw a stone at Cari as she made her way to the bus stop one afternoon. Her popular older sister, Megan, who was not the brightest, had protected her. She pinned the antagonist against a tree until Mrs Evans nabbed the perpetrator.

The teacher decided to try another tack. "Are you interested in frogs and toads, Cari? Is that why you took Joe's?"

"Yes, Mrs Evans."

"And you like to read about them?"

"Yes, Mrs Evans."

"Where, Cari? Here in the library?"

Cari dipped her head. "No, Mrs Evans. We don't get enough time there. I've been going into the lounge room when Mummy and Daddy aren't home. I read their encyclopedia books."

Mrs Evans arched a thinly penciled eyebrow. Formal lounge rooms in this part of the world were strictly off limits to children. "Your parents don't know about this?"

"Please don't tell them, Mrs Evans. They would get ever so mad."

A hot surge of anger inflamed Mrs Evans, a tightness at the base of her throat. It rankled that Brian and Carole Rainsford, and especially Cari's father, Brian, for whom she felt an intense dislike, might be impeding their daughter's education. I need to have a word with them, she thought. But then again, Brian would not have much tolerance for someone with special needs, like Cari.

Mrs Evans knew Cari lived with her parents and sister in an Edwardian-era two-storey house on the edge of a nearby village on the outskirts of Monmouth, in South Wales. Brian managed the local pub, mostly working the bars; Carole oversaw the hotel's kitchen and restaurant. Both worked long and strenuous hours.

What the teacher didn't know was that Cari and Megan spent large periods of time unsupervised. Most days, after school, they would make the short trek to the pub to sit in the hotel's kitchen to do homework or else they would catch the school bus home. Either way, Megan would usually wander over to a neighbor's house to scrounge for food and play with their little girl. Cari either stayed in her room reading a secret stash of books she had squirreled in, or wandered the woods nearby, to classify the plants that grew there. She was fascinated by the lichen and fungi that grew there: the rust-colored Artists Bracket, the tar-like Witches' Butter, and the coral-like Oakmoss, a type of lichen, which grew on a nearby ancient tree. She would jot down descriptions of these species in her notebook, complete with a small drawing to illustrate. This was just how she liked to be. Alone, her thoughts were free to roam the pathways and glens of the woods. She didn't miss the company of other children.

In the silence that followed, the teacher thought about what to do with this offbeat child. Mrs Evans suspected that unlike the surly persona she presented, Cari *did* care about what people thought of her. Her intuitions were correct. Cari's skin was as thin and permeable as that of the frog she'd hoped to dissect. Hurts were stored in the treasure chest of her psyche; conflict left her sad and unsettled. However, the child would have to learn a lesson.

"I want you to apologize to Joe. And you will need to make it up to him."

Cari stared up at her with dull eyes like dirtied glass. Mrs Evans swallowed a pang of irritation.

"I want you to help Joe pack his bag and put his books away after school today. And then …" Mrs Evans struggled to think of a task that was not too onerous a punishment. "I'd like you to help the librarian re-shelve books. I'll ask her to let you stay for a while after you have finished. How does that sound?"

If Mrs Evans had expected Cari to leap into the air with a joyful whoop, she would have been disappointed. Instead, Cari just gave a nod and wriggled off her chair.

She stopped at the doorway. "Can I look at the encyclopedias, Mrs Evans?"

The teacher gave a wintry smile. "You can. But only until four o'clock. Mrs Charles needs to leave then."

The little girl looked hard at her teacher then—her narrow unblinking eyes the color of murky pond water. But then a ghost of a smile lit up her small, pointed face.

The days lengthened as spring turned into summer. The valleys of the Wye River in the month of June became washed a brilliant green, the oaks, beech trees and sweet chestnuts fully clad with their summer canopies of leaves. Perfumed wildflowers lined the walking paths and dotted the meadows near the village school. Mrs Evans didn't have the time to drink in all this Welsh beauty and tranquillity, however. She dreaded the end of the school term—the marking, the school plays to be rehearsed and performed and, most of all, the exhausting parent-teacher interviews. Especially the one she planned to have later in the week with Cari's mother and father.

☤

"Please sit down," Mrs Evans said, indicating two child-sized chairs next to her desk. It was not a bad idea to remind that this classroom was her castle of learning, and she was queen; she took a perverse delight in only offering students' chairs to visiting parents. Brian in turn grunted in mild disgust as his chair strained under his unaccustomed weight. Carole perched primly on the edge of hers.

"You'd think with the amount we pay in taxes, the school could afford to buy some decent chairs," Brian grumbled.

Carole stroked her husband's arm. "Not now, darling."

"Look here, Dora," Brian said addressing the teacher, his face ruddy, his fleshy lips curled into a scowl. "I can't afford to waste time discussing Cari's problems at school. That's your department. You should be sorting this out with extra tutoring or extra lessons, or whatever it is you teachers do."

Mrs Evans took a deep breath and shuffled some papers before starting again. She found her most regal voice. "I do thank you both for coming in today—"

"Waste of time, us both being here." He jabbed the table with his index finger. "This is Carole's business, anything to do with the girls."

His wife remained silent.

Mrs Evans gave a thin, patient smile. "Quite the contrary, Brian. It was actually very important you both attend today."

"How so? Ya reckon she needs to go into some kind of home, is that it?"

"No, no! Absolutely not." Here the teacher smothered a nervous laugh. "Far from it … Cari is probably the most gifted student I've ever had the privilege of teaching."

Now Brian and Carole's attentions were fixed firmly on the teacher. They stared at her dumbfounded, mouths wide open.

"Cari? Our Cari?" Carole whispered.

Brian gave a derisive snort. "What do you mean? The girl collects fungi. She's obsessed with those weird-looking plants. She never talks. She just stares at you with those squinty eyes, she—"

"Did you know that Cari has been systematically working her way through the contents of our school's *Encyclopedia Britannica*?" Mrs Evans thought it best not to tell them that Cari had already perused their own.

The couple shook their heads. Carole had noticed, but thought little of it, that over recent months her daughter had been turning up at the pub a whole hour late most days, if at all, after school finished.

Brian frowned. "And what are you suggesting *we* should be doing about it? We don't have time to give her extra lessons. We certainly don't have the money to pay for extra tuition. That's your job."

"I'm sure you only want what is best for your daughter," Mrs Evans said more coldly.

"Heaven knows we've tried, Dora. I'm right aren't I?" he turned to his wife. "I always thought my daughter must be a bit funny in the head, even when she was a baby. We tried to play with her, get her to react, like a normal bub. She'd stare at us like she was looking through a wall of ice. She'd spend hours trying to untie the rattle attached in her cot. But I've seen nothing to suggest she's smart."

"Please darling," Carole said. "Let Dora finish."

"Over the last few months I have been finding ways to extend your daughter," Mrs Evans said. Her speech had acquired a trill quality. Only those who knew her well identified that her patience was being sorely tested. "Such as giving her extension mathematics daily." Brian looked to be hardly listening. "The other children are working through Level 2 books, while Cari is completing Level 8. With regards to her literacy, she has the reading age of a 12-year-old. She is now reading

The Hobbit. She has exceptional comprehension. Her writing skills are closer to those of a ten-year-old."

Here Carole intervened; her voice sounding strangled. "I need to tell you, Dora. I've been unable to help her. She refuses anything I offer to do for her. I really don't know what to make of her." She fished an embroidered handkerchief from her handbag and dabbed her nose. "She's so unlike our Megan."

The teacher experienced a sliver of sympathy for the woman before her. Brian was known for his right-wing, red neck bluster. But looking at Carole, who would guess that she might actually have a brain under that ditsy facade?

"It's true that socially Cari has much to learn," Mrs Evans said, "but her classmates have grown to accept her … and her quirks."

She didn't tell Cari's parents that she did need to intervene on the odd occasion. Usually when Cari wrangled some unsuspecting victim into a psychological headlock and then started to proselytize like an overexcited politician. These occasions mostly happened when she had found some item that had special meaning for her, such as a rare fungus.

"If you're right, and she's that clever, what do you think we should do then?" Brian sat back on his squeaking chair, arms folded.

"I would suggest you consider moving your daughter to a school better able to cater for students with high academic potential, perhaps in one of the larger centers, like Bristol. Our school doesn't have the resources to cater for students with Cari's high ability."

"But that means we would have to move from Llanishen," Carole said.

Brian sucked in his broad mouth. "Impossible!" He slammed his fist on the table making his wife jump.

Silence descended. Brian glared at the teacher, while his wife's eyes were pleading. She reminded Mrs Evans of a once-fresh daisy wilting from lack of water.

"She won't let me help her," Carole repeated in a soft voice. "And we're so busy with the pub …"

Mrs Evans hesitated, then asked slowly, "Have you considered the possibility of Cari winning a scholarship to a girl's boarding school?" She braced herself for the couple's reaction. "I do know of one facility I think you would both agree is highly suitable. Wistow Grammar School for Girls has an excellent program for gifted and talented students."

Brian lifted his gaze then and studied the woman before him with a new and grudging interest. Carole wiped her eyes with her handkerchief, causing her mascara to run in black brushstrokes down her cheeks. Husband and wife exchanged a glance. Carole then allowed an uncertain smile to appear on her lollypop-pink lips. Brian's expression turned skeptical, then defiant. "She's not capable of what you're saying," he muttered. "I've said it before, and I'll say it again … That girl's not right in the head."

"I will contact Wistow tomorrow," Mrs Evans said, closing Cari's folder. She stood. "I think you will be pleased when you find my assessment is quite correct. Wistow offers a scholarship to Forms 1 and 2 students who show outstanding academic potential. I'm certain the headmistress will be keen to meet Cari, especially when I show her examples of her work."

Later, when Mrs Evans turned off the lights in her small classroom, she revisited this interview in her mind. It pained her that a child would be leaving her rural home, albeit not a happy one, to be cast into the foreign environment of a city school. Brian was not an easy person, no argument there, but she was sure he would do the right thing once he met with the Wistow headmistress. As for Carole … well, she was clearly out of her depth. Any mother would be. She collected her handbag from under her desk, and pondered Cari's future. She couldn't imagine the child ever dealing with people beyond a superficial level. But she loved books and libraries were full of people who struggled with relationships. Yes, that's it, Mrs Evans thought; she resisted the urge to punch the air. Cari would make a fine librarian. And with this rosy career goal for her student in mind, Mrs Evans headed out into the balmy air of an early summer evening.

CHAPTER TEN

Samson

9/12/1996

Blue Opal is a stone that is useful to enhance courage. It also deepens love and soothes the troubled. It can be a stone of mischief; many believe that if worn by an unfaithful lover, misfortune will result.

(*The Magic of Opals* by WO Brown, 1972, p. 116)

After we'd sorted out the mix-up over the contract, which was a great relief to me (how would I explain to my wife if the job had fallen through?), Cari and I settled down to the business of providing Manguri with a medical service. My negative impression of Cari that first morning we'd met proved to be unfounded. I'd imagined her to be difficult and demanding. She wore her mousy, bobbed hair tucked severely behind each ear; her clothes could only be described as drab. When we were introduced, first she frowned, then gave a forced smile. Her body radiated pent-up tension. She reminded me of a surly child pinched hard by a disapproving grandmother for bad manners; every time I spoke to her, I felt a pressing need to clear my throat.

In time we became more comfortable in each other's presence. I began to understand her struggles in dealing with others. She still liked to give the odd strident lecture, which I listened to with respect; she *was* a useful source of current medical information, where I was often, sadly, ill-informed. Her dictatorial manner was incongruous with her petite, doll-like build. She was shorter than me and most other women towered over her.

Despite my initial reservations, I began to regard her as a true friend. Her unwavering honesty and her dedication to doing a good job were qualities that endeared. It was clear that under the surface, Cari had poor self-esteem. She told me about a fainting episode in an operating theater that had happened just before she came to Manguri; this had shaken her self-confidence in terms of being a practicing surgeon.

Early in November Chicken Pete died. Right up until his final breath, he spun a tangled web of elaborate, entertaining stories to anyone who would listen, each more audacious and colorful than the last. While still lucid, he instructed Jack to give Cari a blue opal he'd found during one of his last digs. Cari at first had refused, but Jack wore her down, saying, rightly, that a dying man should not be denied his final request.

Paradoxically, while most people, including some doctors, regard death as frightening and abhorrent, Cari found being witness to Chicken Pete's demise fascinating. She examined him daily. She used a cannula and drainage bag every few days to drain off liters of the thick fluid that seeped into his abdominal cavity. She monitored the effects of his pain-relief medication; she made sure he was kept comfortable. Chicken Pete liked Cari. Her deadpan manner suited his own phlegmatic nature.

When Cari shared Chicken Pete's theory that the only people who came to live in Manguri were those escaping their past, I laughed. In response, Cari frowned. She'd already shared a little with me about her relationship with her boyfriend in Adelaide. I gathered Richard had been seeing other women and she wished to put as many miles between him and her as possible. For my part I was still hesitant to reveal the reasons I had come to Manguri. Certainly, I'd wanted to work in Australia. The generous salary would be most welcome. But the real reason I'd come so willingly—and I do hope I am not seen as a self-serving, unfeeling man—was because I was relieved to escape from my wife.

Growing up in Chennai, my most pressing fear was that I might disappoint my adoptive parents. I always strived to do my best at school and university, and achieved first-class honors in my medical training. However, although they were proud of my achievements, Rosalind and Dr Paul Cherian were itching for me to make them doting grandparents. They rarely saw their existing grandchildren, their daughters having long since flown the nest to marriages in America and Bangladesh. Therefore, always eager to please them, and despite my better judgement, when I passed out from university, I attended a marriage broker with them.

Off we went, into the suburb of West Mambalam of Chennai, to a small office with an ingratiating assistant sitting behind a desk, to pore over catalogues with pictures of pert and attractive young women, paraded as if they were for sale. Some held flowers. All smiled whimsically at the camera and also looked, I suspected, nothing like their true selves. My prospective wife's level of education was deliberated over: not to mention her health, her dental history, her ancestry, her ability to speak English, her astrological sign—all these aspects had to be considered; with any potential bride to be discounted smartly, if not up to scratch.

My parents selected Mercy. She came from a good family and was well educated, having acquired a Master of Arts in political science from the University of Madras, befitting the status of a wife for an ambitious surgeon-in-training. At the time I was happy to be guided by my parents; they loved me and generally made wise decisions on my behalf. When I first met Mercy, she was slender as a sapling and her manner gentle, polite and articulate. She was more than happy after marriage to find part-time work, until my seed would make her heavy with child and she could fulfil her destiny to become a full-time mother.

Yet, best-laid plans often go astray. After trying unsuccessfully to conceive for 12 months, we eventually made an appointment to see Dr Jhadev, a top fertility specialist. This scholarly man announced his verdict to us in his poky office, in clear earshot of his receptionist, nurse and the entire packed waiting room (his orotund words not diminished by the whirring of a wall fan). It was bad news, as I'd suspected all along.

"Madam, you are fertile and quite capable of making a baby. However, Dr Cherian here, is completely barren. He carries a gene mutation that has rendered him azoospermic. In other words, I'm afraid, he cannot make sperm."

The specialist, a squat little man, with an unlikely booming voice, was peering at us over gold-rimmed glasses. Dwarfed behind an ancient oak desk, he whirled his chair around and then fixed his gaze on me, pausing his words for suspenseful effect. "*He*, I am sorry to say, Madam, is the problem."

Dr Jhadev's words dropped on my head like a sack of heavy stones. Mercy, who until this point had always acted like a dutiful spouse, even if she could be a trifle disdainful, also turned and lashed me with a scornful glare. The doctor confirmed all of her worst suspicions. And, he went on to say, I was not just infertile, but I also had a very minor type of cystic fibrosis that causes respiratory illness, a rare condition in India.

We then traveled the route of assisted reproductive technology and in particular, the process of ICSI (intra-cytoplasmic sperm injection), a novel fertility treatment. Sperm were to be collected right at the "factory floor" level, as it were, from my testicle and injected into Mercy to fertilize her eggs. Dr Jhadev was wrong. I was able to make sperm—I just wasn't able to deliver it. Putting it frankly (and I apologize if this sounds crass) there was no "exit chute"—a patent *vas deferens*—for my swimmers. So, I subjected myself to painful tests, and the ongoing extraction of my magical fluids. My wife's eggs were fertilized in a test tube and then the resulting embryos were implanted directly into her womb. But she didn't fall pregnant.

The blame-game began.

Although Mercy never openly verbalized her bitterness toward me, she didn't need to; her manner spoke louder than any words, revealing her feelings of acrimony, disappointment and grief. She was mourning for a child who wasn't to be. And I was the problem: Dr Jhadev had said so.

I became a source of revulsion to her. We behaved in public like any happy newlywed couple. But behind closed doors, as far as Mercy was concerned, there was no point in being intimate. Marital relations to that point had been a furtive dance. I would touch her thick hair each night as we undressed, a tentative test of the waters, and wait for her to flick the wiry black strands of her hair, one way or the other. A slow, sensual toss meant there might be a chance. Conversely, a swift flick, with a shrug of the shoulders, indicated there was no possibility, in Hell or Hades, of any loving action. At first, I found the suspense exciting and bewitching. But, as time went on—this was when we were still ostensibly trying to make a baby—I became increasingly frustrated by her lascivious teasing one moment, only to turn resentful and icily frigid toward me the next.

Since our worries began, Mercy's physique had expanded, like a sponge placed in water. She changed from a trim young woman, into a plump, waddling duck. A love of Indian sweets and a lack of exercise no doubt the cause. I wondered, illogically, if she was trying to sweeten her very blood, that fluid being poisoned as it was by so much unspoken resentment. Nothing I could ever do pleased her. Her acerbic tongue raked me for my incompetence, my ineptitude in all tasks, my lack of fine breeding. This last jibe pained the most. Having been adopted as a young child, I, of course, had no idea about my ancestry.

My marriage to Mercy had filled my parents with sweet hope. Yet, the months passed, and Mercy's belly did not swell. Eventually, I confessed the situation to my father. In response he was his usual reserved self, but his visage flooded with sadness and disappointment.

It was Mercy who mooted the idea of moving to Adelaide, South Australia, having heard of successes in the field of reproductive technology at a clinic there. Acquaintances living in this city reported back, via a network of friends and family, that the lifestyle to be enjoyed there was excellent. My wife now poured her energies into the possibility of moving to Australia. For the first time since it was declared I was "the problem", she began to move with quasi-military efficiency; her manner toward me now tolerant, if remote.

My parents were also keen for us to emigrate after our failed reproductive attempts in India. (And yes, we sought second opinions.) But there was only one thing stopping us, which could be summed up in one word: *money.* The wonders of the modern medical age come at a price and the techniques we needed, which were relatively new, cost thousands of dollars.

Mercy hatched a plan. I would move to Australia, work the prescribed two years, and send back to India some money for my wife (still a young woman in her mid-twenties) and my parents to live comfortably. Then, at the end of the two years, she would join me. Flush with my additional savings, we would try again to make a baby at the IVF clinic in Adelaide.

I'd already been advised that I would need to work in Australia in an "Area of Medical Need". Then I chanced upon an advertisement in one of the medical journals:

Rural Health Australia!

Are you an experienced medical practitioner?

Want to work in Australia? Our international company, Optimal Medical Recruitment Solutions, offers streamlined procedures and support for you to work in a rural Australian location.

A two-year opening is currently available in beautiful Manguri, South Australia. Play golf in the desert, feed kangaroos at dusk, meet with the locals. Gaze at the stars.

Contact us today...

This seemed to offer the perfect opportunity that I'd been waiting for, so I called the recruitment agency the very next day.

On Sundays I summoned the courage to telephone my wife, to let her know I hadn't succumbed in the heat and to catch up on family gossip. She had moved to my parents' home in Chennai. During each haranguing call I felt like a dog caught cowering in a corner, guilt for the sin of being sterile radiating from me like invisible pheromones.

"Oh *Chella Kutti*. You would not like it here. Oh no, no, no. Such heat! It is even hotter than Chennai—it's 50 degrees, Mercy. That's 50 degrees Celsius, in the shade! The sun is like a blasting hot furnace. And the flies too! They are black, sticky ones; they fly into your mouth at every opportunity. The dust, it is in everything! My clothes, my hair! And you would not like the townsfolk, Mercy. They are rough, Mercy— rough! They swear all the time and they drink too much."

"You must stay there. Keep sending the money. Think of me and my *Amma* and *Appa*."

"I will, *Chellam*. I think of you every day."

"I love you."

Did she? Was she play-acting, trying to convince herself, even more than me? Mercy could turn on me with the speed of a spinning top, to remind me I was "the problem", only to whisper terms of endearment a blink of an eye later.

If I was truthful, each telephone call I made to Mercy was a made-up play of splintered truths and exaggerations. I cringed when I thought about what an eavesdropper would think of me gesticulating my horror to her. The reality was, I'd found peace in Manguri, once I had become accustomed to the doggedly gluey flies, the living underground and later, the summer heat. I privately treasured my time with Cari, discussing our patients and medical matters. She didn't demand of me anything other than my opinion about our clientele. I could breathe freely in her presence. I also admired the uncompromising honesty of the nursing staff and their resilience, despite often working in less than optimal conditions. I even warmed to the townsfolk with their stories of adventure and their unfailing stoicism.

Chapter Eleven

19/1/1997

Any wearer of the opal knows their dreams are more powerful.
But the opal has a dark history. In medieval times, due to its
similar appearance to the optical organ of animals thought to
portend evil (cats, toads, snakes, for example), it was likened
to the "mal ocule": the evil eye. Medieval witches and sorcerers
were reputed to use opals to heighten their powers.
(*The Magic of Opals* by WO Brown, 1972, p. 22)

One afternoon, I was asked, as a matter of urgency, to see a 17-year-old Aboriginal girl by the name of Bonny. It was the height of summer and few tourists were in town. Many of the usual staff had headed south to see family in Adelaide, even the hospital was quiet. Only the ol' timers, as they called themselves: Dee, Jo and Marg, the stalwarts of the regular staff, remained on duty.

Bonny was originally from the far west of the state and was on her way to Oodnadatta with her family. She wore a faded blue shirt-dress that flapped around her knees; underneath, her legs were stalks, like an egret's. Her coal-black skin was darker than mine. Most Aboriginal patients were seen in the Aboriginal health clinic before attending the hospital. On this occasion, one of the health workers had the sense to bring Bonny, along with her Auntie Flo, the five-minute drive from the clinic to the hospital. (The term "Auntie" is often used by Aboriginal people as an honorific for any older woman.)

Bonny, typical of many other Aboriginal people of the region, spoke softly, if at all. Her standard answer to questions was "yes", her shy eyes downcast. However, Auntie Flo, being a respected elder, was more forthcoming. Bonny had been suffering abdominal pain for the last day or two that had been getting worse. She suspected the girl might be pregnant. Bonny denied all knowledge of how this could be so.

I collected the terrified girl from the waiting area. She walked into the treatment room hunched over, her thin arms gripping her sides. Her black eyes darted here and there, taking in all the strange sights. She grimaced with pain when she climbed on to the barouche.

One of the nurses had collected a urine sample when Bonny had arrived and was now waving the pregnancy dipstick up and down under my nose like a priest anointing the repentant. The test was positive—and Bonny was bleeding. Not a good sign.

Cari rushed over from the General Practice Clinic and examined her. This was, after all, "women's business". Bonny was in big trouble. Her abdomen was exquisitely tender to the touch, indicating a mass in the lower left region. It was likely that not only was she pregnant, but that the embryo and placenta had set up shop and were growing outside her womb—either in her Fallopian tubes or, more rarely, in her actual abdominal cavity. She needed urgent evacuation to Adelaide. I prayed she wouldn't rupture the pregnancy: this was a life and death situation.

I phoned the Queen Adelaide Hospital and spoke to the obstetrician on duty. The Royal Flying Doctor Service was likewise contacted. An airplane was to be dispatched but it would be at least an hour before one would be available. Cari started seeing another sick patient while we waited. We just had to sit tight.

After I'd made the necessary phone calls, I headed back to Bonny's treatment cubicle. Soph, the scatty young nurse sent to Manguri by the agency, followed behind with IV tubing and a bag of fluid in hand. I announced my presence and pulled back the curtains.

The barouche was stone-cold empty.

"Where is Bonny?" Fear gripped my insides. This girl should not have been let out of our sight.

"I don't know," Soph said. "She was here a minute ago. Maybe she's gone to the toilet?"

"I hope so," I said. I took a calming breath. What was the agency doing sending such a manifestly inexperienced nurse to work in a remote area like Manguri? Marg or Jo would never let this happen. Where were the senior staff? Oh yes, they had gone to the pub. I slipped my glasses off and polished them on my sleeve.

The girl was nowhere to be found. She'd done "a runner" or gone "walk-about". Scared witless by the prospect of flying to Adelaide in the company of strange medical people, she'd upped and left.

"I'm so sorry," Soph said, in the nurses' office. She was almost in tears. "I feel terrible. I should've stayed with her. I know that now."

I momentarily closed my eyes. It was not Soph's fault this had had happened. It was mine. I should have been more vigilant. I placed a gentle hand on her arm. "Auntie Flo will find her and bring her back. Don't worry. Our young patient will be fine."

I later learned Bonny had snuck past the nurses while Auntie Flo was making phone calls from the nurses' station. She'd convinced a cousin sitting in the waiting area to take her to another house further out of town. Auntie Flo had also vanished, presumably to search for her.

I remember this incident as a turning point for Cari. This was the day she reclaimed the confidence that had been missing in action following her fainting spell. But as for me, I felt the burden of responsibility more than ever. A howling northerly wind had whipped up dark, oppressive clouds of red dust that were now barreling toward Manguri. An Aboriginal girl was missing, potentially to bleed to death. Even if she were located, she'd be stranded, unable to be airlifted out, if the dust storm engulfed the town. Her abdomen would fill with bright blood as it spouted from a placental geyser. I was a qualified surgeon, but had a theater furnished with only basic equipment and an assistant suffering a confidence crisis. Not an ideal situation.

The local town crier, Barb, was put to work on the "blower", ringing all the hotels to see if any medical people were in town to lend a hand. Dee, Marg and Jo were called at the pub and hurried back. We had a windfall in the form of Dr Arnold South. A softly spoken anesthetist in his late sixties, he was on his way north from Adelaide to Alice Springs to attend an opera festival. Without hesitation he volunteered his services and rushed to join us. We had to be prepared for all eventualities, *if* we found her.

Cari and I had watched the dust storm hit an hour or so before, from the ambulance entrance. The freakish, mountainous cloud avalanched toward the town looking like some enormous ravenous pink-and-purple cotton-candy materialized from a horror movie. But, instead of eating people, this one devoured fragile topsoil in its path. The sun fought to push its rays through the gloomy haze, reducing visibility to 50 meters. There was no chance any plane could take off. The RFDS plane had landed just before the storm slammed into the town and was now stranded on the airport's tarmac, along with another passenger plane.

It was early evening when a utility arrived at the hospital's main entrance and a man carrying a limp figure ran into the A&E. It was three hours since our patient had absconded. Bonny was semi-conscious, her pulse flickering dangerously fast, her lips blue-gray under the dark pigment of her skin. We had no choice. We'd have to operate.

Together we lifted her onto a barouche and literally ran into the hospital's operating theater and dragged her onto the table. Jo, who had once been a theater nurse, had already set up a surgical tray. By a further stroke of good fortune, the theater was well stocked for emergencies. Dr South commenced IV fluids and a blood transfusion. We breathed a sigh of relief as her blood pressure improved.

"OK, I think we're good to go," he said. He administered the anesthesia. It wasn't long before the reassuring rhythmic hiss of the ventilator filled the theater. Jo, Cari and I scrubbed, gowned and gloved. I would be primary surgeon, Cari and Jo would assist. Dee adjusted the overhead lighting. We draped our patient. We were ready but had no idea what to expect.

I took the scalpel and made a vertical midline incision, to cut down through the layers: skin, the marshmallow of fat, then muscle, fascia, *quickly, quickly.* And then I experienced a lightening of my mental load. Not for the first time, when I literally had my patient's life in my hands, God stepped in and operated through me: I was his conduit. The instruments of His work—my gloved hands—became steady and strong. My fingers worked automatically in a whir of activity, cutting, snipping, dissecting. I was a mute witness.

Cari grabbed the retractors. We moved deeper toward our final destination, to then reach and pierce the glistening peritoneal sac.

"*Righto* then," I said in my best Australian accent, "let's see what we have here."

Where to start looking? Blood coated the slippery sausage-like bowel that propulsed through our exploratory fingers. We poured more saline into the cavity and the sucker slurped away blood-stained fluid. Bonny's pain was located in the left lower side of her belly; there was a good chance this was where our invader had burrowed in. And there it was—a small bluish translucent prawn of a fetus, of at least ten-weeks' gestation, with head and limbs visible inside the bubble-like sac. Looking like a chrysalis, it hung from a bleeding twig of pulsating tissue from Bonny's omentum, the yellowed fatty curtain of tissue covering the coils of her large bowel.

"*Accharyam!* I've got it!" I exclaimed, relief flooding through me.

Jo passed over arterial clamps and sponge holders laden with cotton peanut-gauze. The fetus was intact. We removed it and the attached omentum, which had the texture of a piece of smooth, wet tissue. Sadly, this pregnancy could not continue.

Cari remained glacial-cool during the procedure, saying little as we concentrated our efforts. She showed no sign of nerves.

"BP 110 over 60, folks," Dr South said.

My junior colleague looked up and our eyes met. She allowed a trace of a tight smile that I could just make out behind her mask and plastic shield.

I placed the pregnancy tissue into a jar containing formalin. The pungent smell always reminded me of my days dissecting corpses as a medical student. There was a difference this time though—Bonny was going to live. I willed it with every last ounce of my being.

"What is happening with the dust storm?" I asked.

"I just spoke with the RFDS," Dee said. "We're good to go. Paramedics are on standby just outside in the ambulance."

After we'd closed up Bonny's belly, we stumbled out of the operating theater, peeling off masks and gowns, patting each other on the back.

"You did a most excellent job as first-assistant, Cari," I told her.

"Samson, how on earth did you know exactly where that fetus was?"

I shrugged and silently thanked God for steering me. He never let me down.

Once Dr South was satisfied our patient was fit to travel, Bonny was wheeled out through the ambulance entrance into the hands of the RFDS personnel. In two hours she would land in Adelaide.

"Thank you again, Dr South," I said as we shook hands. "I'm most sorry that your holiday plans have been ruined."

"Don't think anything of it. It was worth it to think we may have saved this young lady's life."

The anesthetist climbed stiffly into the back of the ambulance and the vehicle set off down the hill to the main road. He would accompany Bonny to Adelaide. Cari and I stood outside, still in our surgical boiler suits, a warm wind gently tugging at our clothes. The air was still heavy with dust, but a few stars had begun to twinkle in the ashen night sky.

Then Cari said, in a rare moment of levity, her face now alive, "I think this calls for a celebratory drink, don't you?" And, laughing from relief and nervous exhaustion, she perhaps a little too loudly, we turned the opposite direction, tripping from time to time in the dark, to descend the uneven path of our special hill.

Chapter Twelve

Richard

It has been said that the sparkling color display of opal is like a rainbow that has been struck by lightning. I agree—opal is the visual conduit for magic from the heavens. No other gemstone can seduce like this one.
(*The Magic of Opals* by WO Brown, 1972, p. 4)

Miners may have one or two decent finds in a lifetime— if they are lucky.
(*The Magic of Opals* by WO Brown 1972, p.2)

Did you think I would just slink off and disappear? When Cari had told me she was mine?

I want you to imagine a warm night, a night blacker than the blackest of black opals. Our view is from the peak of a hill. We are alone; there's no-one within a cooee of calling distance. White and yellow lights blink and move in the distance, like slumbering fireflies zig-zagging through a dust-filled haze. Listen to the faint rumble of a plane taking off, tail and wing lights blinking as it veers south. Hear the gentle hum of a generator and a dog pining for its master, howling its sorrow into the night.

Please visualize a man and a woman, standing nearby, oblivious to our presence. Both are living and working a long way from home. Both are lonely. Both yearn affection, yet neither will admit or recognize their desires. Love in this place of the disappeared or faded is an impossible ideal. The man and woman stand close—too close. Then, experience a kiss that whispers the yearnings and disappointments of this place: the ache of thwarted happiness, the grip of desire, the clutch of stubborn grief.

Do you feel it, as I do?

An unplanned, stolen kiss.

A kiss that is wrong. Yet, to this man and woman it feels very right. Overhead, a billion stars wink galactic approval.

Imagine this woman is Cari, dressed in blue surgical scrubs. She reaches her arms around the unknown man. She plants her soft lips on his, her body moving against his.

Can you imagine this tender scenario? Do they spend the night wrapped in each other's arms, in a soft bed, whispering endearments? Do they?

I don't know. I wasn't there.

In my dreams, Cari's lover, who wears the mantle of a thousand forms, sneers at me.

"I am yours, Richard," she had said. "You know I never lie." And like a fool I'd believed her.

I know people questioned why I needed Cari in my life. We were so different. Perhaps it was because for the first time in my life I had been refused by a woman of my choosing. It left a bilious taste that made me retch whenever I thought of her. But there were other reasons too … Let's just say I needed to find her.

I tracked her down. And, just before a suffocating red cloud of dust blanketed the skies over the remote outback town of Manguri, a light aircraft bearing me and ten others, skidded to a halt in a flurry of dust on a desert runway.

I would find her; I would make her understand.
She must understand.
This was not how it was supposed to end.

109

PART TWO

London

United Kingdom

Foreword of the second edition to *Essential Tips for the Young Doctor and Medical Student,* by Professor Albert Crankshaw, originally published 1948

Essential Tips for the Young Doctor and Medical Student has been a bible for all students of the medical profession, since its initial publication in the late 1940s. Packed with practical tips, and pearls of wisdom, such as advice about hospital bureaucracy, this marvellous text helps the young doctor navigate his way.

I well remember my early days as a house officer at King Albert Hospital in the late 1950s. I worked arduous long hours, encountered many ailments with (then) limited treatments, and shouldered the considerable responsibility of the young clinician. Camaraderie with fellows and nursing staff helped. Few, if any, investigations were available, beyond simple X-rays and the use of microscope. As a result, doctors developed substantial clinical skills, fostered by experienced clinicians, such as the famous Professor Crankshaw. I count myself lucky to have been instructed by this superb diagnostician. Lauded and renowned for his clinical skills and his dedication to imparting his knowledge to the next generation of medical officers, this gentle and erudite man loved nothing more than to teach.

Professor Crankshaw's book was written nearly 30 years ago and it is tempting in this current edition to remove sections that seem old-fashioned and anachronistic. There were few female doctors working in Crankshaw's day. Likewise, doctors from non-caucasian racial backgrounds were rare. Professor Crankshaw was never knowingly racist or sexist, and it must be remembered his writings reflect the cultural vernacular and dogma of the times.

Essential Tips for the Young Doctor and Medical Student is Professor Albert Crankshaw's opus and I am delighted that his publisher saw fit to re-release this current edition.

Professor Felix Drummond -Williams MBE PhD (Oxford) 1977

CHAPTER THIRTEEN

Cari

*The young clinician must become familiar with the
neuromuscular causes of difficulties with speech and swallow.
Myasthenia gravis, a chronic disease, can present in its early
stages with dysphagia and dysphonia. Thus, it behoves the
student to be astute and remember this differential diagnosis
when encountering these cruelly afflicted and frightened souls
who present to the emergency department.*
(*Essential Tips for the Young Doctor and Medical Student*, 2nd Edition,
by Professor Alfred Crankshaw 1977, p. 201)

See one, Do one, Teach one!
*This mantra is no doubt familiar to most doctors and medical students.
Good advice for the most part, yes. But it is a wise and humble doctor
who doesn't overstate his expertise. Remember this, young sir, do not
blow your own trumpet; always demonstrate humility. If you do, it is
certain you will be wiping egg from your spectacles, when your bravado
and incompetence is revealed in the probably not-too-distant future. My
motto? Do not teach a skill unless you are proficient.*
(*Essential Tips for the Young Doctor and Medical Student*, 2nd Edition,
by Professor Alfred Crankshaw 1977, p. 10)

I'm sure other people would wonder why an intelligent girl like me could ever get involved with a lothario like Richard. And, not only that, when he did have his later assignation with Miranda, how he could be so brazen as to pick a storeroom in the middle of a busy downtown hospital for it. In short—it's a long story.

We'd worked together at the King Albert Hospital, in London, a little over a year before I arrived in Manguri. I was working on Bower Ward, a medical unit in the western wing. The year was 1995. After our rocky beginning, Richard was a welcome relief from other colleagues: the snide future pathologists and the party-hard, braggart trainee orthopedic surgeons with their sexist jokes, among others.

Richard was not handsome in the conventional sense. Always clean-shaven, his face was divided by a fine aquiline nose, his chin slightly square in a perfect symmetry. He dressed conservatively and always wore his silk royal-blue Imperial College London tie. Yet, he managed to convey an impression of casualness together with an underlying ability to knuckle down when the job called for it. With just the right sprinkling of *joie de vivre*.

If I were to describe him, I would have to say "arresting" would be the best description—if you can say that about a man. Not tall, his build was wiry. His skin smooth, he had eyes that disquieted one minute, then seconds later crinkled at the edges ahead of a slow, crooked smile that banished any doubts or misapprehensions.

At first I was immune. To be honest, I'd felt an intense dislike for him when we first met. But for some unknown reason, and I still don't know why, Richard persevered with his quest to win me over; the tendrils of his charm imperceptibly wrappng silken fronds around my psyche.

I ignored the warnings that Dr Smythe whispered in my head. *He's not good for you, my dear girl. Mark my words.* Because when Richard fixed you with that singular gaze, it was as if only you existed for him. I felt special; Richard had that effect on you. Dr Smythe's voice became humdrum background noise, to be disregarded.

I can't believe I was so blinkered.

This chivalrous man, a wannabe cardiologist, with whom I shared my life, was, I realized later, nothing but a slippery bottom feeder. He worked the system, worked over the system, worked little, in spite of the system. He knew who to cultivate to get things done with a minimum of effort and a maximum of credit to himself. But my Richard was also shrewd. He was not the dandified fool he so dearly loved to play. He knew when to move on to the next rotation. Later, with me in tow.

I think my forbearance was because I knew a side of him that only I was privy to. A tender side. At first, when he touched me in an intimate way, I'd felt repulsion, his touch too… strong. Then he showed a concern for me, a tenderness I'd not known before and I needed to learn how to reciprocate. When things were right, back at the beginning, we snatched precious hours together between shifts, to bunker down in our small unit. There were no lightning flashes of razzle-dazzle. Just my hands cradling his beautiful head.

I never suspected I was destined to be played like a pawn.

But, as time went on, we settled into the boring rituals of any established couple. We bickered about the minutiae of existence. *Peck, peck, peck.* Little birds gobbling seeds of discontent. Nothing was off limits. My snapping frustrations were aroused by his unreliability, and his were triggered by my seeming lack of interest in his career ambitions. But most of all, I think, he was annoyed by my inability to read social situations and play-act the glitzy starry-eyed girlfriend.

We soon turned into strangers. Six months after we became a couple, living together in Adelaide, we drifted apart. The unit we shared became cold and empty. I'd head home after a long day, my legs aching, my head pounding. Then Richard would appear, begging forgiveness for being late. I didn't argue, although it nettled, like a burr hidden in a shoe. Yes, I agreed. Of course, he needed to meet our new friends, in our new city.

Let me take you back, to that day when we first met in London. It was the second day of my working on Bower Ward. When I arrived for work, I met Professor Crankshaw, the crusty in-house senior physician, resident relic of the medicine ward for nearly 50 years. In his tweed suit and daffy bowtie, he looked as if he had been shepherded off a golf course just moments before.

"Ah yes, the new house officer," he said, as if I was in any doubt about my identity. I frowned in reply. He possessed a chaotic set of punk-style gray eyebrows with matching bristly hairs extruding from the nostrils of his bulbous nose. He exhaled, his nostril hairs producing a shrill whistling noise. "Before ward round this morning I'd like you to find a new case to present. It's wise to keep your clinical skills sharp. Yes? Good old-fashioned history taking, and clinical examination. That's the real science of medicine. When I was a house officer, we didn't have expensive tests. We had to use our senses." He tapped his oversized nose with his index finger for emphasis, "and our clinical nous—"

"Would you like me to see Mrs Davis?" I interrupted. "She presented yesterday with a three-day history of difficulty swallowing."

He rumbled a sound which I took to be one of approval and said, "That sounds highly suitable."

Mrs Joanne Davis, the patient on whom I was to sharpen my clinical skills, was an underweight woman with gaunt features. The nurses on the ward informed me, Dr Richard Leitch, my senior, had seen her the previous afternoon. He'd already diagnosed, prognosticated, and informed this hapless lady that the most likely explanation for why food was unable to descend beyond a certain point in her esophagus—a blocked food pipe—was due to an aggressive cancer.

I slipped on my white coat, mentally transforming myself into the kind and compassionate Dr Cari Rainsford. Just like all those familiar doctors in daytime medical dramas.

I went to introduce myself and turned on my Efficient Yet Empathetic voice, the one Dr Smythe would want to hear. "Hello Mrs Davis, I'm sorry to bother you. I'm Dr Rainsford. I'll be caring for you while you're here at King Albert's." I gave an Empathetic Smile.

The lady was desperately trying to swallow. Propped up on pillows, she worked the bedsheets, clutching at them with bony fingers, her mouth making a wet, smacking sound.

I stepped back and observed her. *Why does Mrs Davis have saliva drooling from the corner of her mouth?* This was a very late sign of esophageal blockage.

I stood over her, torch in hand. "Mrs Davis, poke your tongue out at me. Repeatedly."

Her brow furrowed but she did what I asked. In and out her tongue slithered, Komodo dragon-like. After a few protrusions, as I'd expected, the muscles fatigued. Mrs Davis's pink mollusc-like tongue lolled out of her mouth, exposing a shining droplet of mucus that dangled teasingly off its tip.

My palms tingled. I'd read about this as a final-year medical student but had never expected to see a case so early in my career.

"Mrs Davis, I think I have good news." I remembered to smile. "You do not have cancer. I think you have a condition called myasthenia gravis, which is a neuromuscular problem. There is treatment available. When we do ward round I will bring the consultant physician to see you. I will inform of my findings... There is an effective treatment."

Mrs Davis, a verbal cripple by virtue of her malfunctioning verbal apparatus, did not need to say a word. An expression I took to be gratitude flooded her angular features. I noted the drooping of her left eyelid, characteristic of this condition. She looked like an antique doll with a wonky eye; only tipping her head forward would flip her eyelid back into its rightful position. She tried to slurp up a small pool of liquid from the crease below her sagging bottom lip.

On the periphery of my vision I saw that Richard had entered the room. He stood back, resplendent in a white coat; a cardiology-grade Littman stethoscope peeked out of his coat pocket. A half-smile lit his face.

"Good work, Cari," he said. "Thank you for examining Mrs Davis. Professor Crankshaw is waiting to commence ward round. We are ready to go in Room 8."

I followed behind. I knew my place in the medical pecking order. Even the senior ward-sister walked ahead of me. Soon enough we returned to Mrs Davis's room. We assembled at the foot of her bed, a white-clad crowd of nurses, medical students and doctors. We all gazed down at our tremulous patient. I took a big breath. I'd been rehearsing my speech in my head since the beginning of the round.

"Here we have Mrs Joanne Davis, 67 years old, who presented to the Emergency Department yesterday afternoon following—"

Stepping forward, my senior colleague cleared his throat. "Thank you, Dr Rainsford. I will take it from here if you don't mind, as I was her admitting doctor."

Mrs Davis looked from me to Richard through her good eye, and then back to me again. I suspect now she sensed a serious theft of my thunder was about to occur. I stared at Richard in disbelief, not knowing how I should react. I'd never been interrupted before when presenting a patient. And sure enough, Richard summarized my findings—*my findings, my diagnosis!* —with an adroit flourish, in dulcet tones I could only ever hope to achieve. He was concise; he reported an accurate history of the problem; he detailed all the clinical signs present, including the eyelid droop. Then he leaned forward. Hands in white-coat pockets and with a complicit smile, as if about to share a hushed confidence. Each member of the team huddled closer to hear the grand finale: Richard's momentous closing statement.

"Of course, I would suggest a Jolly's test before ordering other investigations. This is likely to be a case of myasthenia gravis, as Mrs Davis has been informed," he said in a low tone.

Yes, but not by you!

Richard presented on this bleak, drizzly London morning in an equally colorless and dingy ward as the consummate doctor he was reputed to be. Professor Crankshaw couldn't help but be impressed. He'd forgotten he'd asked *me* to see Mrs Davis, that very morning. He gave Richard a hearty nod of approval. The nurses stared doe-eyed; even Mrs Davis dug deep into her fast-failing reserve of muscle strength and smiled weakly. Only the pimpled, greasy-haired medical students, to my inexpert eye, looked bored and fidgeted, or strained to gawk at the unwilling victim.

As for me, I withdrew to the back of the pack. My face flamed red-hot; my mouth dried up. I couldn't believe what I'd just witnessed. Had I missed some nonverbal cue that he was about to do this? A senior registrar had—without any compunction, or any generosity of spirit, or even just a shred of professional courtesy—pretended he'd diagnosed a rare condition. He'd cunningly rogered me over. I was breathless after the act, but not in a pleasant way. Instead I felt strange emotions I struggled to identify. Humiliation came to mind. The sheer audacity! He'd taken full credit for diagnosing this woman's rare condition, after obviously performing only a cursory examination, without even bothering to look for more subtle signs. If he had, he might have twigged the real cause of Mrs Davis's ailment. Then, in all fairness, I would have joined other members of the rank and file and chorused his praises.

Thankfully, ward round concluded shortly afterwards, and nurses, students and doctors dispersed. I trailed off to the ward office, only to encounter Richard. He blocked my path.

"That was a productive round, wasn't it? But plenty to do now! We'd best get started as soon as possible," he said. "But I'll have to leave you,

I'm afraid, to write up the notes. I'm presenting at the Grand Round." He gave a ghost of a wink. "Can't be late."

Tally ho old chaps, I sulked, as I gathered charts. I should have known. Richard would be first in line to present the newest and most interesting case at the Grand Round, his scalpel-sharp professionalism in hand.

We soldiered on, visiting other Bower Ward patients, then chasing those in other wards spread throughout the hospital. Not one word of apology was uttered.

I couldn't understand his behavior. *I'd* been asked to present the patient by the professor, *I'd* made the correct diagnosis. He hadn't picked Mrs Davis's myasthenia gravis—I had. Why didn't he just admit it?

After a while I began to wonder if Richard was, like me, unable to read the expressions of others. Unwavering in his perpetual cheeriness, his mouth moved as if his jaw was hinged like a ventriloquist's doll. Out would gush a series of meaningless pre-recordings, empty of substance. Unfailingly upbeat, he joked with the nurses, and flirted and teased the elderly female inpatients. For example:

"Hello Sister! The ward is looking very organized today."

"My, my Mrs Cook! You *are* coming along well. Doctor Rainsford will organize your discharge from hospital tomorrow."

These cheery exchanges wasted time and struck me as illogical and pointless. I've always hated small talk. A social convention, yes. But who in their right mind would think I remotely cared about the weather? When you work a 36-hour-straight shift, you don't even know what day of the week it is, let alone the meteorological happenings outside the hospital's walls. We hassled medicos bore an uncanny resemblance to the dancing bears of China with our clouded eyes and our pagers our electrical prods.

He was always there, always willing and able. At the ready to step in when a disgruntled wife marched up to the nurses' station, demanding,

"Can someone please tell me when my husband will be going home? Thank you very much!"

"Madam," he'd exclaim, leaping to his feet, his arms open and palms faced upwards like a trouble-shooting messiah. "I'm sure your husband won't need to be in hospital much longer. I'll see what I can do."

"Thank you *so much*, Doctor," the wife would simper, her high-pitched strident demands replaced now by gentle cooing—*Ooh, he's ever so good-looking*, she'd be thinking.

And then, a nurse would inevitably sort things.

We settled into a frosty daily working routine. I shadowed that minor deity, Dick the Prick, all day, every day. With his poodle-like hair, some locks prematurely flecked gray, he reminded me of a freshly shampooed and cloying little brown dog trying to mount my leg. Always there, always sniffing about.

But my supervising doctor hadn't counted on meeting his match. That was me, in the shape of a five-foot-two-inch tall house-officer. I could not or would not forgive or forget. Armed with clipboards, paperwork and stethoscope, he was also equipped with an invisible shield no verbal missives could penetrate. My poisonous word arrows fell away like useless duds.

This status quo continued for another three weeks, with the nurses being as terse with me as they were unfailingly helpful to Richard. An icy torrent of dislike drenched me whenever I walked onto the ward. Even the communication skills Dr Smythe had taught me didn't work. They turned their backs, suddenly engaged in tasks requiring their undivided attention. It was official—I was difficult. A complete nightmare to work with. Especially when you compared me with that simply *lovely* Dr Leitch.

I didn't really blame the nurses for the way they felt toward me. The skill of being less sensitive to the imagined, and more resilient toward actual criticism had not yet come to me. What did other people feel? I was unable to put myself in another's emotionally soggy shoes. Social interactions, especially with groups of people, were particularly difficult. I lugged around a crushing anxiety. Pathological conditions and the science of medicine based on logic and knowledge I understood. The gamut of human interactions? Forget it. I tried to settle down, on this ward filled with patients with varying degrees of organ failure and, like the ice queen I was purported to be, to get on with the job.

Richard always found a reason to waylay me. "Cari, I'm sure you would have thought of this, but I want you to check Mrs Alwind's gentamicin levels."

"Yes Dr Leitch—done. I reduced the dose yesterday, remember?"

"Oh, yes. Of course. I knew you'd be on to it. Good work."

My suave senior registrar nearly patted my arm, but backed off when I stared him down, instead rewarding me with one of his lop-sided smiles.

Mostly I kept to myself and out of Richard's way, going about my business with a brisk efficiency he couldn't fault nor yet understand. And then, one morning, when our medical unit was taking new admissions for the day from the A&E, I snapped.

We'd gone to see a new patient admitted in the early hours with a severe pneumonia, in Room 6. A frail 92-year-old lady, she was wafer-thin. Her sallow skin was draped like thin tissue over the scaffolding of her skeleton, sinews and tendons. Oxygen tubing coiled around her face, with small plastic prongs sitting in her nose. Yet her sunken eyes were surprisingly bright.

"Top o' the morning to you, Mrs O'Connell," Richard said, in a poor imitation of an Irish accent. I tapped my foot, irritated. Didn't he know that Irish people don't greet each other this way? This nincompoop clearly knew nothing about the social mores of other cultures.

"Top o' the morning to you too, young man," the old woman replied. Her ill-fitting dentures made a chattering noise as she spoke. Mrs O'Connell was disorientated. The nurses said that as far as she was concerned, she was back in her warm kitchen on her small farm. These smart young things, were just one of the many strange people, some wearing nurses' uniforms, who popped in and out of her cosy cottage.

"I'm Dr Leitch," Richard said.

I jostled in front of him. "—and I'm Dr Rainsford."

His lips thinned. "We just want to have a little look at you. All right then?"

What was she going to do, say "no"?

We helped Mrs O'Connell sit up. I noticed that her IV cannula had migrated out of her hand vein from her left wrist, the leaking blood staining her skin a moldy blue. Without speaking, I procured gloves and gauze and, with a deft tug, removed the offending piece of plastic.

"You'd better replace that as soon as possible," Richard said. He scribbled some orders on a chart at the foot of the bed. If he'd glanced up, he might have noticed that my face had changed color several times, from a light-pink flush, to a glowing red balloon. The gradually widening cracks and fissures under my unsmiling face had finally yielded to the mounting pressure beneath the hitherto dormant volcano of my temper.

"Yes Dr Leitch, I'll do it as soon as I can," I said. "That is, when I've finished admitting the five patients that only arrived this morning. And, when I have completed rewriting Mr Thomas's drug chart. And, when I have…"

Calm yourself my girl, Dr Smythe cautioned from deep within my gray matter. *It's not becoming of you.*

Richard flinched. "OK, OK. I get it! You're pretty busy. I didn't know."

We faced off on opposite sides of the white-sheeted bed. Mrs O'Connell settled herself back on her pillows, obviously delighted with the minor drama unfolding before her. A volley of heated accusations and denials started to pelt back and forth, her head pivoting faster than a chair umpire's at a Wimbledon tennis match.

I spat out my hurts, real or imagined for at least ten minutes. (Patient confidentiality was completely forgotten.) Mrs O'Connell, in an admirable display of fortitude, chimed in with her sage opinions and advice, her soft voice tinkling. At last, I gave voice to the reason I was so riled. I could not let an inexcusable injustice go unheeded!

"How come you said you diagnosed Mrs Davis. It was me who diagnosed myasthenia gravis. You told Mrs Davis she was going to die."

"Now that wasn't a good thing to do, was it dear?" Mrs O'Connell looked pointedly at Richard.

Richard cocked his head, like a puppy denied a toy. "I'm sorry, I have no idea what you're talking about. Now, if you will excuse me, I do have rather a lot of work to do. Unlike some."

He swished open the bed curtain forcefully and started toward the next room. But then he suddenly stomped back to the bedside, his mouth downturned and lips pursed. He looked at me hard.

"So you think I eavesdropped your conversation with Mrs Davis that morning?" He gave a harsh laugh.

"And didn't you?"

Mrs O'Connell clicked her tongue. "Did you dear? 'Twasn't a nice thing to do if you did…"

Richard puffed himself up like a magisterial rooster fluffing his feathers. "As you know, this condition fluctuates from day to day. I'd entertained the notion that Mrs Davis might have myasthenia gravis when I first saw her in the A&E. Her signs then were however … rather subtle. I saw her on a good day. You saw her on a bad day. I thought it safer to assume the worst possible diagnosis then—cancer. And then, if the tests I'd organized were clear, we'd look for other causes of her symptoms. Then, when I saw Mrs Davis with you, of course I was astonished by her clinical signs. The drooping eye, the poor swallowing … all of that."

Usually I was a trusting fool. Not this time. I would show Richard I was not *that* naive. "But why did you tell Mrs Davis she had cancer? If you're not sure, don't say anything!"

"Not a good idea," Mrs O'Connell agreed, with a shake of her head.

"But I didn't. I'm not sure where you heard that piece of information, but that's not what happened."

"But the nurses told me … *you* definitely told Mrs Davis she had cancer. You said she only had weeks to live."

"Not true. I might have told the nurse in the A&E I was concerned, but I certainly didn't say anything to the patient. I'm sorry the nurses gave you the wrong impression, but that's the honest truth."

I calmed my breathing. I began to question the assumptions I'd made. Mrs O'Connell, who was a wise woman with much experience of the human condition, turned to me and whispered almost inaudibly, "I think you may've been a little hard on him, dear."

I felt the flush of rage begin to be replaced by the heat of shame and anxiety. Our Irish patient spoke the truth. Yet again I'd been shown to be a complete idiot. Both Richard and Mrs O'Connell probably thought I had more loose marbles rolling around in my head than in a child's toy box. And they were right. Giving Richard some credit, his expression had softened. I began to feel ashamed of my surliness of the previous few weeks.

"I'm sorry you felt you've been flying solo with all of the ward work, but you seemed happy to be alone," he said. He smiled winningly. "I mean—I'd often look for you to give you a hand, but … I see now I should've tried a bit harder."

"And I'm sorry I've been difficult. I will try not to be so —" the words caught in my throat— "cranky all the time." Being in a state of crankiness seemed to be my default condition.

Mrs O'Connell nodded approvingly and said, "That's my girl!"

She briefly took Richard's hand in her bony fingers; he could easily have smashed these bony sticks into shards. With a consummate respiratory effort her voice became more forceful.

"Come here, dear. You mustn't let her down again, you hear? 'Tis a bad thing when a good girl likes this gets so put out. You have to look after her, you understand?"

"Wise words indeed, Mrs O'Connell," Richard said.

With his hands now clasped before him, he reminded me of a naughty schoolboy waiting to be caned.

We finished Mrs O'Connell's examination, then turned to leave. Before she nodded off into a well-earned siesta, she called out, her Irish brogue a musical lilt. "And dear, don't forget to close the gate after you leave. The sheep got out yesterday." Her head jerked sideways and she began to snore softly.

Richard and I left the patient's room and stood facing each other in the corridor. Following this final exchange, I began to get the giggles. I glanced up at Richard. His eyes were twinkling with merriment. Before I knew it, I was buckled over, trying to restrain big, gulping belly laughs. He began chuckling then, which only made things worse for me. Like a Christmas bon-bon with the string pulled, I went off with a bang. I was almost rolling on the floor, clutching my sides.

Sister Bernadette the charge sister shot out of a side room. "Are you all right?" she panted.

"All's fine, Sister," Richard said. "Mrs O'Connell just made a little joke."

The charge nurse gave me an odd look.

"I'm fine, Sister. Sorry to worry you." I wiped tears away. Then I saw Richard out of the corner of my eye and I was off again in peals of laughter. A rare sound from my lips. Later, I wondered if I'd made a fool of myself, me and my snorting hyaena laugh.

We got back to work that day, and from that moment on, we became a team, collaborating in our efforts and our decisions. Richard was a good doctor, although I noticed he was a procrastinator. I, on the other hand, was happier if we followed the same daily routine to tackle our tasks; I strived to get jobs done quickly. But despite my efforts, geeky people like me have an alternative hierarchy of needs. Hospitals, despite the efforts of the best administrators, are not for the one who thrives on a strict schedule.

I remained my usual serious and reserved self, but I made an effort to smile more. Richard held no malice toward me. The nursing staff noticed the thaw in our relationship, a warming that was a relief for everyone. But I still hung back from being too chatty or too available. I didn't feel comfortable when around too many people. Was I perhaps boring? I probably carried on too long, telling various staff about the patients' clinical signs. However, the nurses accepted me. The new Dr Cari Rainsford was a lot easier to deal with than the old one. They possibly thought I took myself a tad too seriously.

I just needed to lighten up.

CHAPTER FOURTEEN

Richard

Nothing angers me more than when I hear a lazy and disrespectful young clinician refer to a patient by his or her diagnosis. The patient you are about to see in Ward 8 is not, as I have heard recently issued from the lips of a laggard, "The Pneumonia"! That patient—lady, man, or child—has a name. Enough said.
(*Essential Tips for the Young Doctor and Medical Student*, 2nd Edition, by Professor Alfred Crankshaw 1977, p. 12)

Cari's backstory of how we met in London is filled with more holes in the telling than a Swiss cheese. There are always two sides to any tale. It's up to me to fill in the gaps, including how we came to be in Adelaide, before the "Storeroom Incident" as Cari unimaginatively described my liaison with Miranda. Let me take you back to how Cari and I first met and what happened afterwards, from my point of view. I need to confess—I never did tell her the *real* reasons why we left London.

It had been a busy day, the day I admitted that dysphagia, Mrs Davis. I'd endured many disruptive trips downstairs, to see the usual winter ailments that present at an inner London hospital. It was hospital policy that a senior doctor needed to authorize ward admissions, usually after an initial diagnosis and treatment by the junior rank and file. Most of the conditions I admitted were of the respiratory kind. Elderly folk with lungs turgid and stiffened by thick mucus; others with hearts failing, their oedematous legs propped on pillows like water cushions.

"Dr Leitch, I presume? You are seeing the lady who can't swallow." A white-haired nursing sister stepped out from behind the main triage desk. "I'm the charge sister on tonight. Please follow me."

The nurse handed me Mrs Davis's file and headed off, her white rubber-soled shoes squeaking. I hurried to keep up with her brisk pace. After showing me the cubicle at the end of the corridor, she left me without having the consideration to check if I needed further assistance.

Five minutes later another tall nurse waited for me outside the curtained entrance to the cubicle. Dressed in the King Albert's student uniform of navy pinafore and white shirt, she was flat-chested and dreadfully plain, and—oh dear—she was far, far too thin. She watched me for a while through heavily lidded brown eyes, a dark shadow of a moustache tingeing her upper lip as if, bizarrely, she had snorted cocoa, not cocaine, before coming to work. A white starchy nurse's hat swamped her narrow head, allowing only a glimpse of dull black hair underneath. I suppressed a smile. An image had come to me of a seagull alighting upon and shuffling its white feathers on this unwitting nurse's noggin.

"Are you the senior med reg?"

"Yes."

"Good. I'm just letting you know that guy with asthma is back from radiology. In case you wanted to look at his X-Rays before he goes upstairs."

"Thanks. Won't be too much longer. All seems to be organized with Mrs Davis here."

I observed the new patient lying on the barouche. Earlier that day she had been brought to the A&E after she choked on a piece of bread. I smiled. There was no need for me to examine her and replicate ground that had already been surveyed and mapped quite nicely by Cassie Jenkins, the A&E's junior house officer.

"Doctor, may I ask you a question?" Mrs Davis asked.

I turned back to the patient; a hopeful but shrunken eye stared at me side on. I took a deep breath to quell my rising irritation; I didn't have time to field too many questions. Instead I replied, "Of course."

"What's wrong with me?"

I patted her clawed hand. "I'm not sure yet. There may be some kind of blockage stopping food going through. So, tomorrow I've asked the Gastroenterology Department to perform an esophagoscopy. Do you know what that involves?"

"No."

"It's a look down your gullet with a camera. It's painless and you will be asleep. Then we'll know what we're dealing with... Any more questions?"

The birdlike woman shook her head and sucked in a dribble of saliva from her bottom lip. I breathed a sigh of relief; I didn't need to elaborate further. Patting her hand once more, I gave her a tight smile and left the cubicle. It was obvious this was an open and shut case of cancer. I would be astounded if it was anything else.

Out in the corridor Christiaan Grobler, another medical registrar and a South African, bounded toward me like an oversized bloodhound.

"Ah Richard ... It looks like you saw that lady with the swallowing problem. I was held up so I asked the nurses to call you. What did you think?"

"I'm afraid it's not good news for Mrs Davis. I agree with Cassie Jenkins who saw her earlier. She most likely has an aggressive esophageal carcinoma. I'd be surprised if she has many months left. Weeks would be more like it."

"Hmmm, bad luck," he said, his forehead wrinkling. "Let me know if I can give you a hand a bit later."

With that he dashed off again. Was his offer of help genuine?

I found the charge sister and signed Mrs Davis's admission papers. I was about to leave the office when the seagull-hatted nurse waylaid me.

"I couldn't but help overhear, Doctor. Is it true you think Mrs Davis only has weeks to live? I can't believe it. She told me she'd been perfectly well until a few days ago. She told me—"

I held up my hand to silence her. "I'm sorry … Anna." I glanced at the kitsch name tag dangling around her neck. Glittery stars and cutesy flowers sparkled next to her curly-lettered name. "I have a few other patients I need to see in the A&E. Page me if you have any problems." I picked up my file, about to turn away.

"So, if she asks me about what's happening, what do I say to her?"

"You can explain what will happen tomorrow, and anything else she needs to know." I made a show of examining my wristwatch. "I'll be seeing her in the morning. I'm afraid she'll need to be admitted for consideration for palliative care. I don't imagine she'll be able to go home."

The nurse nodded, her eyes downcast. Was she tearing up? *Oh god, spare me.* I might be more tolerant if she were at least pretty, like the nurse rostered in the treatment room. You won't last long in this job unless you toughen up a bit, I thought. Bad things happen to good people. You just need to deal with it.

It may seem odd to hear this from a doctor, but in truth I'd always felt embarrassed by displays of raw sentiment from patients. In fact, I found the whole American style of publicly dumping one's emotions into another's lap to be distasteful in the extreme. However, providing a reality check was regarded by most as callous, so instead I'd mastered how to act. Each day I would don the ultimate Pierrot costume in the form of my white coat, my face and movements mimicking the actions of magical medical actors. Compassion and kindness issued with the swish of a stethoscope.

I smiled consolingly at the nurse. "We'll make her comfortable, don't you worry. I'll make sure she gets the best possible treatment. I promise you—" I glanced at the name tag again "… Anna."

She gave another brave nod. A fragile smile attempted to find its way on to her glum face. I made a hasty departure before I could be delayed further.

℞

The next morning, I had the opportunity to become properly acquainted with Cari, then just plain Dr Rainsford. She was the new house officer on the Medical B unit; I'd only met her the previous day. I entered Room 16 to invite her to join the clinic ward round.

Cari was in the process of examining Mrs Davis, the lady I'd seen the previous evening. This was not usual or necessary just before rounds. I had no idea that she'd been asked to do so by Professor Crankshaw, only learning this minor fact later.

My heart sank. I'd worked with other junior doctors like this before. Always conscientious, always snuffling around like truffle hounds, always asking too many questions. Senior doctors like me are far too busy dealing with the machinations of hospital bureaucracy to field unnecessary interruptions by wannabe-saviors. Like other investigative colleagues who have wasted my time, Cari had "Trouble"—with a capital T— stamped in large letters all over her ill-fitting white coat.

She was listening to Mrs Davis's chest with her stethoscope, her hair bobbed and tucked in a businesslike way behind her tiny ears. Her expression, although a little severe, was not unkind. Absorbed by her patient's clinical signs, she didn't register my presence at first. It wasn't long before I realized she was trying to refute my diagnosis of the previous day. Without having the decency to discuss this with me first.

"I think you have a condition called myasthenia gravis, which is a neuromuscular problem. There is treatment available," she blabbed. Her words gushed out of her mouth, the cadence not matching the grim and somewhat peculiar smile plastered on her face. "When we do ward round I will bring the consultant physician to see you. I will inform of my findings... There is an effective treatment."

Damn it. She was absolutely right.

Looking at Mrs Davis now, in the cold light of day, the drooping eyelid and her tongue weakness were glaringly obvious. This house officer, a first-year doctor, in the space of five minutes, had diagnosed (correctly too) an uncommon autoimmune condition. I stood there waiting. I drew my expression into an impassive veil; I forced my lips into a cryptic smile. I observed this Cari. Her expression had softened, her greenish eyes opened wide. She looked almost pretty, her facial skin luminescent and slightly flushed, a sprinkle of freckles on her nose. It was clear she possessed no dress sense whatsoever: her compact breasts concealed within a turtleneck pullover, her legs unflattered by a frumpy, navy knee-length sack of a skirt.

However, it was an unwritten rule among members of the medical hierarchy that one never showed up, contradicted, or cast a senior colleague in a bad light in front of a patient. I wondered if I should wait or take Cari aside immediately, to douse any delicious pleasure she would be experiencing. Or, maybe a better course of action, if the opportunity presented itself, was to make a benevolent show of false humility. Cari was obviously clever; it had taken her little time to piece together a jumbled clinical jigsaw puzzle. But there was more than that. Oddly, Cari struck me as a young doctor who was genuinely fascinated by the pathology before her.

We left the room. With each footstep I knew there was no chance I would ever confess. To be truthful was clinical hari-kari. I could well imagine the sympathetic digs from my colleagues and their comments. The *Ha-ha, shown up by a house officer? Bad luck old chap.* My equally ambitious colleagues would secretly revel in the evidence of my deficient medical acumen.

Call me a cynic, or what you will, but every year a procession of attractive idealists dress up as house officers in white coats: new graduates spat out at the terminus of production-line medical schools the country over. Fantasies of being able to help people are what lure these ignoramuses to sign up. Yet reality hits, usually after the first year of medical practice. Instead of helping people, we doctors merely delay the inevitable. Thanks to us, demented, space-occupying legions of geriatric patients continue to suck our health system dry, their crumbling bones rattling on and on. As a result of our TLC, drug dependents and the personality-disordered steadfastly persist in their overdosing and their creative self-harming ways. As for the drunken and disorderly idiots who stagger at all hours into the A&E—it's all thanks to us and our welcome mat. The cut up, the beaten up and the knocked up, we treat 'em all.

I wondered when Cari was going to wake up and join the ranks of the disillusioned. Or, more worryingly, if she would discover the vocation of altruism, the medical equivalent of a religious zealot, working long hours with inversely proportionate low pay. Year in, year out. Those thankfully rare and well-meaning misguided souls I disliked the most.

I looked forward to the day when I would be a world-renowned cardiologist, seeing the rich and famous with their stiff and clogged coronary arteries on Harley Street. But first I had to endure the arduous journey there. The long hours of on-call, my insipid co-workers and the boring dinners to celebrate the departures to maternity leave of various nurses along the way. Even having to do demeaning work on general medical units, while waiting for vacancies to appear for highly sought-after training positions. I continued to enchant these same jejune souls; I dazzled with my competence. I resisted the urge to appear burned-out and jaded. I needed to continue to be the highly skilled and steady doctor I was.

The medical team commenced the ward round. Doddery Professor Crankshaw, the head physician, led the way. It wasn't long before the usual motley collection of medical staff, students and nurses were back in Room 16, facing Mrs Davis.

I glanced at Cari. She clearly regarded this as her big moment to make an impression, her pointed face had colored again. She took a deep breath.

"Here we have Mrs Joanne Davis, 67 years old, who presented to the Emergency Department yesterday afternoon following—"

I stepped forward. "Thank you, Dr Rainsford. I will take it from here if you don't mind, as I was the admitting doctor yesterday."

I continued on. This was my greatest and most celebrated skill, the art of holding the floor. And looking around at the expectant faces of the staff admiring my oratory ability I knew this brief presentation was going to be no exception. I enjoyed the reverence from the attentive junior staff and the adoring nurses, and the grudging respect from my senior colleagues. Some junior doctors dread ward rounds—specifically, the droning of interminable facts and figures, just in case the consultant physician has a burning need to be in possession of some irrelevant data. I, however, savored those times when I worked the crowd.

I observed Cari retreat behind the wall of zitty medical students. Hopefully, she now realized the error of her ways. It wasn't acceptable for her to put forward an alternative diagnosis. Even if, as luck would have it, it was the correct one.

After ward round finished and a brief delay for Professor Crankshaw to congratulate me on my excellent presentation, I attempted to make light chat with Cari and, in an admirable display of my forgiveness, cheer her up. I was not one to bear a grudge. The young house officer evidently didn't share the same mindset. She glowered when I attempted small talk. This wasn't going to be easy. But I had to make sure she knew that I, her senior registrar, was the boss. We commenced our morning rounds and I made sure she was kept busy. She appeared to resent the work I asked her to do. This was another bad sign; my inexperienced colleague obviously didn't take well to instruction. With a sinking feeling I remembered we were going to work together for three months.

☤

A few weeks passed. Cari hadn't expected to meet her match in me, but she had. The more morose, sullen and withdrawn she was, the more upbeat, conversational and indefatigable I became. It was maddening her. It was almost humorous to watch her stifle her poisonous responses to my helpful comments. However, I had to admit Cari was an excellent doctor. She toiled through her daily tasks with minimal assistance. Her calm dealings with patients and relatives engendered respect. But the forcefield of her aloofness repelled any attempts by the nurses to be friendly with her.

Finally, Cari spontaneously erupted, after three weeks of simmering tensions, like a purulent boil bursting. It was in response to a simple and not unreasonable request, when I requested an IV cannula be replaced. This made her bristle with indignation.

"Yes, Dr Leitch, I'll do it as soon as I can."

And then she let off a barrage of hurts and complaints—every imagined affront she had endured during the three weeks we had worked together. I looked at her in astonishment. It was the most I'd ever heard her say. I attempted to humor her, to appeal to her sense of reason: this only inflamed the fires of her indignation more. And all the while, the little Irish lady with pneumonia we had gone to see, chipped in her useless demented opinions.

At last, Cari revealed the real reason for her animosity.

"I don't know why you pretended you diagnosed Mrs Davis's myasthenia gravis," Cari said. "I was the one who diagnosed the condition, not you. You told Mrs Davis she was going to die." Her normally pale

138

face had flushed scarlet, her eyes blazed, making her hazel-green irises look distinctive, even alluring.

I was flabbergasted—I should have been the one stripping shreds off her character, not the other way around. I reminded Cari of the fluctuating course of Mrs Davis's condition and why I'd put forward a different primary diagnosis.

"But the nurses told me … *you* definitely told Mrs Davis she had cancer. You said she only had weeks to live."

This time, I could defend myself with complete honesty. I hadn't informed Mrs Davis of any diagnosis, other than a suspected blockage in her swallowing pipe. I certainly hadn't worried her with any news that she had a terminal illness. I thought back to that evening in the A&E Department. That silly tall nurse who had questioned me as to what she should say, if Mrs Davis asked any questions. In all likelihood, she was the fool who prematurely scared the poor lady. *Not guilty, Your Honor!*

I had won. Cari couldn't argue against scientific logic given her deductive mind.

At that precise moment, deep within, some stirring of undefinable attraction toward her flickered into life. Cari was a strong woman. She was clearly highly intelligent. She didn't tolerate fools easily. When I thought about it, she could be bloody difficult. But just at this moment she looked vulnerable, her fine little nose glowing a soft pink, although when she looked up, her eyes were still bright with lingering defiance. But then her gaze slowly lowered and she bit her pale lower lip. I allowed a sympathetic smile. I'd watched the aura of her indignant pretensions inflate about her, to then pop and shower her with feathery shame. It had been a good fight, but the best had triumphed. As was right. As was just.

A new emotion began to flare within me. No longer did I want Cari to be relegated to kow-towing at my feet while I barked orders from my golden throne. Now, I wanted her seated beside me. Because Cari and

I could be so good for each other. We would be a formidable team: her sparkling intellect and my superior social skills would complement and nourish the other. I needed a woman who understood my thinking. Cari's appearance was somewhat deficient, though not beyond repair. But, after our uneven start, how to win her over?

And bless me, if the pneumonia in Bed 6, who was enjoying every minute of Cari's tirade and eventual capitulation, did not throw the switch to illuminate a part of Cari's psyche that was rarely on view to be appreciated: her sense of humor. The old Irish lady grabbed my hands and made it very clear that the ball was in my court. I mustn't let her get away, she said. I nodded my head in complete agreement—this was serious business. Eyeing Cari at that moment, she started to smile at the absurdity of our exchange. Just an ever-so-slight upturning of her mouth's corners, but it changed her tight, withdrawn expression completely. Her face now came alive, as if she was Sleeping Beauty looking around in wonder after being wakened by her prince's kiss. It was contagious. I found myself starting to relax and smile too. Finally, the little Irish lady revealed the extent of her delirium when she implored us to make sure we shut the gate properly when we left for the day. This tickled Cari's funny bone; she spluttered a little giggle before losing it altogether, to the point where I had to take her into a side room to calm down.

The weeks and then months passed. Cari and I worked in easy synchrony, like the squeeze and empty of a baby's heart. Increasingly I found her useful; she calmed me in indefinable ways. If I played my cards right, she would continue to do so. But I also found— surprisingly— that I wanted Cari in my life. Her straight-faced manner made me laugh, I was never quite sure if she was taking the mickey. Yet, even so, she calmed me. So, it was a shock, late one afternoon, when I remembered she was finishing her rotation that very day.

"It's your last day. I absolutely insist, we must go out to celebrate. I won't accept you suddenly have other plans," I said, hamming up the tragedy of the situation. I'd followed her into the ward's doctor's office after dodging trolleys laden with empty dinner trays in the passageway, and relatives of patients dawdling before the start of visiting hours. Cari picked up and looped the handles of her handbag over her shoulder, in readiness to leave. She froze, indecision mapped on her face.

"Oh, come on. It's just one drink." *Careful—this was a make or break moment.*

She gave a tentative brisk nod of the head. Before she could change her mind, I linked my arm through her own, which she held in an awkward rigid way, and we headed out into the misty, cold night. We ended up at a local pub and I began to talk to her in a way I'd never done before with a woman.

With her direct, undiplomatic questioning, Cari pulled no punches. I peeled off the jovial and uniform veneer I wore like a protective surgical mask, all day, every day. It felt how I imagined a tender-skinned serpent would feel, after shedding its hardened old skin. Cari listened without making mollifying or sympathetic comments. She occasionally smiled, as if remembering that this was what she ought to do. She then told me a little about her life. She had supported herself through medical school with the income from a small scholarship and an inheritance from her father's estate. He'd died from a stroke when Cari was 17 years old, when she was completing her A levels. After the pub closed, we stood outside in the chill night air of Hammersmith and agreed to see each other again.

This is how my relationship with Cari began. We were an unlikely pair, I admit. But during the early months together, our different personalities aligned and attracted. Her cool manner often put people off; they misread her. Instead I wondered if people were perhaps unnecessary to her—the science of medicine was all that mattered. And did she ever feel compelled to impress anyone, including me?

As I got to know her, I realized Cari could sometimes be volatile, like that time she blew up at the bedside of the Irish lady. She was not unlike one of those sea mines from the last war that still occasionally wash up on lonely beaches, metal spikes hidden under kelp, in readiness to blow the unsuspecting to smithereens. And she had a delay timer too. She could sometimes mull over an innocent comment for days before detonating.

She relaxed more as time went on. Although her sensitivity was challenging at times, she intrigued me. My feelings for her went beyond just a desire for a partnership of mutual convenience. I was strangely attracted to this young, interesting doctor, whose intelligence may well have been on a par with mine.

Chapter Fifteen

The student of medicine must balance the workload of study
and examinations with rest and recreation when time permits.
Find a rousing new hobby that is good for the constitution and
nervous system, such as one of the many outdoor recreations
(sailing is a terrific hobby).
(*Essential Tips for the Young Doctor and Medical Student*, 2nd Edition,
by Professor Alfred Crankshaw 1977, p. 66)

Cari had no difficulty entering the surgical training program, as she had planned. She began to work longer hours, with many on-calls. She would return at night, often wearing, unusually for her, a look of excitement as she described how she'd assisted with various surgical procedures.

Meanwhile, I secured a position as a registrar physician on the cardiac unit at King Albert's. We discussed whether to share a pad together, but for the time being we decided to stay put in our respective places, never finding the time to make the big move. I never revealed that my unit in fashionable Kensington was owned by my parents and I didn't pay rent.

Our period of contentment was short-lived. My final clinical exams were fast approaching, and I needed to put my head down and do some study. Although the verbal presentation part of the exam was easy if one was a first-class orator, actual knowledge was still needed for written papers.

Most trainee specialists, shuttling down the bumpy runway of exam preparation, regularly visit other units to practice clinical *vivas*—that is, oral patient examinations. The week before my scheduled exam, I spent an entire weekend devoted to doing just that, at another London hospital. Instead of the usual offerings of the elderly with heart failure and smoker's lung, one of the patients I was assigned to see was a young man. Eighteen years old, he'd survived a cardiac arrest on the football field, thanks to the quick-thinking actions of a nearby spectator. Admitted only the day before, although battered and bruised, he was in commendably good spirits after his ordeal. After I examined him, I concluded that he most likely had a rare but deadly heart condition, hypertrophic obstructive cardiomyopathy.

After I'd finished seeing the young man, I presented my clinical findings to a pallid-looking cardiologist. Dr Liddard was clearly an Oxford old scholar, with his cut-glass Queen's English accent. In his late thirties, he wore a gray Italian-made suit and fashionable glasses, his thin ash-blonde hair combed back off his shiny forehead.

"Well then, Dr Leitch," he said before pausing to give an incongruent honk of his nose on a white linen handkerchief. "I'd like to know more about the inheritance of this particular condition. What genes in particular would you be interested in? You have already identified this as an autosomal dominant disease." He rocked on the heels of his black patent leather shoes as he eyed me, his chin resting lightly on a tee-pee of interlaced fingers.

I gulped. I had no idea beyond what I'd already said. "M-M-Must be new developments I'm not aware of," I stammered.

My interrogator smirked then issued a curt nod of dismissal. With a swipe of his fingers he motioned me away as if he was flicking a leech off his skin, his attention diverted by the gray-green screen of his desk computer. For him, I had ceased to exist.

I left the cardiologist's office, ripping off my coat jacket and loosening my tie as I went. A dark-haired attractive nurse, standing outside, looked up from a patient file she was reading. She would have heard our conversation.

"How did you go?"

Why do you ask? I felt like saying. *I'm bloody annoyed. He asked unreasonable questions.*

She did not wait for my reply. "I think Dr Liddard is tough, but fair. If you do well with 'im, you pass exam." She spoke with a faint Italian accent.

I shrugged and gave a rueful laugh. "Didn't do so well, I'm afraid."

"Better luck next time, hey?" Her playful brown eyes remained on mine.

I sighed but still mustered a brilliant smile. "Yes," I said. "Better luck next time."

This episode niggled. How dare he—just a junior consultant—embarrass me? That evening I visited the hospital library and searched Medline on the library's computer. The relevant journals were in stock and I was able to acquire the pertinent articles. Although the information was dense and obscure, at the end of two hours of careful study I knew any doctor would be hard pressed to fault my knowledge on this particular topic. So, it was with great surprise and with secret delight, on the day of my final exam I was asked to attend the same hospital, and—you've guessed it—see the same young male patient I'd seen the week before.

You're possibly thinking I had an unfair advantage over the other candidates, and that, if I had a shred of moral fiber, or an ounce of decency, I'd admit the coincidence and request a different patient. Or, even better, a different hospital. But the cold, hard reality is this: I had knuckled down and done the relevant study. I had put in the hard yards. And there was no way I was going to relinquish any leverage I had over any other equally ambitious wannabes. Those try-hards would act exactly as I did. All good looking, all possessing just the right measured tone of concerned voice, we all shared the same connections and we'd attended the best schools. So, save your moral outrage for someone who deserves it, or wants to hear it. You're not familiar with the competitive oily environment of the London cardiology scene. If I stepped on and crushed a few egos to get what I deserved after years of hard work, so be it.

I entered the young man's room. Let's call him James. He'd planned to go home the previous day, but as a magnanimous gesture, had agreed to stay the extra day for the physician exams. A flash of recognition crossed his face when he saw me. I nodded at him; he winked back. He was in on the game.

"Good morning James. I'm Dr Leitch, and this is Dr Cornish and Dr Andrewartha." I indicated the much older examining physicians standing behind me. Luckily there was no sign of the chap in the Italian suit from the previous week. "Thank you for agreeing to participate in my examination today."

James nodded, smothering a droll smile.

The exam commenced. I was sharp, yet smooth. I was sleek and faultless in my detection of the clinical signs and relating these to the management issues at hand. In another room, the two older doctors cross-examined me. It wasn't long before we were discussing the structure of genes that encoded sarcomere proteins. Within only a few minutes or so it was apparent my knowledge of the inheritance of familial cardiomyopathy was far superior to that of my examining doctors. They also knew it.

I'd nailed it. It was in the mailbag: signed, sealed, delivered. This exam was mine. A heady flush of exultation swept over me—I needed to remain calm.

Finally, Dr Cornish, in a thin ragged voice, said, "I thank you for attending, Dr Leitch. Your examination was of an excellent standard. I will be recommending you for a prize after your meritorious performance today." He smiled drily. Dr Andrewartha rasped his agreement.

We shook hands, I voiced my suitably gracious thanks and, while leaving the ward, I visited James's room. Seated on his bed he was waiting to leave; bags, cards and chocolates piled next to him. His freckled face broke into a grin when he saw me; he gave a knowing thumbs up. His enthusiasm was infectious and I reciprocated. I was just turning to leave when a young woman approached me in the corridor outside. She looked familiar.

"Aren't you Dr Leitch?"

My feminine assailant was slender, but with soft curves, her complexion as silky as the skin of warmed custard. Dressed in the more informal nurses' uniform of this particular establishment, her full breasts swelled against her closely fitting white shirt.

"Yes …" I tried to place her. "I'm sorry. Have we met before?"

"Of course." The woman gave a coquettish smile. Her small white teeth contrasted with the deep red of her lip gloss. "I'm Allegra Rimo. You're Richard, right? I was here last week—remember? I told you Dr Liddard was tough but fair."

"Of course, Allegra! How nice to see you again. Quite a coincidence isn't it? Two weeks in a row."

This was dangerous territory—and she clearly knew it. She pointed to James's door.

"Didn't you see him then? You know … that boy with the cardiomyopathy?" Her shoulder-length hair had fallen loose from a clip, a lock of thick hair fell forward, peek-a-boo, across her face. Shaking it back with a flick of the head, she folded her arms across her shapely chest and eyed me expectantly.

I glanced around. We were alone in the echoing empty corridor. "Yes, that's right… Really must get going now, although it's awfully good to see you again. I'm due back for a meeting at King Albert's in half an hour. I—"

"And isn't there some little rule...one that says you cannot have for the specialist doctor exameenation..." her speech slowed, her velvety Italian accent now thicker. I was holding my breath "... a patient you have seen already? Hmm?"

She stood waiting for my answer; a mistress in the art of patience. She clearly found the situation to be delightful. I'd better play along. She was astonishingly attractive, her olive skin glowed against her burnished black hair. Her beautiful kohl-lined eyes were fixed on me, her full lips pouting in mock disapproval. I couldn't help but find her Latino looks quite luscious.

I felt my body stiffen in response. "I wasn't aware of that."

"Oh, come now, Richard. Surely you know that is against ze rules."

I stood there, stunned. She had me, for want of better words, by the short and curlies—a big handful of them. She wasn't going to let go. There was no point in arguing with her.

There was no way of wriggling out of this situation, other than doing what I was best at.

"Allegra," I said. I put my arm around her. "I think we should talk about this over dinner. Are you free tonight?"

She gave an enigmatic smile. Visions of eating juicy sweet strawberries suddenly filled my head, the juice running down my chin and then into the valley between her round breasts.

"Yes? We can talk about this, then. Is that all right?"

Allegra slowly indicated her prurient agreement. And, if I ended up sleeping with her, surely this would be in both our interests. After I'd safely deposited the piece of paper with her address and phone number in my pocket, I touched her hand in a final fleeting caress. I fled before questions could be asked by other staff.

Did I think about Cari, I hear you ask? Well, yes, I did in actual fact. But I had a split personality: Dr Jekyll and Mr Hyde; the price of brilliance. One side of me, the Richard accessible for public perusal, the show pony, belonged to her. I couldn't promise her the dark, hidden side; that wasn't available to anyone. Cari owned the uncomplicated Richard, the respectable Richard, the Richard my mother could show off. As a promising London cardiologist, I needed to use any means available to get what I surely deserved. Cari should surely support this. She understood the importance of this particular exam result to my future. And after all, we didn't have any binding agreement. No guilty thoughts. This was how it had to be.

CHAPTER SIXTEEN

Gloucestershire, England UK

1979

White light forced its way through a narrow strip of an opening in the dormitory's heavy floor-to-ceiling curtains, to lighten and make luminous the innocent face of a sleeping boy. He'd been dreaming, a technicolor nightmare of playing schoolboy rugby. Drenched through, the boy was pinned down under a morass of heaving bodies. A stench of sweat and urine assailed his nose, his mouth was filled with gritty mud.

He jolted awake, blinking in the glare, before registering the high-pitched voice of 12-year-old Richard Leitch.

"Time to get up! Breakfast at seven. Shoe and bed inspection at 7:45. Rugby at 8. Any late comers are reported to Hammond. Get moving!"

Fifteen other dorm residents mumbled futile complaints against the early wake-up call, like they did every day, blankets tumbling from bunk-beds.

The boy, nine-year-old Timmy Snodgrass, flexed his legs and groaned. His dream of being wet was reality; he was soaked. Flannelette pyjamas clung to his legs, the skin of his toes wrinkled in the cold urine.

Richard, the head boy, came over and leaned on the strut of the bottom bunkbed. He picked up one corner of the sheet, his nose wrinkling, and showed it to the others. "Snodgrass, not again! When are you going to grow out of this bed-wetting caper?"

Some boys sniggered. Timmy climbed out of bed, sighing, and stripped off the offending linen. He carried the pile to the laundry hamper in the corner of the room, his legs chafing under his sodden pajamas.

Four strikes. There was no hope of evading The Wack, Mr Hammond's wooden ruler that he used to cane misbehaving boys. Mr Hammond, the boarding house headmaster of Marden College for Boys, took a dim view of miscreant bedwetters. He'd surely have kept count over the last week and it had been three times already. Timmy had once tried to convince Mr Hammond he wasn't doing it deliberately. The glowering headmaster, his bottom lip resolutely downturned, only threatened to beat him more if he didn't lift his game.

Later in the day, the small boy, with a pile of clean sheets, was again stopped by Richard Leitch as he skulked back to the dormitory. Like Timmy, Richard was dressed in the formal school uniform of green-and-white-striped blazer, white shirt, green tie and shorts. If seen from a plane passing overhead, the boys at this institution would look just like a swarm of green grasshoppers.

Richard was clutching a pile of Timmy's *Computer World* magazines, which were usually kept hidden under the younger boy's mattress. When Timmy had stripped the bed of its wet sheets that morning, he'd failed to notice that a tell-tale corner of one magazine jutted out.

"What are these Snodgrass?" Richard asked. He didn't seem angry—more curious.

Timmy knew it was against school rules for boys to purchase magazines without approval but given his miserable track record to date with Hammond, he'd chosen to ignore this directive. He dropped the linen and tried to snatch back the contraband.

"They're mine! Give them back!"

Richard spun in circles, a whirling dervish, holding the magazines high above his head. "I'll decide if you can have them back if you tell me what's in them."

"Why do you want to know? So you can go tell your best friend, Hammond?"

Richard halted. "I won't. That's if you tell me what's in them."

Timmy sighed, held out his hand and Richard thrust the stack toward him.

"They're just magazines about computers and robotics, and stuff like that."

"So why are you hiding them?"

Timmy's eyes started to brim with tears. He turned away. "I … I don't really know. But they're mine. I'm the only one who likes this stuff. The other boys would rip them up." His face reddened.

Richard jerked one of the magazines back from Timmy's hand and started to flick through the pages. "Do you understand this stuff? What's all this rubbish about a Smalltalk programme?"

"I do understand it. And it's not rubbish either. My dad thinks computers are going to be the way of the future …" Timmy's voice faded out. Usually at this point grownups patted him on the head and made condescending comments about how the youth are always such dreamers. Richard instead passed the magazine back to Timmy and regarded him with a cool gaze.

"So—making anything at the moment?"

"Yes, as a matter of fact, I am," Timmy replied, unable to contain a note of pride in his words. "I'm making a walking robot. My dad— he works with computers—is helping me. And, I'm learning all about robotic design."

"You think you could show me how to build one?"

"What?"

"Build a robot, idiot.'

Timmy gaped at Richard. "You want to learn how to build a robot?"

"No, stupid, I want to build a bloody house. Course I want to make a robot. Didn't I just ask you if you could help me?"

"But why?"

"Because I have a school project I need to get done. I'm stuck for ideas. So, I'm offering you an opportunity. You help me build it, I'll make sure everyone knows. I'll even have a word with Hammond so you can keep your magazines."

"Really?"

"Really," Richard said. "I promise." He held out his hand to shake, and after a moment's hesitation Timmy reached forward and grasped the older boy's slightly damp hand.

The head boy concluded this meeting with a warm feeling of satisfaction. He'd been struggling to come up with any original ideas, and now Timmy Snodgrass, the scrawny white-haired, bedwetting geek who lived in the corner of the dormitory, had delivered him his original project—without even a whimper of dissent.

That night, in the dormitory after homework, Richard and Timmy got down to business. It could be about any subject, and students from other years were allowed to participate. As long as each project displayed creativity and had some item, be it poster, model (or maybe robot), to display at the stultifying show and tell evening for the parents of the Form 7 boys, the requirements would be met.

After Timmy's initial terror at the idea of working with Richard, he now felt a rush of excitement. Richard understood what Timmy had in mind. Timmy had always assumed that Richard was just another pretty-boy sap, the sort that some of the masters were rumoured to invite to their country homes for weekend visits.

After that, Timmy saw Richard in the dormitory every day. Richard was his usual off-hand self; he could turn this on and off like a lightbulb, especially when the masters were close by. Timmy had to hand it to him. Richard knew how to be prefect perfect, complete with polished black shoes, antiseptically clean knees and spotless green-striped tie. Always likeable and pleasing; no wonder he sucked in teachers and parents alike.

Timmy sometimes wondered if the rumours were true, if Richard was Hammond's special pet. But he discarded this as just the stuff of jealousy. The head boy never mentioned Hammond other than in a voice tinged with scorn. He didn't give Timmy any hint of any special favors.

For Timmy's ninth birthday, in that year of 1979, his father gave him a book: *Build Your Own Working Robot*. On exeat weekends when the boarding-school boys were allowed a brief escape to their family homes, Timmy and his father spent hours tinkering in the shed in their backyard, following the manual's instructions. A lack of cash forced improvization. Most of the small circuit boards they used had been discards from the polytechnic where Timmy's father worked.

On one of these weekends Richard had arranged with Timmy that they would spend the time together at the younger boy's family cottage. The presentation was only two weeks away. They would return to the school at the end of the weekend with what they had built and continue to work on the robot in the evenings. Timmy's father, Mr Snodgrass, came to collect the boys in his small car. Richard saw Timmy visibly relax in the back seat after they left the school's grounds and, as the miles sped by, become more talkative.

They soon pulled up in front of a fallen down fence with thick bramble roses and an overgrown garden strangled with weeds. Mr Snodgrass lugged bags from the back of the car and climbed the few steps on to the cottage's small porch. He crashed the side of his body several times into the dwelling's jammed front door, until it finally relented, and he nearly skydived into the hallway. The boys looked at each other and both stifled giggles. He threw the boy's gear inside.

"I guess I'd better leave you to it then," Mr Snodgrass said. "Let me know if I can be of any help."

Timmy was off already, with Richard in hot pursuit. They headed around the ivy-choked side path, to face a wooden shed with a sliding door, which opened after a hefty shove. Richard followed Timmy into the shed's dark fusty confines. A naked lightbulb swung on a single wire, cobwebs hung in the corners and between the window louvres.

"This is it!" Timmy said.

He pointed to a collection of small circuit boards, wires and twisted scraps of gray metal scattered across a plywood bench. A soldering iron lay nearby. Richard stopped and looked at him, dumbfounded. The results of Timmy's labours looked more like a passer-by, only moments before, had lobbed a live hand-grenade into that dimly lit space.

Richard walked around, to pick up and examine the various tangled bits of metal shrapnel. He picked up a few wires and dangled them off his index finger. "This is it? This scrap is a robot?"

"Yes," Timmy beamed. "I know we have still got heaps to do, but we're missing some of the TTL logic chips. Dad's been trying to get some more from work but …"

Richard looked at him with outright disbelief. Timmy continued talking, but his tone reflected the growing self-doubt casting a black cloud over his optimism of only a minute before. "… But he can't always get them."

"Well then." Richard's face lit up. "We'll just have to get the bits we need, won't we?"

"How are we going to do that?"

"My dad, of course! Dad knows everyone. I'm sure he could get some. I just need to call him."

Timmy nodded, still a little unsure, but his eyes started to shine. "You'd be willing to do that? It's not cheating either, is it? We still have to assemble it, don't we?"

"Absolutely," Richard said. "Absolutely."

The boys set to work, and with the how-to book propped nearby and solder iron at the ready, they rapidly assembled the robot's parts. Timmy's father gave advice and pitched in when the boys' efforts stalled. Later, when it was time to stop, Richard borrowed the telephone in the cottage's hall and rang his father.

"OK, all fixed," Richard said, rubbing his hands as he sat down for a well-earned hot chocolate.

The boys and Mr Snodgrass headed off to dinner at the local pub that night. Richard was friendly and respectful but said little about his family or himself. He didn't explain why he was boarding at Marden College. Instead he wanted to quiz Mr Snodgrass, learning that Timmy's mother had died when Timmy was only five years old. Mr Snodgrass, a gentle man with a caved chest above his paunch, now boarded part-time with another family in Bristol near the polytechnic; hence Timmy's dispatch to Marden College.

"You're damn good at working out those diagrams in that book," Richard said to Timmy. The trio were waiting for their meals to be served. "Instead of hiding yourself away like you do, the school should know you're an expert at this robot design stuff."

Timmy felt a pink flush at the base of his neck creep upward. "Thanks … But the teachers don't understand anything about computers. I'd probably just get in trouble for wasting their time."

"Don't be an idiot! I think if you do something well, you should show it off."

"Yes, son, I quite agree," Mr Snodgrass said happily. "You can help Richard demonstrate the robot at the parent-teacher night. Maybe the school could introduce a new subject, electronics, or something like that."

"You know I don't like standing up and talking, Dad," Timmy mumbled. "I can't help it. I get nervous. The other boys laugh at me. And then you know what happens …" He leaned forward and whispered in his father's ear. Mr Snodgrass gave a doleful smile and wrapped his arm around his son's shoulders. He pulled his son's weedy body in close.

"It won't be forever, my boy. As soon as I get a better paying job, we'll get a housekeeper. Then you can come home again. In the meantime, you and I—we just have to stick it out, don't we?'

Timmy sucked in his lower lip and gave a half-hearted nod.

"That's the spirit." Mr Snodgrass tousled his son's hair. "Oh, good. Here's our food. I'm quite starved, aren't you?"

He's just a graying version of his son, Richard thought, as he watched the man and his son wolfing down their meals. Sharp pincers of jealousy nipped at his throat. The Snodgrass cottage might be falling down; Timmy's clothes might be shabby and too small; Mr Snodgrass might look a bit like a vagrant. But he could sense an invisible shielding bear-hug between father and son. Richard kept it to himself that he'd been sent to Marden College virtually as soon as he was out of diapers.

The weekend over, the boys were dropped back at the boarding house. The other dorm residents noted with interest that Richard had returned from Pissy Snotgrass's house. Rumors began to circulate that Timmy was somehow under Richard's protection. Perhaps Timmy was working with Richard on some secret project? There was even speculation by other more suspicious fellows that Timmy had become Richard's obliging fag.

℞

The afternoon before the big night, the parent-teacher presentation evening, Timmy went to the art room where the robot had been deposited to check all was ready. The robot was far from perfect. Bits of dulled metal were welded onto the outer casing; the inner bits skewed. But, even so, it had mostly been his work. Who would've thought "Pissy Snotgrass" could pull this off? he rejoiced inwardly.

He sailed past the usual colorful masks, the brilliant orange and green paintings, the dioramas assembled for the big night. He arrived where he'd stationed the robot only that morning, to find the stand empty. There was no sign that any creation—living or inanimate—had ever inhabited that small section of worn linoleum flooring.

Timmy stood there momentarily crippled, a sense of blinding panic overwhelming him. His bladder started to scream to be emptied. He clutched his groin, his eyes darting around, at a loss where to start looking. His pulse quickened. Was this a nasty practical joke? After a few minutes of slamming cupboard doors and in a haphazard fashion looking behind other displayed projects, Timmy gave up. He had no choice. He'd have to enlist the help of Richard. He'd know what to do!

Timmy raced back to the dormitory, to find Richard lying on his bunkbed. He cleared his throat. Richard glanced up, startled by the sight of Timmy panting. Some of the other boys lazing around also stared openly, their interest dragged away from books and homework.

"The robot's gone!" Timmy said, willing his bladder not to rebel at that inconvenient moment.

Richard turned and pulled a humorous *Oh really?* face for the benefit of his fellows and became briefly cross-eyed, before returning his attention to his book. The other boys obligingly snickered. "No, it's not." He spoke in the same dismissive tone he reserved for a silly little child asking silly little childish questions. "I just organized with my father to have a few bits replaced, that's all."

"What do you mean? There was nothing wrong with it!"

Now Richard looked up sharply and gave the smaller boy his full attention. "In my opinion it was a bit of a dog's breakfast. And as it was my project, I could do what I wanted … It will be back tomorrow, in time for the show."

Timmy stood blinking at the foot of the bunkbed, not knowing what to do or say, his eyes filling with tears, watched by Richard with some irritation.

Why was he so upset? It could only improve the robot—right? Why did he act as if some evil act had been committed, and he'd become a willing accessory? Richard grimaced and flicked his hand, like Timmy was an annoying gnat buzzing in his ear. Some of the watching boys giggled quietly and turned back to their activities. Timmy knew what they would be thinking. Stupid, geeky Timmy had been getting a bit too big for his booties—and this would teach the prat a well-deserved lesson. It was never too early to teach kids the big lessons of life.

The next evening, Timmy waited with his father in the brightly lit main school hall crowded with people, young and old. The pleasant chatter of excited boys and parents filled the balmy air. The official opening was about to begin: the inaugural exhibition of the boys' projects titled *Creative thinking 1979: a new dimension.*

Three masters, including Mr Hammond, were seated on the stage behind a desk. Muttering to each other, they surveyed the gathering audience. The boys were each going to receive a score for their efforts.

Timmy sat a short distance from the stage and away from the sheet-shrouded robot, which had reappeared as guaranteed. Richard stood next to it like he was an armed guard. He'd shot Timmy a warning look when Timmy had entered the hall.

The younger boy felt dully resigned that Richard was going to take full credit for his creation. No-one would ever believe he could have had a hand in bringing this funny walking robot to life.

Timmy's father, sitting next to his son, looked more like Pinocchio's toy maker than an electronics whizz in his brown corduroy trousers, and yellow-and-red-checked flannelette shirt. He placed his hand on Timmy's shoulder and repeatedly squeezed and released it, as if trying to milk tension from his son's body.

Timmy looked over to where Richard's parents were, yet to take their seats. He couldn't help but stare. Barry Leitch looked like a pumped and cocksure American wrestler—all loud-mouthed confidence and greasy testosterone, making up for his lack of height. He wore a large gold medallion on a thick chain buried in a dark forest of chest hairs, his shirt unbuttoned two notches for full effect. He scanned the audience with a look of bitter triumph.

In contrast, Helena Leitch exuded movie star glamour. She reminded Timmy (who had watched old flicks with his dad) of Grace Kelly, with her honey-blonde hair twisted into a chignon above her alabaster neck. Timmy thought he'd never seen a woman who looked so refined. Her blue eyes flitted discreetly over the gathering. She sat with her fashionably thin body, suited in pale gray silk, turned away from her husband. However, a frown of embarrassment or haughtiness (Timmy couldn't tell which) soured her swanlike features.

The evening got underway. An expectant hush fell over the assembled crowd. One by one, each project was announced, and the student teams were invited on to the stage, to offer a quick demonstration and say a few words. Timmy waited, his breath catching in his throat. He was beginning to feel even more nervous. Suddenly it was very important to him that his robot worked. What had Richard done to it?

"And now, our last demonstration of the night," Mr Hammond boomed.

On cue, the audience woke up and cheered—the presentations were nearly over. Richard stood, in readiness for his turn on the stage.

"Will Richard Leitch please bring his project up: a walking robot, folks!"

A warm wave of surprised applause and chatter swept over the audience.

Richard leapt onto the stage with a few agile bounds, his confident grin that of a future celebrity, or game show host. His father moved the robot onto the stage, still covered with its white sheet.

"This is Bobby, a robot that's been modified from the original design of Buster—a prototype designed by an American, David Heiserman."

The audience responded with polite clapping. A hush descended. Richard scanned the assembled boys and parents, his arm poised in readiness above the sheet to flick it off. A showman, in make-believe top hat and tails, he could be pulling white rabbits from hats. He basked in drawing out the hovering suspense, to a drumroll only he could hear.

"Get on with it!" complained one impatient boy at the back.

"Indeed, I will. Ladies and gentlemen, I give you Bobby!" And with a flick of a wrist, *Ta Da!* There was Bobby in all its naked metallic glory, clattering and spinning over the wooden floorboards of the stage.

The crowd responded with enthusiastic clapping. Timmy felt a profound sense of relief; his robot worked. But then a smoldering anger worked its way from deep within his bones, to seep through his visceral layers, to finally flush his hot face.

The robot was altered. Gone were the rough and ready bits, hewn together. Now polished, and smooth—just like Richard, and devoid of any soul, if indeed it ever had any—just like Richard. The head boy stood with arms folded, his smug smart-arse expression unleashing an overwhelming hostility in Timmy. The younger boy suppressed an urge to run toward and knock Richard over and punch him hard on the nose.

Catching a glimpse of Timmy's murderous expression, Richard stopped the robot by placing it in the machine's docking station.

"Of course, I've had some help building this robot from Timothy Snodgrass and his father Peter Snodgrass."

The audience clapped again.

"Come on up Tim!" Richard urged, in his best TV presenter voice. He leaned over the edge of the stage, to extend a friendly hand.

Before Timmy could protest, he was being pushed up onto the stage, his father giving him an encouraging squeeze of his arm. He faced the audience, his round mouth opening and closing; all thoughts of violence and retribution gone as if his memory cells had been scorched by an electricity surge. A silence filled the hall.

"I …, Uh …, I…" Timmy's words were curled up in his voice box, refusing to leave.

And then—a terrifying panic. He needed to do a piss. Badly. His bladder had been nagging him for the last hour; he'd ignored its calling. Timmy started to lurch toward the stairs, but it was too late. An invisible hand reached inside his pelvis and was squeezing and twisting and wringing his soggy orange of a bladder. A warm trickle quickly became a gushing yellow torrent running down the inside of his shorts before pooling in his left shoe.

A deathly quiet filled the hall. Then a few titters of disgust and frank jeers sang out from the audience's delighted boys. Timmy began to sob hot tears of shame, humiliation, anger, loss. The next minute he was being hoisted off the stage by his father.

"Come on, son," Mr Snodgrass said in Timmy's ear. He was being carried off like an over-tired toddler. "Let's get you out of this place. It's no good for you here …"

Timmy buried his wet face in the warmth of his dad's shoulder that smelled of charred grilled meat and sour soap. It smelled good. It smelled of home. It smelled of all that was right. Timmy lifted his face to fleetingly observe his father staring at Richard. His father's benign expression had changed into that of a fierce Hakka warrior, his normally complacent eyes burning into his son's young enemy.

But Richard didn't appear to notice. Helena Leitch had retrieved a camera from her silk handbag, her delicate nose crinkling at the sight of the yellow puddle lapping at her feet. The head boy posed happily, his biggest cheesiest smile on display. He was oblivious to everything other than the camera capturing him for posterity.

Timmy knew then he'd get his sweet revenge. He'd show Richard. How long it would take, he didn't know.

CHAPTER SEVENTEEN

Richard

Many doctors meet their future partners through the workplace.
Hats off to the good nursing sister who eases the workload of
the busy young doctor. But beware the temptations of the flesh,
young sir. You need to maintain professionalism at all times and
keep your private life just that—private.
Of course, one must avoid at all costs,
the lure of ladies of ill-repute.
(*Essential Tips for the Young Doctor and Medical Student,* 2nd Edition,
by Professor Alfred Crankshaw 1977, p. 66)

I continue my story of what happened, after that specialist's exam when I blitzed the competition out of the water. There's no surprises really. I slept with Allegra, as anyone would sensibly expect.

I take you now to a winter's afternoon at her flat. After I'd enjoyed some downtime, I'd nodded off. I glanced at the clock when the wail of a distant ambulance siren pulled me from my state of blissful slumber. *Holy crap!* It was nearly two o'clock.

I jumped out of bed and located my briefs and woollen trousers lying on the floor's shag carpet. Tangled pink sheets and items of clothing were strewn everywhere, a sign of the hurry in which they'd been shed.

Allegra's bedsit was not how I would have imagined the boudoir of a Latino bombshell to look. All pastels and pseudo-Laura Ashley: curtains, bedspread and ribbons, gratingly quaint and *so English*. And cheap English too. At least in bed she'd lived up to first impressions. She was an Italian wildcat—fierce and insatiable.

"Richard …" Allegra opened drowsy eyes to study me. She lay back on the bed draped in a gown, one leg outstretched, the other crooked, the small swell above her pubis gleaming with perspiration. A waft of musk tickled my nose. "You 'ave to go so soon?"

Milky winter afternoon sunlight streamed through the room's gray-smeared window. The view of terrace houses and the dirty street front of Cricklewood Broadway contrasted with the clean lines and curves of her smooth skin.

"You know I have clinic. I told you when I arrived."

"Yes, but so soon? I thought we'd spend a little longer together."

Allegra pouted at me; her lips swollen. I noted a faint rash on her neck: lovers' burn. She sat up and carelessly let her silk gown fall off her shoulder. The wild cat knew the effect this would have on me. I shook off her temptations and located my trousers.

"We can do this again later in the week."

"When, Richard?" She sat up and looked at me with a sudden blaze of defiance. "When? Am I just your little quickie during daylight hours?"

I noted there was now, inexplicably, no trace of her Italian accent. She sounded as English as a punter placing a bet at Ascot.

She spun around, dragging bedclothes with her, nearly knocking the white bedside lamp sideways. Tugging her floral gown to herself, she glared at me. "When are you going to take me out again? … I'm happy to go to the movies, or a pizza restaurant. I don't ask for much. I just want to go out." Allegra was breathing deeply, her bottom lip trembling. "Are you ashamed of me?"

To my dismay, there was a film of tears in her brown eyes, making her irises look like runny caramel.

"You know I can't spend much time with you at the moment."

"Why not? What's wrong with me? Am I not clever? Am I not good looking?"

I'd taken Allegra out for dinner that night after the clinical exam, as promised. Wined and dined at an expensive Italian restaurant, and bedded later that night, right on schedule. One restaurant dinner was more than enough.

I snapped, "I've already told you. I'm at an important point in my career. I don't have time to be involved with any woman."

"But you are involved with me!"

"Yes, I know." I sighed and reached over and took her slender hand. "When I have my consultant position I'll take you out on dates. Until then I have to work a lot of hours. I'm not going to be much of a boy-friend, I'm afraid."

Allegra lifted her gorgeous wet eyes to look at me. "You promise?"

I pulled her into a tight embrace. "I promise. I'll make it up to you."

☤

I left the poky bedsit and returned to the cardiac clinic at King Albert's. I hurried past the main desk to avoid the frowns of the senior nurses; I was 45 minutes late. I had only just pushed irritating thoughts about Allegra and her increasingly needy behavior aside, to concentrate on seeing my scheduled patients, when my pager sounded: an outside call to be taken. Picking up the phone I dialed the switchboard number.

"Dr Leitch."

"Darling, is that you? It's Mummy. I'm ringing to remind you that we will need to be picked up from Paddington this Friday."

"Oh yes, Mother … haven't forgotten."

How could I overlook this? I was going to be presented with a medal for my outstanding performance in the physicians' exams, at the hospital's annual charity ball. And, for the first time, my parents would be meeting Cari.

"We are still meeting Cari?"

"Yes, Mother."

I wondered if she sensed my eyes rolling. My mother was revealing the real reason why she was calling me. She would be desperate to meet the woman who had snared her son's heart. Cari was not what my mother would be expecting to meet, so I was not looking forward to that first introduction.

I could understand her point of view though. Cari wasn't pretty. Always serious in manner, her struggles with small talk and her tendency to answer banal queries abruptly—as if the questioner was a complete idiot—was at times a problem. But I still found her sharp intellect and her dry view of the world interesting. Sex at times was a touch mechanical; she keenly observed what did what to what, often announcing results as if she was calling a horse race. Still, I liked her. I knew the Allegras of this world would fuel and quench the fires of desire that still burned within me as needed. My addiction to sideline sex could remain a secret. But I wanted Cari in my life for the long haul. At least she could keep up with my intellectual powers—even if at times I felt like a participant in a Kinsey study during our so-called moments of intimacy.

I leaned back in my swivel chair after bidding my mother goodbye, my head resting backwards in my hands, feet up on the desk, to reflect how I'd found the perfect work-life balance. Sex by day with Allegra (during office hours too, I smirked), and a challenging debate about intellectual and other interesting matters over dinner at night with Cari. Then I remembered Allegra's clinginess. I shivered. I needed to end this liaison before she could create real trouble.

A hag dressed in a senior nurse's uniform opened the door to the small office, her mouth hardening and forehead creasing just at the sight of me.

"Sorry, Sister." I jumped up. "I just got off the phone to my mother."

"Well, I'm sure, Dr Leitch, she would be very pleased to know you are working so hard."

I hurried off to collect my next patient.

Bitch.

Four days later, I was back at Allegra's bedsit. I was just peeling her red T-shirt over her generous breasts and pressing my hard body against hers when the hospital's mobile phone rang. This black leather brick of a gadget, the latest release of 1995, had been issued to senior medical staff only that week. We were expected to carry it with us whenever we exited the hospital grounds.

"Leave it," Allegra panted, taking the phone from my jacket and examining it to find the off-switch.

"No. My parents are coming from the country today to see me. They might be letting me know there's a delay."

What was I saying? Allegra might get ideas that she can meet them!

Eyes widening, she wordlessly passed the phone to me.

"Richard … it's Cari."

"Dr Leitch here."

Thankfully Cari didn't notice my formal address.

"Where are you?"

Before I could reply, she continued an obviously rehearsed announcement in a clipped voice.

"I'm very sorry, Richard. I won't be able to attend the hospital function tonight. I've been asked to assist with a laparotomy. It's scheduled to start at seven. Dr Tomlinson especially requested I stay on to help. I know you were hoping I'd be there to see you get your award and meet your parents, but … *Duty calls.* It's an honor to be asked by Dr

Tomlinson …" She paused, then said uncertainly, "I thought you'd be OK about it?"

I didn't answer her. The phone heavy and damp in my hand, my attention was diverted elsewhere. Allegra stood before me, in her black lacy bras and matching panties, grinning voluptuously like a sleek Italian Cheshire cat. She held out a gilt-edged card that had fallen from my jacket pocket.

"It's fine. I completely understand. Good work. I have to go now. I'll catch up with you later."

I pressed the end-call button before she could reply.

"Richard!" Allegra was clutching the card to her bosom like a prized golden trophy. "This is an invitation! You didn't say anything about going to a ball!" She began to read haltingly. "R-Ree-chard L-Leit-ch and partner are i-invit- invited to at-attend the ann-u-al King Al-bert's—"

She was blushing a little. I didn't know she could hardly read. Poor Allegra: all beauty, no brains.

"It's a work function," I said matter-of-factly.

Allegra shook her head in disbelief at this ridiculous statement, her caramel-brown eyes shone. She finished reading silently, mouthing the words, her face crumpled with concentration.

"Don't be silly. It says, 'Dress: Black tie.' How lovely! What should I wear?"

It was *fait accompli,* like it or not; she was coming with me. All thoughts of our lunchtime link-up were forgotten. Allegra floated away, chattering to herself, and left me standing next to her bed, frustrated, as she flung open her wardrobe in the far corner of the room. I could hear the scraping sound of coat hangers and the rustle of dresses as each item was pulled out for consideration.

Sheesh, that was close, I thought. If Cari hadn't canceled, I would have had some real explaining to do. Now, instead, I was going to be saddled with Allegra as my partner that night, unless some miracle happened. How was I going to explain her sudden apparition to my parents? They already knew I was seeing Cari.

⚕

That evening, after I'd collected my parents from the railway station, I thought to phone Allegra. My parents had gone to unpack in the spare bedroom.

"Hello Richard," she said huskily. Perhaps she was wrapping and uncurling the coiled telephone cord around her hand, her pink tongue licking her full lips next to the telephone's mouthpiece. Maybe, she was still wearing the same matching underwear …

"I'm just ringing to make sure you really want to do this. I mean, my parents are quite stuffy," I said this quietly, in case my mother overheard. "I wouldn't want you to feel uncomfortable in any way."

Allegra giggled. "I'll be fine. Can you pick me up soon?"

Good god! There was no way I wanted my parents to share a ride with Allegra. This was going to require some planning. I would have to find an excuse for not taking my parents … OK, they could take a taxi.

"All right, say about 7:30? But Allegra, my parents are conservative. Please wear something a little boring, OK? Not too much cleavage."

She sighed. "Oh, Richard. Please give me some credit. I won't embarrass you. We'll have some fun tonight."

Yes, but afterwards, Allegra, I wanted to say. Not before.

⚕

Later that evening, my Italian paramour and I made our way from my red Audi to a large white marquee located in the hospital's adjoining park. Her stilettos sank into the soft grass along the pathway; her body sashaying as she paused to extricate each black shoe. Her olive skin gleamed under the overhead street lamp, the low light setting off her glossy black hair. Her features soft, she gave me a coy smile, like a modern-day Venus de Milo. She was wearing a long black velvet wrap over her full-length strapless dress. Laughing, she let the stole fall from her shoulders as we walked, allowing it to drape her hips.

"See Richard? No cleavage!"

I nodded with relief. Allegra looked stunning. She wore a small garnet stone in each tiny perfectly rounded ear, a matching drop necklace nestled in the groove between the faint swell of her breasts. Her black hair was swept up, held in place with combs, fine tendrils escaping to hang over her long neck. The effect was subtle, classy— less is more. Shame our liaison was not going to be for much longer, I thought.

I'd secured a prime parking spot as a senior registrar, so the walk to the marquee was only a short one. This had been transformed as if by magic into a royal ballroom, complete with crystal chandeliers and a dance floor. I stopped at the opening, a parting in canvas folds. Allegra took my arm. A waiter appeared bearing a tray of glasses filled with champagne.

"Let me take your wrap, madam," she offered. "Welcome. Do you have your ticket? Good. Let me show you your table."

Allegra took my arm and we followed her. It looked as if a wedding reception was taking place. Each round table positioned around the dance floor was dressed with crisp white damask linen, each chair swathed in a matching gauzy fabric. A large bouquet of roses was placed in the middle of each setting, with sparkling silver cutlery laid out and an assortment of crystal glasses. A band was setting up on a small stage. Murmurs of appreciation and admiration filled the air. *Darling, you look ever so lovely!* The fragrance of exclusive European perfume drifted over the assembling crowd, to accompany vigorous hand shaking and genteel back slapping.

My parents were already seated at their assigned table across the room. Christiaan Grobler, the other senior medical officer, bustled his way over and blocked my path, his wife prim at his side in sensible white lace, her elbow locked in his.

"Hi Richard," he said smiling. He shook my hand, his white square teeth contrasting his perennial tan. "Good to see you. Cari joining you tonight?"

Before I could reply, Christiaan's eyebrows lifted, his mouth forming a small 'o'. He was staring at Allegra standing behind me, her body lightly brushing mine. I turned around. The demure wrap removed, she revealed her glittering sequinned dress in its entirety, complete with a thigh split I'd not noticed before. It looked as if a ninja had just moments before cartwheeled across the dance floor and slashed the fabric of Allegra's dress to her hip with a scimitar. She revealed a curvy leg.

Christ. Was she wearing underwear?

Allegra smiled saucily at Christiaan, and then at me, before introducing herself as "Richard's friend". Christiaan's wife tightened her hold on her husband's arm. I bade them a rapid good night, after securing the promise of a dance from Christiaan's conventional-looking spouse, before more damage could be wreaked by my loose cannon of a sexpot.

"What the hell do you think you are doing?" I said, at the same time smiling bashfully at other guests streaming past. "I told you to wear something conservative."

"Oh Richard …" Allegra pouted, like a petulant teenage girl. "You told me not to show too much décolletage. I'm quite respectable, I think. And besides, you're being a bit silly." She gestured vaguely toward the other women. "Look at all the other ladies. I'm not out of place."

I scanned the room. Not one female would rival Allegra in the wanton drop-dead-sexy competition. She smiled gaily and flashed more leg at a tuxedoed older man sauntering past, who immediately tripped over his feet. Allegra giggled.

"Stop it! You're going to cause heart attacks!"

Allegra laughed again. "More business for you, Richard!"

Then her face changed abruptly, to an icy scowl. She tiptoed to purr into my ear, her breath hot. "Who ees Cari?"

"My sister. She's also a doctor," I whispered back. Allegra bobbed her head, willing me to continue. "She was going to come tonight with my parents, but she had to work."

Out of the corner of my eye I saw her merry smile once again. She unsuccessfully tried again to pull the edges of her dress together.

The beautiful fool had bought my story.

Yet, I'd been thinking about Allegra since she had read that invitation earlier. How the heck did she manage to work as a nurse? Maybe Allegra was not really that dumb. She just needed to bat her eyelids and no doubt someone else covered over the semi-literate tracks she left behind. And, why did her sexy Italian accent turn on and off like a broken streetlamp?

We walked over to my parents' table. My father, Barry Leitch, looked hot and uncomfortable squeezed into a penguin suit too small for his chunky frame, his belly constrained by a sagging burgundy cummerbund. Black hairs sprouted above his tight collar. He resembled an American gangster from the 1920s. Seeing Allegra, he brightened and gazed at her with thinly concealed desire. His black eyes traveled up and down her body resting on any flesh that was still on show.

I gave a calm and collected smile. "Dad, this is Allegra Rimo, my friend."

To give my father credit, he swallowed any surprise at the sudden appearance of Cari's replacement. He stood slowly and brought Allegra's hand to his lips.

"Allegra Rimo, this is Barry and Helena Leitch."

"Pleased to meet your acquaintance," Allegra replied.

"*Make* your acquaintance," I corrected.

My mother remained stolidly seated. I thought of her as an ethereal aged goddess with gossamer-thin hair set in a French roll, its color matching the silver silk gown she wore. A constitutional lack of warmth toward her fellow humankind was likely responsible for varnishing the external shell she presented to the world. She was frowning at me, a fine crêpe of wrinkles spreading like tiny birds' feet from the corner of each carefully made-up eye.

I pulled out a chair at the table next to my father and Allegra sat down, pulling at her dress to cover her legs.

"How do you know my son, Allegra?" my father asked.

"We met when he did his clinical examination at my hospital. He came to see a patient on my ward, where I work as a cardiac nurse. We started talking after the exam... and the rest is history."

"And where are you from originally? I detect a trace of an Italian accent."

"Originally Genoa. I came to London after I finished my nursing exams."

"You plan to stay in England then?"

"Yes, I love it 'ere. Especially since I met Richard." She gazed at me fondly and stroked my hand.

I noticed my mother's thin body tense. Sporting the same frosty expression Cari often wore when she was deep in thought, her pale cheeks were sunken pockets of flesh next to pink lips pursed in the shape of a love heart. But, unlike Cari, who had no appreciation of her public persona, my mother was fully aware she could curdle cream with a single glance. Every ounce of energy my mother possessed she channeled, emitting a powerful stream of negative vibes: green flares shooting toward a woman whom I suspect was an updated version of a prototype of secretaries my father would have employed (read—enjoyed) in previous times.

The evening continued. My father was engrossed in Allegra. I was relieved that at least he was happy to "meet" her acquaintance.

I led my mother onto the dance floor after the main course had been cleared. She glowered back at her husband, who was still seated and whispering in Allegra's ear. My date, in turn, was pulling away, laughing, before dipping her head to hear more.

"Where is Cari? I thought you were seeing her."

"She was called in to work, Mother. Allegra's just a friend."

She squeezed my leading hand tighter, producing a mild burning feeling, then steered me toward the other side of the dance floor. "A friend with fringe benefits by the look of it."

"Just a friend, Mother."

I spun her round suddenly, causing her to gasp, expertly catching her before she fell. You can't choose my bed partners ... *Mother*, I thought. Even if my bedfellow was increasingly reminding me of an Italian fishmonger's daughter, with her constant and shrill "Reechard!"

Back at the table, Christiaan Grobler made his way over to me, followed by a tall man.

"Richard," Christiaan said. "I'd like you to meet Dr Max Wolsey, from Australia. Max is presenting at the cardiology conference this week. You are going?"

"Of course. I'm very much looking forward to it."

Max Wolsey was a large man with a square-cut jaw. A vast smile occupied most of his broad face. He reminded me of a non-verdant Jolly Green Giant from the TV advertisements.

"I've been interested in your work on coronary artery remodelling after myocardial infarction," I said as I shook his enormous hand.

Max looked impressed. This was cutting-edge stuff, only just published in *The Lancet*. "I hear you're being awarded a prize tonight. Congratulations."

I nodded my suitably humble thanks.

"Perhaps you would consider taking up a cardiology fellowship position in Adelaide in the future, where I'm based. We'd certainly have room in the department for you. Christiaan here has been telling me about some of your research proposals, which would fit nicely with what we're doing."

Had he indeed?

"In fact, I'd be delighted if you think seriously about joining our team as soon as possible. We've just come into a substantial grant."

Well, well. This was a windfall of a proposition. The struggle to get prestigious jobs in London continued, regardless of how many decorative ribbons and prizes I earned.

Max moved off to join his table again. I looked over to see prehistoric Professor Crankshaw shambling over to the stage. His body bendy and frail, swimming in a dinner suit too big for his shrunken body, he hesitated when he got to the podium. I leapt from my chair and assisted him with climbing the few steps. I returned to my table, a rush of anticipation filling me.

"Ladies and gentlemen, colleagues and invited distinguished guests," the physician said, after tapping the microphone with his index finger, his papery voice filling the room. "Welcome to the annual King Albert's Charity Ball. I'm sure you're already aware, this year, we are raising funds for the Red Cross. Dig deep, ladies and gentlemen, for a good cause. But in particular, we host this evening each year to honor the hard work of our staff here at King Albert's. And we also take the opportunity to acknowledge academic and research excellence." Professor Crankshaw took a fortifying mouthful from his wine glass. "This year to present prizes our staff has earned, we are especially thrilled to welcome a rising star in the cardiology world, Dr Max Wolsey, from South Australia. Max is in London to present his research next week at the International Society of Cardiologists."

Polite applause sounded.

"And also, a representative from the College of Physicians has kindly joined us tonight, Dr Steven Liddard. Welcome, doctors."

More applause filled the marquee as both doctors stood up and made their way on to the stage. I knew Dr Liddard somehow, but from where, I could not quite place.

"Tonight, we have the honor of presenting the Merrett award for the highest-placed candidate in the recent College of Physicians' Examinations. Our very own Dr Richard Leitch performed brilliantly not only in his written examinations, but also during his clinical viva. His detection of the clinical signs and understanding of hypertrophic obstructive cardiomyopathy were reported to have been outstanding. Well done, Richard. You are a worthy recipient of this award."

The clapping this time was more enthusiastic. I stood and weaved my way between the tables before running up the podium's steps. I smiled modestly at the audience.

Max reached forward and warmly shook my hand. "Congratulations, Richard."

"Good work," Dr Liddard said. He slowly looked me up and down. A flicker of recognition passed over his features. Extending a regal hand for me to shake, he leaned forward and said in my ear, "Quite a coincidence, don't you think? That you saw a patient with exactly the same rare condition only the week before your clinical exam?"

"Indeed, quite," I murmured. I glanced around. No-one else had heard him.

And then with a sudden lurch in my chest I placed him. He was the same cardiologist I'd seen at the trial exam, the week before the finals. The one who had gloried in my dearth of knowledge. He was also the one who could—if he chose to— conduct a simple investigation to reveal I hadn't come clean about my already knowing James, the patient with the heart condition. *He and Allegra Rimo.* In partnership they could complain to the College of Physicians, or worst still the Medical Board. I would be failed, my name forever sullied.

Small embers from hot coals of evidence scattered in my wake were starting to glow, and flames were taking hold.

"Would you like to say a few words?" Professor Crankshaw asked.

I ambled over and stood before the lectern. I looked at my parents seated at the table near the stage. My father had coolly draped an arm around the back of Allegra's chair. My mother regarded me with an accusing expression. Allegra herself looked serene; she wore a teensy smile. She would know who Dr Liddard was.

For once, my words dried up. I stood there, a silence filling the room. I cleared my throat. "Thank you Professor Crankshaw, Dr Liddard and Dr Wolsey. It is an honor to be the recipient of this prize. I thank my family and colleagues. Thank you."

My face reddened, I hurried off the stage.

"Thank you, Richard," the professor said, after a brief pause. My sudden exit and curtailed oration were unexpected. He knew I loved to give a good speech as the much as the next man.

The awards continued. I sipped from my glass of Chablis and settled my racing nerves, watching other buffoonish winners approach the stage, sporting big grins of pride. An amiable Max Wolsey congratulated and shook each recipient's hand. Watching him, the offer of joining his team in Australia was becoming increasingly tempting. I could see it all. I could undertake research at the prestigious Cardiology Centre at the Queen Adelaide Hospital for the next year or so. Under the supervision of the famous Dr Max Wolsey, no less. And, in the meantime, Dr Steven Liddard and Nurse Allegra Rimo would forget there ever was a Dr Richard Leitch.

Finally, the speeches concluded and the music and dancing recommenced. I took the opportunity to suggest to my father that we have a brief father-son chinwag outside. My father gave a grateful nod. His nicotine blood levels had fallen to a dangerously low level, and not even the distraction of Allegra was enough to stop his mouth twitching in a menacing way.

The cold night air hit us with a chilly slap as we stepped out of the tent and headed toward the grassy hillock some distance away.

"Gotta give up the cancer sticks, Dad," I said as he puffed up the slope. His face was perspiring and his flecked gray hair damp, a few thinned remnant black curls of his youth sitting lank on his forehead.

"I'm too old to worry about that, son."

He lit up a cigarette and exhaled a cloud of smoke, before taking another puff.

"How's the tire business?" I asked.

"Not so good, I'm afraid. Your mother thinks I should sell the company. But I think we just need to work smarter, not harder. So we'll see."

My father continued to smoke in silence. Other tuxedoed men had stolen out to join us, the slope adjoining the marque dotted with flares of guiltily inhaled tobacco. Somewhere a woman shrieked laughter. Jazz music surged and ebbed as the flap to the large tent opened and closed after disgorging its occupants.

My parents owned a tire manufacturing business in Gloucester. Asset rich—they owned a mansion, fancy cars and a few other toys—but hit hard by the '87 share crash, they had never fully recovered. Mother was my father's first and only secretary.

My father chuckled, his mood improved with his replete nicotine blood levels. "Congratulations, son. You worked hard for that prize. Any idea what you're going to do now?"

I shook my head. "I've got a few ideas, but nothing too definite."

"Your mother thinks you should be aiming to work at St Vincent's. She thinks it's more prestigious than King Albert's."

"I think I can decide my own career, Dad," I said, my jaw clenching.

He held his hands up in a pacifying gesture and cast a shrugging look of respect toward the marquee. "Just being the messenger... but your mother is a smart woman, son. Listen to what she says." He gave me a sharp slap on the back and grinned. "You're doing a good job, though. Keep it up. We always knew you'd rise to the top of the pack. It's good to have a bit of fun …" his tone now serious, I knew he was thinking of Allegra, "… but there's a time when you gotta settle down." He dropped his cigarette butt on the damp grass and extinguished it with a stab of the sole of his shoe.

An idea dawned. I thought of Allegra, Cari and the mess I'd found myself in.

"Dad, there is something you can help me with."

"Anything, son."

"Tonight, I had a decent job offer to work in Australia. I'm thinking I'd like to take it. But I just need to tidy up a few loose ends here first."

After we'd discussed how to tidy my "loose ends", we headed back. I saw Max Wolsey standing at the bar, pouring the contents of a large beer down his gargantuan throat, his Adam's apple bobbing up and down. I made my way over to him.

"Max, I would be delighted to take up your offer," I said.

He choked on his beer with happy surprise. "That's wonderful news." He wrapped his bear paw around my hand again, to shake it up and down. "When can you start? The sooner, the better."

"I can start as soon as you want me to. There's nothing keeping me here in London."

Max's brow furrowed slightly. He'd spotted Allegra, now entwined in the arms of my father on the dance floor, but he remained silent. No doubt, he too had a woman stashed in every conference port. After some discussion about the details of whom to contact in Adelaide, South Australia, and more enthusiastic hand crushing, I said my good-byes. This was all going to work out OK in the end, I thought.

Wild fire alert: stand-down. Under control, doused.

Later that evening, I lay next to Allegra's smoldering body in her bedroom. I ran my hand up and down her firm thigh that had teased me all night long. I licked her neck while inhaling her floral perfume. Maybe I should wait to tell her my news, I mused. Another 30 minutes wouldn't change anything. One more time for the road. I had to leave her happy—not wanting.

Common sense prevailed. Some time later, after we had given into carnal urges, with me finishing off the dress's slash job, I staggered from her place into a biting cold night air, nursing a smarting and rapidly ballooning purple bottom lip. Allegra had a surprisingly strong right hook, I noted wryly. However, despite her over-reaction, I was pleased with how the events of the evening had panned out.

I summarized the state of play as it stood in my head:

Allegra—sorted.

Dr Steven Liddard—unlikely to cause trouble, if I was out of harm's way in Australia.

Cari—not a problem, if I sold the virtues of a move to Australia in the right way. I wanted Cari to come with me to Adelaide. I'd miss her wilting observations, her astute powers of reasoning. There was nothing keeping her in London. She complained from time to time about her mother, who, now widowed, had discovered an assertive and punctilious side. It was her irrefutable right and mission to offer innumerable suggestions to Cari about how her daughter should conduct herself in all walks of life; all unwanted, all rejected short shrift. Cari would believe me when I told her this would be a good move. This was important for me and my career and, therefore, it was good for her as well. But how would I explain the bloodied lip? The drive back to my unit would give me the time and solitude to plan my explanation—not to mention the sales pitch—how to sell a move halfway across the world.

CHAPTER EIGHTEEN

Allegra

*The occasional more-learned nurse may develop a skill in
reading the electrocardiograph, given careful instruction.
However, the diagnosis of the cardiac arrhythmia must be left to
the keen eye of the physician. The best nurse knows her place, at
the bedside of the suffering ill and wounded, holding the hand
and wiping the brow.*
(*Essential Tips for the Young Doctor and Medical Student*, 2nd Edition,
by Professor Alfred Crankshaw 1977, p.100)

Editorial note: The opinions of Professor Crankshaw do not reflect those of editorial staff
or of the publisher – Professor Felix Drummond -Williams MBE PhD (Oxford) 1977

Cari and Richard have told their London story. Now it's my turn,
the other woman, to tell the truth of what happened later that
night when my "lover" gave me the heave-ho.

After Richard scrammed over 30 minutes earlier, I was left alone in
my bedsit. I nursed a glass of wine and contemplated whether to pilfer
the remains of a toffee-fudge ice cream hidden at the back of the freezer.
I looked at my brand-new dress, purchased only that afternoon. It now
lay crumpled on the floor, ripped to the waist, ruined. Alternately sad
and angry, my murky emotions marbled together; ha! Making my very
own brand of vitriolic Allegra Rimo ice cream.

How could I be so stupid! Why, oh why, had I started to trust him?

I knew Richard was capable of bending the truth. But, in some crazy kind of way, I'd thought it was going to work out differently between us.

Truth time. Richard's not the only one capable of keeping secrets. Yes, my name is Allegra Rimo. Born in London, from hard-working Italian stock: my father a brickie, my mother a housewife. Both speak little English. After the war they settled in Manchester, before moving south in the swinging 60s. In other words, my Italian accent is a complete fake. I speak with an East End accent, as well as any other native of Hackney, where I'd spent most of my childhood.

I hide another secret. I can't read well. Severe dyslexia to blame. I'd left school as soon as I could. When I was 17, to escape a boy chosen by my parents, I traveled to Genoa, my family's home city, where I had cousins still living. I studied nursing, after smart talking the admissions officer. Fortunately, despite my poor literacy, Italian was my first language. I discovered there, to my surprise, I was an excellent nurse. I enjoyed the work: the ever-changing faces of patients, watching the eternal progression from sickness to health, and back again; the banter one minute, the hand holding the next. The literacy wasn't the great problem I thought it would be; I double-checked all medication orders. The other nurses thought I was a nervous Nelly, but it didn't impede my work in any way.

I'd worked in the cardiac unit in the Genoese hospital. I was terrified at first, we were expected to read heart monitors. But strangely, in my topsy-turvy brain, the flowing lines revealing the inner electrical streams of the heart, made perfect sense. I had a talent for reading these squiggles, above that of my colleagues, and for interpreting even the trickiest. However, I didn't pass the course due to a case of severe nerves while sitting the final exam. I haven't officially earned the certificate framed on the wall above my bed. That's a forgery, thanks to a sleazy Italian chap from the education office. He'd ogled me most days when I passed his desk on my way to the wards. One chilly night, in a dark medieval alley, I passed some lira his way as we'd arranged. I allowed him to grope my breasts with his rough hairy hands, his garlicky breath rank on my neck. Then he passed over my certificate. No questions asked.

I returned to London; my parents were getting old and needed help. I applied for a nurse's position at a local hospital. The HR manager was a fat and lazy flub. As long as I was a British citizen, spoke reasonable English (accent nil) and had the required paperwork, I'd get the job. Again, no questions asked. I did have outstanding references from the nursing director in Genoa and I was soon employed in the cardiac ward. That's where I met Richard. It was on the day he came to practice for his clinical exams. The day I decided I wanted to meet him and perhaps get to know him. The same day the silly ruse of the fake Allegra began.

What's a smart girl doing, dressed up in a nurse's uniform by day, play-acting at being the sultry Italian temptress by night? The reality is this. When you're told all your life, "You are dumb. You can't read because you are dumb. You will never achieve anything in life, because not only are you dumb, you also can't read," you'd better believe it. So, let's put it this way. You begin to use any wiles you have up your pretty little sleeve. You use your sex as a weapon. That first day I saw Richard, he intrigued me. His crooked smile, his charm, his humor … my undoing. This feeling intensified the second time I saw him, the day of his clinical exam. But I knew he'd only truly hook up with me if he thought I was his equal in social standing. Even if I'd met him the usual way, like he'd chatted me up at a bar and bought me a drink. Get it? Proper upper-crust English boys just don't date a working-class ethnic bird like me. He'd never be interested in an East End slapper (even a pretty one) of Italian background. And I wouldn't blame him: I had baggage, and a heavy load at that.

This slapper (me) came complete with aged dithery parents with limited English. This slapper (me) would head to her parents' home in the mid-afternoon, to find a kitchen either flooded or blazing hot. Overnight her wide-awake wandering mother would turn on the kitchen sink faucets to wash non-existent dishes, or heat the gas oven in preparation for a long-forgotten batch of *Giugiuleni* biscuits (her specialty). This slapper's father spent his days playing cards in happy oblivion, drinking grappa with his other doddery Italian mates, in the downstairs lean-to while her mother dropped pans and created noisy chaos upstairs.

"Mama, what are you doing? You have been cooking again. It's lucky the kitchen isn't on fire!"

I would scrub baked-on dishes clean, my mother following behind wiping up the items and hiding them away in wrong places.

Poor little Italian slapper. Despite your beauty, you're no great catch. Don't get ideas above your station. Look at the way Richard's mother's eyes glided over you. She had you pegged as a husband-stealing cheap floozy, or worse, as if you were just a stoned hooker in the street to be stepped over, an imposition on her day. Richard's father was kinder; he enjoyed being transported in your arms back in time to his own virile youth when he probably enjoyed a series of affairs, one after the other— good-time girls more than happy to fill the void when the last diversion was found to be wanting, or, just wanting more.

You, beautiful Italian slapper, are just a convenient summertime fling for someone like Richard. He'll screw you over and throw you in the trash as soon as he's finished with you. Just like he would a napkin wrapped around the cone of a delicious gelato. Here one minute, gone the next.

Be the temptress, my inner voice commanded. Later that evening, sipping champagne together in that posh restaurant that overlooked the brown River Thames, he'd murmured how glad he was he'd met me. *Enjoy it while it lasts. He might be your ticket.* And, if you needed to make his acquaintance via his cheating at the clinical exams, well … that was fine too. Just maybe, one day, he might glimpse the good girl beneath the sultry sex siren. I won't lie either. I enjoyed playing the vixen, flaunting the vamp. *Lady in Red.* My life empty of excitement, speeding one way toward a final destination of filial duty and spinster-hood, I'd had no success meeting decent men. At least with Richard I enacted my fantasy of being an Italian bombshell. And didn't he just lap it up.

Somewhere in the back of my mind, I wondered if Richard's atten-tiveness was anything to do with his failure to notify the College of Physicians that he already knew that patient, the boy with the heart condition. But I chose to stay mum. Don't mess with me Richard, I could say to him. I know your dirty secret. Did he think this whenever I teased him? Was I becoming too demanding? I'd noticed his fleet-ing look of recognition, then fear, when he shook Dr Liddard's hand at the ball. And, if the cardiologist had spotted me, he would probably recognize me as the nurse who accompanied him sometimes on ward rounds. But did Richard really think I'd be so shallow as to dob him in, at first opportunity? *Let he who is without sin cast the first stone.* That's what my Sunday school teacher used to chant whenever we ran to her tattling our tales of woe, real or imagined.

You have your own little secrets, don't you Allegra? You're not going to tell on Richard … or are you?

Then he plunged my face into ice-cold reality, after the ball, back in my bedsit, with a brutality that left me speechless. We'd been lying on the floor in the warm glow of lamplight, next to my velvet settee, my head nestled on his chest, fine gray and brown hairs tickling my cheek. Smelling of stale cigarettes and warm champagne, he wrapped his arm around me. I felt safe and secure, warm and soft. We'd made love with an urgency that had taken my breath away. I felt adored, a goddess to his Adonis. He was running his fingers through my hair; his other hand stroked my leg.

I sighed in happy contentment. "I had such a wonderful evening."

"I'm glad. My father was very taken with you." He then chuckled softly. "But I don't think my mother really ever recovered from the sight of your dress."

"She's a silly stuck-up cow," I said. My hands flew to my mouth. But Richard didn't seem offended. Instead he patted and fondled my head like I was a kitten lazing in his lap.

"That she is, but she's still my mother."

"Why do you hate her so much?"

"Pardon me?" His voice now had a chilly edge to it.

I giggled, my nerves showing. "I see way you look at her. Like she is … poisonous weed. You want to pull her out of the ground and throw her away." I pretended with my free hand, to pull out a mythical plant with a heave.

Richard burst out laughing. "You're funny. Of course I don't hate my mother. Maybe I was feeling a bit cross with the way she was behaving toward you … That's all."

I breathed a sigh of relief. All was forgiven. We lay in silence, the warm caress of Richard's fingers across my thigh almost lulling me to sleep.

Then with an abrupt movement he withdrew his arm and stood, his gaze bright eyed. He pulled me off the floor to sit with him on the settee.

"Allegra, you know I've become very fond of you these last few weeks."

"Oh yes, Richard. I have also loved our time together."

He gazed at me with an indulgent smile. He took my hand and cradled it in his own.

"What is it you want to say?" my voice squeaked.

"I have something to tell you."

My heart started to beat faster. "Yes?"

His gaze lowered.

"Some news, I'm afraid." His words sounded a dull dishwasher gray.

I glared at him. "What is this? News?"

"I've had the job offer of a lifetime." He started caressing my fingers, light strokes of deceit. "I've been asked to move to Australia to take up a prestigious research position. I'll be working with one of the most eminent researchers in my field."

I swallowed hard. Tears started to film my eyes. "When?"

"Next month. I'm sorry Allegra, my plans don't include you. I want to throw myself into this research without the distraction of a … partner." He shrugged. "Sorry."

"What? You bring me home for a quick little fuck and then you tell me?"

"That sounds rather vulgar. I wanted us to finish on a happy note."

"More like a happy ending for you!"

Then I socked him and sent him packing.

I'd told no-one of my daytime liaisons, my secret hook-ups between shifts. Other nurses had never warmed to me, especially the married ones, so this pain I carry alone. Pull yourself together, Lady in Red. Blink away those tears. Notch this one up to experience. *Focus.* You are a good person, you're not a slapper. You can do better. You will do better. No more users. No more losers! I needed to pour my efforts into my career as a nurse. I would be that good girl in uniform, I would believe in myself. I'm not dumb. I just have trouble reading. Tell yourself that, repeat after me. *I'm not dumb. I just have trouble reading. Repeat after me.*

Chapter Nineteen

Richard

The young doctor must be open to opportunities that advance his clinical skills and love of learning. This may entail travel to exotic far-flung parts of the globe, often to work with unsophisticated indigenous primitives of dubious moral character. Singledom will present challenges to those vulnerable to the deprivations of intelligent and decent company. Therefore, it is sage advice to make a good match early in one's career. Although 'One must not mix business with pleasure' as I have already stated, a marriage between a doctor and a nurse of good character will certainly protect the junior clinician from temptations unbecoming. Just make sure you are not rostered on the same ward—at the same time.

(Essential Tips for the Young Doctor and Medical Student, 2nd Edition, by Professor Alfred Crankshaw 1977, p. 66)

Editorial note: The opinions of Professor Crankshaw do not reflect those of editorial staff or of the publisher – Professor Felix Drummond -Williams MBE PhD (Oxford) 1977

The following day I decided to tell Cari my plans. An afternoon off work was a luxury; I was exhausted, especially as the night before was a late one. I'd gone into the hospital for ward round as usual that Sunday morning. I ran a hot bath when I returned home to my flat.

Surprisingly, Cari decided to join me. However, my energy was sapped, my bones ached. Following my energetic previous evening, sex was *not* at the top of my to-do-list.

"What happened to your face?" she asked, in relation to my fat bottom-lip.

"Would you believe I walked into a door knob?"

Her expression conveyed that she thought I was a complete moron. But she didn't enquire further, other than to say I should have applied ice. I lay back in the warm water, in the oversized enamel bath. Cari faced me, waggling her toes through the fine lacework of bubbles glistening the water's surface. Closing my eyes, I inhaled the heady scent of rosemary and sage from bath salts I'd added. Steam enveloped us like a warm blanket, the taps and mirror trickling with droplets of condensation.

"No sleeping on the job," Cari said, after a while. Reading others' non-verbal cues was never her strong point.

"What job?"

She gave me that look again. "I think you should find that out for yourself."

I sighed. "I've been busy all morning. Can't a hard-working doc get the occasional break?"

In reply Cari splashed me, this time directly into my face, the suds stinging my eyes. Her face determined, her mouth a straight line. The bubbles adherent to the cerise nipples of her small breasts twinkled like a million tiny stars. She neatly climbed out of the bath, the water sloshing over the edge. She wrapped herself in the towel strewn on the floor among discarded clothes and shoes.

"Well, come on then. You have work to do."

I groaned in mock dismay. Cari could be stubborn, and there was really no point in arguing. "You're a hard taskmaster, Cari Rainsford. Leave me alone."

She pulled a face, half-frown, half-grimace. She poked out her pink tongue like a small child's and held out her hand. "Up you get, lazy bones," she said awkwardly. This playful speech was not something she'd usually say.

She pulled me out of the bath, and I kissed her, her teeth and tongue meeting mine.

We made love on the sodden bath towels that afternoon, on the hard-tiled bathroom floor, my earlier reticence forgotten. Cari kept her eyes open as if she was reveling for the first time in all of the sensations, a dripping tap our only musical accompaniment. No scented candles, no sexy or romantic music. Just ourselves, wrapped in each other.

"You're mine, don't you ever leave me," I whispered to her afterwards. She cradled my damp face with her cupped hands, her serious gaze open, searching my eyes as if she was trying to assimilate every last ounce of me—my skin cells, my hair follicles, the pigments of my irises— into her memory.

"I *am* yours, Richard," she said. "You know I never lie."

She gave a small gasp of surprise when she said that, as if she also had discovered an unknown side to herself, the revelation of being able to give and receive naked tenderness.

"Please come with me to Australia, Cari. I have had a job offer and I think it would be good for me … us … if I accept. As soon as possible." I looked into her deep-green eyes. What I said was true. Her face colored and her eyes widened—the only clue that I had surprised her. Without speaking, she gave a vigorous nod.

PART THREE

Queen Adelaide Hospital

South Australia

CHAPTER TWENTY

Cari

28/8/1996

*Long hours in the operating theatre is part and parcel of the life of
a junior doctor. The wise surgeon thus ensures sufficient rest breaks
and refreshments are taken by his assistant. Take up this offer, young
sir. No-one respects the fainter, especially when through heedless and
un-necessary deprivation a syncope is the result.*
(Essential Tips for the Young Doctor and Medical Student, 2nd Edition,
by Professor Alfred Crankshaw 1977, p. 104)

We had been living in Adelaide for a few months when the Storeroom Incident happened. It was a Wednesday on the 21st of August at 1:42 pm, to be specific. I was heading down in a utility lift to the main cafeteria before starting my General Surgery clinic. This was usually a sensible decision; I often took the back way behind the A&E Department to avoid other doctors who wanted second opinions or to indulge in idle gossip. The lift lurched to a stop on the ground floor. Its doors slid open with a soft whoosh.

I was about step out when I recognized Richard, dawdling at the far end of the corridor. I was mildly bewildered; he didn't usually frequent these parts. He had his back to me and was talking and laughing with a nurse who looked familiar. Taking her arm, he opened the door to a utility room that I knew stored IV fluids and other supplies. Something made me hesitate. I'm not sure what. I saw him make a shifty glance over his shoulder, just as the doors of the lift slammed shut, almost jamming my extended foot. He hadn't seen me. Trapped inside the lift, I fumbled with the buttons of the operating console. The doors at last opened again. I leapt out. He was gone. I hesitated to follow him. Some foreknowledge pinned me in place. But then, as if jerked along by an invisible chain attached to my torso, I stumbled the 20 meters or so to the storeroom.

I'm sure many would think I was a fool to not get on and open the door. But I needed to assimilate, to contemplate, to make sense. Here are the facts: fluorescent light bounced off walls, spotlighting that particular door, as if lit up just for me. The door was painted a caramel-beige, the smooth chrome of the doorknob cool to the touch. A steam autoclave located in the A&E wheezed behind the wall and echoed its wet sounds along the corridor. I heard the wail of an ambulance, its siren escalating in intensity, as it pulled into the driveway of the adjoining A&E.

I stood frozen. I heard muffled voices behind the door, then a moan.

I understand now, many years later, that my reluctance to confront Richard was borne out of some subconscious knowledge that our dying relationship was already taking its final breaths. Not only gasping for air, but choking with a death rattle half the hospital could hear. Back then, my conscious self was totally deaf to its demise.

Dr Smythe, always a font of reliable advice, whispered to me from the inner reaches of my subconscious. *My dear girl. You won't know what is inside that room unless you take a look inside.*

I ignored her. Maybe Richard was shooting up drugs? I knew of one doctor who had done such a heinous act in an A&E backroom and had been caught.

Minutes passed.

Get to it Cari!

I heard a groan. I opened the door. Just a little, and then, a little more.

Before me was a small room—a dark cave filled with bags of IV fluids, packets of suture materials and a few tubby torpedoes of oxygen bottles lined up along a wall. There were two occupants: Richard and the nurse.

They were kissing.

My eyes took a moment to adjust to the gloom. Richard's back was to me. A white shirt just covered the top of his butt; his charcoal-gray pants hung around his ankles.

I couldn't breathe. My chest was on fire. Knees shaking, my legs turned to jelly. Head spinning, I couldn't move. Acrid bile rose into my mouth and swirled around. I grabbed a bench to steady myself, sending bits of medical equipment scattering. A plastic gadget that looked like a cannula fell to the ground.

Startled by the noise they pulled apart. Richard was swaying and seemed dazed. Turning towards the door, he at last registered my presence.

"Oh shit. Cari!"

He tugged his clothes on, glancing over his shoulder. Although I could only see glimpses of the nurse, her firm mouth told me she was furious they had been disturbed. Straightening, she pushed him away and tucked her white uniform shirt back into the band of her skirt. She wiped the residue of blood-red lipstick across her cheek with the back of her hand, leaving a smudge like sunburn. She pushed past me forcefully, knocking my hip against the corner of the bench. I gasped with pain. Then I heard her footsteps tapping away quickly along the corridor.

I knew her now.

Miranda Baird.

All I could do was stand there. I heard a choking noise—it was coming from me. Irrelevantly, I thought, my symptoms could be anaphylaxis, with a swollen tongue and spasming throat.

"Are you all right?" Richard asked.

What a ridiculous question!

He was still trying to adjust his state of dress; his zipper would not pull up. I shook my head; my tongue was in a stranglehold. I tried to slow my breathing. The room was chilly, yet my face burned. There was a smell of rank sweat.

"I'm so sorry …" was all he could say.

I channeled all my studied knowledge of soap opera scenes.

"You bastard!" I shrieked. I flung out my arms in a theatrical fashion and spat in his face. "Get out of my life! Do not darken my door ever, ever again! We are finished Dr. Richard. Leitch!" And with that final declaration, I turned and bolted, to promptly throw up in the basin of a toilet cubicle in a bathroom further along the corridor.

Dr Smythe made a late reappearance as I bent over heaving, alone in that small dim room. *Well done, Cari. I'm so very proud of you. He doesn't deserve you. You have done the right thing.*

I flushed the loo and dragged myself to the corner of the bathroom, next to a sink. I closed my eyes and put my hands over my ears trying to zone her and the entire world out. I fell to my knees on the hard terrazzo floor and curled into a fetal position against the dizziness. Slowly I began to rock my upper body: back and forth, back and forth, back and forth.

℘

Long minutes passed. Eventually, I climbed to my feet. The sensation in my fingers and hands had returned; my breathing almost normal again. I splashed warm water from the sink taps on the now smarting skin of my face. I must have looked as if I'd been sobbing, but I hadn't. I took a long, critical look at myself in the cubicle's mirror. I was pale and my pupils were dilated.

I was scheduled for an outpatient clinic, but it would be impossible to work. Clinic, and the multifarious grumbles about my no-show from the various staff who worked there, would have to wait. I needed time to think, to process. Just now, I couldn't face anyone or act rationally.

Richard and Miranda. How long had that been going on for?

I needed to find the charge sister of the unit and somehow plead an excuse: a migraine, period pain, anything. My explanations would be received with all the warmth of the air in the basement's mortuary. In this job, attending your own funeral was not a plausible explanation for missing clinic. I glanced at my wristwatch, not sure what to do. Clinic was beginning in five minutes. I needed to hotfoot it two floors above if I was going to inform the staff I was taking the afternoon off. I pushed the door open and peered outside—just in case Richard was having second thoughts and had followed me.

The echoing corridor was empty except for a middle-aged woman in a white uniform pushing a clanking linen trolley toward me. She halted when she saw my head poking out of the doorway.

"All right dear?"

I nodded in reply and pulled the Reassurance smile. Seeing this, the woman proceeded on. At the end of the corridor she stopped, and glanced back.

I left the bathroom and turned toward the lifts foyer. My pager sounded. I groaned. I yearned to do my work efficiently and well, but that tweeting black destroyer of my best intentions always had other ideas. This portent of trouble, carried deep in my pocket, was the metronome for the pace of my day. I could be called in the hospital, anywhere, anytime. It bleeped like a cricket chirping, louder and louder, a crescendo of whirring and vibrations.

I groped wildly to reach it in my pocket, but I was slow and clumsy, unable to silence its clamant call fast enough. Number 71 flashed up on the small screen.

The Emergency Operating Theater.

My pager was not only an acoustic form of acid, burning holes in my schedule, but was also a beacon for any inquiring souls needing to find me—a location-divining device. If I didn't answer, someone would find me, regardless. I found a wall phone and dialed the number.

"That you, Cari? It's Linda." I recognized the voice of my theater nurse friend. She didn't wait for my response. "We've got a cardiac tamponade, secondary to a dissected aortic aneurysm, ready to go and can't find the on-call cardiothoracic reg. Can you give us a hand? Just till we find Cam Bryant?"

"I'm not on call and … I'm not feeling that great," I said. Holding a retractor for Joan Backhouse, the city's only female cardiothoracic surgeon and boss of Cam Bryant, was known to be challenging at the best of times. "I've got a migraine. I need to go home. I was about to cancel afternoon clinic." Despite still feeling slightly disorientated, I felt a momentary surge of pride at my ability to concoct a convincing lie.

"Oh … sorry to hear that. But we really need to get going. The patient crashed in A&E. Dr Backhouse wants to start his repair. She's really pissed we can't find him."

I sighed my agreement. This was bad news. *Really* bad. This guy on the theater table had an excellent chance of meeting his maker. A dissected aortic aneurysm is a life-threatening condition. It occurs when the main artery that supplies blood to the body has a major tear along its inner lining. There's a risk of cardiac tamponade, when blood flowing in a backwards direction fills up the space between the muscle of the heart and its outer slippery sheath, the pericardium. This causes the heart to no longer be able to pump blood, causing shock to set in, then death.

Oh, for goodness sake … Pick yourself up, my girl, Dr Smythe said.

Phone in hand, my head started to pound; the fable of my migraine was becoming a throbbing reality. And I'd never assisted with this type of surgery before. My mouth opened like an automaton. "Just for a little while, OK?"

"Yes Cari," Linda said, relieved. "You will be fine."

I hurried upstairs and dashed into the scrub area. The theater atmosphere was tense. Thick chemical laden air was shattered by the sounds of the puffing ventilator and the crashes of falling metal, as surgical instruments were unbundled and dropped onto green-draped trolleys. Linda, who was a senior scrub nurse, was already scrubbed and assembling the instruments needed on draped trolleys. She gave instructions in a low voice. Scout nurses scurried about; more packages were unloaded.

Dr Backhouse was also scrubbed and in theater garb. In her green gown, wearing a paper mask with special telescopic loupe glasses, she looked more like a goggle-eyed pest exterminator than a surgeon. Lying on the theater table, already draped with green theater sheets, was the male patient. Linda saw me and shook her head, holding a gloved finger to her mask, signaling that Dr Backhouse might ignore me if I stayed quiet.

It was wishful thinking. Dr Backhouse's eyes migrated over to where I stood. She gave me the once-over.

"For Christ's sake. A first-year trainee assisting with a tamponade? Where the hell is Cameron Bryant?"

"No idea," Linda said.

Dr Backhouse muttered expletives and returned to fiddling with her glasses.

I scrubbed and donned gloves. Then, after whirling around for a nurse to tie my sterile gown, I stepped up onto a small stool on the other side of the table. The head surgeon lifted her eyes briefly as I positioned myself. With a reputation for being "one of the boys", she didn't tolerate fools. She'd been known to reduce medical and nursing staff to tears, usually when equipment she needed was not available or up to expectation—or worse, when her assistants were found wanting.

The theater lights cast a bright white arc over the operating field. I felt unpleasantly sticky and warm. I attempted unsuccessfully to lick my dry lips under my mask. The surgeon slopped brown iodine solution onto the patient's chest before taking the scalpel from Linda's outstretched hand. She cut along the femoral artery and vein, and cannulated both.

"Simon Marsh. Forty-two years. Fit and healthy," Dr Backhouse said, as she worked, as if she was speaking her thoughts aloud. "No medical history, not even a smoker."

"What happened?" I dared ask.

"He's a teacher at a primary school," she said. "He was on the oval. Complained of terrible chest pain. Collapsed a few minutes later; then arrested in A&E. They did well to bring him back." She paused to meet the eye of a young man, the perfusionist, sitting behind the operating table, next to the bypass machine. "OK John, get going."

The perfusionist hooked up the blood-filled tubes and the process of cooling the patient's blood began. The bodily temperature needed to be reduced to slow his metabolic rate, then the bypass machine could take over the pumping job of the heart. The machine started up, blood swishing through pipes into the depths of the machine, to be pumped out, a rich shiraz color, and be returned into his body. Simon Marsh's vital functions were now reliant on a machine. In his deeply anesthetized state there was no way of knowing if it was not already too late. His brain had more than likely suffered hypoxic damage. But Simon Marsh's heart continued to beat, despite the blood being circulated elsewhere, as if it planned to defy the odds, remonstrating with my pessimism.

Dr Backhouse made a midline incision over the sternum. She didn't concern herself with bleeders along the way—that could wait. Then, wielding a sternal saw, which emitted a high-pitched squeal, she cut down on the breast bone, a lower munching sound made as it met bone. It chomped through, until it reached the fibrous outer layer of the pericardium. The shrill noise of the saw indicated it had reached its intended destination.

We waited for the cooling. Retractors were placed to expose the boggy-looking blue pericardium bulging through the small space, like the breast of a blue wren. Dr Backhouse enlarged the area, to improve her view of the major blood vessels around the heart.

"Pay attention." Dr Backhouse looked up suddenly, her eyes met mine. "The root of the aorta is aneurysmal. Don't touch it or it'll blow. I'll suture in an aortic root replacement, then we can drain the blood off."

The coronary arteries were mobilized and a mechanical heart valve inserted. A smell of burned flesh filled the air as cauterized small blood vessels sizzled at the touch of the diathermy probe. My gown heavy against my body, I attempted to cut suture material short. My clumsy shaking hands would not cooperate.

The surgeon's face knitted in concentration as she checked her handiwork. Satisfied, she clamped off the aorta. I held the sucker in place in readiness to catch the deluge of cruddy coagulated gore.

"OK, here we go …"

She plunged the scalpel in.

Immediately, the plastic instrument I held spluttered into life, noisily guzzling a bloody mess through the attached opaque tubing. The heart, now fully visible through the gaping hole, was a beefy-red giant cardiac eye, weeping and blinking tears of congealed blood.

"We're down to 18 degrees," the perfusionist announced.

The anesthetist injected a lethal potassium-rich solution into the bypass machine's blood-filled tubing. This was to stop the heart, to allow Dr Backhouse to finish the repair job by placing a Dacron graft to the bulging artery wall. Without warning, the feeling of sweatiness and the sensation of my gown being glued to my skin worsened. Intense nausea and giddiness washed over me; a cold sweat drenched my upper body. The theater table became a bucking bronco, I reached forward to grab its edge.

"Cari, you OK?" Linda's query dragged out as if in slow motion. The room was swimming. "You're not looking … too … good …"

The sight of that piece of rhythmically contracting meat cooking under the hot lights and then slowing—as if finally giving up—was my downfall. And fall down I did. I didn't fall in the graceful swooning fashion of heroines described in novels. They daintily lose consciousness, smitten hearts racing at the sight of their beloved, with stars or playful seraphs with fluttering wings encircling their peripheral vision. Instead, I fell down in a crashing, blundering, piss-your-pants, black-out-cold kind of way. In short, I fainted. Something I'd never done before. I careened backwards and ploughed into a surgical trolley. Dr Backhouse's exasperated "Oh for fuck's sake!" was the last thing I heard.

When I came to, I found myself in a cramped A&E cubicle. I had no idea how long I'd been out. I remembered only being lifted by unknown hands, then an awareness of flying and bright lights flickering.

"Hello you."

I opened my eyes to see Linda looking down, a heavenly white light haloed her. A drip inserted in the back of my hand, however, confirmed I hadn't shot off to the next life. A nurse was pumping up a blood pressure cuff wrapped around my other arm. A momentary squeeze, then hiss, as it released.

Linda's eyes held an expression I couldn't read. Maybe she knew I was in deep trouble; irrevocable trouble of the brown variety. Trouble of the kind that is a bottomless hole with smelly slippery sides and no foothold to climb out.

"God, I'm so sorry, Linda." My words came out as a croak, my mouth still bone dry.

"Don't worry about it. Cam Bryant turned up just as you blacked out. It worked out OK. You just scared us to death. A nasty fall … I thought you'd cracked your skull."

I fingered the lump on the top of my head and swallowed painfully as the events in theater drifted back into my consciousness.

"So, what happened? You've never fainted before," Linda said.

"I hadn't eaten all day."

She rolled her eyes. "Big deal. You hardly ever get time to take a break most days."

A feeling I recognized as dread and despair settled within. It was true, I couldn't argue with logic—I was incompetent. I started to cry. *Surgeons can't be fainters!*

"Oh Cari, my poor darling," Linda said. She reached for a tissue and dried my eyes. I continued to sniff, and she watched me, her brow knitted. "Something really bad must have happened."

I closed my eyes. "I just fainted, that's all."

"Cari, come on. Aren't we friends? Spit it out."

The nurse, her eyes bloodshot from hours of theater-light glare, waited for me to reply. Linda was my closest friend; in fact, she was my only friend.

I opened my eyes to stare at the plasterboard ceiling. "I walked in on Richard having it off with Miranda Baird this afternoon." *There,* I'd said it. A flash of what I'd seen rushed past me. I reached for the vomit bag and started to dry retch. When I'd calmed, Linda poured me a drink and caressed my hand.

"Richard was kissing Miranda Baird?"

"No, no. Worse than that—"

"Richard was doing *Miranda*?" Linda whispered.

"His pants were down, and he had her against a bench."

"But where?"

"In one of the storerooms just down the corridor from here."

"Bastard." Linda regarded me without speaking. I watched her wide and generous face move through a myriad of emotions even I could identify, from anger to concern, then back again.

I started to cry again.

This was a very different Cari to my usual persona. Normally I was cool and collected; I could handle any emergency. My facial expression and composed voice gave little away of any inner turmoil. I'd once been told by a hospital psychiatrist that I possessed a "flat" or "blunted affect". His words meant nothing to me. As far as I was concerned, he could have been describing the state of an economy.

"No wonder you're so upset," Linda said.

"I don't know how I feel. I had no idea this was going on."

"Well, I'm feeling bloody angry. I can't believe his audacity. You going to kill him? Or do you want me to? And by the way, I'm not joking."

I stared at her, not sure whether she was speaking the truth. "What happened to Simon Marsh?" I asked, hoping to change the subject.

Linda stopped grinding her jaw and half-shrugged. "Too early to tell, I'm afraid. The ICU guys don't think he's going to do very well though. He didn't show any sign of waking up when they tried to bring him around." She exhaled softly. "But Cari … It's not your fault if he doesn't do OK. You know that, don't you? Anyone can faint in theater. That guy was dead man walking when he went to work today."

She ran a hand through the matted curls of her blonde hair, flattened from hours of being confined under a paper theater cap, and rubbed her reddened eyes. A fine skin groove cut across her forehead where the cap's elastic had dented her skin. "I think you'd better come to my place for dinner," she said, after a while. "Or better still, stay with me for a few days while you sort out the Richard situation. And don't you say, 'I don't want to be any trouble!' because you won't be."

I wouldn't have said that anyway, but I didn't argue. She was right; this was the best solution for me at the moment. I nodded, every facial and neck muscle cramping. After arranging my transport for later, Linda gave a wan smile, before slipping off to prepare the emergency theater for its next customer.

Chapter Twenty One

*Examinations are always a time of stress for any medical student
or junior doctor. A nutritious diet, plenty of sleep and a balance
between recreation and study is the right recipe for success.
Those friends not engaged in study or of a frivolous nature will
often hinder one's efforts and should be respectfully kept at arm's
length. The student must exercise temperance.*
(Essential Tips for the Young Doctor and Medical Student, 2nd Edition,
by Professor Alfred Crankshaw 1977, p. 10)

That evening my friend took me to the unit I'd shared with Richard, only a kilometer from the hospital, to pack up my meagre possessions. I still felt oddly sick and dissociated. I placed the key in the lock of my front door. It swung open with a loud creak. Linda stood behind me, her hand resting under my elbow, half-pushing me, half-holding me upright. There was a gush of cool mildewy air in my face. I realized I was holding my breath.

"Good, he's not here," Linda said, peering around the door frame. I stood frozen. "Let's get your stuff and get out of here."

This was what I needed to do. Best not to linger. Used coffee cups, and plates in the sink smeared with the remnants of toast and strawberry jam, were the only signs a living, breathing relationship had been resident earlier that day. The telephone answering machine in the corner flashed a dull red light.

"Crap—it's probably him," I said. "Leave it."

Too late. Linda had already reached over and flicked the button.

Darling, it's Mummy. I haven't heard from you for such a long time. When are you going to take time off and give me a call? I've got good news: Megan is pregnant again! Six weeks gone. Give my love to Richard. OK then ...

The recording cut out mid-sentence, the echoing voice from overseas fading with it.

"Wow, that's all I need," I said. My mother was the last person to whom I felt like justifying my actions. "And that's for Mum to call and find out we've broken up. She thinks the sun shines out of Richard's—"

"You don't normally worry that much about what people think, do you?"

"That's not true, I do actually. But it depends. It's just ... Mum will start up a barrage of phone calls. She'll go on and on about how I should go home. Back to Wales. Then she'll get my sister involved."

A black look settled on Linda's face. I'd been almost shouting.

"OK, sure. But you will have to tell her sometime."

I got busy. This untidy unit was a symptom of the disarray of my life. I threw rubbish in the bin and piled more dishes into the sink. Linda dried after I'd slammed the washed crockery onto the drainage board. She admonished me at one point for cleaning up yet again after "that bastard."

We piled clothes and toiletries into suitcases. Richard could keep the white goods and the television. It was all his, anyway. The unit didn't look much different after we'd collected my gear. There was no evidence in pictorial form of our life together, although there were several pictures of him, skiing in France and collecting various awards, stuck on the fridge. On the desk his framed university degrees were proudly displayed, and the award certificate he received when he'd won the medal for excellence in his physician exams.

The clean-out complete, I stormed outside to the catacomb-like mailboxes at the front of the units. I flipped the lid of my unit's box.

There it was. Tucked neatly into a pile of bills, a letter addressed to me from the College of Surgeons in London. The letter I'd been dreading. The letter informing if I had passed or failed my primary written surgical exam.

Dragging my feet, I took it inside and sat on the bronze leather lounge suite. The cushion behind me hissed with a slow expiration as I sank into it, like the sound I imagined toxic gas released from a tear in the ballooned flank of a long-dead beast would make. I flipped the envelope several times in my hands, not really wanting to know what was inside. When would this dreadful day end?

"I think it might be my exam results," I said.

"Open it Cari."

Linda sat down next to me, a burst of air also gusting from under her backside. She wrapped a doughy arm around my shoulder. A big woman, her dimpled arm encased me with a reassuring soft mound of warm fat, feeling not unlike an inflatable flotation device.

I ripped the envelope open and pulled the waxy document out.

Dr Cari Rainsford *Royal College of Surgeons*
2/22 Chester St *221-226 Leicester Square*
East Adelaide 5777 *London SW553*
South Australia *United Kingdom*

10/8/1996

Dear Dr Rainsford,
This letter is to inform you that you have been unsuccessful in obtaining a satisfactory result in the UK College of Surgeons Primary Written Examinations 1996.2, held in Adelaide on 21/6/1996. If you wish to appeal this decision you can contact …

I stopped reading and let the letter fall limply into my lap.

"I didn't pass."

I shook my head with disbelief. How did that happen? Admittedly my study attempts were half-hearted. I'd not found the routine to put my head down in the previous months and just get on with it. It wasn't easy when I was always working, and on any free afternoons Richard had wanted to visit friends.

"Bugger," Linda said.

We sat in silence, digesting the news. What was I going to do now? I'd come to Adelaide to take up a surgical training post. After my spectacular back-flipping performance no-one in their right mind would consider having me on their books, in any surgical post, ever. Would the Director of Surgical Training want me back? A trainee who not only had failed her primary exam—no-one failed this—but who now had a reputation for conking out when the going got tough in theater.

We threw my gear into Linda's car and drove to her small Victorian cottage, a few kilometers south of the city. It wasn't long before Linda was busy chopping vegetables for salad, while I sliced crusty bread. Andrew, Linda's husband, was cooking outside, the sizzle of steak hitting the hot barbecue plate heralding the tempting cooking smells that wafted through the kitchen window minutes later. He came into the kitchen to fetch cooking utensils and Linda passed him a beer, before fixing him with a cold stare. He then made a hurried escape, banging the back door behind him. Even I could tell Andrew knew his affable presence wasn't welcome. His wife had serious business to attend to with me: my interrogation.

"OK," she said, holding a long knife that glinted under an overhead bench light. "Tell me exactly what happened today."

I rehashed the story without skimping on details. She remained silent but continued chopping as I talked, her lips pinching and eyebrows raising now and then.

When it was clear I'd spilled all, she put the knife down and looked me squarely in the eye. "What made you and Richard get together in the first place anyway? You're so different."

I explained everything: Mrs Davis and the Irish lady, me becoming hysterical with laughter in the corridor, the nurses disliking me, that night in the pub, his cooking dinner for me a week later at his place. Then afterwards walking alongside the Thames near the bridge, his arm around me.

"But that still doesn't explain why you two got together."

"I've no idea. Or what Richard ever saw in me. I kind of got sucked in. I thought I liked him... I thought he liked me. I now wonder if I was just his pet project, until someone more suitable came along."

It was true. Richard had begun to find faults with my appearance: the way I ate, the way I talked, how I wore my hair, even how I slept.

"Linda," I said. Her face was more flushed than usual. Was she angry, moved, or merely feeling hot? "I've never told any friend this, but I find it really hard to read people. It's like … I think I just believe everything people tell me. So, when Richard said he loved me, I believed it. God knows if it was true or not. I spend a lot of time trying to work out what people are really trying to tell me. I feel so stupid sometimes."

"Oh Cari, you're hardly stupid. But why would he lead you on like that? Richard's a smart man. It doesn't make sense."

"I know. But the reality is, things weren't going so well."

"Don't defend him," Linda said. "Look … I know he's a good doctor, even if he's good at worming out of the boring stuff." She paused, for a brief moment. "In fact, Sandra in the Cath Lab says he's right up there, when he wants to put his mind to it … She told me last week how he diagnosed a patient with a seriously rare heart condition. And you have to respect him for that—not his being lazy, of course."

"When I think back, I did everything, while he got all the credit."

"I can imagine. But Cari, it's true what you said about not reading people. That does make sense. When you first started doing the surgical lists, I thought you were a stuck-up English bitch. You didn't want to talk to anyone … always so serious. But then I noticed you were just focused on doing a good job. You weren't trying to impress anyone. I liked that about you." She resumed her chopping. "Maybe Richard was attracted to you by the fact you didn't fall into his arms when you first met."

"What? You think I played hard to get?"

"Exactly."

"Anyway, we're entirely finished. The hard part is knowing what to do now. Whether I should go home—wherever that is—or grit my teeth and stay in Adelaide."

"What do you think you'll do?"

"I don't want to go home. Not yet. I like it here in Australia. And I've learned a lot. But I'm not sure if the hospital would like me to return after what happened today."

"I'm sure that will blow over within a week."

"Yes, but how will I face you-know-who?"

"Ignore him."

"Easier said than done."

Linda looked at me, her gaze unwavering. "I think I have the perfect solution for you," she said slowly. "How would you feel about working in the Outback. You know, up north?"

"In the bush?"

"Yes. I'm thinking the remote north, say somewhere like … Alice Springs?"

"But why?"

"I grew up in Port Augusta. I did my nursing training there. I only came to Adelaide to get my theater certificate. But then I met boof-head over there …" Linda pulled a humorous face. She twisted her head in

Andrew's direction. "So, I ended up staying. The point is, you need a break from Richard."

"I do."

"Second, you need to get more experience, while studying for your exams. And the perfect place to do that would be in a small, quiet rural town, where you'll be treated like a princess. You'll get paid heaps and you can study to your heart's content."

Linda's face had become even more red and sweaty. Although only in her early forties, she looked like she was in the throes of a never-ending climacteric hot flush. She was grinning. Probably too much wine, I thought.

"OK," was all I could think to say. "I would never have thought of that."

"Think about it. There's nothing keeping you here. Richard doesn't even need to know where you've gone."

"But I'm not that experienced. I mean, I can do appendicectomies, I've done a laparotomy under supervision—but I still have a lot to learn."

"Cari, trust me. You'll love it. Country people are incredibly friendly, and they're tolerant. They're just grateful to have a doc in town. You can put your head down when you're not working and study as much as you like. Think about it—no distractions. Especially of the male variety."

Linda is an astute and sensible woman, Cari, Dr Smythe whispered. I startled. I never quite knew when she would be listening in. *What a splendid idea!*

Linda prattled on. "You'll get experience and see conditions you'd never see here. Well, you'll see those things here," she said, "after the senior doctors have sorted them out."

"I certainly will have a good think about it. Where do I sign up?"

Linda chuckled. What was so funny? Then I realized she'd misinterpreted my sudden eagerness as a sarcastic dig at her over-enthusiasm.

"I have tomorrow off. Why don't we pay a visit to a doctors' recruitment agency? We can find out if any contracts are on offer. You never know, maybe the hospital will let you do a rotation in some area of medical need."

Linda was 100 percent spot on. This was the answer I needed.

Quite so Cari, Dr Smythe agreed.

Linda and I clinked our glasses of white wine together; we toasted my good fortune. Although I suspected most women my age would be a bawling mess by then, instead I felt numb.

But strangely, after a while, new emotions like champagne bubbles began to form and fizz just below my conscious recognition. I puzzled over their meaning, before recognizing that not only was I experiencing fear, but also the stirrings of relief and excitement.

Maybe it was the wine, but flowery fantasies of being a country doctor entered my head: a grateful mother whispering her thanks for saving her young child's life after she had been bitten by a snake; a young man clasping my hand, because my quick-thinking actions had rescued him when he'd choked on a piece of meat.

Stop it, I chided myself—some of Richard had obviously worn off on me.

Andrew barged open the backdoor with a clank.

"Right ladies, enough chit-chat," he said. "The steaks are getting cold and I'm starved. Time to eat."

So further thoughts about my future were pushed aside and, in an unexpectedly famished state, I tucked into the spread before me, smiling and laughing at all of the right times in response to Andrew's non-sequitur jokes.

Linda took me to a medical recruitment agency the next day, as promised. There, I met with the woman who ran the show.

"The people in the country are desperate for decent doctors!" the recruitment agent trilled as soon as I explained the reason for my visit.

"You'll love it! So much good experience to be had. Perfect for a young thing like you!" Dressed in a business suit with padded shoulders to boot, she was all business, no mucking around. *Jobs, jobs!* For anyone who spoke English and didn't have two heads.

Quick smart, she organized a three-month contract to be drawn up before I could change my mind, to work in Manguri, a remote opal mining town 900 kilometers north of Adelaide. Populated by 600 people, this town had a well-equipped modern hospital complete with a theater and surgical facilities.

I signed my name on the contract and wondered if I was running away, my tail between my legs. The more I reflected on my time with Richard, the evidence was mounting. The unexplained absences, the excuses. I asked myself, how long had he been lying to me? Bare-faced lies I never questioned, like an innocent kitten lapping up the tainted milk he dished out. He could rely on my gullibility, my naive trust in him.

I wondered if Richard planned to take Miranda to medical dinners and various functions we'd attended, now he was a free agent. How many other women were there? Was Miranda the first?

I wasn't even sure if I was making the right decision. To leave the security of a major teaching hospital to head off into the Australian Outback—*crazy*—that's what my colleagues would think. I'd been to visit the Department of Surgery to say goodbye. The other doctors I spoke with were dubious, or downright worried. If news about Richard's dalliance had been minced by the hospital's gossip mill, they gave no clue. They worried for my safety, for my lack of friends. I hadn't even told my mother.

But it was too late to turn back now. I made a vow to myself: I was going to work harder; I was going to be a better surgeon and doctor. Never again was I going to get myself involved with a man who could turn me inside out and discard me, like one who indifferently whips off a used and smelly sock at the end of a day.

Tossing and turning, trying to sleep on that final night, I rode what I knew as cresting waves of excitement, to peak and then crash again into troughs of doubt and reservation—the future unknowable, the past unalterable. Gifted a second chance I could start again. I too, could be a free agent and drive change.

PART FOUR

Manguri

South Australia

CHAPTER TWENTY TWO

Cari

20/1/1997

It takes many years of experience for a miner to silence the chatter of the brain when prospecting. Opal magic is perceived by only the most attuned. Those blessed to be water diviners will find ancient sea beds, but few will hear the soft call of the most valuable deposits. More often than not, an amateur bypasses the best finds.

(*The Magic of Opals* by WO Brown 1972, p. 2)

Don't be fooled by showy opals that dazzle the most color. They may be rendered of little value by deep fault lines through the substance of the gem, invisible to the naked eye. These opals are often worthless; not only in monetary value, but also for the wearer's emotional wellbeing. It is rare for these trickster stones to be truly malevolent, but they have been known to bamboozle even the most wary. These stones seek the healing powers of water and hence, figuratively, they may parch the wearer's soul. In short, beware.

(*The Magic of Opals* by WO Brown 1972, p. 24)

The next morning after our excitement with the Aboriginal girl, Bonny, one of the nurses I didn't know so well, Rae, came up to me in the nurses' station. She had just finished her morning tea.

"Cari," she said, her mouth twisted into a giant, all-knowing smirk. "There's someone in the staffroom waiting to see you."

Rae headed off before I could respond. Someone to see me? My heart sank. Usually that meant a visit from the local constabulary to notify a death of one of the townsfolk. However, as I chased Rae, I could hear rowdy laughter and a babble of excited voices emanating from the staffroom. Perhaps it was someone's birthday, and the cake was about to be cut.

I rounded the corner, past the main entrance, to find a gaggle of nurses: Dee, Soph, Jo, Di and a few others lounged around the table in the staffroom, with Richard seated at the head of the table. Dee was leaning forward, rapt, chin on hand, gazing at him. And Richard was smiling the smile I remembered, the one that made most females (and the odd male too, for that matter) go dizzy.

I stopped dead in my tracks. He looked good. Dressed in a casual white shirt unbuttoned at the neck a few notches and sleeves rolled up his tanned arms, the fair hairs on his legs were a sleek fur below his khaki shorts. His brown hair was swept off his forehead in soft curls, more ruffled than I remembered, like a rakish English lord's. He wouldn't have looked out of place in an aftershave advertisement.

My erstwhile flame had evidently been regaling his new fans with some amusing story. He stopped mid-sentence and stood to face me.

"Hello Cari. It's, it's really …" He squared his shoulders and smiled at his audience as if apologizing. "It's really good to see you."

My mouth, working on the wad of words that would not form, opened and closed a few times, until a gagging sound emerged. "What are you doing here?" I finally managed.

Remember your manners, Cari. Even if he is a snake, Dr Smythe prompted.

I forced a smile.

He grinned. "I came to see you, of course."

Dee stood. "Cari, why don't you take the day off and show your friend around? It's pretty quiet. I'm sure Samson won't mind covering for you."

I stood there, dumbfounded. Samson had followed me into the tearoom, and I watched Richard regard him in an oddly challenging way, like a first encounter between two strange dogs. Then Richard relaxed, his famous smile once again lighting up his face. He stepped forward to introduce himself in a low voice. Samson responded with a stiff half-smile. Extricating his hand, he started to scan a piece of paper pulled from his pocket. He then passed me a pager and mobile phone with his other hand, without raising his eyes. "Yes, please do," he said in a flat voice. "Take the day off."

Dee nodded her agreement.

"I have work to do," I said. "Samson can't be expected—"

"It's quite fine with me," he said. He shrugged, his attention still elsewhere. "I'll call you if we need help."

"Go on Cari," Dee said.

It was strange, but within the space of a few seconds Samson made a sudden recovery from whatever had bothered him. He looked up sporting an exuberant smile, his teeth flashing white against his brown skin. "Please! Please! I must insist. Go enjoy yourself. We will be fine. Everything is well under control."

So, it was decided. Led by Dee, the nurses reluctantly trickled past to resume their work, casting sideways glances in my direction. Soph licked her lips wetly and winked at me as she wiggled by.

I felt confused by Samson's yo-yo behavior. I mustered my most pleading expression, my eyes begging him. I didn't want to see Richard! Why couldn't he understand? Instead he also shouldered past after giving my arm a quick insistent tap, to leave me standing next to my ex.

When we were alone Richard clapped his hands together and beamed at me from ear to ear like a happy drunk. "That's great, isn't it? A whole day with you. We've got a lot to talk about. We've all been very worried... Especially your mother. She tells me you've hardly written. She's been beside herself!"

I sighed in response.

⚕

Ten minutes later, we were at my front door. The trip to the bottom of the hill was mostly in silence, apart from the shrill unrelenting diatribe in my head, thanks to Dr Smythe.

Well, he wasted no time, did he? The hide of him. Insist he tells you the real reason he's here, Cari. Remember this, my dear. People may say one thing and mean something completely different. Look deeper.

Once inside the lounge of my starkly furnished dugout, with not even a reminder photograph of family on display, Richard faced me and took my hands in his. This was so unexpected I froze. He didn't speak straightaway.

"Tell me, what are you really doing here?" he said. "You're such a long way from home. I know, I was a complete tosser giving into Miranda."

"What are you saying?" I snapped. "You just happened to give into Miranda? Don't you have even an ounce of self-control? You could have pushed her away. You should have told her you were already with me. That's what most people do. That's what I thought when we were together. You don't just think, here's an opportunity, *whacko*! I'd better not waste it!"

Good girl! Dr Smythe cheered.

Richard stepped back, his shoulders sagging. He let my hands go. "It was a mistake. I've regretted my actions every day since it happened. But you didn't need to run away."

"I didn't want to be in the same city as you, let alone the same hospital, Richard. I had no choice."

"I know. I shouldn't have done what I did …" He took my chin in his hand and guided my eyes to meet his. "But you know what? Not being together has made me realize how lost I am without you. Please … Give me another chance. And if you won't do that, at least let's be friends. We had some special moments, Cari."

Now, I know I'm not good at reading people. I know I'm an imbecile when it comes to whether someone is pulling the wool over my eyes, or "telling a porky" as Barb would say. But I wondered, looking at him, if he might just be telling the truth. There were no puppy-dog eyes or running his hands through his hair in that carefree way, as if he was a raffish fighter pilot—not even a sunny smile to brighten anyone's day. Instead he fiddled with a dried wildflower I'd left lying on the table. It crumbled at his touch. I'd picked it up walking one day with Samson, thinking I'd look up its name.

Despite the hurt Richard had caused me, despite my loud proclamations I never wished to see him again, flashes of memories of good times weaseled their way uninvited into my brain. Like the time we lay in the bathtub and I'd discovered what it was like to cherish, and to be cherished by another.

Be careful Cari. Don't trust him, Dr Smythe warned.

I sat down unsteadily at the kitchen table.

"I appreciate you've come a long way to see me. But this is a bit of a surprise. I need to think about things."

"No pressure." He moved over and put his arm around me, before giving me a gentle squeeze. "Let's spend today and tomorrow together. That's if the hospital will let you have the time off. I'm sure that nice Director of Nursing will. But we'll have evenings free, even if she doesn't."

I nodded my assent and got up to turn the kettle on.

That day Richard and I played at being tourists. Despite having lived in Manguri for a few months I'd never visited an underground mine before, or really learned about opals. Perhaps it was time I did. After we'd driven around the town in my rickety car, we headed out to Patty's Old Timers mine.

Patty, a tubby Scotsman, was our tour guide. After he'd shown us through the mine's tunnels and demonstrated the workings of a tunnelling machine that resembled a giant apple corer, he showed us how to divine for opal. Water-divining rods held in each hand looked like TV antennae but were really bits of straightened copper wire.

Richard was enjoying himself, a hound on the scent. He scampered along the yellow and white tunnels, the rods swinging in when he located a seam of the compacted prehistoric water which was the raw opal, like the feelers of an opal-seeking insect.

"It's easy," he said, indicating I should follow. "Just walk over here."

In my hands, the rods flopped like idle knitting needles.

Richard chuckled and painted my nose with a daub of white dust. "Sorry, Cari. It seems only the 'truly blessed' can water divine."

The tour finished. Patty suggested an area of the minefields where we could "noodle" for opals safely. I was not so sure.

"It's so hot," I complained. "And no-one ever finds anything."

"Let's just have a go, shall we?" Richard said.

Fifteen minutes later, on the road that ran out to Eight Mile Creek, we found the public noodling area. We squinted into the sun's rays, that ricocheted off the piles of bleached yellow rock and shale. A scorching hot northerly wind had picked up, smelling faintly of dead animal. Richard set to work some distance away, crouched over, scraping through the small sharp stones. I gave up after a few minutes, my hands grimy and my mouth annoyingly dry. My only afternoon off not studying for my exams and here I was sifting a pile of dirt looking for a mythical opal.

"Cari! Cari!" Richard straightened up. "I think I might have found something!"

I ran to where he stood. When I reached him, he snatched his fist away and hid it behind his back, then danced away out of reach like he was hopping over hot coals. Laughing at my puzzlement, he stepped forward and pushed the cool stone into my hand with a wry grin. I examined it closely, turning it over in my palm. The gem was highly polished—surely not a recent find.

"But where did you get it? You didn't find it here."

"You're right. I wanted to see if I could trick you. It's a black opal … the most expensive kind. I bought it earlier today. I want to have it made into a ring for you."

I looked at the beautiful jewel, a burst of dark green and blue erupting within, like a miniature gas flame explosion in the depths of outer space. Richard stared at me, all mirth forgotten. I struggled to identify the feelings his intense gaze generated. My face flushed hot.

"I'm not sure if I can accept this."

"Accept it as a token of my gratitude to you."

"Gratitude?"

"I realize now I want to be a better person. And you're responsible. No more lies—I promise."

"OK. Whatever happens, no more lies. Please?"

Richard grinned in reply. I placed the gem in the jeweler's box he produced and tucked it deep in my pocket. We made our way back to my car, both laughing at how easily he'd fooled me with his opal gag.

CHAPTER TWENTY THREE

Samson

Aboriginal dreamtime legend holds that long ago the rainbow serpent came to earth. Where the rainbow touched the ground, the stones began to sparkle and glitter in all its colors. It is little wonder then, that the magic of the creator is trapped in these glorious stones.

(*The Magic of Opals* by WO Brown 1972, p. 22)

Fake opals can be difficult to spot. A plastic veneer over the surface disturbs the light, altering the play of colors. Large patches of color or a snakeskin pattern is a giveaway. However, there are clever imitations on the market. Ask yourself—how does the opal make you feel? Real opals enliven those who are sensitive to its magic; fakes afflict the wearer with an awareness that one is an impostor.

(*The Magic of Opals* by WO Brown 1972, p. 4)

It's difficult for me to describe my feelings when I walked into the staffroom that morning. Cari was already standing there, facing Richard, having apparently arrived only moments before. She blinked a few times but her face betrayed no emotion. Richard was speaking in a low tone; I could not catch his words. A minute of deafening silence followed, and I held my breath in delicious anticipation of a showdown. But then Cari smiled a radiant, full smile, baring all of her small teeth, as she asked him, "What are you doing here?"

A feeling of cold misery washed over me. I stood there, flummoxed, a nervous grin on my face. The truth is—please forgive me, I'm not proud of this—I could no longer deny my increasing affection toward my young colleague. With Cari I could be completely free; she didn't make demands of me. She didn't carp in my ear day after day, like a disappointed princess promised an undelivered kingdom; nor did she reach inside my soul with fat, grasping fingers to rip out and discard every shred of joy or hope. Cari was my soul mate, my friend. My partner-in-arms. My confidante. I knew she would be unfailingly honest. Always, under any circumstance.

But Cari was not my lover. I had no rights over her. Moreover, I was married. Why shouldn't an old flame turn up, to stoke the bonfire of love to burn white-hot?

Good for her. She could sleep with Richard that night, in that den of luxury at the underground motel. *Not my concern.* So, what did I do? I pushed her straight into the greedy tentacles of that honey-tongued sorcerer by encouraging her to spend the day with him. I won't trap you, or tie you down, I thought. But it devastated me to think Cari could be seduced once again by Richard's shallow magnetism. She'd be swallowed up in his octopus embrace, lulled by his soft kisses, killed softly by his words.

CHAPTER TWENTY FOUR

Richard

The opal minefields contain powerful magic that can also disorientate. Be careful! Always stick to properly marked tracks. Never travel alone and always notify of your position. Ignore this advice at your peril.
(*The Magic of Opals* by WO Brown 1972, p. 2)

After I gave Cari the black opal, we spent the afternoon in my hotel's bar, which was, unusually for Manguri, above ground, overlooking the hotel's swimming pool. Dressed in a light cotton skirt and tank top, her mousy hair falling in untidy strands around her face, she greeted a few locals lounging around. Her manner was more friendly now—interested but not gushy. She'd definitely changed.

We sat near a front window, heat radiating off the tinted glass, despite the aircon.

"How long do you plan to stay here then?" I asked, sipping my gin and tonic.

She idly trailed a finger through the condensation frosting of her beer glass.

"Another year. I have a contract." Her face gave no hint of how she felt about this imprisonment.

"Another year? My god. What will you do after that? You can't stay in this hellhole forever!"

One of the customers propping up the bar had heard me and glanced around, scowling.

Cari's eyes narrowed. "I actually like it here. I've learned a lot. And I've yet to sit my exams. I haven't studied as much as I wanted... I'm always working." She blushed a little.

"I heard you hadn't passed. I'm not surprised really," I reached forward to stroke her pale arm. "But I reckon you wouldn't learn much here."

"Oh, that's not true … Samson's an excellent teacher," she said. Her eyes momentarily shone. "You should've seen him operating yesterday. It was *amazing*."

I raised an eyebrow. I felt like asking, *Who are you? What have you done with the real Cari?* "Really?"

"He saved the life of a young Aboriginal girl. I've never seen anything like it."

An acid twinge burned the back of my throat. I knew Samson's sort. Raised in India to wealthy, medical parents, schooled at the best institutions, servants at beck and call. Strict adherence to hierarchy was the only principle these sickening sycophants recognized. He was probably a second-rate surgeon who didn't cut it (excuse the pun) in his hometown.

Cari was off on a monotonous soliloquy. "Just the other day we removed a lesion on a young guy's forehead. He was only in his thirties. Nasty melanoma. Samson and I did it together. The patient's gone off to Adelaide for further treatment. But I guess you wouldn't see any surgical cases now … Oh!" she halted, spluttering, as if she'd just remembered I was there. "How's it going with your research?" She didn't wait for my reply before grinding on. "And then there was this guy with a nasty foreign body in his eye. I couldn't get it out using the slit lamp, but then Samson had a go …"

She had no stop button. I had the complete lecture: how to do rotation flaps, toenail wedge resections, cortisone injections into inflamed joints, and more.

"How very interesting." My eyelids felt like they were weighted with dumb bells. She didn't notice the dripping sarcasm in my voice. I don't think she even twigged when I stopped listening altogether. Sure—this new animated Cari was a welcome relief from the waxen Madame Tussaud variety. But when was she going to shut up? I'd not come all the way to Manguri to be lectured on the vagaries of dermatological barnacles or other conditions. Try telling Cari that. Her voice motored on, her face assuming its usual expressionless mask. Apart from her earlier uncharacteristic animation, I couldn't believe she was the same woman who had shown enough chutzpah to spit in my face the day she'd caught me with Miranda.

What did I ever see in her? I'd stewed with jealousy when she left, conjuring up a thousand lewd scenarios involving imaginary strangers. Now I knew these imaginings were the head scramblings of a rejected man. Cari didn't care about me. She wasn't capable of caring about anyone but herself, though listening to her anyone would think she did. But why would she care about any of this motley collection of half-baked outback characters? If I thought about it, I should really be angry with her. Put yourself in my shoes. Cari had scuttled off to Manguri with no thought for anyone. I was the one who told her mother she'd left. I was the one left to field questions as to her whereabouts. As a matter of fact, she should also be damn grateful. I'd provided her with opportunities she would have totally missed if it weren't for me. I was never her Svengali but I had helped her to reach her potential in every way. She should remember that.

To be honest, it wasn't just losing Cari. Everything sapped me dry. The constant brown-nosing, the sucking up to whoever decided what research grant would be awarded, the administrator who decided your fate. Always needing to be brilliant to escape the fate of mediocrity. My career in Adelaide hadn't panned out as I'd imagined. What really broke the camel's back were those letters from the UK Medical Board and the College of Physicians, only the previous week. The funding grant for my research project had been withdrawn. Now I was just doing a junior registrar's work. News of my liaison with Miranda must have leaked out, probably via the letterbox mouth of that bossy elephant Linda, Cari's friend. I'd endured looks of intense disapproval from my colleagues ever since. And Miranda herself was also causing trouble, with her outrageous allegations. Most people would think my behavior in the recent past was wrong. But you could just describe it as a minor lapse in judgment. With all the stress I'd been under, it was completely understandable. If Cari had simply looked the other way, I wouldn't have ended up in the hideous mess I found myself in.

I knew one thing for sure. I needed to convince Cari to return to Adelaide to straighten things out. Cari was key to saving my reputation. I'd have to forget that her staid image reminded me of those portraits of an aging Queen Victoria. When I gave her the black opal, it looked like my plan was working. I'd watched her face light up with pleasure and satisfaction. She became animated, looking for a split second scarily like my mother. She'd stood there, lost for words, just turning the opal over in her palm.

I thought about Miranda and the Storeroom Incident. It was she who had led *me* on, I planned to say to the board at the Queen Adelaide. She'd been showing me leg non-stop for the whole week before, in the Cath Lab. She'd flashed me her cleavage whenever she leaned over a patient during angiograms. That's distracting at the best of times. But try keeping your focus when you're attempting to identify on an over-head viewer which coronary artery is gummed up. What was I sup-posed to do?

On that Wednesday I'd invited Miranda into that storeroom behind the A&E, telling her there was a new angiogram cannula I wanted to try, and I had a few packets stored there. She would have known that was a fib. Even Cari might have questioned my motives. My frustrations had been boiling away all week. This was my opportunity; we had a break between patients on the list. She'd fluttered her eyelashes in reply to my crass invitation, for god's sake!

The storeroom's air was frigid and smelt of rubber and disinfectant when I opened the door. I flicked a switch which cast a dim light over the shelves of equipment. Miranda gave a small gurgle of approval when I located the correct package. "This does look useful, Richard!" She smiled and held the tube of plastic up to the light. I took it from her and placed it on the bench alongside. I shuffled forward, to lift her skirt and run my hand up her leg. She was wearing lace panties.

Without speaking, I pushed her backwards against a bench. She looked surprised but I saw her eyes round and pupils dilate with desire. With my finger I traced the map of her femoral artery, under the elastic of her panties. "You see?" I murmured in her ear. "The *Flo-Max Cannula* allows easier access to the important places …" I yanked her shirt out of her waistband.

"What are you doing?" She pushed me away, her eyes puzzled. "I'm sorry, Richard. I think I may have given you the wrong impression. I just wanted to look at that cannula."

"Sure you did, Miranda. That's why you came in here with me."

I pressed against her urgently now, forcing her legs apart with my knee. I silenced her protests with my tongue. She'd been leading me on all week! I hoped anyone listening in wouldn't hear her soft moans. I quickly unzipped my pants and let them drop to the floor. My mouth covered hers, I pinned her buttocks hard, forcing my groin against her own. Only the filmy lace of her panties separated us. But then she gave me a fierce shove and momentarily, I lost my footing.

"I don't want this, Richard …"

I recovered and lunged toward her. "Yes, you do," I breathed in her ear. I kissed her again, her struggles only exciting me more.

It was the sound of that plastic cannula hitting the floor that announced Cari's presence. She stood there, like a department store mannequin, staring blankly at us as if she was watching a TV movie. Only her sudden red flush told me she understood what was going on. God knows how long she had been standing there, frozen.

My surprise at her presence caused me to jump backward. Miranda's eyes were ablaze with anger and shock, lipstick smeared across her face. My heart gave a jolt. What was I thinking? This could damage things with Cari, who I still regarded as an important part of my life. Why, oh why, could I not keep my hands off sluts like Miranda? That was because women like her led me on. No-one could blame me for this unseemly situation. Especially Cari.

Cari poked my arm with her finger, yanking me back to reality. I was still seated in that aircon-blasted grimy front bar in Manguri. Just as in the rest of the town, there was a coating of red dust on everything, even me. Cari leaned forward and sipped at her beer. She had asked me a question and was now waiting for my reply. I cleared my throat.

"Sorry? I didn't quite hear what you asked?"

She rolled her eyes toward the ceiling briefly. She then gazed at me with a patient and kind expression, as if she was addressing a small child. "Are you staying here at this hotel, Richard?"

"Yes," I replied, puzzled she needed to ask. "But I'd much rather be back in Adelaide. Preferably with you."

"I can't do that," she said quickly. "But I'm happy to spend tomorrow with you, if you like." She stood and gave me her usual wooden smile. "I'd best get back to the hospital, Richard. I have a sick patient I'd like to check in on." She turned and marched off, before careening around as an after-thought. "Good night, then."

I blew her a kiss and she replied with just a faint purse of her lips. I finished my drink as she headed toward the pub's heavy swing doors. She had a quick chat with a local on the way, who laughed aloud in reply to something she said. Cari the comedienne, I thought. No, that wouldn't be her. But no-one could ever say she wasn't a good doctor, I thought grudgingly.

It was a surprise the next morning when Dr Samson Cherian turned up at the reception desk with a glum expression, to announce he was to be my appointed tour guide for the day. His junior colleague had been called to the hospital to see a woman who insisted on only seeing a female doctor.

"Women's business," he announced solemnly.

Cari would join us as soon as she was available, he told me. He was charged with the responsibility of her clapped-out car and to ferry me wherever I wished to go. I wasn't happy about this turn of events, but I accepted Samson's explanation. (Remember? Cari's mantra: *Duty calls.*) But I'd read about the area called the Brittle Hills and was, despite my irritation at this news, intrigued. I shrugged and after some discussion, we made our way to Cari's parked car.

We headed out of town into a weird landscape, some 30 kilometers north. Towering white monolithic rocks looked as if they had once been meteors, flung from the heavens onto the red soil. We could have been on the red planet. We parked the car at a lookout, to survey a bleak terrain that stretched away forever. The sun bore down on us like a blowtorch; our eye sockets felt sucked dry, our skin toasting. The wind gusted, kicking up red dust. Samson said little, other than muttering his appreciation of the beauty of the panorama. He swatted without success at buzzing flies that zoomed in a pulsating nebulous halo around his glossy black head.

Maybe he's in love with her? I thought. *The dirty dog.* I saw the way he'd glowered at me in the staffroom. The silly fool, a long way from home, working closely with an unattainable colleague, had stupidly fallen …

Only minutes before at the lookout I'd tried to drop hints to him in a roundabout joking kind-of-way—nothing too obvious—that maybe he'd developed feelings for his younger colleague. And he'd bitten back angrily. From the way he overreacted I could have been accusing him of sleeping with one of the town's prostitutes. But he quickly controlled his indignation and even opened the car door for me after we'd descended the hill.

"Let's go visit the minefields, shall we?" I said in my most jolly tone. We were driving back onto the main road, 20 kilometers from Manguri, near the turn-off to Wynga. The Indian turned his worried eyes to meet mine. "I'm not sure, Richard. The minefields are prohibited to tourists."

Ah, a worrywart.

"And besides, Cari may have finished at the hospital. Wouldn't you like to go back now?"

"Not yet. This place is amazing. Don't worry, we won't go too far off the highway. We'll just take a quick look." Despite some annoyance about Cari not joining us, I wasn't lying. This landscape strangely beckoned; I had to see more. "We'll be fine. Cari won't mind. How often do you get to visit an actual true-blue ridgy-didge minefield?"

Samson didn't reply. Instead he concentrated on the straight road ahead. Eventually however, we reached a turn-off onto a dirt track, next to a large sign warning of the area's perils. I insisted we stop so Samson could take my photo with my shiny new camera.

Such a queer landscape. Black holes here, there and everywhere. Yellow and white piles of mine excavations stuccoed the open expanse; patches of gravel tarred the red clay earth. A few straggly mulga trees grew between mounds. The car ploughed over rutted and twisting trails, juddering and bounding along like one of those exhibition monster trucks with oversized wheels. Samson's mouth had become a thin line, his eyes stretched wide and dark, his fingers curled tightly around the steering wheel. It was obvious he'd never driven on roads like these before.

He slowed to a near halt. "Is this far enough?"

I suppressed a small laugh. This *was* turning into an amusing expedition. "No, no. Keep going. It looks very interesting over there."

At last I decreed it was time to stop. Samson sighed his reluctant agreement. We got out of the red Ford and wandered around the pitted landscape, the earth opening up as if a million fires from the underworld had blasted through.

"Samson, let's take some photos."

I took the camera and snapped a shot of the Indian surgeon jiggling on the spot near the parked car. His head started making funny little movements, nodding forwards and sideways like one of those wobbly toy dogs people stick on car windshields. He had the grim, harried look of an innocent man about to face a crowded courtroom.

"And now one of me."

I passed the camera over and started walking backwards to find the perfect backdrop. Samson squinted through the camera's viewfinder, his finger hovering over the shutter button. His entreaties for me to take care were muffled by the camera, clenched in front of his face.

"Hang on," I said. I made a deliberate show of moving around the terrain, pausing to examine the position of the sun and the angle of the shadows. "Yes, here we are."

I stopped next to a large yellow dirt pile, the wind blowing sand off its peak, like a chimney fuming white smoke. A large fissure divided the adjacent ground. I stood on one leg, broadly grinning, the other was outstretched near the edge of the drop, as if in a merry state of alacrity, I was about to take an eternal step into the unknown.

"Brilliant," I said.

Click, click.

We returned to the car. With an expression of unmitigated relief Samson passed the camera over and opened the driver's door. He climbed in.

"Hang on a minute. I just want to get a shot of Cari's car."

I moved away, my eye trained through the lens, the car now ten meters away in perfect focus. Samson leaned out of the car window, his face tense, his arm bent upright in salute as if halting traffic. I snapped the shot, then grunted with dissatisfaction. That would make a lousy photo; I needed to get the sun behind me. I prowled around; a few feet here, a few feet there.

Then I had it.

I'd found the perfect shot, the light sublime. The shale of each mullock pyramid sparkled grimly, as if reflecting Samson's pessimistic mood.

"Say *cheese!*" I clicked the button, but my shoe slipped on the loose surface. *Damn it.* "Sorry Samson, not happy … Think it's gone out of focus. I'll take another one."

The Indian surgeon's face now expressed something like horror but he stayed in the car. To gauge the best position, I glanced up but was blinded by the sun. I blinked a few times, to dispel shooting stars in my outer field-of-vision.

Samson opened the car door then and made to get out. "Is all well? Should I help you?"

I sensed irritation beneath his superficial kindness, yet I blanked him out. Suddenly, getting this picture was the most important thing in the world. "I'm fine... Just gotta get another. I'll be quick."

I held the camera to my face, disorientated for a moment. Like black magician's cloaks flung across the red earth, the crazy shadows of the mullock piles confused me, as if they were scheming with the terrain's gaping black holes, seemingly opening up to deep dungeons below. The earth glittered, shot with rainbow colors and speckled with dazzling lights. I carefully framed a final shot of Cari's car.

And then, the earth gave way.

There was nothing really, nothing particularly momentous about that final step. Just a small startle as my foot pitched sideways to become weightless. A brush of crisp cold air softly kissed my cheek. I plunged down, down, only to flatten the perfectly formed skeleton of a kangaroo corpse stretched out at the bottom of the shaft. Its tattered body exploded on impact, gray bones scattering like a game of knuckles.

Too late, I heard Samson screaming as my body disappeared into the darkness, "Please be careful Doctor Richard!"

And then nothing. Only cool oblivion, that was all.

CHAPTER TWENTY FIVE

Samson

Any adventurer to the minefields of Outback Australia is advised to take extra care. Many tourists and miners have fallen to their deaths down abandoned mineshafts. The opals below the ground may bewitch, causing foolish behavior. Opals can be an agent of karma. Beware!
(*The Magic of Opals* by WO Brown 1972, p. 2)

The few minutes after Richard reeled backwards down that hole, his body sucked into a vacuum, were the longest of my life. I stood over the maw of that black cavern. I could just make out Richard's slumped body, his head thrown back at an impossible angle. The drop must have been at least ten meters. Sprawled on his back, his arms flung out and legs akimbo, he could have been meditating in a yoga class. But the blood spilling out of the back of his head into the sand told a different story: Richard was stone-cold dead. His camera lay nearby half-buried in the dirt.

At first, I'd yelled. My voice made bleating, desperate calls. "Wake up Richard. I'll get help."

Frantic words spilled from my mouth, only to be buffeted about in the surging wind. Failing me, failing him. Standing there with no-one else around for miles and miles, I sounded pitiful. My pleas useless.

Get up Richard.

Panicked, and initially paralyzed, I looked around. A man had just died. The ancient landscape was a silent, unchanging witness to this tragedy. The wind grew stronger, its whistling interspersed with low moans and peals of demented laughter. Red dust whipped my exposed legs and arms. Playful eddies of fine powder swept along the dirt road and formed whirlwinds. Pieces of dried saltbush were being kicked around like footballs, the players ghosts of long-dead miners. A brown goanna was the only living creature in my vicinity. It stood up like a soldier being called to attention, emerging from behind a rock near the hole. It eyed me warily, its gray tongue testing the air before it scurried away.

The sun's glare had grown fiercer. I was wearing a baseball cap and sunglasses, but even with that protection it was difficult to make sense of the alien landscape. The shimmering white-knuckled Brittle Hills were a faltering memory in the distance. Closer by, a dense clump of mulga clung to the banks of a long-dried creek, roots hanging on like a skeleton's black fingers.

Rolling loose in the back of the car was a clear plastic bottle half-filled with water and a few foil candy wrappers lay on the floor. These would have to suffice to act as markers of our route. I'd have to drop them at intervals, like a child leaving a trail of the spoils of a night-time candy jar raid. Cari's utilitarian car was not unlike Cari herself, and wasn't filled with the kind of decorative junk, which now, paradoxically, would have been useful. I placed the drink bottle on the edge of the dig and built a small cairn out of pointed yellow rocks around it to guide the rescue service. The hospital's mobile phone was useless here. There was no reception.

There was nothing else I could do. Now I had to get into the car and drive back to town, following the narrow dirt tracks. I could not allow myself to get lost. I chastised myself silently as I drove, but I nursed a brewing anger that I'd acquiesced to Richard's stupid demands to see the minefields in the first place.

Oh, the irony! Only a short time before we had turned off Richard insisted I take his picture right next to that large warning sign! Why, oh why, did he not heed the sign's message? Had I been merely a court jester, a simple distraction easy to overlook? And why did I go along with his foolhardy plan? Because Samson Cherian was afraid to say "no", that's why. Always schooled to do what he was told. Rarely questioning or arguing. At the end of the day he was just a poor little street urchin from the back slums of Chennai, rescued and nurtured by decent people. Gratitude and subservience: his eternal cry.

I passed over two intersections. Stopping for seconds only, I placed the candy wrappers under rocks at the entrance of each turn-off. I tried to maintain a steady speed over the corrugations and the bouncing pot holes until I was back on the bitumen of the main highway.

My first stop when I arrived in Manguri was the local police station. I raced up the cement ramp at the front of the local constabulary's headquarters and barged through the heavy doors. The air was heavy with afternoon languor. I dinged hard on the call-bell at the front desk to rouse a police officer, who was dozing with his feet propped up on the front counter. He stirred and smiled when he recognized me. Only the week before I'd seen a maddened young man who had been out of control, hearing voices in his head and smashing bottles on the street. He was taken to Adelaide in an ambulance. This policeman had brought him in.

"Dr Cherian! What can I do for you?"

I tried to slow my breathing.

"I'm afraid there has been a terrible accident. A visiting doctor from Adelaide... I was taking him sightseeing and he wanted to see the minefields. I told him this was a foolish idea, but he was most adamant." To my ears these words sounded trite, the pitiable whinging of a tired child.

The young constable, who had been smiling, suddenly took notice. "Has he fallen down a mineshaft? Is that what you're saying? Where?"

"A few miles off the main highway, near the turn-off to Wynga. By that big sign … warning you about the dangers."

The young constable's eyebrow shot up, but he kept his counsel.

"He was taking a photograph and he walked backwards before I noticed. And that was it." I stopped and took a big breath, trying to control the knocking of my heart. "I think he's dead. His neck looks broken. It is very hard to tell. I can only just make out his body at the bottom of the shaft."

The constable turned and shouted, "Sarge! I think you'd better get out here."

I was already acquainted with Sergeant Stuart. He was a gray-haired man in his mid-fifties. With his roly-poly build he looked as if he'd last chased a crook 20 years before. He sauntered toward me from an office out the back, wiping the greasy remains of a late lunch from his fingers onto a brown handkerchief. His belly flesh was visible through the straining buttons of his blue shirt.

"G'day Doc! What seems to be the problem?"

I repeated my story. Mentally I was kicking myself. In my panic I hadn't thought to slow down on my way into town and check the mobile reception. An ambulance could have been on its way had I been able to ring ahead.

Now I stood helplessly at the counter. I listened to the background sound of a large wall clock, which was giving a forlorn tick-tick-tick. It seemed time here ran at a different pace to what was happening out there, in the real world of good and evil. Maybe I'd somehow found myself launched into a parallel universe. Maybe I would tumble suddenly back into my normal zone and wake up to find a mocking Richard sitting in Cari's car next to me, heading back into Manguri.

Sergeant Stuart radioed the ambulance station and the Mines Rescue Service officers on duty, bellowing the details into a handset held near his crumb-specked mouth. He let them know the call out location was very uncertain—somewhere near the turn-off to Wynga. All the while he fixed me with a calculating stare. Five minutes later I was sitting in the passenger seat of a police 4-wheel-drive, and we were on our way. The Mines Rescue Service and ambulance personnel had also been contacted and were going to meet us at the prophetic warning sign.

I used my mobile phone to call the hospital, hoping to speak with Cari. Dee answered.

"Cari didn't come in today," she said. "Didn't she tell you? She rang me this morning and told me she was going sightseeing with her friend."

"I'm afraid I don't understand," I said. "That's not true! She phoned me this morning and said she had to go and see a patient, a lady who would only see a female doctor. That's what she told me."

"No, that was last night. The patient was having an early miscarriage. Cari organized for her to go down to Port Augusta."

"Then why did she say she was going up to the hospital this morning?"

"Beats me," Dee said. I had a mental image of her shrugging. "Maybe she just wanted to take the morning off—*alone.*"

"I still don't understand. It's not like Cari to not tell the truth. Why would she not say so?"

"I don't know." A note of impatience had crept into the tone of her words. In my head I could see her multitasking: juggling the phone; signing a drug order; the keys on her skirt jangling as she unpinned them to open the DDA cupboard. "Anyway, if there's nothing else, I need to get back to work. And it would be really helpful if you can come in."

"I'm afraid I have some dreadful news. I won't be in for some time—"

"What? What's happened?"

"A terrible accident—'

The conversation died. We'd moved out of mobile phone range. However, Sergeant Stuart contacted the hospital on his CB radio as he urged the hulking vehicle on. We were still on the bitumen road heading north, past the thousands of mini pyramids of dirt and rubble spat out from the digs below, sirens wailing even though the road was deserted. He raised Jo, who was on duty in the A&E and explained that we were going out of town to the northern minefield area near Eight Mile Creek. The mission: to search for and retrieve a "Caucasian male, early thirties, by the name of Dr Richard Leitch. A victim of falling into a disused mineshaft."

I heard a small gasp of shock over the speaker.

"Is that Cari's friend?" Her voice sounded tinny over the airwaves.

I took the microphone from Sergeant Stuart. "Jo, it's Samson speaking. Yes, it is Dr Leitch. Can you ring Cari and ask her to come in urgently? We will need to notify his next of kin."

"Will do. I'm very sorry …"

"Yes, well let's wait and see. Let us pray for a miracle."

"Copy that. Over and out."

I placed the microphone back on its clip, not quite sure what she had meant.

We met other emergency personnel at the turn-off and headed across the dirt tracks that criss-crossed the deserted minefield. Great clouds of white and red dust billowed behind each vehicle, obscuring vision for following drivers. The temperature inside the cabin was rising, despite the car's air conditioner. It must have been at least 55° Celsius (130° F) in the shade, fanned by a strong northerly wind. Sergeant Stuart said little. He continuously mopped his wet brow and glugged water from a drink bottle.

We had no difficulty finding the first turn-off in the maze of small trails and dead-ends. But here is where our difficulties began. In my panic to seek help I had not marked the second one. I had completely missed it. But I knew I must have passed three intersections, not two. Each small trail looked identical to the last. Our convoy of emergency vehicles was aimlessly wandering across the flat, featureless bush.

Thousands of holes and fissures lined the roads, most with a pile of mullock standing as sentry, others just ditches or sheer drops gouging the flat earth.

Our convoy separated after a while. I hadn't checked the mileage on the odometer when I left the minefield earlier, so I could only give a vague approximation of the accident site. And now I was less and less sure. Was it five kilometers, or only three? I should have put more markers out. I should have used my clothes. I should have never agreed to this foolhardy venture in the first place.

A cavalry of local miners came to volunteer their help. The CB radio crackled as instructions and directions were flung around. Dusty utilities and heavy trucks joined the search, driven by young and old men, some with thick European accents—Greek, Italian, German, Croatian—others Australian. Vehicles were now moving in all directions, looking for foil candy wrappers. They may have got buried beneath the dust for all I knew.

The longer we looked the more disoriented I became. And with the passage of each unfruitful and tortuous minute, I became uncomfortably aware that Sergeant Stuart may—quite understandably—not believe my story. Think about it. An ex-lover of the local female doc turns up one day unannounced (half the town would know all about that via the local bush telegraph) and is spurned. In the fevered imaginations of the town's gossips she has fallen tragically in love with the married Indian doctor she works with. Or maybe he had fallen in love with her. They hatch a plot. The unwitting ex-lover is tricked by the Indian doctor (alias me) into visiting some remote minefields, where a tussle ensues near to an unmarked shaft. Easy to make it look like an "accident".

I felt the heavy weight of Suspicion slide an arm companionably around my shoulders, hugging me close. And then Suspicion's bedfellow Guilt— I won't deny I had feelings for her—crept in to lay its head in the crook between my neck and shoulders, like a cosy date at a cinema. *Suspicion and Guilt.* We were going to make a quarrelsome threesome. If I shook one off, the other would then tighten its embrace. Things looked bad for me, that was for sure. Despair surged through me but I forced myself to pay attention, to keep looking out the window for that one tiny marker—I owed Cari that.

It was late in the afternoon when the last foil wrapper was spotted, and a short time later my cairn and drink bottle.

We'd found Richard.

It took some time for Richard's corpse to be loaded onto a stretcher, and then winched out of the hole. In death he looked nonchalant. We could have been out on a training exercise and he'd volunteered to act the role of tragic tourist stranded at the bottom of a mine. His body had grown cold in the pleasant temperature of the mineshaft. Now, as he lay on the ground, flies were already busily massing on his boggy welter of congealed blood and matted scalp hair, like a crawling clod of blueberry jam. I averted my eyes. We wrapped his corpse in a white sheet, loaded it into the ambulance and drove steadily back into town, all urgency now forgotten.

The volunteers then dispersed, scurrying back to their nests. They reminded me of the foraging ants I used to examine in my schoolyard. I wondered how many of these underground workers were burrowing in that honeycomb of a minefield at any one time.

The first person we met back at the hospital was Dee. She took me aside and quizzed me for the details of what had happened, and where.

"Is Cari here?" was my only question.

"She should be back shortly. She came in when you first radioed. When was that, at about 2:30? But then she went to her flat after you radioed there were some problems locating Richard... There was no point in her hanging around here when there was nothing she could do."

We commenced a medical record and I certified Richard's life extinct. This would be a police coroner's case and so I could not officially certify his cause of death as a fractured neck. When I'd finished examining Richard, my head was pounding. I took the paperwork for completion with me into the staffroom. Sergeant Stuart was already seated there. Dee made us a strong cup of tea. She offered us sweet biscuits and words of consolation.

Cari arrived ten minutes later, her expression as unreadable as ever. She looked like one of those life-sized cardboard cut-out photographs of movie stars you see in the foyer of a cinema. Was she so devoid of emotion? I had a sudden urge to grab a thick marker and draw a sad mouth and eyes, or an image representing consternation or shock.

"I'm so very sorry, Cari," I began, as she entered the staffroom, my voice breaking. I couldn't meet her blank eyes.

"Why apologize? It was an accident, wasn't it? You didn't do anything wrong. But what were you doing out at that part of the minefields? Everyone knows it's dangerous there."

"I mean, I'm very sorry for your loss. I feel I failed Richard and you. I should have been more vigilant. I argued with Richard about going out there, but he was determined. And then when we arrived there, I begged and begged him to be careful …" The words poured out of my mouth.

She frowned. "Samson, all I can say is that Richard is, I mean *was*, used to getting his own way. What happened was his responsibility." She gestured airily, and then smiled at me strangely—that smile she used when she thought it was required, not to express any cheerfulness.

"I'm OK. I got here as fast as I could," I said. Cari gave me a quizzical look; I had spoken my thoughts aloud. I tried to settle my shaking hands.

After a few minutes silence, Sergeant Stuart spoke up.

"Dr Cherian, and you too, Dr Rainsford—you will both need to come down to the station and provide statements. I'm sure you understand this is just a formality. Dr Leitch's body will need to be sent to Adelaide for an autopsy by the police coroner. So, please excuse me," he stood up heavily from the table where we sat. "I'd best get the process started. I understand Dr Leitch's parents have been contacted?"

Dee replied, "Yes, I got their contact details from The Queen Adelaide. I rang the number and spoke with Richard's mother. It was about seven o'clock in the morning over there, in the UK. I must have woken her up; it took an age before she answered. She sounded really put out. After I'd convinced her the call was genuine—that I really was ringing from an outback town in Australia—I told her what had happened. The line went dead. At first, I thought she'd fainted. When she came to she told me her husband was indisposed and wouldn't be available to assist with arrangements—whatever that means."

My heart swelled in sympathy. Telling a parent that their child had passed away must be the toughest job of all.

"Perhaps I can come down to the station with you shortly, Sergeant?" I offered. "I would just like to see to some business here first. I should only be ten minutes or so."

"That's fine, Doctor. I'll come back for you then."

Sergeant Stuart bid us a grave farewell and left the three of us.

Cari remained silent, staring at the table before her. I felt an angry pulse throbbing at my temples. I rounded on her.

"Where the hell were you this morning? You didn't need to see a woman in the A&E." I gestured toward Dee, whose eyes widened at my brusque manner. "I was told there was a patient you had to see! Yet she came into the A&E last night. You lied to me!" I leaned forward, jabbing my index finger on the table. Dee recoiled a little. Cari, however, didn't seem put out in the least.

"I just wanted to be alone, Samson," she replied. "And I knew Richard wasn't going to understand that."

I began to wonder if Cari would make a good spy, her frozen face not revealing any of her thoughts or feelings. How well did I really know her? Was she actually capable of experiencing emotion? Maybe I'd given her attributes that were completely false. Perhaps this Asperger's

Syndrome diagnosis of hers, was a complete fabrication. Maybe the truth was—I was shocked that I could even entertain the thought— she'd wanted Richard dead! That repugnant idea began to germinate and take form in my subconscious.

Maybe I'd been *set-up*! Would she really do this? Maybe Cari herself had cooked up some weird, murderous plan for Richard. And I, the unsuspecting middleman, was going to carry it out. Suspicion and Guilt down in the basement of my subconscious were cheering my paranoia on, having a grand old time.

Don't be ridiculous, my sensible, clear-thinking self responded. *It was an accident.*

But I couldn't ignore a nagging recollection. If I was completely truthful, as Richard was taunting me in his upper-class English accent, I too—just that very morning—had felt a fleeting urge to push him down a mineshaft. But I wasn't actually going to do it, was I?

"But why did you drag me into this mess?" I willed myself to calm.

Out of the corner of my eye, I saw Dee slinking out of the room. She looked back at me, her shoulders drooped, her eyes soft. She would have some idea of how I felt.

"I had no idea Richard was going to fall down a mineshaft, now did I?"

Finally, some sort of response from her. More anger erupted within me. It was as if years of frustration, humiliation and being put upon had reached a critical mass: my emotions gushed out in a frothing mess. And it felt good. *Really* good. I knew my friend Suspicion was giving Guilt a high five, both would have huge grins. Instead, I felt the seething bitterness and indignation of the self-righteous. I couldn't and wouldn't let it go. My words were like knives.

"Maybe you didn't, but you decided to get your Indian lackey to play chauffeur for the morning. Then you could hide away? Is that it?"

"Absolutely not! I just thought that if I kept my wanting to be alone to myself that would be better for you. Because Richard may have asked you awkward questions. I didn't know this accident was going to happen!"

"Well, you didn't think, full stop, did you?"

Cari flinched, then stared at me, fury blazing in her eyes, her steel-plated armour finally cracked. *Good.* She is human after all.

"You think I'm incapable of logical thought? Well then, if you're so damned intelligent, why are you here? Why are you not working in a high-profile job somewhere in India, instead of being stuck here in this backwater?" She glared at me, daring me to answer her, her arms folded. "At least I have a reason: I'm in Manguri to get away from Richard and to study for my exams. What's your excuse? Have you committed some crime in India that you are running from? Remember what Chicken Pete said? There's always a reason why anyone's in Manguri, and it's usually because he or she is escaping something or someone."

"Don't turn it back on me, Cari," I growled. "This isn't about me. This is about the fact that you lied to me!"

"How could I know this was going to happen?"

At that moment Dee made a reappearance at the door. "Doctors, please. We can hear you in the nurses' station."

Cari was looking at me, mouth sucked in, as she answered. "I think we've finished, Dee. Now I'd like to have a look at Richard. Just to confirm how he actually died."

"I'll come with you," Dee replied. She frowned at me over Cari's shoulder. Why was she looking at me like I was the one to blame? Cari was the one who had lied!

A few minutes later, I passed the A&E, in the company of Sergeant Stuart. I heard Cari talking to Dee. She was examining Richard's body behind the curtained cubicle.

"Yes, he clearly has an upper cervical spinal fracture, judging by his neck instability. And a nasty depressed temporo-occipital skull fracture too. I would say he died instantly."

She could have been talking about what she'd eaten for lunch. Did this woman not possess a drop of humanity? And only yesterday I'd felt jealous because she had seemed so pleased to see Richard. Was that obvious display of pleasure when Cari first saw Richard also a complete lie? Anger churned within me. It was Cari's fault I was in this mess.

It was all her fault.

One hour later, I staggered exhausted from the police station after being interviewed by Sergeant Stuart. I rehashed the story I'd already told and repeated to him, word for word, entire conversations, which he recorded with an old-fashioned tape recorder. He also wrote by long hand in an exercise book as I dictated my statement. Sergeant Stuart said little; he seemed satisfied all was in order. Cari had not yet been interviewed.

I stood to leave.

"There's one thing I don't understand," the sergeant said. "Why were you showing Dr Leitch the sights, and not Dr Rainsford? I understand he was visiting Manguri to see Dr Rainsford. Why was Dr Rainsford not able to show her friend around herself?"

He must have read my mind. Despite my anger at Cari, I felt an unexpected sense of protectiveness. I couldn't repeat the heated staffroom exchange we'd just had.

"Cari rang me this morning," I said wearily. "She asked me to show Dr Leitch around because she had to see a patient at the hospital."

Sergeant Stuart nodded. He knew how hard we doctors worked. Time off to sightsee was a luxury.

We shook hands. The sergeant followed me to the heavy doors that led outside.

He opened the door for me before briefly placing a rough hand on my arm. "Dr Cherian, please look after yourself," he said. "You and Dr Rainsford both work long hours and often deal with stressful situations.

And now, with what has just happened, it's sometimes enough to... push you over the edge."

I jerked as if I'd been kicked hard in the groin. Why did he put it like that, after what had just happened? I forced my face into an expression of blank inscrutability.

"Let me know if I can be of assistance. You know where we are."

Despite my nervous tension, I laughed with him at his lukewarm joke. It was true. There was no escape from Manguri.

I walked the 20-minute hike up the dirt path from Main Street to my dugout, to eat an evening meal Barb had generously thought to leave in an esky at the front door. The wind had dropped. Although it was still warm, the sun had mellowed. Cari's car was not in her carport. She was either at the hospital or had driven to the police station to give her statement. She would have some explaining to do, I thought.

But the image of Cari squirming as the truth was wormed out of her didn't cheer me. Instead I felt uneasy, agitated. I had no appetite, and my saliva struggled to wet the food in my mouth. I'd grown used to eating Barb's sweet curries, yet I still craved the delicious combination of spices and flavors that my wife, an excellent cook, regularly concocted. But not this day. No food, no matter how appetizing, had any appeal. I forced myself to eat and drink, but the food lodged in my throat, making me gag. In my mind's eye I saw an image of Richard laughing at the spectacle of me retching like a dog with a bone stuck in its gullet.

I sat outside under the pergola, on the metal chair that rocked from side to side, and opened a bottle of beer. It was odd to be drinking alone. The beer, although bitter and cold, didn't refresh me. The daily Manguri sunset show was performing its usual spectacular rainbow display, but in my distracted state I couldn't relax to enjoy it. Also, there were more sticky flies than usual.

The bitumen road that led to the hospital wound around the base of the hill. From my vantage point I could see any comings or goings to and from the main entrance. Richard's body had not been moved as yet. This would depend on RFDS flight availability to transport him to Adelaide. He'd now be lying in the morgue. There was no sign of Cari's car. I drank some more, not because I was beginning to enjoy it, but it was something to keep my hands and mouth occupied. Maybe if I screamed it would fill the void that was opening within me. I felt some of the tightness leave my neck and back. I spread myself more comfortably. If I was a better doctor, I reprimanded myself, I'd go up to the hospital and check on the welfare of my inpatients. But my happy work ethic had been sucked away, down into that abyss with Richard.

A little later I saw Cari's car turning off the bitumen road to make its way up to her dugout. A minute or so later, the vehicle pulled into the carport close to where I sat, showering me with red dust. She got out of the car, her brown purse dangling from her shoulder. She gave another strained smile. "Mind if I join you?"

I nodded but it was half-hearted. Although I wanted to ask questions, I suspected I would have felt better if I was tucked up in bed, my velour bedspread pulled over my head.

"Any beer left?"

I turned my head to indicate the fridge inside. She returned a minute or so later with a bottle in hand.

"Well, I did the police interview," she said, as she collapsed into a chair.

"How did it go?"

"OK, I think." Cari slapped a fly on her cheek. "Well, you know, the sergeant asked lots of questions. I answered him as best I could."

Good! We could all move on and put this unfortunate incident behind us. I breathed a sigh of relief.

"Sergeant Stuart said he's asked the CIB from Port Augusta to come and interview us."

My heart sank. "What? That's the Criminal Investigation Bureau! Remember that CIB detective investigating that break-in last month? That means the sergeant thinks this isn't a routine accident. That he thinks it's suspicious!"

Cari stretched out her arms and settled back in her chair. "Does it? I don't know why he would've got that idea. You told me what happened. How Richard wasn't looking as he walked backwards, taking that photograph. Why would he think it wasn't an accident?"

I felt like strangling her. How could she be such a naive fool?

"Because Cari, obviously you and I have given different stories," I said through gritted teeth. "You still haven't told me what you were doing when I was taking lover boy around."

"I can't."

"What do you mean?"

"I can't."

"You can't or you won't?" The volume of my speech was rising. Suddenly, I was standing over her.

"Both. I made a promise."

"To whom? Don't you understand? I am in big, big trouble! It could look as if I murdered Richard! I know that I didn't. It was an accident. How can you sit there and lie to me?"

"I'm not lying, Samson—"

"But you're not telling me the truth either. *What* were you doing?"

"Can't say ..." And with that she abruptly stood up, leaving her unfinished beer behind, and walked over to her dugout, quietly opening the front door and closing it behind her.

I kicked the table's leg and the whole thing flipped over. Beer fizzed and soaked into the red dirt. I restrained a yell. How could I face the detectives tomorrow? They would ask about my feelings for Cari. They would ask the same questions, until I'd doubt myself. They would be looking for a motive for murder.

So, Dr Cherian, you wanted to stay in Manguri and lead a double life, with Dr Rainsford by your side!

Was that true? Had I?

But you are married, Dr Cherian.

Yes, I am. And I am faithful to my wife...

But Richard came along and upset your plans.

No! As I told Richard himself—there was nothing going on …

"Guilty, guilty, guilty …" Suspicion and Guilt joyously caroled in my ear.

I went inside and made preparations to retire for the night. I couldn't ring Mercy; I was too wound up. The air seemed to be alive with static electricity. If not for my hair oil, I'm sure each strand would have been standing on end.

I tried to settle; I tried to sleep. There was no peace from my underground psychic civil war. Sweating, I tossed all night; my old anxiety about being compressed underneath thousands of tons of dirt returned, a hundred times worse. I could feel the walls of the dugout crashing down on me, squeezing and pressing every last molecule of air from my lungs. And then, like a video stuck and looping on rerun mode, I replayed over and over the sight of Richard falling backwards, his smug and arrogant look being replaced by one of absolute terror. He fell like a stone dropped into a black well. But now his fingernails were raking at my arms—he was pulling *me* down, down. And, in the aftermath of the rockslide that crushed our corpses, fell a shower of the finest opal dust, drizzling prisms of light. The walls of our shared tomb were splashed with a myriad of colors, of a most exquisite Manguri sunset.

Chapter Twenty Six

Cari

Wear opals daily. Not only will the beautiful appearance of the gem soothe any jaded soul, but the wearer will be more astute toward others' true motives. Opals are known to be helpful if one wishes to be invisible. Not literally, but figuratively. The opal allows the wearer to become perceptive to the dreams, auras and feelings of others. Opals guarantee safety to the wearer.
(*The Magic of Opals* by WO Brown 1972, p. 2)

The first thing I did when I returned to my dugout after my day playing tourist with Richard was to pick up the phone and call Linda. I knew she would help me. We hadn't spoken for a few weeks.

"Linda, you're not going to believe this," I said. "Richard's in Manguri."

She gasped. "Did I hear you right? Richard's with *you*?"

"He's staying at one of the hotels. He got here yesterday, just ahead of a huge dust storm. We spent today sightseeing. I've just had a drink with him in the hotel bar. I decided to play along and be nice."

"Well, well … And what explanation did he give for finding you?"

"He says he wants to try again with me. That he made a huge mistake letting me go. He said he's regretted it every day since. He even gave me an opal to make into a ring."

"Ha! And you actually believe that? The hide of him."

"I don't know what to think."

This was true. Since I'd lived in Manguri, something had changed me. The locals seemed to be born with inbuilt bullshit detectors, especially the nurses. Any slight stretching of the truth, any twist in a yarn, any subtle discoloration of the facts, would inevitably be met with an initial scoff, accompanied by an emphatic gesture of hands on hips. Then, a loud cry of, "Bullshit! Now you've told us 'the truth', what's the real story then?" Some of that cynicism must have rubbed off on me.

"Well, let me tell you this," Linda said. "I nearly called you, but I thought it would just upset you. You're very right not to trust that bastard. There's a rumor floating around The Queen Adelaide that Richard's in big-time trouble."

"What kind of trouble?"

"One of the ladies who works in the theater office told me that Miranda Baird is filing sexual harassment charges against him. She even has the gall to claim that Richard tried to rape her in that storeroom last year."

"What? It looked entirely consensual to me." As I spoke, minnows of receding memory streaked past, darting away before I could snatch them. I took a deep breath to check my beating heart.

"So, why would she say something like that?" Linda asked.

"And why would she lie like that?" I puzzled.

"Maybe Richard dumped her. You know, all of the excitement of the chase had worn off for him."

"Maybe. So, what do you suggest I do now?"

"If it was me, I'd go through his things and see if there are any letters or documents referring to the case."

"But that would be snooping! I can't do that!"

"Think about it. You need to know what he's up to. How many times do you think Richard lied to you? I'd say daily. How could you know if he's ever telling you the truth? You can't trust him, Cari. Maybe he's trying to butter you up, so that you'll agree to come back and testify on his behalf."

"But why not just come right out and ask me? I'd tell anyone who wanted to know. Miranda was obviously enjoying what took place in that storeroom."

However, even as I said them, my words sagged with a lack of conviction. Had I got it wrong?

"Ah, but that would be too simple," Linda said. "Maybe there's other stuff you don't know about."

This was also true. Over the last few months I'd realized there was plenty I didn't know. Even my basic-learner model bullshit meter was emitting an unrelenting, annoying shriek.

"How could I even get a look at his stuff?"

"Break into his hotel room," Linda said, "when he's not there. Get someone to take him out for a while. Maybe that nice Indian surgeon you told me about? Richard won't suspect a thing. Tell Samson—that's his name, isn't it?—some cock and bull story about how you have to work up at the hospital for a while, and then ask him to take Richard to see the sights in your place. Samson won't suspect anything. And, don't breathe a word about what you're doing. It's best you leave Samson out of it. Knowing Richard, he'd twist the truth out of him and work out what's going on."

I swallowed hard. "I don't like lying. In fact, I don't think I can—I'm no good at it."

"I know. But you can do it, Cari. Think, it's for the greater good. Not just for you, but for Samson as well. Because if you tell Richard just that you want to be left alone, Richard will probably ask Samson lots of awkward questions when he takes him out tomorrow. *Kapiche*?"

"Sorry?"

"Do you understand me?"

"Yes, Linda." I sighed.

Echoes of Dr Smythe's words to me as a schoolgirl replayed over in my brain. I returned to a conversation we'd had when I was about 15, about the difference between a white lie and a malicious lie. We'd been sitting in her front parlor. I was following Dr Smythe's example of politely sipping strong tea from a cup and saucer that she'd placed before me, while nibbling arrowroot biscuits.

"Cari dear," Dr Smythe said. "Sometimes we just have to lie to save people's feelings. For instance, let me ask you. 'How do you like my shoes?'"

I studied her practical brown lace-ups, with a square toe. They looked like something she might have inherited from an elderly aunt.

"I don't much. They look like old ladies' shoes."

Dr Smythe's mouth puckered as if she was sucking on a sour lemon, then she tittered, a soft lady-like hee-hee.

"Oh dear … That was certainly honest. I only bought these last week. Now, let's try that again. Let's pretend I paid a small fortune for these shoes—I can tell you they weren't cheap—and that I'm extremely proud of them," Dr Smythe opened her arms in a theatrical manner as if she was a diva in a Wagnerian opera, about to launch into an aria. Her voice climbed an octave higher.

"Now, when I say, 'Cari dear, how do you like my shoes?' how do you reply? Go on Cari. Tell me a nice, juicy, big fat lie. Tell it so I believe you."

I leaned forward to inspect those ugly brown shoes. I put on the thickest, most obsequious voice I could muster.

"Oh, Dr Smythe, are those shoes new? They're lovely. They look very expensive!" I looked up at her with an expression that I hoped conveyed extreme conviction.

"Good girl, Cari!" Dr Smythe clapped her hands in open delight. "That was terrific! Now when someone asks you, 'How do I look? Does this dress make me look fat?' Do you tell the truth? *No!* You don't! Your friend would be terribly offended."

Dr Smythe sat back to regard me, breathing heavily. She leaned forward. Her voice soft, but sure. "You tell your friend a sugar-coated white lie. You say, 'You look gorgeous. That dress really suits you.'"

☤

"You there, Cari?" Linda's voice broke into my thoughts.

"Yes, sorry. I was just thinking. I guess it's OK to tell Samson a white lie, isn't it?"

"Precisely. The less Samson knows, the better. Actually, don't tell anyone. Nothing will go wrong. It'll be worth it to know the truth about what that pig has been up to."

"Thanks Linda, I appreciate your help." And I meant it too. I could have gone on innocently believing every story Richard had told me.

☤

The next morning, a Tuesday, bright and early, I rang Samson with my plausible story about a woman in the A&E wanting to see a female doctor. Tourist patients often irritated hospital staff. In the outback you were lucky if you saw *any* doctor, male or female. Ergo, it was an easy lie, the part of our planned scam that I'd been dreading the most. I just repeated the scenario and details as we'd practiced the night before. I also promised to see his other patients to save him a trip. I planned to keep my word on that—as soon as I'd completed my mission in Richard's hotel room, I'd head to the hospital.

I could tell Samson wasn't exactly keen to be guide to Richard that day. But he grumbled his assent after I reassured him I'd call as soon as

I was able. Then I drove to the swanky hotel where Richard was staying and spoke to the hotel's concierge and desk clerk. I knew Tom already. He was the son of the hospital's head cook, a lanky carrot-haired youth dressed smartly in the hotel's uniform of suit and tie, the only establishment in town where anyone did. He carried an air of nervous officialdom about him. This may not be easy, I thought.

"G'day Doc, back again?" Tom had been on duty the previous afternoon when Richard and I had walked past to go to the hotel's bar. "How can I help you today'?"

"Hello Tom," I said, trying to smile in a relaxed manner. "Doctor Richard Leitch who's staying here—"

"Oh yes! The doctor from Adelaide you were with yesterday."

"Richard rang me this morning, after Dr Cherian had picked him up to go sightseeing, to say he'd left his camera in his room. He was wondering if I could pick it up for him. I'm going to meet him later this afternoon."

Tom scratched his chin. "Sure, but why doesn't he just come back and get it himself?"

"He's got another tour booked at 11," I said. "He just thought it would be easier if I collected it."

I looked Tom directly in the eye as I spoke. He reached behind to retrieve a key from a pigeonhole.

"OK, sure. Just give me a minute, I'll come down with you. Room 101."

Tom, a native of Manguri and a resident bullshit spotter, had swallowed my loopy story, hook, line and sinker! But I hadn't factored in that he might actually want to accompany me into Richard's room. That could spell disaster.

But then he looked up at me slyly, before peering up and down the length of the reception area. He leaned toward me over the desk and whispered, "Second thoughts, would you mind if I just gave you the key? I have to sort out a mess-up with a conference booking. And seeing as you're our local doc, I know I can trust you not to pinch anything, eh?" He winked at me.

"Of course not!" I said, uncertain how I should react, but feeling a little offended even so.

"Sorry, Doc. Only kidding … There ya go …" Tom slid the key across the marble desktop. After giving me a tight grin, he turned back to his office duties.

Wow—that was lucky! I hot-footed it down the plush carpeted corridor and disappeared into the stairwell before he could change his mind.

Richard's room was located underground, one floor below the main reception. A few minutes later I unlocked and opened the door and flicked on the fluorescent lighting. Richard had traveled light. He'd told me he expected to catch the last plane back to Adelaide the next night. There was only a small valise parked on the luggage rack at the end of his bed, and a fluffy white towel and slippers strewn on the floor.

Typical, I thought. Richard had expected someone else to tidy up after him.

I spotted a black leather satchel lying on a desk in the corner and made a beeline toward it. There was a large wall mirror above and I caught a glance of myself as I rifled through the bag's contents. I looked the complete antithesis of how a burglar should look. A small, plain woman with biscuit-brown hair wearing a pink blouse and navy cotton skirt stared back—hardly the popular image of a spy. With shaking hands I pulled out and scanned various pieces of paper: mostly unrelated receipts and one or two crisp reprints of articles. Maybe, I thought with a sinking heart, this was going to be an utter waste of time.

But then I pulled out an envelope with a letter dated from only the previous week, from the Department of Cardiology at The Queen Adelaide Hospital. I quickly read the contents. What Linda had heard was true. Richard was being requested to attend an interview to answer allegations that he had repeatedly made comments of a sexually harassing nature to a nurse, Miss Miranda Baird, over the previous five months.

… Miss Baird alleges that this harassment commenced when she worked in the angiogram suite. She further alleges on 21/8/1996 you attempted sexual intercourse with her, without her consent. In view of the serious nature of these allegations, it is requested that you meet with the Director of Training, Dr Janice Williams, and the Chief Executive Officer, Mr Brice McManus on 23/1/97. (That's in two days' time, I thought.) *You may bring a legal representative and a support person as required …*

What rot, I thought, as I slipped the envelope into my handbag. Even Richard didn't deserve that load of baloney being thrown at him. But then I remembered my phone call with Linda the previous evening and the cold stab of uncertainty I'd experienced. Had I misinterpreted what I had seen that day?

And if Miranda was lying, why didn't he just come right out and ask for my support? Why beat about the bush? Perhaps he really did mean it when he said he'd regretted his behavior toward me and had therefore broken it off with Miranda. Was this a case of Miranda being a sore loser and seeking her own revenge? If only I could remember exactly what I had seen! I decided there was no time like the present to try jogging my memory.

I'd seen self-hypnosis on TV and thought I'd try it then and there. I put the satchel down and lay on the unmade hotel bed. Richard's imprint still dented the bedsheet, his wood-smoke smell faint on the pillow. I concentrated on slowing my breath. A dig in my hip reminded me that the jewelry box enclosing Richard's black opal was still inside my skirt pocket. I repositioned it inside my shirt, next to my heart, and then closed my eyes. I soon felt a pleasant warmth in my fingers and toes, which then blanketed my whole body. I gave myself permission to go back in time, to that storeroom. I recognized the premonitory tightening of my throat and increasing thud of my heart, but I banished those perceptions firmly. I was once again in that small dark room. Richard's back was to me.

He was kissing Miranda. Forcibly. Brutally.

As in a darkened theater when the lights suddenly go up to illuminate a dazzling stage, I now saw the reality. What I'd witnessed all those months ago had not been a consensual act. Now I knew Miranda really had been trying to push Richard away. Her anger wasn't directed at me—it was meant for the man who was assaulting her.

I pulled my vision away from the scene and allowed myself to return to the present. I opened my eyes; I was back in the cool silence of Richard's hotel room. How did I misinterpret Miranda's facial expressions and actions in that storeroom so badly? *Damn it.* My head had been truly elsewhere, most likely stuck on the Planet of Ice Queens (or Ice-creams, as Samson would have said).

With trembling legs I got off the bed and lunged at Richard's bag. I shook it out. Maybe there were more documents. And sure enough, two more thin envelopes spilled out. One was marked from the College of Physicians, and one from the UK Medical Board.

Dr Richard Leitch
2/22 Chester St
East Adelaide 5777
South Australia

UK College of Physicians
Hartfordshire Place
Regent's Park
London NW! 4LE
United Kingdom

3/1/1997

Dear Dr Leitch,

I write to inform you that an allegation of professional misconduct has been made in relation to the College of Physicians' clinical examination held on 19/12/1995 at the Greater Sinclair Hospital. In view of the seriousness of these allegations it is requested that you contact this office as soon as possible.

Yours sincerely,
Professor Alfred Tilbrook-Smart MBChB (Oxford) MRCP AOM

My jaw fell open. Professional misconduct? Richard? In London?

Richard was confident that he'd done well in his clinical exam, now over a year ago. He'd told me of the cardiac case he was assigned and how he'd easily answered the examiner's questions. He'd even hinted that he might be awarded a prize—which did happen, at the charity ball. But cheating? Is this what the letter was alleging? I'd never suspected Richard of academic cheating, but then, I never suspected he would sexually assault someone! The UK Medical Board letter provided more detail.

UK Medical Board
22 Regents Rd   London SW 24M

28/12/1996

Dear Dr Leitch,

This letter is to notify you that Professor Alfred Tilbrook-Smart of the UK College of Physicians has recently contacted this office to report a serious allegation of unprofessional conduct during the final clinical examination for the Fellowship of the College of Physicians, held on 19/12/1995. It is alleged by Miss Allegra Rimo of Cricklewood Broadway, Kilburn, formerly cardiac-care nurse, and Dr Steven Liddard, Department of Cardiology, Greater Sinclair Hospital, Hampstead, that you had prior knowledge of the patient you presented during this examination. Under Rule 25, sub-clause 3a of the Code for Examination Professional Conduct, this is considered a serious breach of proceedings.

I request you contact this office as soon as is practicable, in order for this matter to be resolved without delay.

Yours sincerely
Professor Felix Drummond -Williams MBE PhD (Oxford)

My chin could have been scraping the soft pile of the room's plush carpet, my mouth had fallen open so widely. The words on the page danced before me. I tried to pull my thoughts together. Richard already knew the patient he saw in his final exam. But how? And then I remembered that he'd gone to the Greater Sinclair Hospital only the week before. In the exam he must have seen a patient he already knew from that previous visit. And who was Allegra Rimo? And who was Dr Steven Liddard?

I quickly stuffed all the documents in my handbag. I'd have to own up to Richard later that I'd swiped them. But it wouldn't be hard to confront him now. He couldn't exactly get too angry given how badly he'd mistreated me. And now I also knew the vile truth about Miranda. Richard was not just a bad person; he was evil, I realized. I was shocked at this sickening and sudden insight—but that was the truth.

I headed back to the main desk to return the key.

"Find the camera ok, Doc?" Tom asked.

I patted the handbag at my side and tried to smile. "Yes, thanks Tom. I'm sure Richard will go back to Adelaide with many happy memories from his visit to Manguri."

"Glad to hear it, Doc," he said, then paused. "Everything okay?"

I nodded but didn't meet his concerned gaze. He returned the key to its pigeonhole and after a brief silence went back to his work.

There! I had done it again! This fibbing business was getting easier by the minute, I thought. But instead of experiencing jubilation as I stumbled back to my car, bitter tears pricked at my eyes.

Chapter Twenty Seven

*In the 14th Century opals were believed to be the cause of
famine and pestilence, even the Black Death.*
(*The Magic of Opals* by WO Brown 1972, p. 22)

*Crushed opal can be reconstituted and made into a pretty piece
of jewelry. But like a shore damaged by a hurricane, the magic
of the original stone is destroyed.*
(*The Magic of Opals* by WO Brown 1972, p. 98)

I headed from the underground hotel to my dugout to store the black opal safely in a bedside drawer. I then went up to the hospital to see Samson's patients as I'd vowed, although my focus wandered and I was slow to complete tasks. I was on the verge of heading home again when Jo rushed into the staffroom, white-faced.

"Cari! I just had a call from Sergeant Stuart. He tells me that he and Samson are heading to the minefields. Richard's fallen down a mineshaft!"

I felt my knees give way. "Fallen down a mineshaft? Where?"

"Somewhere near the turn-off to Wynga. They're going to have to find the site and that might not be easy …"

"How did it happen?"

"He slipped while taking a photo. I can't believe it," Jo said. "He was so … full of life yesterday."

"Is he all right?"

"Samson thinks Richard may be dead. Cari, I'm so sorry."

I felt my breathing become shallow. The room seemed to spin.

"Do you need to sit down?" Jo asked.

"I'm OK," I answered. "Is Samson hurt?'

"No, he's fine. He just sounds... completely shaken-up."

A bark of a laugh escaped me. Suddenly, I saw a comical image of Samson being shaken, while Richard lay deservedly crushed. (*'Cari!'* Dr Smythe scolded me.) I twisted my face back into the Worried look. "Sorry. I always laugh when I'm anxious... I'll just sit in the staffroom until we hear more."

"Let me know if there's anything I can do for you." Jo reached forward and squeezed my hand.

I waited in the heavy, stifling air of the tearoom. I felt strangely wired, as if I'd landed in a scene from one of the hospital soapies and hadn't learned my lines. Or, for that matter, how to act in the first place. My mind was racing. Maybe Richard had decided to end his life? Perhaps the pressure of Miranda and people in London accusing him had become too much. I made my way back to the nurses' station.

"If it's OK with you," I said to Jo, "I might just head home. I won't be long."

I needed to know what had happened back in London and, in particular who had made those allegations. The evidence couldn't be denied—Richard had lied to me about everything. "I have a few calls to make," I added.

Jo's brows drew together, and she looked at me sideways through narrowed eyes. "Sure," she said slowly. "We'll call you if we hear anything."

Armed with my handbag, containing Richard's incendiary documents, I headed down the red hill at the back of the hospital on foot, the wind slamming its furnace breath into my face. Ferreting out the whole truth had become my driving motivation. Somehow, I knew Allegra Rimo was the key to this riddle.

The first phone call I wanted to make was to the Cardiac Unit at the Greater Sinclair Hospital. They'd know how to contact Allegra. Half-jogging, I reached the final 50 meters to my dugout. The sticky heat seared my throat with every breath, although inwardly I was numbed by an icy uneasiness. Strangely, although what had happened to Richard was shocking, images of Sampson's face looking anxious popped into my mind's eye. If I were Samson, I knew, I'd be angry at Richard's stupid recklessness.

I tried to concentrate on the task I had to do. I rang International Telephone Directories and was connected to the London hospital. The whirring echo of the ring tone sounded both alien and familiar. It was five am, UK time. I spoke to a nurse who explained that a nurse rostered for the morning shift knew Allegra and I had to call back.

Drat the time difference, I thought.

Dee knocked on my door some time later. Over an hour had passed. I'd been sitting at the kitchen table with my forehead resting on the table, rerunning the morning's events in my head.

"I just thought I'd pop down and check on how you are," she said. She poured a glass of water. "Phew, it's hot, isn't it? They say there's a storm on the way."

I tapped my fingers on the kitchen bench, impatient with her small talk. "Have you heard anything?"

"No, sorry Cari. No news. The sergeant just radioed there's some difficulty locating your friend. What were they doing out there? Everyone knows that area is dangerous."

"That would have been Richard's doing. He would have convinced Samson that he absolutely had to go there. Samson wouldn't have known how dangerous that mine field is."

"I've been wondering why you weren't the one showing Richard."

"To be honest, I just needed some time to think … just by myself. Richard is so dominant. I can't think straight when he's around."

And you don't need to know about my sleuthing either.

Dee half-smiled, her eyes welling. "I can certainly understand that. You weren't to know this would happen. Poor Samson though. How must he be feeling?"

I sat back down, unable to say anything at first. My mouth felt stuck, as if it was chewing an indigestible cud of words. One good thing about my condition was I knew my face didn't betray my dilemma.

I finally spluttered, "Would it be OK if I stay down here? I think I need a rest." I lied. I didn't actually feel tired at all.

"Yes, of course. Good idea." Dee gently touched my hand. "I'll call you as soon as we know more."

After Dee had left I stood outside surveying the valley below. The wind had dropped. Now ominous purplish-gray clouds were building on the horizon, heavy with rain. In the outback this was common. Northerly winds brought baking heat and dry dust from the surrounding deserts; then, from the tropical north, monsoonal storms followed a week or so later. Torrential downpours then washed out roads and flooded plains, often lasting weeks. If this happened, the task of retrieving Richard would be almost impossible.

I tried the hospital in London again. This time, my call reached the nurse who knew Allegra.

"That snake! He's the reason she's no longer working here!" the nurse cried, after I'd explained that I knew Richard and I needed to speak with Allegra. "Allegra is a nice girl, and not a bad nurse. She didn't deserve what happened to her."

"Oh." I didn't know what else to say.

"I'll need to speak with her first. Call back in ten minutes."

I rang again as instructed and the nurse gave me Allegra's details. I dialed the given number.

"Hello?" Allegra answered on the first ringtone. "Are you calling me about Richard Leitch?" Allegra's accent sounded foreign, maybe Italian.

"I am."

"Who are you?"

"Allegra, my name is Cari Rainsford."

"Cari... I know that name! Aren't you Richard's sister?"

"No, no. I'm a friend of his," I said.

"A friend? Then I don't want to talk with you!"

For a horrible moment I thought she may hang up. "No please—wait! I really need to speak with you!"

There was silence at the other end, and then, "What is this about?"

"Allegra, it's a long story. Richard has had a terrible accident and is seriously injured."

I heard a sharp intake of her breath.

I continued. "I was Richard's girlfriend in London. We moved to Australia last year, but we broke up."

"And he told me you were his sister ... Why are you calling me now?"

I explained how Richard had arrived in Manguri only two days before, and that I'd found some documents in his room relating to professional misconduct. And that her name, and Dr Steven Liddard's, were there in black and white, typed on that expensive paper sent from the UK Medical Board. I couldn't tell Allegra about my confused feelings, nor did I tell her about Miranda. Yet I needed to know everything he'd done. Why, after all this time, was he being reported for cheating in his specialist exams? Was it true?

"Richard Leitch took away my livelihood and my reputation," she said in a quiet voice.

"What do you mean?"

"I was there when he took his specialist exam. I saw him cheat. I confronted him about it afterwards. And to keep me quiet, he treated me for a while like a princess. He took me out to dinner ... No wonder he did so well in that exam. Richard already knew the patient from the practice exam he did only the week before. He is a liar, Cari. A rotten liar."

Was a liar, I thought, and a potential rapist.

"What exactly happened?" I asked.

"Richard got spooked that night at the King Albert's Ball, when he was awarded a prize by Dr Liddard. He also knew Richard from that practice exam. It all went wrong after that ball."

I remembered that night. I was supposed to have attended but was called in to assist with a surgical case.

"You don't believe me, do you?"

"Allegra, listen. I do believe you … Richard had an affair with you?"

"Yes."

"That night at the ball—were you there?"

"Yes. I sort of invited myself, just that same day."

That would explain some of the odd looks I noticed afterwards at the hospital. My co-workers were embarrassed to see me. They'd figured out he was playing the field.

"And you didn't know about me?" I persisted.

"No! I swear I didn't. If I'd known he was seeing someone else, I would've sent him packing. But I had no intention to report him for cheating, ever. And that's the honest truth."

"I would have thought it very appropriate to have reported him," I rebuked her. And I meant it. Cheating was reprehensible.

Allegra sniffed wetly. "But I liked him. I just thought it was a bit of a game. And Richard's a good doctor, I think... When he's actually treating patients, that is."

I heard the derision in her laugh.

She sighed and continued. "Dr Liddard told me later he had his suspicions at the ball that Richard must have cheated. And then that bastard— Richard, that is—dumped me, that very night, after we'd gone back to my place and made—" She halted there and was momentarily silent before continuing. "After that night he had me investigated by a private detective."

"Really? Why would he do that?"

Allegra started crying.

"To shut me up. To discredit me, in case I ever decided to report him. I had no idea he would do such a thing. It was a complete shock when I was contacted by the director of nursing, a month later. The hospital found out I didn't have legal nursing qualifications and I was charged. They asked me if I could prove I was a qualified nurse."

"And you're not?"

"No," she said. "I'd worked as a student nurse in Italy. I was good at my job. But I couldn't pass the exams. So, then I got a forged nursing certificate. I worked in London for a few years, then I was struck off. I'm never allowed to practice as a nurse in the UK—ever. But, instead of jail, I got community service."

I rubbed my eyes. I had trouble collecting my thoughts. It all seemed so shady and wrong. Allegra had also duped the authorities.

"After the court case, I tried to find other work. Nurse's assistant, private nursing, even waitressing. But once any potential employer found out about what I'd done, they ran a mile. I got very depressed. My mother needed to go into in a nursing home. We had no money."

"So what happened then?" I asked.

"I ran into a nurse I'd worked with—the same one you spoke with earlier today—and she told me that she thought a man had been following me. This guy pretending to be a patient's relative had been hanging around the ward asking creepy questions about me. I'd actually seen him! I just laughed it off. But then I heard on the news on TV later, when things were going really badly for me, that Richard's father was being charged with fraud and corruption. Barry Leitch had been using private investigators illegally to dredge up stories about his business competitors."

"Richard's *father* was charged with fraud?" How much crazier could this get?

"Yes! And he's going to jail, the sleazy bastard. I started putting two and two together," Allegra said. "The apple never falls far from a tree. I thought, if Richard's father uses private investigators, why not Richard? Maybe that creepy guy had been a private detective. I decided then to go and see Dr Liddard."

"He was the doctor who already knew Richard and he had been at the ball."

"Yes. We'd worked together on the cardiac ward as well. I explained everything. He was horrified when I told him my story. He didn't think Richard should be allowed to get away with what he'd done. Dr Liddard started his own investigations. Somehow, he got hold of my file. And I was right. I was set-up, Cari. *Set-up!* It turns out that the same firm Richard's father used was the one that investigated me. Even a copy of the letter from the detective was included in my file, passed on to the hospital by an anonymous concerned citizen. But I know that 'concerned citizen' was him—Richard. He wanted me gone. *Finished! Vamoose!*" Allegra was now shouting, all trace of an Italian accent gone. "His reputation was more important than mine. Richard is a bastard like his father, a total bastard!"

"You decided to report him?"

"Yes! And I hope he rots in hell!"

That may be happening sooner than you think, I thought, but I bit my tongue.

When she calmed, I said haltingly, "Allegra, there's a chance Richard may be dead."

I heard her gasp. As steadily as I could manage, I told her what had happened.

Renewed wailing surged down the line. "I wanted him to get into trouble—but I didn't want him to die!"

I nearly said, "Make up your mind!" but Dr Smythe gently reproached me from the far depths of my cerebral cortex. *Not a good idea to point out her words are contradictory at this moment, my dear.*

Dr Smythe was right, as usual.

I hung up after promising to call Allegra as soon as I had any news and headed back up to the hospital. The ambulance had just arrived. I found Samson and Dee in the staffroom. Samson was sitting down, his forehead resting in his hand. Dee was placing a cup of tea before him. His pallor was obvious, even through his dark skin. His worried eyes were unfocussed, staring off in to space, but immediately became alert when he saw me. He swiftly lowered his gaze.

A police officer sat across from him. He coughed to get my attention. "Dr Rainsford, my name is Sergeant John Stuart. I am very sorry for your loss," he said in a deep bass voice.

I dropped into a chair, not sure what the appropriate response was. I folded my hands in my lap and waited. It was Samson who spoke first, with an apology for what had happened. He wouldn't accept my comment that he was in no way responsible. He even became hostile when I tried to reassure him, making me feel I was somehow to blame. But I wasn't even there!

The police sergeant left, and our conversation became heated. Samson started demanding answers. Feeling my face grow hot, I tried to stay calm.

Don't tell anyone. Linda's words echoed in my head.

I'd assured my wise friend that I would keep my exploits in Richard's room a secret. But as Samson grilled me, a strange discomfort roiled within: wasn't it wrong not to confide in him? But I wasn't really lying, I reasoned (although I had told him a porky—a white lie to protect him—when I said that I was needed at the hospital that morning.) I just wasn't telling him everything. (*Richard nearly raped someone!* I wanted to shout.) Samson was the only innocent and truthful person in this whole debacle. He didn't need to be involved.

Where are you Dr Smythe? I thought in desperation. *I need you!* She'd know what to say.

I tried to explain. "I wanted to be alone, Samson. And I knew Richard wasn't going to accept that at face value."

But my Indian friend wasn't buying it. Eyes blazing, he stood up and towered over me, just as my father did when he was drunk, when I was a small child. Looking at his face, all of my efforts to remain passive when someone was insulting me flew out the window. Like a panicked pigeon scrabbling and trapped in a dark cardboard box, all my composure now shredded into ribbons.

I said words I regret now. I drove my quiet peace-loving friend away. Samson had only shown me the greatest generosity of spirit in the time I had known him. And, ultimately, I let him down. I had no idea how my secretive behavior, my skulduggery, would affect him.

But I was in a quandary. I'd promised Linda I wouldn't tell anyone I'd entered Richard's room. Also, I knew I would have to be interviewed by Sergeant Stuart. What was I going to say to him? Best to keep all this to myself, I reasoned. I needed time to think. I needed to see the body, to know if it was really true—Richard was dead.

Seeing Richard as a corpse a little while later, swaddled in a white sheet on the stretcher in the A&E, was like seeing any other lifeless body. He could be any old, cold, stiff on the slab. No longer the Richard I'd known. I felt no particular grief as I examined him. Only the scientific excitement I always enjoyed when I deduced how someone's life had been snatched away.

It was a few days later that I did experience something I recognized as grief for Richard: a wistful memory of an innocent time. But this low mood was tempered by the knowledge that Richard had, in the end, only wanted me for one purpose. He'd needed me to champion his innocence. Maybe, he'd also wanted me back on his arm to present to the world the respectable young doctor again. At the end of the day, our whole relationship was a sham.

Later the sergeant took me to the police station and asked me a lot of questions about my relationship with my ex-boyfriend, and where I had been when Samson took Richard touring. He even started asking very personal questions about how Samson and I felt about each other. What did this have to do with Richard falling down a mineshaft, I felt like asking him.

It didn't occur to me in my numbed state that my asking Samson to take Richard sightseeing looked suspicious, especially when I was so evasive about my movements on that day. I was instead—foolishly—terrified I'd be charged with criminal trespass and the theft of those documents from Richard's room. The police sergeant told me he needed to requisition my car. He asked me to wait while he made some phone calls. In my confusion I didn't register the implication of those words until he returned to announce that he'd asked the Port Augusta CIB to make further enquiries, given the "unusual" nature of the accident.

That night, after a terse conversation with Samson outside his dugout, I rang Linda to fill her in about what had happened. After she'd recovered from my news (she dropped the phone), we discussed the interview I was to have the following day with the CIB detective.

"I don't understand," I said. "Samson told me that we could be in big trouble. But it was clearly an accident."

"Cari! Think about it! The police might think you were in with Samson on some kooky plan to get rid of Richard."

"You're kidding me."

"I'm not. Cooperate fully with the police. Show them the documents you stole and explain why you were in his room. Then they will see it was just an accident."

"But they might charge me with breaking and entering."

"Isn't that better than being under suspicion for murdering someone?"

Linda was right. I needed to come clean. Hopefully the detective would accept my story.

The following morning, bleary-eyed from lack of sleep, I fronted up for the interview with the detective who had flown from Port Augusta. Detective Brodie was an older stocky man with a round head and shiny scalp that looked like a polished bowling ball balanced on his thick neck. His eyes were almost closed as he flashed a broad smile in greeting. He extended his hand for me to shake.

I was fascinated by his appearance. The milky white rim of *arcus senilis*, sometimes seen in a person with high blood cholesterol levels, encircled the irises of his faded gray eyes, when I could actually observe them open. He also had a small *pterygium*: an overgrowth of tissues adjacent to the cornea of his left eye, a legacy of years of squinting into the harsh outback light, looking like an albino fly had landed there. A large *xanthelasma*, a yellow waxy collection weighted the skin fold of his left upper eyelid. Small broken blood vessels wove under the contrasting scaly pink skin of his moon face.

Maybe I should offer this man a blood test, I pondered.

"Are you with me, doctor?" Detective Brodie asked, interrupting my inspection. He grinned.

Detective Brodie's jocular manner perplexed me; it wasn't what I'd expected to encounter in a crime investigator. The detective's expression then clouded.

"Before we begin our interview, I need to tell you that I am shocked you examined Dr Leitch's body without police present. In future, if there's to be a coroner's investigation, don't." He muttered something about incompetent local coppers not adhering to correct police protocol.

He then led me into a small office with a plain table scattered with recording gear and notepaper. The air stank of stale coffee and burned toast.

"Detective," I began, before he'd even asked the first question. I slowly lowered myself into the chair he indicated. I willed my hands to stop trembling. "I need to let you know that I secretly entered Richard's room yesterday."

The detective now regarded me with an alert expression reminiscent of a tiger with its tail twitching about to pounce on an unsuspecting prey. He pressed a button on the tape recorder, murmured some details into the microphone before nodding to me. "When you are ready, Dr Rainsford."

Opening my handbag, I produced the documents I'd stolen. I then confessed all, without pausing for breath, including my conversation with Allegra.

"Slow down, Dr Rainsford! There is no hurry," Detective Brodie implored at one point. Otherwise, he sat back and listened to my story.

How Linda and I hatched a plot to ransack Richard's room, to see what he'd really been up to.

How I'd tricked Tom at the hotel into giving me the key.

How I'd urged Samson (who knew nothing) to take Richard sightseeing.

How we had no idea that Richard would fall down a mineshaft—we honestly didn't. And especially, how Samson was completely innocent of any wrongdoing.

More than anything—and it was really important that the detective knew this—how Richard had been completely dishonest with me and with others. Finally, that I'd sprung him assaulting a nurse in a store-room, and this was why I had broken up with him and fled to Manguri.

When I finished Detective Brodie beamed at me again, his puffy eyes again narrowed to horizontal black commas. His smiling disconcerted me. This was serious! He whistled softly though his teeth as he breathed out, as if he'd been holding his breath the entire time.

"Well, your Dr Leitch was a bad, bad boy, Dr Rainsford."

"Yes, he was," I agreed. "And his death was an accident."

The detective picked up an envelope containing some color photographs that Richard had taken. The camera had been retrieved from the mineshaft and Sergeant Stuart had had the film developed. The detective pushed each picture toward me.

The first was a photo of me with screwed-up eyes peering into the sun, my face contorted into a grimace. I was trying to pull a Photograph smile. A background of red dirt and gray gravel shimmered, a wide blue sky above. Then, another snap of me taken from some distance away, contemplating a mullock pile at Patty's mine. Photos of the township of Manguri were next and then panoramas of the Brittle Hills, with one picture of Samson looking like he was a big-game hunter with his ramrod stance and his cap pulled low. More followed. One of Richard flashing a jaunty grin, in the foreground of a flat landscape with piles of old mine rubble scattered about. He was wearing the blue shirt and cotton khaki shorts he'd died in. He looked every bit the worldly, comfortably well-off young go-getter he had professed to be. Then, a jokey irresponsible one of Richard playing the clown. He was standing next to a crevice with a big goofy grin. His foot was lifted, as if ready to take that final step. Then at last, the final picture that Richard ever took. Silently,

Detective Brodie slid it over: a blurred photograph of a small red car, with Samson looking at the camera, looking dismayed. Even I could recognize his distress. Only his head could be seen poking through the window and one arm extended, palm open.

"Dr Cherian told us that Richard was taking a photograph of him at the moment he fell," Detective Brodie said, his face now serious. My heart slowed with relief; this was the proof that Samson was nowhere near Richard when he'd fallen. "This is that picture. There will be no charges laid. Dr Leitch's death was clearly a tragic accident. However, I will caution you," he added. "I could charge you with breaking and entering, and possession of stolen property. And Dr Cherian will also be cautioned that he must not enter prohibited areas, such as the mine-fields. That area is out of bounds to tourists."

I nodded my understanding and tried to smile. The detective knew I was telling the truth. Now, I could come clean with Samson and repair our friendship.

However, the warm surge of relief vanished when Detective Brodie leaned forward, his words soft. "I will also advise you, Dr Rainsford, this conversation is police business and is strictly confidential. Also, the last thing Dr Leitch's family need is that his activities, however distasteful, should become widely known. Keep the details to yourself."

The detective then stood and vigorously shook my hand. "I'm sorry we've had to hold this interview, Dr Rainsford. You may have gathered that Sergeant Stuart spoke to Tom, the hotel receptionist, about Dr Leitch's last movements. So, I'm sure you understand that when the sergeant discovered you had arranged access to Dr Leitch's room through Tom, at about the same time Dr Leitch died, he was required to refer the matter to us." He grinned again, the facial equivalent of a no-harm-done shrug.

I left the police station a short while later and made my way to my parked car. A gloomy light had settled over the town. Increasing cloud cover signaled a pending storm. As I drove home, in the now humid air, I felt uneasy that I wasn't allowed to tell Samson the whole story. I'd given my word to Detective Brodie, however. I couldn't tell anyone the truth that Richard had really come to Manguri to lure me back to Adelaide, so to cover up for him. But at least Samson and I could resume life as we'd known it, before Richard's appearance had threatened to destroy our friendship—once Samson knew he was conclusively cleared of any wrongdoing.

CHAPTER TWENTY EIGHT

Samson

*Visitors to the Australian opal fields must remember these
are treacherous places. Weather changes, such as severe
thunderstorms with flash flooding, or severe dust storms, are
not unusual. Travelers through the area must expect that roads
can be cut between major towns. Always carry provisions and
camping equipment if traveling in inclement weather.*
(*The Magic of Opals* by WO Brown 1972, p. 3)

It was early afternoon when Cari returned from her interview with
the detective. I'd been inside my dugout, forcing down a sandwich
made with stale bread from the hospital's kitchen. It was so dry my jaw
muscles ached. I heard her car thrum into the carport, the tyres squealing a bit as she came to a halt and cut the car's ignition. I pretended I
hadn't heard her pull in as I waited for her to rap on my screen door.
Damp gray light cloaked the valley below. I heard a distant rumble of
thunder.

"Samson, you there?"

"Yes. Wait a minute."

I hauled myself out of my chair and flung the door open. There she
stood, wearing her standard white blouse with an ill-fitting navy skirt
and worn flat shoes. Her critical green eyes meandered over my face

and body. I hadn't shaved that day, or ironed my white shirt, which I remembered had a small tomato stain on its collar.

"You look terrible," she said.

Blunt as always!

"I'm very tired. What do you want?"

"I thought you should know that no charges will be laid against either of us. The CIB accepts that Richard's death was an accident. They know you were in no way responsible for what happened."

"Good," I said. "And now are you going to tell me why you've been keeping secrets from me?"

"I can't do that."

"Why not?" I felt my temper start to rise. Keep calm, I told myself.

"The detective asked me not to tell anyone."

"Why not?"

"Because I know some things about Richard that they think I should keep private."

"And you think I'm going to go spread lurid stories about your lover about, is that it?"

"No, Samson. And Richard isn't, I mean, wasn't, my lover. Not any more …"

I stared at her in disbelief. *But he had been once!*

She tried again. "I gave the detective my word I wouldn't reveal certain things to anyone."

"So, it's fine to lie to me! I don't deserve an explanation?"

Cari stood stock-still outside the door, just staring intensely at me.

"I'm sorry you were caught up in this. I had no way of knowing that Richard would do something so dangerous …"

"Cari, are you actually capable of feeling sorry for anyone? From what you've told me of your condition, people with Asperger's syndrome usually can't feel another's pain. Now, if you've finished, then please go and leave me alone."

Her eyes narrowed at this and she frowned. It was hard to tell if she was feeling wounded or angry. I knew that her expressions were often a poor guide as to what would fly out of her mouth next. I slammed the door behind her, feeling riled and paradoxically guilty at the same time. It was as if there were two Samsons occupying my body. My usual self had been pushed into a corner by an outspoken and irritable grump. At the moment he was doing all the talking.

The next morning, I trudged up the hill to the hospital to commence ward round. Over the previous long night, I'd heard the patter and hiss of raindrops on my pergola. A deluge of rain had hit us in the early hours of the morning. Normally, the sound of rain soothed me, but not this time.

There was no sign of Cari. Her red car, streaked with mud, sat under the carport looking abandoned. The galvanized iron roof above it must have leaked. The morning sunlight, filtered through rain clouds, made the township below look eerily dim and violet-hued. Rivulets of muddy water ran down gullies next to my path as I made my way, my unsuitable black leather shoes slipping on the muddy terrain. The skies threatened to open again. I hurried my pace.

That would be right, I thought. Cari had caused untold distress with this Richard business, yet she'd decided to have a sleep in.

I glanced at my watch—seven o'clock. Cari liked to commence ward round at eight; she was a stickler for punctuality. I was actually 50 minutes earlier than usual. However, I assumed Cari would agree that after the last few chaotic days we needed an early start. (But then again, Cari would never be known for thinking beyond herself, I griped uncharitably.)

I arrived at the hospital wet and disheveled; my shoes and trouser bottoms soaked. Marg was in the nurses' station, with the agency nurse,

Soph. They had just finished the night duty handover, detailing the inpatients' progress.

"Good morning, Dr Cherian," Marg said. "You're here bright and early." She passed me a towel and laughed. "You look like a drowned rat."

I swallowed my irritation at being compared to a gutter rat. Why had I never noticed before Marg's annoying habit of finishing every sentence with a rising inflection?

"Perhaps we should wait for Cari before we start the round," she said.

"I'm keen to get started," I snapped.

"Of course, Doctor …"

We checked out our inpatients, although in my torpor I was struggling to concentrate; my thoughts sluggish, my focus poor. Marg gave a running commentary on each patient's progress, providing relevant medical information, with some jarring, gossipy detail thrown in.

"Mrs Jonavich and her congestive cardiac failure, she's doing well following her diuretic therapy. She complains about everything and wants to be waited on hand and foot … Here we have ten-year-old Todd Morris with his abdo pain, but he's fine Doc, he's had some breakfast. I think he can go home … Now Patty the mine owner with his emphysema; he responded well to those nebs … And Dirty Harry, he's back again with that ulcer that won't heal up. We'll take the dressing off later and show it to you. God, he's got a filthy mind … All the nurses hate him."

I half-listened to Marg's commentary. Everything was so mind-numbingly dull. These patients and their revolving-door complaints. The same things day after day: the conditions caused by smoking and drinking, ruined hearts and lungs failing and filling with excess fluids, damaged organs struggling on against the odds. Skin eroding and granulating to heal to only then erode again, because the Dirty Harrys of this world did not bother to look after themselves. These wastrels suctioned up precious hospital resources and staff time. They did not eat properly, they drank too much, they knocked shins and ulcerated their limbs when they should know better. What was the point? I felt drained by the hopelessness of it all.

"Are you OK, Dr Cherian?" Marg asked after a while. "You're looking a bit peaky. Do you want to take the day off? It's horrible what happened, you must still be feeling the shock—"

"I'm fine."

"Seriously, take the day off. We'll manage."

"I said I'm fine!"

Marg looked at me startled, then affronted. I knew I sounded unnecessarily sharp.

The morning dragged on. I signed forms, ordered medications, authorized discharges.

It was nearly time to break for lunch when Marg came over to me. I was sitting in the nurses' station, filling out paperwork.

"Samson, would you mind checking Dirty Harry's leg? It's looking very red."

I followed her into his room.

"G'day Doc!" Dirty Harry greeted me. "Those bloody nurses. They're paid to worry. It's just a bit flared up after my shower, that's all."

Sighing, I examined the man's swollen leg, which resembled a waterlogged mini-zeppelin. The skin had the texture of an orange past its use-by-date, with a color the bright crimson of a boiled lobster.

I stood at the end of his bed, my arms folded, a pulse started throbbing in my temple. This infection was manifestly inexcusable.

"Have you been keeping your leg elevated? Have you been taking your tablets?"

"Steady on, Doc!" Harry protested. "Course I've been taking my bloody tablets. You reckon this lot would let me not take them?" He looked over at Marg for support.

The senior nurse frowned at me. "It's no-one's fault. How about we commence some IV antibiotics and see how he gets on over the next few days?"

I grunted my assent and snatched the medication sheet she held out. I headed to the nurses' station before she could put me in the firing line with more worries. Now the nurses were telling me how to do my job!

Mags, another nurse, approached me, her usual smile wavering. She bit her lip.

"Dr Cherian, I'm sorry to bother you, but there's a problem with one of your drug orders." She hesitated. "Did you really mean to order 1500 mg of cephalexin to give to that baby? Normally it would be 150 mg. I haven't given it, just in case."

I stared at her in horror. The dose I'd prescribed was ten times what it should be. In my state of fatigue, I'd written the wrong number of zeroes. An understandable error, but for a doctor, an unforgivable one. Without speaking, I took the medication sheet, crossed out the offending zero, and tossed it back.

"Thanks Doctor. Don't worry. That's an easy mistake to make."

If that was meant to make me feel better, it didn't. I was a doctor for goodness sakes. I couldn't afford to make blunders like that. I muttered my thanks and the nurse gave a hasty nod. She glanced over her shoulder at me as she hurried away.

I didn't see Cari at all that morning. She had rung Dee to say she was seeing patients in the General Practice Clinic and asked if I could see her inpatients. Was that the truth? Or had she found something more interesting to do?

☊

On Monday evenings, as an informal get together, the hospital staff often gathered at one of the few meeting places above ground in Manguri, the Italian Club. Cari usually drove us to the venue which was located south of the hospital. Ordinarily I looked forward to these social occasions. It was a break from my hit and miss cooking efforts, and a chance to socialise and get to know the hospital staff better. Doctors, nurses, kitchen hands and cleaners, we all sat together to enjoy the Monday night special: plates piled with roast lamb, gravy and potatoes, then apple pie and ice-cream for dessert. Trays laden with glasses of cold beer circulated, with wine or shandies for the ladies (excepting Cari— she drank beer). We all pitched in our 20 dollars and any money left would pay for the hospital's annual Christmas party.

But the rain had started again. The unrelenting drip and pit-a-pat galled me; my clothes felt damp. There were now mud pools outside my front door. I didn't feel like going. I lay on my couch, the mindless buzz of the television my only company. Cari gave up on me after pounding on my door a few times. The sound of her car sliding and splashing through the rivers of mud outside faded as the motor throttled to join the main road. Looking around my well-furnished but comfortless dugout, I had never felt so alone in my whole life.

CHAPTER TWENTY NINE

Plague and earthquakes devastated Venice in 1348. The hapless opal was yet again blamed—it was then a favorite gem of Italian jewelers. Mysterious deaths were directly attributed to this "stone of dread".
(*The Magic of Opals* by WO Brown 1972, p. 23)

The days and nights following the Richard incident started to become more alike. It was as if all color and joy had also been sucked down that mineshaft. My sleep fragmented. Dreams were crowded with people I'd worked with, or Cari or Mercy. My biological parents even made a special appearance, their images blurred and unreal, and, sometimes, the director of the children's home where I'd lived as a young orphan. A taunting Richard regularly dropped in. My visitors appeared in snatches of conversations, gibbering and chattering in my head, like an untuned radio. Or silent visions flashed across my brain, played out in full cinematic color. There were random scenes: Cari lit up by bright theater lights holding a surgical retractor, or Richard falling backwards from various angles, as if recorded by different cameras strategically placed for best view, with him begging me pitifully to rescue him as he fell.

Every night I laid my head on my pillow, praying for restful sleep and release from my daytime anxieties. Time as a construct lost meaning. Most nights the clock ticked over slowly, the hours seeming to stretch out forever. I watched the morning sky lighten outside my window with a sense of relief. I felt lucky if I'd had an hour of fitful sleep. But I had to get myself up and get through another day. Occasionally, I slept as if I was unconscious, my body exhausted, the sleep of the dead. Those nights I did not dream, nor did I feel rested when I awoke.

Feelings of guilt plagued me. I should never have driven into that derelict minefield. I should have stood my ground against Richard; although, in his eyes, I was just an Indian manservant. The scourge of confusion and being overwhelmed pinned me down. Everyone always wanting something. The nurses relentlessly calling at all hours about sick patients, Barb wanting me to prop up her ego by praising her dreadful curries, Mercy wanting a father for her child—I couldn't even manage that. Dee urging me to stay on in Manguri and not bugger off.

Only Cari expected nothing of me. And, inexplicably, that made me angry too.

☙

"Tell me the truth," Richard had said to me only an hour or so before he'd fallen. I had taken him to admire the view from a promontory over-looking a valley, 20 miles or so from town. "I won't be upset or angry with you."

We were standing near the edge of a cliff, a sheer drop before us. The ground disappeared to scoop out to the plain below, from which the enormous phosphorescent rocks of the Brittle Hills rose like a cluster of white sessile polyps in the distance. I'd driven Cari's car to the highest lookout to view this natural wonder.

This scoundrel that Cari had allowed into her life (and possibly had loved), fell silent then, allowing me to dwell on exactly what his words alluded to. The buzzing of flies mingled with the whistle of the hot wind that rushed upwards and towards us, fleeing the valley below.

He pirouetted to face me, an angry intensity stamped on his face. "Have you and Cari been an item?"

My heart began to race, my mouth suddenly bone-dry. "What do you mean?"

"You know. Have you been spending 'special' time with Cari?"

He smirked. But any malice was now wiped from his face, as if removed by a sudden gust of wind. He gyrated sensuously like a flamenco dancer, in an obscene gesture.

"Most certainly not. I am married. I would never cheat on my wife," I said.

He stopped and stared at me. "Oh, come on. I wasn't born yesterday, Samson. It would be perfectly understandable. She's smart. She's interesting …"

There was the briefest of pauses. He didn't offer the suggestion that Cari was attractive. "It would be impossible to resist the temptations of the flesh out here... And why would you?" He twisted his lips suggestively, letting me know there was no question in his mind how he'd behave if he were in my position. "The quiet lonely nights, just each other for company. It would get cold in the evenings in Manguri. *Brrrr!*" He wrapped his arms across his chest. "No-one would ever need to know, your dugouts being so close."

"I find your questioning most insulting!" I cried.

"I apologize," he said. He hung his head in a gesture of penitence, but I could detect the sly lift of an eyebrow. "I'm only pulling your leg. I'm an idiot, aren't I, to have such vulgar thoughts? No hard feelings, eh? I know you'd never have a *liaison* with Cari." He said these last words lazily, as if he was suddenly bored with his silly charade. "You're not that kind of man, are you, Samson? And Cari is also not one to be unprofessional, I know that."

At that, he shrugged hard and strode away toward Cari's car, the matter seemingly dismissed.

I felt annoyed and perturbed as I watched him march off. I picked up a handful of the white scree at my feet and, hoping to vent my building frustration, threw each stone as far as I could into the shimmering heat below. Had Richard sensed something from the tension of my bearing in Cari's presence? Maybe he suspected that my staunch pragmatism belied my confused feelings.

After my handful of stones had been discarded one by one over the edge of the plateau, I reluctantly rejoined Richard in the car.

I knew he toyed with me.

The rain, as expected, was continuous. After four weeks flash floods washed away the roads further north. Creeks filled with fast-flowing yellowish water and burst their banks. The red plains began to resemble a giant brown inland sea. Even landing planes on the bitumen runway at the airport was hazardous—the planes skidded like rocketing speedboats as soon as their wheels touched the ground. Like the cold drizzle that soaked into the dirt outside my dugout, I couldn't shake the pervasive feeling that something terrible was about to happen. I started to double, then triple-check my work. I became slow and inefficient. Even so, unfathomable anger churned when the nursing staff tried to interfere.

One afternoon, a month after Richard's accident, Dee called me in to her office. Indicating a chair across from her desk, she didn't beat around the bush. Her concerned eyes held my gaze as I took my seat.

"Samson, my staff and I are very worried about you."

"What do you mean? I'm working to the best of my ability. You know that."

A fanciful image came to me of getting up and going home to my dugout to sleep, to curl up under my slippery purple nylon bedspread. I felt so tired I didn't care if the walls of my dugout collapsed and crushed me as I slept. Indeed, this fantasy held a macabre appeal.

"When did you last have a decent night's sleep?"

I didn't reply.

"I want you to take a week off work. Cari and I have already discussed it. She's more than happy to look after your patients."

"Cari? You discussed me with Cari? You can't trust anything she tells you. No, no. She might tell you that she will look after my patients, but how do I know she will?"

Dee's face hardened. "That's very unfair of you. Cari has only ever demonstrated the utmost concern for you."

"Oh no she hasn't!"

"Oh yes she has! And since the accident you've not been yourself. I'm not asking you—I'm telling you; you need a break. And I want you to see a doctor, to help with your sleep."

"Who? Cari? Is she the good doctor you suggest I see?"

"There's a psychiatrist who visits Port Augusta every month. I hope you don't mind but I took the liberty of calling his office."

"What?" I exploded. "Have you and Cari worked this out between you? Does she think I'm cracking up because I didn't like the lies she told me!"

"Calm down, Doctor," Dee said. She pressed her lips together. "I made an appointment for later in the week when he's due for a visit. That's if we can get you there. The Cooper Creek looks as if it's about to flood. That will block off access for a few days."

What had Cari called Manguri? "A bloody backwater." And now I could be stranded in this godforsaken town waiting for floods to ease. I fidgeted in my chair, unable to keep my feet still.

Dee fished a small key out of her pocket and opened the top drawer of her desk. She found a plastic bottle.

"I probably shouldn't be giving you these, but here are some Valium tablets. At least they might help you sleep. We all need a bit of help sometimes, Samson … Please take some time off. We'll manage." Dee's brown eyes searched mine; she smiled weakly. "And go see Dr Rajesh. I'm sure you will like him. He's also Indian; but he's lived in Australia for a long time."

By studying the bottle in my hand, I could avoid Dee's gaze. I murmured my assent. I finished my day's duties and headed down the now treacherous track back to my dugout, jumping over puddles and sliding through the mud, the drizzling rain pearling and clinging to my clothes and hair. I knew Dee meant well. However, I couldn't tell her that seeing another Indian doctor about my anxiety was tantamount to admitting I was a total failure. Not for the first time, I felt hopeless. I wondered if living this lie of a life was worth all the effort.

I took the tablets and, for the first time in a month, I laid on my bed and drifted into a peaceful doze. I knew the anxiety still waited, a patient presence, bunkered down outside my dugout in the thick fog. Yet, for a short time, I had some respite from nagging doubts.

Later in the day, I showered and forced myself to eat a light dinner. I tried to watch television, but the local channel was only showing a soap opera rerun. I stopped watching after ten minutes. The heavily Australian-accented dialogue spouting from the mouths of the pretty yet overacting actors was impossible to follow; the storyline also too improbable.

The ABC was showing another program about the devastating floods up north. The commentator predicted the flooding Cooper Creek would cause heavy damage to roads and cattle stations. There was no feed for stock, but the local salt lakes were expected to fill for the first time in decades. A mouse plague would inevitably follow, she cheerily suggested, to invade large tracts of farmland where wheat was being sown. All doom and gloom, famine, floods, pestilence.

The next day, after another restless night, despite taking two more of the tablets, I spent the day again trying to read and watch TV. Since I'd arrived in Manguri six months earlier, I'd visited the hospital every day; now my days felt starkly empty. I dared not go out. I knew word of my melancholy would have spread like wildfire. I couldn't face the kind yet uncomprehending faces of the townsfolk. I didn't particularly wish to see anyone else either. I couldn't be bothered; I was too exhausted. I had nothing to say. I didn't care that I'd stopped shaving. I couldn't raise the energy to wash myself or my clothes. Parcels of hospital food started to appear at my door each evening, dropped off by a loyal Barb, who gave up knocking after a few days. I ate little, however. My clothes hung loosely on my shrinking frame. I'd leave the mostly untouched plate outside my front door, for it to disappear the next day. I refused to answer the door to anyone, especially Cari. She knocked several times a day, but I ignored her.

CHAPTER THIRTY

*If you are heartbroken, the opal is the gem for you. This stone
is known for its power to restore hope, love and resolve painful
memories, and is revered for its ability to allow introspection. Inner
truths may be revealed, even those unpleasant. The Ancient Romans
believed it brought good luck and great success. Lovers, beware.
Opals are only powerful if you remain true to your partner.*
(*The Magic of Opals* by WO Brown 1972, p. 66)

The day that I was due to see Dr Rajesh was particularly fraught. The road to Port Augusta was still closed. Dee rang me and asked if I wanted to fly down with the RFDS to see the psychiatrist. Not wishing to cause a fuss, I convinced her, with an Academy Award winning act, that I indeed felt much better and this was not necessary. However, this particular afternoon, I couldn't calm. After giving up on watching the fuzzy screen of my TV, I decided to go for a walk through the town, despite the gloomy conditions. It had been over a week since I'd last left the dugout. I donned a raincoat and set off at a furious pace up the hill past the hospital. The rain had finally eased after a month of downpours. A thick mist fogged the town.

Eventually, I reached the underground Serbian church. The muddy shingle carpark and pink sandstone external walls gave little indication of the beauty and tranquillity within. It had been nearly six months since I'd last stepped into a church, and my friend Guilt delighted in giving me a sharp rap over the knuckles. I was raised a Catholic and my adoptive parents and I had attended mass most weeks in Chennai. However, since my move to Vellore, before coming to Australia, my church attendance had dwindled to nothing. I thought this was understandable then, given the long hours I worked. This was a pathetic and inadequate excuse, I well knew; I should have made more effort.

I'd always regarded God as being like a dear old friend, always in my thoughts. When I did make the effort to catch up, we renewed our acquaintance as if we'd never left off. The truest of friends know there is no need to see them every minute of the day. Yet, perhaps I had misread the situation. My stomach gave a lurch.

Perhaps God felt a little … taken for granted. Maybe he felt my soul had reached dizzy ecclesiastical heights and he no longer needed to actively participate in any spiritual guidance. I was a self-obsessed soul who had wandered off, not looking back, or even around him, fueled by my own ego, blindsided by my petty personal problems. Plenty more willing and grateful souls out there needing to be shepherded, God may have surmised. So, perhaps it's like when you look up an old friend that you haven't seen for some time. They might show some shock, indifference or confusion when you just pop up out of the blue. It takes time to reconnect because you've changed. Or your friend's changed, or something is different. It's never like it was before. Your friendship becomes based on nostalgia. Remember when we did this? Remember when we did that? Maybe this is how God regarded me when I dropped in at His house for a fleeting catch-up.

God was only rightfully acknowledged when I performed surgery; when he stepped in and operated through me to save lives. Then I knew he was with me—and I gave thanks. But was that enough to satisfy our Lord? Surely I needed to repent my sins and pay penance.

No! God wasn't like that. God was pure, unadulterated love. God accepted me warts and all. The Lord was a forgiving God. He knew I was a sinner, yet he still loved me. Get rid of those scandalous thoughts right now that God had abandoned you to look for new souls to save. God wouldn't do that.

But, the recent events in Manguri had planted a nagging seed of doubt. Maybe Richard had been an emissary of the Devil, sent to test my resolve. Perhaps my inattention had allowed a rent in the spiritual fabric between the world of the living and Hell, allowing a stealthy Richard to slip through. Maybe Cari, by virtue of her re-acquaintance with him, had already sold her soul. Cari had seemed unfailingly honest before he arrived in town. Now, she could lie with an unnerving ease, as if she'd been born to it.

The chapel was empty. My footsteps echoed on the floor tiles, my breathing amplified in the quiet cool. The ceilings had been scalloped out by a tunneling machine, the walls built in a roughly hewn rosy sandstone. Carvings of Christ stared impassively over the altar. I turned to look at the lead-glass windows behind the pews. The vivid red and black Sturt's desert pea, the state's floral emblem, was depicted in the upper panes, to brighten the somber church. The windows beneath showed images of the Virgin Mary and the apostles. The artificial lighting tossed licks of orange onto the walls, reminding me of the flames of a Hindu funeral pyre. Normally I would have been in awe at such beauty. But that day, I couldn't shake the feeling that even the Virgin Mary was judging my character from the shadows. Although God was willing to put up with spiritual neglect, she would not be so easily appeased.

I tried to pray, but the anxiety I'd managed to keep at bay in the dugout, had resumed its place at my side as soon as I entered the church. My heart pounded. The Apostles gave me a contemptuous stare, as if they were waiting. The Virgin Mary glowered a look of pure scorn. It was the same withering expression of contempt Mercy gave me each morning when I departed for work. What do you want me to say? I felt like yelling. I willed my mind to still, my breathing to steady.

"You're a hopeless husband, Samson," Richard whispered in my ear.

I turned around, panicked. The chapel was empty. I pawed the air but didn't feel any draft of icy air. No ephemeral apparitions materialized in my vicinity.

"You can't see me. I'm all in your head." My soon-to-be nemesis then sighed and said, "Poor Samson. I know everything about you. I even know you were locked in that toilet when you were just a wee little tyke. Dear me. And you still don't like dark, confined spaces, do you?" He guffawed, then cleared his throat, his tone becoming businesslike. "Now listen up, Samson. The nurses, the townsfolk and that extraordinarily long-suffering wife of yours, are all in complete agreement. You should leave Manguri before you cause some other disaster."

"I have no plans to leave!"

"Don't bother trying to argue with me, my dear fellow. Their decision was unanimous. The nurses also think you are a second-rate surgeon, did you know that? You have been such a disappointment ..."

"Please shut up," I said under my breath.

"Even Cari hates you now. Can you blame her, the way you've been treating her? She can't help being a little—how should we put it—insensitive? That's just how she is. And yet you have been yelling at the poor child."

"Please go away." My breath was coming in hot ragged bursts.

"You're the problem, Samson. They would be all so much better off without you," he whispered. "Hopeless, useless!"

"Shut up!" Desperation screamed out of me. "Leave me alone!"

A door behind me opened and Barb burst out of a backroom.

Great. Just who I need. I lowered my head. I didn't want to have to meet her eyes.

"You all right, Doctor? I thought I heard you shouting. I'm doing the flowers for the church. Hope I didn't frighten you."

"I'm fine, Barb."

I got up out of my pew and pushed past her. I ran out of the church, sensing the Virgin Mary's eyes like hot daggers in my back. But I couldn't help it. I needed to escape the feeling the walls were closing in. Barb stared after me open-mouthed, her arms laden with blooms of yellow wattle and deep-red bottlebrush.

Richard tittered as I crunched over the white gravel of the carpark. "Well, well. It's going to be all over Manguri now. *Tsk-tsk.* The local doc is hearing voices."

In my imagination I could see him striding next to me, a look of smug frivolity lighting his face. But then, turning on me, his face dissolved and rearranged itself into that of a nightmarish clown. "I shouldn't have fallen down that mineshaft, you idiot. It was your fault. But you know that, don't you?"

It was true, although I hated to admit it. No wonder Satan had singled me out for special treatment. As I blundered home, Richard's evil sniggers ceased, leaving me in a state of fearful agitation.

I'd never heard voices before. Maybe I really was "cracking up", as I'd heard the Manguri nurses refer to patients who cowered in the A&E, suffering paranoid delusions, begging to be saved from demons, biker gangs or aliens. Or, besieged by unrelenting auditory hallucinations— voices that only those unfortunates could hear.

I needed to get back to my dugout. I needed to calm down and sleep again. I needed more of those sleeping pills. And I needed to pray. I needed to pledge to the Lord that I would do better; he was my protective armor. He would look after me. But most of all, I prayed Richard's voice wouldn't return.

Perhaps I should see that doctor in Port Augusta.

However, as I hurried down the hill, I began to have suspicions that Barb was following me. I spun to look behind from time to time, hoping to catch her out. But, other than a piece of rubbish, an empty biscuit packet she had left behind, I saw no sign of her presence. Another tray of food had been placed next to my front door. I lifted the metal lid off the plate to see some cooked chicken and soggy vegetables floating in a brown soupy gravy, a meal obviously pilfered from the hospital kitchen. I didn't dare eat it. Who had left it there? Not Barb; she was at the church. Maybe Cari or Dee? Maybe it had been poisoned from sitting outside, incubating staphylococcal toxins, or who knows what other pathogens, although the temperature in Manguri had dropped with the rain. Or maybe, some tasteless chemical had been added to the unappetizing dish.

Richard snickered. "They want you dead."

I had to agree with him, although the sound of his voice made my blood boil. But there was no argument; I had little to offer the world.

In my confused state I fleetingly entertained the idea of visiting the hospital to see how my patients were getting on. But then, with a frisson of anger, I remembered that Dee had made it very clear to me the week before that my services were no longer wanted. Perhaps the idea of my visiting that doctor in Port Augusta was another convenient way for Dee, Cari and all of the nursing staff at the hospital, to see the last of me.

Ha ha! I have you now! I thought.

They were all in on it. They had snuck tiptoeing past the Lord, arm in arm. Cari, Dee and her minions wanted me locked up (a psychiatric hospital would do) to keep me quiet. Cari was in full cahoots with the Devil. A modern-day equivalent of Delilah, she'd lulled me into a false sense of security. She would hand me disempowered to the Philistines, to metaphorically gouge my eyes and bind me in shackles. Richard had been sent by Beelzebub and that deceitful Cari had sold her soul. She and a spell-bound Dee were now doing his filthy evil work, with their schemes and their lies. Despite how the people who worked in that sin-bin of depravity tried to humor me, I could see in their eyes a look of fear. They were afraid of me. But to reveal Cari as the Devil's succubus would be like kicking a hornet's nest: hurting her would only incur more pain from them all. I had unearthed their deceit.

Inside the dugout, there was no sign that any intruders had visited. I breathed a sigh of relief. I lifted up the curtain of my front window in the kitchen and surveyed the area under the pergola and the exterior of Cari's dugout. Her car wasn't there. I quickly dropped it, in case spies were lurking outside. She would be up at the hospital informing on me to Dee. The other nurses would be pitching in, regaling Dee the DON with tales of how Dr Cherian was making mistakes—how he wasn't fit to be a surgeon.

Yet, as I paced around my room, another voice, Mercy's, reminded me that Cari, Dee and the nurses were quite correct: I wasn't cutting it as a doctor either.

"She's right, you know. I keep telling you, but you won't listen," Richard said. He gave a stifled yawn.

I sat down and sobbed; cries that left me filled with more tension than ever. Maybe Dee, Cari and the nurses were being truthful, a little voice twittered. I must be clinically depressed. This was causing me to become paranoid, to question the motives of others who were only concerned about me.

"Don't be ridiculous," Richard spoke up. He cracked his knuckles. "You aren't thinking straight. The truth is you're so hopeless everyone— understandably—wants to get rid of you. Then they can get someone who really knows what they're doing. You could've killed that baby with that medication. Killing someone isn't hard … as you well know."

He was wrong. That dose of antibiotic I'd prescribed wouldn't have caused harm. But it was just the start. I'd been lucky. This time.

I couldn't sit still. I needed to keep moving. I hadn't telephoned Mercy in weeks. Last time the phone had rung, its shrill ring piercing the air, I had pulled its cord from the wall.

I took more of Dee's pills and fell asleep fully clothed on top of the bed. I awoke to the sudden sensation of jerking and vibrations coursing through my body. I glanced at the clock; it was four am.

An earthquake! The rose-colored walls would soon start to cave in, with bits crumbling off, before entire sheets sheared off the walls. Then boulders from the heart of the hill would come crashing in, smothering me. I would be pulverized, compacted, desiccated. To be found millennia later, like a Pompeiian fossil. An object of scientific curiosity for the Dr Cari Rainsford types of the future.

I leapt out of bed and barged through the front door, the screen door slamming behind me. The rain was holding off. Some clouds had parted to reveal the speckle of a few stars in the otherwise inky sky. Not even the purr of a diesel generator broke the heavy silence. My heart rate gradually decelerated; I tried to steady my shallow breathing. I looked behind. There were no billowing clouds of dust, or chasms of dirt opening up in the red dirt under the pergola.

I must have screamed in my terror, because next thing Cari walked from the front door of her dugout. The door banged behind her; she was pulling on a cotton bathrobe. She wielded a small flashlight, to trap me quivering like an ensnared rabbit in its beam.

"I apologize," I said. "I had a bad dream. I am sorry I disturbed you. Please. Please go back to bed."

"As long as you are OK, Samson."

"You should tell her you're hearing voices," Richard piped up. "Then they can put you in the looney bin where you belong."

"I am quite well," I replied.

"Go on, tell her," Richard said. "You don't trust her, do you? She's changed, hasn't she?"

Concern now lined Cari's face. Yes, she was different to the impassive woman I had first met!

"Are you sure, Samson?" she asked.

"Yes."

Cari slipped off back to her dugout, shaking her head as she went. I shivered in the cold. I had a sudden urge to follow her, to wrap her in my arms, to tell her how much I missed our talks and our walks.

"You are a married man," Richard reminded me.

Yes, but Cari had been my friend.

Then in a rush, my heart started hammering again. The Devil had taken possession of the truthful Cari I'd known. This new Cari, this lying dishonest Cari, was in league with Lucifer. I couldn't share my feelings of despair with this despicable impostor.

The next day, I tried to keep my mind occupied by trying to read medical journals and writing letters. I started writing an indignant letter to Dee, protesting how I'd become aware that the food her staff was trying to feed me was poisoned. If she did not order her staff to desist, I would be reporting her to the police.

But then I despondently remembered. I had not even been able to save a fellow medical man from tumbling down a mineshaft. Sergeant Stuart would never believe me if I darkened his door with those allegations.

"You were even a terrible tour guide," Richard sniffed, sounding bored.

Maybe the staff had installed listening devices when I'd rushed out of the room that previous night. *Ah, yes.* That was a clever ruse, making me believe there had been an earthquake. I knew they would be scheming to send me away, telling me I was certifiably mad. But I would outsmart them. I needed to find a way.

I examined a framed photograph of Mercy on my bedside table. She was wearing a dark green sari that disguised her rolls of fat. A collection of fine gold necklaces hung from her thick neck. Black wire-rimmed glasses sat squarely on top of her flattish nose, distorting the shape of her large brown eyes. Mercy was also unlucky to have a dark staining of the skin around her small unsmiling mouth, below the lighter pigment of her cheeks and forehead. It looked as if she'd dribbled her morning coffee. The skin's discoloration just matched the black of her long wiry hair, which she tied back, like a young child, on each side of her head. She never plucked her eyebrows, which sat in a black caterpillar fuzz above her spectacles.

The picture I looked at had been taken not long before I left our home in Vellore. I stared at it, mesmerized. It portrayed a young woman who appeared exhausted. I'd never noticed this before. Put simply, she'd given up caring. Worn down by my failure to deliver the goods, in the shape of a plump, chubby-cheeked babe, Mercy had allowed herself to blow up, like a poorly groomed heifer. In contrast, the Mercy I first knew, had been, not attractive exactly, but presentable.

And then realization kicked in. It wasn't just my infertility that had been the problem. It was my chronic neglect of her. This revelation came as a sickening blow. While I'd spent protracted stretches tending to the sick and injured, I had left Mercy alone in our small unit in Vellore, surrounded by the heaving maelstrom of people that populate India. She was left to occupy herself, isolated, stranded. She had no transport. She'd left her job thinking she would have children to tend to. Her family lived in Chennai, two hours away. She rarely saw them. The trip there was exhausting, so visits were not as frequent as she would have liked. Being a shy person, Mercy was effectively imprisoned in her own home. She was also committed in a marriage to an indifferent man whom she barely knew. No wonder my wife became so embittered.

"You have also been a hopeless husband," Richard agreed.

"I know. You keep telling me. I wish you would just shut up!"

I could see an image of Richard leaning back, carelessly resting his moccasin-clad feet up on my sofa, hands under the back of his head, elbows jutting out. All nice and comfy, and right at home in my lounge room. "She truly would be better off without you. But you know that already, don't you?" he said.

My head drooped. Tears streamed down my face, the droplets catching in the rough bristles of my scruffy beard. Richard spoke the truth. Mercy *would* be better off without me. She'd find a new husband who would be proficient at giving her what she wanted most of all: a baby. Maybe I should just give everyone a helping hand and put an end to all this fuss. I was perfectly capable, thanks very much, of disposing of myself. When, where and how, was up to me.

"It's only a short walk to the opal mines," he added.

Again, he was right. Twenty minutes walking, depending if there was a head wind. I could head west, along the back way; I wouldn't be spotted. Plenty of deep digs out there. I could almost hear the beckoning song of the opal, as if there were sirens of the deep resident there.

"Hopeless, useless! Hopeless, useless!" Richard chanted.

"Shut up! Shut up!"

"There's only one way to silence me, Samson. You know what you have to do."

As he muttered those words, I heard a creak as the outer screen of my front door opened, then a sharp knocking on the inner wooden door. I lifted the curtain of the adjoining window above the kitchen sink and peeked out, to immediately drop the gauzy fabric. The two witches were standing there. Dee was doing a fine job of looking worried. Cari's fair face was an imponderable mask, as always. She held her handbag under one arm. I could see it contained some documents. Dee stood by in her nurse's uniform.

"I thought I heard shouting," I heard Dee say.

"Yes, so did I," Cari said in reply.

They banged on the door again, but I was cowering in the dark of the bathroom with the lights off. I ignored the tiled walls inching closer, waiting to squish me into a car wrecker's cube.

"Shall we try again?" Cari asked.

"Well, we have no choice, do we? If he doesn't answer then, I think we'll have to get Sergeant Stuart to break in."

I knew it! Sergeant Stuart could then take me to jail. No-one really believed that Richard's fall was an accident. They all wanted me gone, locked up, to throw away the key. It all made perfect sense now.

"And they are absolutely right to do so," Richard said.

After they'd left, I knew I could no longer go on. The good folk of Manguri would be in a better place without me and, my poor Mercy was in extreme need of a new husband.

However, I needed to be clever to escape from that witches' coven up the hill. In particular, the main stirrers of that boiling cauldron of trouble: Cari and Dee. I paced the room, deciding what I should take with me. A small snap of Mercy, my important documents—just in case there were problems identifying me—and my wallet. I rummaged in my bedside drawer until I found the small piece of potch I'd found while noodling on my first day. I wrote a short note to the *bona fide* Cari. Hopefully Lucifer would now leave the real Cari alone, as I would be gone.

Dear Cari,

This small souvenir from my time in Manguri is for you. When you are true to yourself, you are like this seemingly plain stone—truly precious inside.

You will be forever in my thoughts and my heart, in this world and the next.

Samson

I took one last look at the room that had become my prison cell for those few weeks, the abode of a desperate man. The floor was littered with soiled garments and coffee-stained cups, my bed unmade. Soggy towels were strewn in the bathtub. I knew I looked a sight, but I didn't care. My hair, uncombed and lacking oil, was standing on end; my clothes dirty and smelly. I quietly opened the front door and closed it behind me. I set off toward the West Road, the hot wind lashing my face. I walked as fast as I could. Even the flies zoomed past my hurrying self as if they sensed the urgency of my mission.

"Finally!" Richard said. He whistled and hollered a rousing pukka hurrah.

I didn't look back.

CHAPTER THIRTY ONE

Cari

Opals can convey painful truths that, for the pure of heart, can ultimately free the spirit. Those who are not ready to bear these verities may be struck down with despair.
(*The Magic of Opals* by WO Brown 1972, p. 92)

"We have to do something, Cari," Dee said, that morning Samson disappeared. We were sitting in the tearoom; Jo at one end of the table, Dee at the other. I was filling my cup with water from an urn. I'd already spooned in the International Roast coffee powder that is a fixture on hospital staffroom shelves the world over.

"I agree," Jo said. "Barb came and saw me yesterday afternoon. She heard Samson talking to himself, then shouting. Over at the Serbian church. She was doing the flowers there."

"Is that woman everywhere?" Dee asked.

I added, "And then, this morning, about four o'clock, I heard him screaming and his front door slam. He thought there'd been an earthquake."

"I think he must be suffering paranoid delusions," Dee said. "Maybe he thinks we're all out to get him."

"That would fit," I said. "He's not answering his door. I haven't seen him leave his place in over a week."

Dee sighed. "It's all my fault. If I hadn't insisted he take that time off …"

"But it was getting dangerous," Jo said. "Samson couldn't make up his mind what medications to order. He kept checking his work, like he was scared he was going to make a mistake. And then I heard he accused one of the nurses of tampering with his tea, saying she'd added something to it."

"You didn't tell me that!" Dee said.

"Sorry. Barb told me only today."

"I think he has a psychotic depression," I said. I modulated my voice to sound gentle and thoughtful, like one of those wise TV doctors. "That's the medical diagnosis for someone who is so depressed he or she starts to hear voices and experiences delusions of paranoia. That would explain why he's talking to himself."

Good work, Cari, said Dr Smythe. I didn't react. Since that day when I'd needed her and she hadn't helped, when Sergeant Stuart spoke to Samson and me in the tearoom after Richard's accident, I'd tuned my former counsellor out. It was time to stand on my own two feet, I'd decided. To give her credit, she'd mostly taken the hint.

"Poor Samson," Dee said. She cradled her forehead with the palm of her hand, her head bent over. "Richard's accident really shook him up. I think he felt responsible."

"And I wish I'd been more understanding," I said. "I didn't realize how he'd feel."

"Yes, it's the only explanation," Dee said. "What should we do?"

"I don't think we have any choice. He has to go to a psychiatric hospital in Adelaide. I'll have to certify him if he refuses to go. The Mental Health Act stipulates that an unwell person can be detained to hospital if he's a danger to himself or others. Samson is a suicide risk, Dee. He's not eating—you see how he's refusing those plates of food you leave for him. Who knows how his mind is working."

"This is so dreadful. A lovely man like Samson. We have to force him to go to hospital, against his will... Can you imagine how he'll take that?" Dee's eyes reddened as she swallowed slowly.

"We don't have any choice. He may agree to go to hospital if we're lucky, often people do, and we can avoid any unpleasantness. But we have to send him. With or without his agreement."

"OK. I'll get the paperwork," Dee said, standing. "Do you think we should ask the police to attend with us?"

"No. Let's see how we get on when we knock on his door. He might answer."

Dee and I drove down the hill in her car. Not unexpectedly, he didn't answer the door, although we heard faint shouts.

"I think we'll have to ask Sergeant Stuart to attend," Dee said as we headed back, her voice quavering. "Do you feel as useless as I do?"

I didn't know what to say in reply. Why useless? We were trying to help.

We headed back to the hospital and rang the police station. Dee managed to locate the sergeant and an hour later she explained the situation in her office.

"I suspected Dr Cherian wasn't going to cope well with Dr Leitch's death. But I never imagined it would get as bad as this," Sergeant Stuart said, after he'd wiped his face with his sleeve.

Silently, we walked outside to the police car in the hospital's parking lot, the forms I needed in hand. The day was sparkling clear, the sun brilliant, the air crisp. Galvanized iron roofs in the valley below had been rinsed by the rains of the previous few weeks and gleamed in the bright sunshine, the sky now a washed sea-blue. Rills from small pools of water streamed down the slopes next to the tracks. Green shoots of wildflowers already speared the red earth. Once or twice I lost my footing on the slippery path, my concentration as atomized as the water vapor of the rapidly drying brown mud that squelched under my feet.

"We're going to have a mass of flowers soon," Dee said as we climbed into Sergeant Stuart's vehicle, her face drawn. I reached across and squeezed her hand. At my gesture a glimmer of a surprised smile flashed across her face.

Minutes later, we hammered on Samson's door. The door handle was firmly jammed.

"Dr Cherian, open up. Sergeant Stuart here. We're very worried about you," the sergeant called.

There was no movement of the kitchen window's curtain.

He tried again. "I'm going to have knock the door down if you don't answer."

Still no sign of life. I became aware there was a tightness in my chest. *Please be all right. You are my friend.*

The sergeant rapped on the door again.

Dee ran her hands through her cap of dark hair. "I wish Barb hadn't lost that spare key."

Sergeant Stuart fetched a crowbar from the car's trunk and I cringed as he wedged the tip into the door, splinters of wood showering the doorstep. A few minutes later he'd gouged a raggedy gap in the frame as if he were splitting firewood and reached inside to unlatch the lock. I breathed a sigh of relief. We were in.

The Samson I knew was a man who was fastidiously tidy. I gasped when I saw the squalor he'd been living in. Unwashed dishes and half-empty food tins were strewn in the kitchen, dirty clothes and towels dropped at random. The air was a miasma of rotting bananas and stale curries with a hint of rancid coconut oil. I remained standing in the doorway, reluctant to step inside. Dee, standing next to me, swayed for a moment in horror and clutched my shoulder.

Sergeant Stuart returned a minute later, mopping his brow with a damp handkerchief. "All clear," he said.

Dee exhaled loudly.

We trooped outside.

"What do we do now?" I asked.

"I'll radio the patrol car and ask them to look for him. Sign the forms if you wish him to be brought in, doctor. It does make it a lot easier for everyone concerned."

"I hope he didn't go to the minefields," Dee said in a faint voice.

"He won't have got far," Sergeant Stuart said. "We'll find him, don't worry. But first I need to check if he took his wallet or any personal items. Maybe he's done a runner."

He returned a few minutes later, carrying a note. "Looks like he has. He left this for you, doctor."

I read the message in his fine handwriting, then examined the piece of potch that accompanied the scrap of paper with a shaking hand. The rock was not much bigger than a small coin in my palm. An iridescent shimmer of red and green weaved through the milky substrate like a fairy's fire burning within.

I felt a powerful swell of emotion. For the first time as I regarded the gemstone I realized that my ex-boyfriend Richard had generated within me an unquenchable thirst for reassurance. I'd needed those times when I felt like I was all that mattered in his world; that I was loveable. But the crashes left me anxious and rudderless. I'd felt then I wasn't worthy of his consideration or his tenderness; his disdain of me was well deserved. I'd believed then it was all my fault because I wasn't able to read his expressions, his nuances. I'd thought if I could change in some way, I could become what he wanted. I now knew—*really* knew— this was all just an act. Richard was a living, breathing lie. It wasn't about me.

But Samson. I thought about his kindness, his unassuming manner, his honesty. His acceptance. For the first time in my life, looking at that worthless stone in the palm of my hand, I knew I was feeling love. Pure and unconditional. And untainted.

I passed the letter to Dee. Her face, usually wearing an expression of energetic competence, wilted. She'd also grown close to Samson.

I felt tears begin to flow unchecked down my face, salty in my mouth, a fount of sadness I couldn't staunch. And then we were both howling like small children because, of all the people in Manguri, she knew how I was feeling.

Samson had taken his passport and his wallet, but there was no indication of where he'd intended to go. An overnight bag and suitcase lay empty on the floor of his wardrobe. No clothes had been packed. A photograph of a young dark woman on his bedside table, probably his wife, stared blank faced and tight-lipped into the room. She wasn't about to snitch on her husband. Sergeant Stuart contacted the airport and the bus station, and made general enquiries, but there were no recent reports of anyone buying tickets matching his description.

Dee and I steeled ourselves for the inevitable. Samson may be found any day at the bottom of a disused mineshaft, but then again maybe not. There were thousands of potential tombs biding time disfiguring the flat red terrain. He could plunge down and dispose of himself in a split second, to be lost forever.

Dee tried to contact his wife. His address in India had been in Vellore, but there was no response to her repeated attempts to find his next of kin. It was as if Samson had vanished off the face of the planet.

Two days later, I was shopping for food in the refrigerated cool of the local supermarket, trying to carry on as usual, when I saw Jack, Chicken Pete's son. I'd not seen him since the day his father had died.

"G'day Doc!" he said. His dirty and trenched face lit up with a good-natured smile. "Did Dr Cherian make it OK to that conference?"

"Sorry?" I gripped the supermarket trolley I was pushing. *Conference?*

"Yeah. I picked him up on Thursday. He was heading out on the West Road. Said he was walking into town." Jack chuckled, merrily oblivious to my sudden state of paralysis. "I said to him, 'Doc. That's not the way to into town, you've missed the turn-off.' And I offered him a ride. He said he wanted to get to the bus stop. He was going to Adelaide for a two-day conference. Of course, you'd know that already, Doc. But you know what, Doc?" His voice became softer and sounded puzzled. "He didn't look that good. He didn't even have a bag. When we got into town, I said to him, 'Is there anything I can do for you, Doctor Cherian?' And he said—" Jack lowered his voice and did a commendable imitation of Samson's formal prosody, "'It is true, I am not feeling well. Would you please be most kind and go buy me a ticket?' Then he pushed some money into me hand. And I said to him, just joking-like, I hope I didn't give him ideas, 'You're not buggering off are ya Doc?' But Dr Cherian gave me a look as if he was a bit down on his luck, so I shut me gob, and went and bought him the ticket."

"We've been worried about Dr Cherian," I said. "We haven't had any word from him. He didn't tell me anything about a … conference. We've had no idea where he is."

"It looked to me like he *was* doing a runner," Jack said, with all the knowledge of a Manguri veteran who had witnessed the hurry of unforeseen departures before. "And who was I to stop him?"

I took a big breath and looked at the diesel-stained man standing before me, his shopping basket slung over his arm. A flare of emotions, a mixture of relief mingled with an urge to throttle him for not contacting the hospital with his concerns, was threatening to be let loose.

"Did he say exactly where he was going?"

"Nah, sorry Doc. I just saw him get on the bus, cos that came by not long after. He was real quiet, didn't say much. Just shook my hand and thanked me, then said goodbye."

Jack rubbed the back of his blackened neck with his free hand and frowned. "It never occurred to me that people might not know where he was."

My heart skipped a beat. Samson was alive!

I pulled the Thankful expression. "Thanks Jack. That's really helpful. This gives us something to go on with. I'll let Sergeant Stuart know you saw him."

Jack's eyebrows shot up under his baseball cap. "Sergeant Stuart?"

"Yes, Jack. We've been *that* worried," I said. I headed off to the checkout to pay for my groceries.

Within hours Sergeant Stuart ascertained that Samson had taken the bus to Adelaide. He'd bought a plane ticket to Singapore, and had left Australia the day before, supposedly to return to Chennai in India. We discovered that Samson's wife, Mercy, had moved away from Vellore, not long after he moved to Australia, but this line of enquiry dried up. We rang the Christian Medical College where he had previously worked, but the staff in the Department of Surgery had no idea of his whereabouts.

"There is nothing else we can do," Dee said. "It's up to Samson to let us know he's all right."

Chapter Thirty Two

*Good luck, peace and prosperity will find anyone who believes
in the magic of opals.*
(*The Magic of Opals* by WO Brown 1972, p. 1)

Life went on in Manguri. After a week of Samson's absence, Dee contacted the Health Department. Another temporary doctor was sent to the town, to share the on-calls and provide me with collegial support. This time, there was no argument from the bureaucratic heavies.

It wasn't the same though. The doctor they sent, an older man, although pleasant enough, was a sloth. He didn't care about the welfare of the town's folk and was only in Manguri because he'd negotiated an extremely profitable contract. He kept to himself; we never shared a beer. Every day that went by, the sun setting as always brilliantly in the west, I missed Samson more.

I decided to remain in Manguri, much to the horror of my mother. She found the whole Richard incident shocking and distasteful, and felt I should return home on the first plane. I didn't tell her the truth about what Richard was really like. The less she knew, the better.

Sergeant Stuart had quietly pocketed those pictorial souvenirs of Richard's last living hours and had allowed me to choose which snapshots I wished to keep. (He should have forwarded them, with Richard's body, on to his mother in England, but I made no comment about this oversight.) I decided to keep all of the photographs. There was no point in pretending that what had happened was a mere figment of my imagination. I'm sure others would have regarded keeping the reminders of Richard's final movements as morbid, but in the end, I was glad I took possession of them. One photograph of Samson I liked, in particular. He was facing the camera, his cap pulled low, the Brittle Hills shimmering in the background. However, even I could see he looked ill at ease.

Dee asked me to keep Samson's belongings in my dugout until we had a forwarding address. The relieving doctor had moved into Samson's dugout. Although Dee had quietly organized for hospital cleaners to give the small flat a thorough once-over, the new occupant grumbled about a lingering smell of Brut 33 and coconut oil.

I still had the black opal that Richard had given me. I wondered what to do with it. It was reputed to be the stone of truth but clearly the gemstone's powers had failed on him. Before the accident I'd purchased a pink opal—the opal of peace—that I'd planned to give to Samson as a memento of his time in Manguri, perhaps for him to give to his wife. But during those final days he'd become so suspicious of me, the time was never right. I decided instead to have a necklace made out of both opals. The jeweler cleverly placed both stones together. I wore it every day—a kind of Yin and Yang hug, echoing those symbols of truth and peace.

Manguri became known as a center for excellence in rural medicine. We negotiated with the teaching hospitals in Adelaide to introduce a rural doctor training-scheme. Suitably experienced doctors worked rotations in the town. Dee and I also ran conferences. Samson had educated me well in performing most minor surgical procedures and, with experience, I felt more confident in managing the emergencies and traumas that are the realities of working as a doctor in the bush.

Before I knew it five years had passed. It was time to leave. It was time to spread my wings and look for further education elsewhere. I was "doing a runner" or "buggering off", as Diesel Jack would have eloquently described my departure. I was 31 years old.

My image was added to the photographic montage of smiling faces in the staffroom. It was a photo of a humorless me, staring intently at the camera, caught by Jo in between seeing patients, my Photograph smile missing. Samson was already there, with a photo taken of him when he first arrived. He was smiling, but his eyes looked anxious, as if he was about to be jettisoned off on a terrible and ill-fated outback expedition. In his picture he was seated like a visiting dignitary and was surrounded by other staff standing behind him, all smiling cheesily. I recognized the setting as Joe's Greek Taverna.

I never forgot Samson. Most evenings I dwelled on the puzzle of where he might be, as I watched the sunset painting the horizon with its vivid rays—that scene changing later to the city's dull polluted skies. I hoped he was happy.

And I also wondered whether he ever thought of me.

There are no goodbyes for us. Wherever you are,
you will always be in my heart.
- Mahatma Gandhi

PART FIVE

Chennai

India

There is no doubt about it. Opal song will steer the attuned to where they are needed.
(*The Magic of Opals* by WO Brown 1972, p. 1)

Medical students and house officers, in fact, any doctor, no matter how junior or senior in rank, must remember the privilege of wearing the badge of white coat. Always bring compassion, sympathy and understanding to any dealing with your patient. To ease suffering is the prime ambition of all treatment.
(*Essential Tips for the Young Doctor and Medical Student, edition 2,* by Professor Alfred Crankshaw 1977 p. 2)

CHAPTER THIRTY THREE

Cari

1/9/2015

A good death is the goal of palliation. This can be achieved by meticulous attention to medications; in particular, the liberal use of opioid analgesia such as morphine and heroin, and anticholinergic medicines, such as hyoscine for the drying of secretions. The gentle touch of the hand on brow can alleviate sorrow. However, it is best to keep bad news from the patient, until the very end. Best to carry his or her burden, young sir.
(*Essential Tips for the Young Doctor and Medical Student, edition 2,*
by Professor Alfred Crankshaw 1977 p. 2)

I bring you now to the present time. I'm seated near the back of a plane, in economy class. I'm en route to Chennai, formerly the city of Madras. Most of the Indian passengers around me are elderly; some wear name tags. Being in my mid-forties, I feel like a relative youngster. I am travelling to the Indian subcontinent hoping to find my old friend, thanks to a surprise letter received only yesterday from his wife, Mercy Cherian. I pull the sheet of paper from my pocket and scan it again. I've already read it several times.

Dear Doctor Cari,

I write this letter with a heavy heart. This letter is to inform you that Samson, my husband, has terminal cancer. He most likely has only days to live. Please forgive the directness of my words. I know of no other way to let you know. I ask you—no, I beg of you, Doctor Cari … Can you please gift him your presence? I do not believe he will die with a full and peaceful heart unless he is secure in the knowledge that you have forgiven a misdemeanour. One committed by him, against you and your colleagues. I know this is much to ask of you, but Samson always spoke highly of you, with much sentiment and warmth. I hope you share these feelings toward him. Samson has told me scant detail of why he returned to India in such haste. I know he felt great shame then, which has endured to this day, that he left the township of Manguri and yourself in less than ideal circumstances. He never revealed to me the cause of his great consternation. I do not need to know his reasons. We have shared a happy life and marriage. However, I am sure he is still troubled by his unfinished business. Please Doctor Cari. Please help my husband die with peace in his heart, knowing he did a good job in all his endeavors. Please help me bring my dying husband solace.

The letter continued with the practicalities: Mercy's address and phone number. It had been sent to the hospital at Manguri where Dee had recently retired. She had forwarded it on to me by express post after calling me first. We had maintained contact time to time over the years and she remained a true confidante.

Dee and I had once shared a love for a humble man who was now dying.

There was no question in my head. It was a foregone conclusion that I would be on a flight to India as soon as humanly possible. But forgiving Samson? What for? Samson had the clinical features of a depressed person in the weeks following Richard's demise, but he was certainly not to blame for what had happened.

If anyone was at fault it was me, I thought, my heart spasming a little. How things could have turned out differently if I'd just confronted Richard with my suspicions as soon as he'd arrived in Manguri.

I am awoken from a light doze by a female steward wearing the airline's tight sarong-style uniform. "Miss … Stow your tray table please. We will be landing in Chennai shortly."

The plane's flashing wing lights rend the starless black of the outside tropical sky. Coalesced lights skirting a shoreline below come into view as we near the airport, to enlarge and scatter like a dropped strand of diamonds.

Thirty minutes after we have disembarked, after collecting baggage I'm in the back of a car feeling as if I have run the gauntlet. A hundred frantic faces greet me at the outside of the terminal, behind the bars of restraining gates, looking like caged animals. I meet a driver and we jostle through the crowd. I'm taken to the Rainforest Hotel in Adyar, near the main business district of Chennai.

I've organized to meet Mercy at the private hospital in Vellore, where Samson is now a patient, the next afternoon. Mercy has offered for me to stay with her but I've chosen to stay in a Western-style business hotel for the first night, to give myself time to acclimatize.

A tall man wearing a traditional Indian white uniform salutes me as I alight from the car. A gold braid is wrapped around his head, with a ribbon pointing to the sky. He could be moonlighting as an Indian Hiawatha. I check in. The hotel is a tall building set among a storm of construction work happening all over the city. Inside this five-star hotel, I could be anywhere in the world.

"How are you, Doctor?" a uniformed man behind the counter asks.

I adopt the Reassurance smile. "I'm fine," I say. "Just jet-lagged."

The man's head wobbles in reply. My heart sinks. I have enough trouble interpreting facial expressions. Now I'm having to deal with head wobbles and the multitude of emotions this can convey to my untrained eye.

The haunting song of the Call to Prayer from the neighboring mosque wakes me at dawn the next morning, although my room is high on the hotel's ninth floor. An hour later a driver collects me in a small white taxi. We head off on the two-and-a-half-hour drive to Vellore in a dusty morning light, along a three-lane tarmac road which never bends. An ancient air-conditioner spits chlorinated water at the front passenger seat; I'm glad I chose to sit in the back. My driver beeps lazily at cars and trucks that straddle lanes and move across with no rhyme or reason. Squealing motorbikes, piled high with people, livestock and baskets, weave between motorized rickshaws puttering along. Oblivious human cargo chat on mobile phones. We pass several ambulances, crawling along, lights flashing and croaky sirens warbling.

This road is more congested than any peak-hour traffic I've ever encountered. When we stop at traffic lights, the occasional ragged beggar makes his way through the stationary vehicles and taps on the car's window. One old Indian wizard, his fine cobwebby white beard billowing from the lift of exhaust fumes from passing cars, waves his walking stick at me. He shouts obscenities when I look the other way.

My driver is firm. "We must not encourage this dangerous practice, Ma'am. Do not give them money. It only encourages them."

We pass rural scenes. Cows pull carts laden with hay, goats graze by the verge of almost fluorescent emerald-green fields of rice. My driver turns and enquires at regular intervals, "Are you comfortable, Ma'am? Is the air conditioning set right for you? Ma'am, you need water?" And I try to reassure—all is just lovely thanks, and how much further?

It is election time in India. Wherever I look the roads are lined by billboards, showing images of candidates. Most hopefuls look like they have boogied off the set of a Bollywood musical. A picture of an older thick-set woman with a kind face, her black hair parted severely in the middle, pops up everywhere. Her complexion is fair and she has a red teardrop biddy between her eyebrows. She wears a red or purple sari. I see pictures of her offering beatific smiles or grins of rapturous delight. Sometimes she stares out from those cinematic screens with dark impatient eyes, appraising all those travelling past. Some images show her shouting through a microphone. A damn good explanation would be needed by any renegade not voting for her! In my imagination, she is Mother India. An unexpected urgent desire fills me—to be taken into her arms.

Finally, the rocky outcrops that herald Vellore come into view. White temples are more frequent and large bridges span buildings below. The traffic is even heavier. We move at a snail's pace. And then, after more zig-zagging and stopping and starting and horn tooting past crowded markets and stalls teeming with brightly clad people, we pull up into the parking lot of the biggest hospital I've ever seen. The entrance to the hospital is crammed with a morass of people, all moving with unhurried purpose.

"Please follow me, Ma'am," the driver says.

Old dark-skinned men in torn and faded kurtha and dhotis amble past, while women in bright saris tote babies and drag round-eyed children behind. Some stop and stare. It's not usual to see a solo Western woman here. We walk past various whitewashed buildings. At any other time, I'd have pleaded to be allowed to visit the clinics inside, including the one for leprosy and hand reconstructive surgery and the prosthesis workshop. I have difficulty following my guide through the crush of bodies.

The private hospital foyer is even more crowded. We push our way through and head toward the stairs. ("Are you OK with stairs, Ma'am?

It will be quicker.") We climb three floors and suddenly there we are, in the relative peace of one of the private medical wards. I wonder how it will be to meet Samson again, having not heard a word from him or about him in 18 years.

A young nurse wearing a crisp white sari comes out from behind a desk in the foyer. She greets me with a wide smile and holds her hands in a prayer gesture.

"Hello! Hello! Are you Doctor Cari? Mrs Cherian told me that you will be arriving today. Please follow me."

She turns and glides away serenely, not waiting for my reply. We walk along corridors that are a hubbub of activity and noise. This is a Christian hospital. The yellow walls are plain except for framed psalms and Biblical pictures.

She stops at the end of a corridor, and says, "Please wait here. I will speak with Mrs Cherian."

I breathe deeply. My heart is thumping. Family members and patients stroll along the corridor, trailing drip stands and drains, they pause and eye me curiously.

"You may come in, Doctor," the nurse says.

She ushers me to an open door and before me is a large woman who fills the entrance to Samson's private room. Her girth is almost as wide as her height; her coarse black hair is pulled back into a large bun. A darker pigmentation of her chin set against the lighter color of her cheeks gives her face a pied appearance. She must have poor vision: her dark eyes look blurry behind the thick bifocal lens of her glasses. Her face lights up at the sight of me.

"Doctor Cari! *Vannakkam!* Welcome, welcome!" she says. She bows surprisingly gracefully, her hands placed in the prayer gesture. "I am so pleased, so very pleased, you could come! I am Mercy Cherian. I have not told Samson you were coming; I have kept it a surprise. Please, please do come in."

I follow her into a room with two beds: one for the patient and one for a relative.

And there he is: a shell of his former self. His heart flutters visibly through his rib cage, beneath his thin blue gown. His famous black hair is streaked gray and patchily thinned due to the effects of failed chemotherapy. His mouth is hidden behind an oxygen mask. His rebellious cowlick is sadly no more. He is hooked up to a drip; a glass bottle administers dextrose solution through plastic tubing. I greet him.

"Hello, old friend," I manage to choke.

He looks up and his filmy dark brown eyes momentarily widen. A smile plays across his features, and for an instant there is a flash of the Samson I knew.

"Cari, Cari," he whispers. He takes my hand and squeezes it with his bony fingers.

I feel emotion flood within. My throat constricts and an ache spreads across my chest as I fight tears.

Mercy drags over a chair and indicates I should sit. Having attended to me, she reseats herself on the other side of the bed.

"You have traveled … a long way to see me." Samson's chest rises and falls with the effort of delivering this short speech. He squeezes my hand again, but even this exhausts him. Mercy lifts his oxygen mask and she spoons water into his mouth. He splutters as he swallows. "I am glad you have come," he says after a minute or so. His breath forms a misty condensation on the inside of the plastic mask.

"It is lung cancer, although he never smoked," Mercy says, her words heavy with the Tamil accent. "Samson always had problems with his chest. So, when he was short of breath and coughing more, he assumed it was a severe bronchitis."

I vaguely remember Samson telling me, early in our acquaintance, that he had mild cystic fibrosis. In this condition, the airways fill with mucus. Respiratory infections often fester. Given he was rarely ill when I knew him, I had forgotten this detail.

"He did not seek treatment until the cancer was well advanced." She faces him and says more loudly, "Samson, I asked Doctor Cari to come."

"And I'm glad your wife asked me." I take a big breath. *Say it.* "I wanted to see you again. I never apologized to you for what I did. I treated you badly as a friend."

He swallows several times, his eyes round and staring. His skin looks darker with the sickness. The sharp ridges of his cheek bones jut beneath his hollow eye sockets.

"I was wrong," he finally croaks after a heavy silence, broken only by the rattle of his breathing. He begins to cough and tears fill his eyes. Gasping, he continues, "I left Manguri. I left you alone... I was sick in the heart ..."

Mercy reaches over and grasps Samson's hand. She brings it to her lips.

"What do you mean?" I say. "*You* didn't do anything wrong. I'm the one. I should have told you the whole truth about why I asked you to take Richard that day."

I look down at him and realize that I have leapt up from my seat. Tears brim over now; the 18-year-old stopper is off. I sit down again. "Please let me explain, so you know the whole truth. You truly were blameless. I should never have asked you to take Richard out that day."

I glance at Mercy. She is listening intently, frowning. She has no idea what I'm talking about.

"No, no, I should not have—" He struggles to sit up but collapses weakly against his pillow.

"Please believe me!" It's suddenly urgent to unburden myself. "Let me explain why I needed you to take Richard out in my car that day. If anyone is to blame it was me."

Samson stares at me. He is shaking his head violently. His mouth puckers as if he is trying to say something. The hollow at the base of his neck sucks in with each gurgling breath. All the while, he plucks at his white sheets making small tents, his fingers unable to still.

I assess his clinical signs. *Pain.* He must be trying to ask for pain relief. I wonder when Samson was last administered morphine.

He makes another weak attempt to sit up.

"Hush, my darling," Mercy interrupts. She sniffs noisily and rearranges Samson's pillow. His face is white with strain. "You will exhaust yourself trying to speak. Let Doctor Cari finish what she has to say."

"But—"

Mercy places her fingers to his lips as if he is an errant schoolboy. "Hush, my darling. Enough."

She nods at me to go on.

Time to pull doctor rank. "Perhaps I should stop," I say. "It is clear to me he is in a lot of pain."

Mercy's eyes narrow momentarily, then she gives a half-smile. "No, Doctor Cari. This is a pain of the heart, not from the cancer. You will bring him healing. Please continue."

I glance at Samson. His terror of not being able to catch his breath is obvious. His sparrow chest rises and falls rapidly. I look at Mercy. She nods again, her gaze resolute and fixed on me. I take a few calming breaths and begin. Then I recount in meticulous detail the events of that terrible day and admit that I had lied to him, my Indian friend, when I conned him to take Richard sightseeing. I explain why I did so and that it was only later that I realized how Richard had just used me—and others—in his quest to avoid disgrace.

At the end of this speech Samson remains silent. But his face has changed. He's given up his struggle. The skin over his forehead relaxes. His eyes close and his breathing eases.

"He is at peace now," Mercy says. She sighs then sits up taller. "He can now leave us with an untroubled heart." She reaches across Samson and places her cool hand over mine lightly. It is surprisingly petite and adorned with fine gold rings.

I sit there for a while. Mercy leaves us and I awkwardly hold her husband's skeletal hand. I have seen this simple gesture bring comfort to the dying. He dozes. The nurse arrives, a silent white angel; she squirts morphine through a needle attached to the wrinkled skin of his belly. I avert my eyes. She leaves, a quiet click as the door shuts behind.

A tiny old woman wearing a lurid pink sari enters a few minutes later. She waltzes around the room with a mop and bucket, sloshing lemon-scented floor cleaner under my feet. She hums a soft tune to herself. Meanwhile, I watch Samson. He is in a deep sleep now. His breathing is more even. The rattle of mucus in his throat is a gentle background to the cleaner's tune.

꙰

I didn't tell Samson that I'd been to see a psychologist a few years after I'd left Manguri, hoping to find a remedy for the unshakeable heaviness of my own heart. The psychologist, Erica, a wise woman in her late fifties, had quickly intuited the issues I faced on a daily basis. I told her all that had transpired in Manguri. I described the characters of both Richard and Samson.

"Richard had a narcissistic personality disorder with a hefty dose of psychopathy," she told me after our first session. She then explained how she had come to this conclusion. It made sense of everything. I wondered why no-one had taught me about personality disorders earlier.

Erica also explained why Samson would have reacted as he did to Richard's death. The isolation, the heat, the differences in culture, his heightened sense of responsibility toward others, including Richard— all factors. And maybe worst of all, there was the violation of trust I had battered him with—a violation that he was unable to deal with.

She suggested, kindly, that I should have ignored the detective's request and simply told Samson the truth.

"But he made me promise! I gave my word I wouldn't divulge the truth about Richard …"

"Sometimes rules are meant to be broken," Erica said mildly. "Maybe this was one of those times."

I'd left the psychologist's office that day completely bereft. I'd ruined a close friendship; I had driven a good man away. I'd caused untold suffering. Just because I was a stickler for rules, however inappropriate the occasion. And, to make matters worse, I'd been unable to track Samson down after he disappeared. I'd tried but it was as if he'd never existed.

I drift back to the present. Samson is still asleep. The hum of voices in the corridor outside the room soothe me. I become drowsy too. The air is humid and warm. Mosquitos skim the air; a whirring fan on the trolley is blowing ripples across the bed's white sheets.

Mercy returns and places a cup of milky sweet chai before me. Then, nursing her own cup, she fills me in about what had happened over the intervening years. On his return to India, Samson had worked as a surgeon in a mission hospital in a northern mountainous region. He was a respected and competent surgeon and enjoyed his work.

"After he left Manguri he returned to Chennai very depressed, his thinking confused. He refused to see a doctor—out of shame I suppose—but he slowly recovered by himself. He did not work for six months. However, I'd saved the money he sent over from Australia, so we were able to live in comfort."

I sip my tea and Mercy continues, her speech rising and falling with its musical Tamil accent. "Once my husband was better, he realized his thoughts had been like those of a madman. He was embarrassed by his paranoid behavior. He believed he had let you and the people of Manguri down. He had broken his promise to stay for the length of his contract, you know, so the hospital wouldn't close."

"Samson was a good man." I correct myself, "I mean, Samson *is* a good man."

"He returned to me a kind and loving husband. He became the husband I knew he could be. We were not able to have our own, so we adopted three beautiful children. You will meet them today. The oldest boy, Bernard, is 12 years old; he is clever like his father and also wants to be a doctor. And then we have two daughters: a ten-year-old, Mary, and a six-year-old, Lydia. They are staying in Chennai but will be arriving tonight."

Samson's eyes flicker open briefly.

"Please do us the honor of sharing a meal with us, Doctor Cari. Please also meet my mother and father."

Later in the day, I visit Samson's family who are staying in the nurses' home. Walking there from the private hospital, we are stopped by various staff who have worked with Samson. Every person asks us to convey their good wishes to him. Mercy talks as we sidestep the thick current of people moving along.

"Samson's parents have passed. You knew he had been adopted?" she asks.

I shake my head.

"Yes, when he was six years old, from a children's home. His real family abandoned him there. His adoptive father, that is Doctor Cherian, died some time ago from heart disease; his mother from old age. Doctor Cherian's own children live overseas and Samson did not see them."

Later that night, we are seated at a small table. Food is produced as if by magic. I am introduced to an elderly but spritely couple, Mercy's parents. They smile constantly. I smile back so much the muscles around my mouth begin to ache. They speak little English. We eat rice with coriander and peas, yellow chicken curry, naan breads and raita. I eat with fork and spoon; the family use fingers, scooping rice and curry into mouths with a neat aplomb. I marvel at how not a crumb or drop is spilt. More chai is served.

I meet Samson's children. They shake my hand one by one. Mercy is right—Bernard is bright, his English excellent. He peppers me with lots of questions about Australia. Do I have a kangaroo at my house? Do I go to the beach?

All the while, Mercy's parents continue to smile and I doggedly smile back, heads wobbling slightly (I suspect mine too). The two girls stare at me, wide eyed, stunned by the unfamiliar appearance of a white woman wearing jeans and a T-shirt at their table.

Before I know it, the evening is over. I am staying at a small tourist hotel in Vellore, with Western-style toilet and shower. Mercy takes me to the hotel in a motorized rickshaw that weaves through the congested narrow streets. We pass flower stalls festooned with chains of golden marigolds and street vendors selling spices. I smell whiffs of coriander and frying onions. At one point, our small vehicle does an impossible U-turn at a busy intersection, to be met with an onslaught of honking cars, buses and revving motorbikes. Mercy next to me laughs and grasps my hand when I shriek. I promise I will return to see Samson tomorrow. My last day. Finally, Mercy leaves me and returns to Samson's bedside.

The next morning, I'm back at the hospital. Samson has deteriorated overnight. Only a few days before my arrival, after consulting with his doctors, he decided to stop treatment. Barely conscious, his breathing is more labored, but he is less agitated.

I spend the morning sitting alone with my old friend. Mercy goes to make phone calls and get some sleep. I begin to talk. I speak of what only Samson and I can know. Our private jokes, our sunsets sharing cold beers, our walks through the township of Manguri. I reminisce aloud about the humorous things that happened and the interesting people we'd known: their funny stories, and often times, the sad ones. I talk about our friendship, and of how much this man lying before me had meant to me. I speak of how the staff at the hospital had respected him. And how Dee grieved to learn of his final illness.

I tell him about my life. I'd happily surrendered my plans to become a surgeon after I left Manguri; I never re-sat that exam. Working in the remote north had changed me in indefinable ways. I was more confident not only in my medical competence, but also in my judgment of people. I decided I did actually like my patients awake. I *did* care about their emotional trials, their pain. I returned to The Queen Adelaide Hospital and then worked at other institutions for several years. I undertook formal training in palliative care medicine. For the last five years I'd worked at a hospice on the outskirts of the city.

I briefly mention my failed two-year marriage to an ambulance paramedic, Martin. I speak of Dee, and of Barb, who is still very much with us, being the unofficial news service of Manguri, although she is now in her late seventies.

And although Samson's eyes are closed, I know he's listening.

I cry from time to time, but my tears are interspersed by silly laughter. I readily identify my emotions: sadness, grief, and even happiness. And I'm glad. My heart is light. I can breathe easily for the first time since the day that Samson disappeared.

The hospital provides me with a curry lunch on white china. Mercy has gone to spend some time with her children; they are due to return to Chennai that afternoon.

At last, I run out of things to say. Samson is exhausted. He sleeps deeply, his limbs twitch every now and then, despite the medication. It's almost time to leave.

340

Mercy returns later in the day with the children. They are frightened by the sight of their father. The girls start to cry and cling to each other in the corridor. Bernard, being older and brave, sits next to his father and asks me questions. Is he in pain? Does he know what we are saying? Samson struggles to speak, but the effects of the medications drag him under.

I have booked a driver to return to Chennai that night. I don't wish to be present when Samson passes. This time belongs to Mercy and her family.

I stand. Samson has been lucid for short intervals so I know he can hear me.

"Goodbye, old friend," I say. "I will see you in the next life. You are the kindest person I have ever known. I truly love you, Samson. Thank you for seeing me."

And I lean over to kiss his cheek, which has the delicate, dry texture of an autumn leaf tumbled from an oak tree, and I press his feeble hand. His eyes fight to stay open. I can tell he is berating himself that he is unable to respond. Mercy is weeping now on the other side of his bed.

"Don't speak," I whisper in Samson's ear. "You don't need to say anything. There's nothing to say. But I will never forget you and your family."

Then I straighten and on sudden impulse, reach inside my blouse to feel the cool stone of the opal necklace I had fashioned in Manguri. The overhead hospital light picks up the vivid glints of green, orange, and purple in the black opal, the gentle pink in the other stone making a soft contrast. I fiddle with the chain and undo the clasp. I cradle it for a brief moment and then push it into Mercy's hand.

"I had this made after Samson left Manguri. I bought the pink opal there." I point to the stone in the setting. "I wanted to give it to Samson …" I then add hurriedly "for him to give to you. But then he left, so I had these two stones set into this necklace. The black opal was given to me by someone … else. Whenever I felt down or worried, I would hold the necklace and I'd remember Samson and Manguri. It made me feel better about things. I'd like you to have it."

Mercy wipes her eyes with her free hand and then examines the piece of jewelry. "It is exquisite," she says. She lightly kisses the stone. "It somehow makes me feel … peaceful. Thank you."

I place the chain around her neck and close the clasp.

"And now, when I look at the opal, I will think of you," she adds. "I will always remember your honesty and kindness. Thank you, thank you, Doctor Cari." She indicates Samson, now sleeping peacefully. "Thank you for releasing this man from his own chains."

Mercy and I hold hands and this time we can't let go. We are both crying.

I struggle to articulate my own gratitude. "*Thank you*, Mercy." I say. She clasps my arm. She smiles. And I smile back. I see now, I can read it in her eyes, that Mercy knows and understands the truth. She rests her hand on the opal necklace. I had chains as well, but no longer. *I needed this too.*

I turn and head down the hallway; the seated nurses look up briefly as I walk past the main desk, and then without fuss they go back to their work. Life goes on: healing and comforting the sick, the injured and the dying.

Chapter Thirty Four

Peace and a lightness of spirit, for those who choose to hear the melody of opal song and surrender themselves to its magic.
(Concluding sentence of *The Magic of Opals* by WO Brown 1972, p. 229)

"Mum? It's Cari. I'm in Chennai in India," I say. I am ringing from the departure terminal in the Chennai airport. My mouth is dry. I attempt to lick my lips, but my tongue feels like sandpaper. I'm not even sure why I'm doing this, given we haven't spoken properly in years.

"Cari, is it really you? What are you doing in India? What time is it there?"

"Ten o'clock at night. I was seeing an old friend. He has cancer. He's not expected to live very long."

"I'm sorry to hear that," she said slowly. "He must have been important to you, for you to travel all the way to India."

I felt for the small piece of potch Samson had left for me, which I always carried deep in my pocket.

"Yes, well... We were never romantically involved, but we were close in Manguri."

Mum doesn't say a word. Doubtless she still thinks I wasted five years of my life in that remote dustbowl.

"Are you coming home?" she asks after a heavy silence.

I take a big breath. "I've been thinking it might be a good time to return to Wales … to see you. Today I asked the hospital if I could have a month off. I'd only organized four days to come here. When I phoned the admin officer, he said that I had so much holiday leave accrued, they were going to have to force me to take it anyway … So, I'll come, if it's OK with you."

"Oh Cari. It's been too long."

"Yes, Mum, it has been."

I'd returned to the UK for a brief visit when Martin and I had first married, five years ago, for Mum to meet my new husband. It was my first visit home since I had left London. We had visited the small flat in Monmouth that she'd rented after my father died. She would have been in her mid-sixties then, but had changed little, appearance-wise, from ten years earlier, the last time I'd seen her. She'd ditched her standard plaid skirt and jacket for white linen pants, loafers and a crisp white shirt, the collar turned up, to show off her long and wrinkle-free neck. She wore her hair in a teased shoulder-length bob, the color faded now to an attractive soft silver. In comparison, I was an ugly duckling-spawn. I looked as if I didn't care about my appearance, which was actually true.

My husband and my mother formed a ready alliance, after her initial disappointment that he was not a doctor. Joining forces, the not-so-subtle goading started. All jokingly of course, about babies, and working part time. But within an hour of being in her presence I realized I'd made a mistake. And it wasn't just about my returning to the UK to visit my mother.

But now, from this place that is midway between my birthplace and my adopted home, I know it's time I saw her again. Neither of us was getting any younger; she would be well into her seventies. And, when I thought about all those years my mother existed in survival mode with my father, she did what she'd had to do. If being a doormat to my overbearing dad gave her breathing space, then, who was I to judge?

I needed to put the past behind me and start afresh.

"I went to the Chennai Cancer Hospital today," I blurt out, without meaning to. "I met with many of the patients there." My saliva is flowing again, the words are easier to enunciate; this is my familiar territory.

"But they don't have a hospice. Most of the patients go home to die, with just their families looking after them."

I'd been accompanied by the briskly officious director of clinical services at the cancer hospital. Row upon row of patients in dark open-air wards: chemotherapy recipients, those recovering from surgery, others marked by the march of fungating tumours chewing through layers of skin, some grotesquely disfigured by inoperable oral tumors. A hush descended over each ward as I entered. Each large hall was lined with beds filled with the sick or dying; all eyes trained in my direction. Some patients smiled nervously at me. Many lit up like Christmas trees at the sight of the little white woman with her entourage on a grand tour, strolling past each bed like a visiting queen of England. Others looked away.

At each bedside we stopped to examine the medical records. I commented favorably about the standard of medical care at every opportunity. Instead of issuing the Royal Wave when I met each frail patient and relative, I placed my hands in the gesture of prayer. I could feel the sadness of those who knew the futility of arguing against fate wash over me. These poor people, despite having nothing, still gifted me with the warmest—and often most toothless—of smiles.

One patient spoke with me. A younger woman, looking to be in her thirties with fierce staring eyes and wild black stubbled hair. Her emaciated form was clad in a blue sari; her remaining teeth looked decayed and lopsided, like a row of leaning gravestones. She told me through the Director that she was dying of breast cancer, to leave behind small children.

"Pray for me," she said in Tamil.

"I will pray for you," I answered, when it was explained to me what she'd asked.

The woman in the next bed began to cry. The Director's eyes widened at my lack of tact. "She wants you to pray for her too," he whispered.

"Tell them I will pray for them all," I announced. I wondered if I should mimic the signing of the cross and utter a benediction. At the same time, I felt like a fraud. What these people needed were not prayers or false prophets, but a heavy cash injection into the hospital's coffers. Money to be spent on sick patients—not fattening the wallets of notoriously corrupt administrators.

The wards were furnished with beds that would not have looked out of place in Florence Nightingale's Crimean hospital. Rattly steel beds with peeling paint faced each other in rows along the walls. There were no partitioning curtains for privacy, and only antiquated equipment. Each doctor I met was gracious and polite yet downright rushed. I didn't bother them with my inane first-world medical worries.

"Money cannot be spent on the dying, Ma'am," my driver softly informed me when we exited the grounds of the hospital in his van, after I'd expressed surprise that there were no hospice wards. "There is not enough available to be spent on the living."

"It would be very different to Adelaide, I would imagine," Mum says, pulling me back to the present. I look around, I'm clutching a public telephone in a cubicle in the airport's departure lounge.

"Yes. Very different. It's difficult for me to comprehend, how the dollar drives everything. It's got me thinking that I might come back to India and do some charity work."

My mother takes a sudden intake of breath. My words tumble out in a rush. "While I've been waiting for my plane, I've been reading about that IT guy Timothy Snodgrass ... How he's given everything away to be a full-time philanthropist, a bit like Bill Gates. Perhaps I should get in touch with his organization … They're trying to help poor people here. Perhaps I should start up a hospice or something in Chennai?"

Mum doesn't say a word. A leaden silence weighs down the telephone in my hand.

I'd picked up a Times magazine in the airport's newsagent, after I'd checked in my bags and been through immigration. The picture on the cover of Timothy Snodgrass, a self-made multimillionaire from the UK, caught my eye. I'd flicked through the magazine's pages while I waited, perched on one of the departure lounge's conjoined plastic chairs, one ear half-cocked for my plane's boarding call.

A small man in early middle age, Snodgrass had just been awarded *The Times* annual "Person of the Year". I was surprised to find that he was born in a village in Gloucester, not far from where Richard had grown-up. Perhaps they had even known each other. He reminded me of the Dalai Lama. His impish smile was that of a child's, yet his sparse hair, salt-and-pepper blond and steel-gray, topped by a monkish bald patch, revealed his true age of 46 years. Yet he was still an enigma, his eyes a mere impression behind the shield of a pair of thin spectacles. I gleaned from the magazine's article that, along with his glamorous wife Belinda (an ex-beauty queen), Timothy had decided to give away most of their hard-earned money to charity. The man known for making "geeky" cool, had enjoyed a stellar career to date. His robots and computer software were innovative, even "life changing", or so the magazine enthused. He'd even been awarded a Nobel Prize, met the Queen and rubbed shoulders with movie stars and celebrities. But he'd wanted to do more. It was time to give something back to the community, he opined in the article, "to leave a real legacy".

Reading this article, I'd felt a swell of emotion. This wealthy man, one of the world's richest, with a big heart, inspired me. If he can do it, so can I, I decided then and there. I had to do something to help those suffering people I'd seen earlier in the day. But first, I had to see my mum.

℞

I'm shocked to find my cheeks are wet. A few children racing past the phone cubicles playing chase crash to a halt and stare at me. A mother sitting nearby scolds them in Tamil and pulling faces at each other, they slouch away.

"Cari, you're a good person. I'm looking forward to hearing about any plans you've got," Mum says at last. Her words sound odd, half-strangled.

"Thanks Mum." I wipe my nose with a tissue and slow my breathing.

"I'm really pleased you're coming home."

"I'm glad I'm coming too. We'll talk properly then."

"Yes, so we will," she says. She laughs softly. And, after a while, I join in.

I hang up, after explaining my flight arrangements and other details, and hoist my bag on my shoulder, to proceed through another security check. I blend in with the herd of passengers being processed at the disembarkation gate, then it's off to Heathrow, London.

Epilogue

1990 (Seven years before Richard visited Manguri)

A vast landscape stretches as far as the eye can see, an arid plain of sparse gray scrub. The soil is a burned cake of red clay, its surface cracked by wind and bouts of torrential rain. Small lizards emerge tentatively—it's too hot. There is no cooling wind to fan the animals sheltering under scattered pockets of small trees. The sky is cornflower-blue, empty; not a cloud shadows the stricken traveller lost in this harsh wilderness. And, when the wind does come, it's not a gentle breeze. The fierce sweep of the whirly whips dust into funnels of red. The white dust from bones of dead native animals is sucked into this swirling vortex, to later drift back to earth and coat the bleached leaves of saltbush. This landscape is a desert in the midst of the driest state, in the driest continent.

A red-furred kangaroo shelters in the cool of a low mulga bush. She is waiting for the night. The desert comes alive then; secretive and camouflaged inhabitants emerge, to feed and find water. The kangaroo is dozing, her suckling joey snug and safe in her pouch. Disturbed by the movement of a brown snake, she startles and skitters off at breakneck speed. She bolts through low scrub and mounds of white shale fissured by deep pits of an abandoned opal minefield. The kangaroo loses her footing on the edge of one such crevice. She panics, she scrambles to recover. Then, momentarily weightless, her body crashes to the base of a disused mineshaft. Her splayed carcass rests ten meters below the red crust.

Yet, here in the desert no life is wasted. A blowfly, body tar-black, wings shimmering green, her belly heavy with eggs, smells the air and likes what she finds. She descends on the kangaroo, to deposit her load.

THE END

Acknowledgments

Anyone who has visited the Coober Pedy opal fields in the outback of South Australia will know that this spectacular landscape was the inspiration for my debut novel. I thank the people of Coober Pedy, in particular Kathy Kruger, the staff at the local hospital and the Lookout Cave Underground Hotel, for answering my many questions about this fascinating town.

There are numerous websites that detail the spiritual benefits that opals can bring, including crystalsrocksandgems.com, crystal-cure. com, gemstone meanings.com and angelfire.com. I thank the authors of these websites for the inspiration you gave me when writing the quotes from my fictional book, *The Magic of Opals* by WO Brown. Having purchased my own opals in Coober Pedy I now also believe opals are truly magical!

Although I am a medical doctor, I am indebted to Drs Chris Sexton, Julian Vaile, Jee-Yoong Leong, Shanthi Saha and Chanh Huynh for providing technical advice (apologies if your info didn't make the final cut). Allayne Webster, Margaret Faux, Shauna Carroll and Fred Guilhaus— you deserve especial mention. You read my early clumsy writings and encouraged me to keep going. I value your friendship. Readers who gave invaluable feedback include Anne Hueppauff, Prue Chapman, Sally Brown, Kate Putland, Sharon Macpherson, Sue Pagram, Peter Herriot and Malene Smith—my many thanks. Likewise, my writers' group: Steve, Heather, Samira, Penny, Chris, Sally, Vicki and Ken, your constructive feedback has helped improve my writing and I would struggle without you.

I was lucky to visit the Vellore Christian Medical college in Vellore, Tamil Nadu, India in 2013. The generosity I was shown was humbling and I sincerely thank Dr Jacob Chacko and his lovely family for hosting me and showing me the hospital.

Thank you, Valerie Mobley, for making editorial suggestions. You have an eagle eye. Also my big thanks to Rommie Corso (Hardshell Publishing) for doing a fantastic job of bringing the book together, and to Peter O'Connor from Bespoke Book Covers for the beautiful cover.

Writing a novel is an exercise in endurance and I thank my family for running alongside me all the way and making my dream come true. My wonderful husband Michael has supported and indeed carried me when I looked to be throwing in the towel. Thank you, my love. With gratitude, I dedicate this book to you.

Adele Lande